LOCUS ORIGIN

— MERILLIAN —

Books by Christian Matari:

Locus Origin – The Never Born
Locus Origin – Merillian

LOCUS ORIGIN®
— MERILLIAN —

CHRISTIAN MATARI

OZOM BOOKS

Published by OZ-OM Books.

ISBN 978-9935-9067-4-8

www.locusorigin.com

To my amazing father, whose affection for science fiction
is truly contagious.

ACKNOWLEDGEMENTS

For the tireless dedication of my editor Luke John Murphy, the spectacular artwork of Mark Molnar - which never ceases to inspire - and the amazing advice of my friends Björgvin Björgvinsson and Jón Thorsteinn Jóhannson, and last but not least, to my sweet Nino, for putting up with me during all of this, I owe my deepest thanks. Your continued support is nothing short of amazing.

Prologue

Space: so vast and unyielding, an endless, unforgiving abyss. Yet it brings hope to those such as us who would otherwise have none.

Was it truly out there, somewhere amidst the billions of stars, billowing radiant nebulae and endless clouds of stardust? Every night my dreams are the same: a city among the stars, a bastion of hope, always beyond my grasp. Each morning I awake drenched in sweat, though I know not why. There is nothing in my dreams to cause such distress. Still, the more I reach, the more blurred the memories of my dreams become. Subtle details seem to shift and change, forever altering perception. Yet I know it's out there. I can feel it. Some would call it faith.

Despite having known such pain and sorrow in my short and meager existence, there are those who would say that I could know little of faith. Yet I find it in the strangest of places, not only within my own self, but in those with whom I share this voyage, my friends, my family. Though their numbers have surely diminished, my faith grows stronger. Where others would see only the emptiness, I see a path, a journey of the mind, the body and the spirit. Even death itself is just another journey, for we are all born from these stars. We are simply returning to the beginning.

Chapter 1

The few faded reeds jutting from the base of the gravestones swayed on the tender breeze. The ground was covered in a thin layer of powdered snow which had fallen throughout the day. Overhead, the sky was overcast in dark, billowing clouds, throwing the eerie shadows of barren trees across the small cobbled path.

Takahashi leaned on his cane, a constant reminder of his frail and failing body. He wore a long thick coat of woven wool, dark grey in color, with a high collar. His russet leather shoes had contracted streaks of white along the soles from where they had made contact with the snow.

"Just a little further," said the driver, a squat stoic man who had escorted him towards the grave despite Takahashi's protests.

"I know where it is," Takahashi snapped, shooting the man a stern glare.

"Yes Sir," the driver responded, wearily averting his gaze.

Takahashi drew a few labored breaths before continuing on the path. It had been months since last he had visited his wife's grave. Given his stature, one would assume he was simply too busy to visit more often, but the truth was that he had been avoiding it. He dreaded coming here, being reminded of all that which he had lost.

On a gnarled branch high overhead a pair of small robins quarreled, huddling together for warmth. The path climbed steadily amidst rows of ornately carved marble head stones. Only the privileged were buried here, according to customs dating back to earth. Those without

2

proper means had to rely on cremations, or unsanctified burial outside the city limits.

Takahashi had secured a plot on a high hill overlooking Sol. Though he knew his wife had long departed this earthly realm, he found at least a small measure of comfort in knowing that he had appropriated such a calm, scenic location for her remains. He and his daughter Mariko had never visited the grave together, not since the funeral at least, but he knew that she visited often, and hoped that she thought the plot suitable. He would have preferred a simpler plot, somewhere out in the countryside, but he knew Mariko wouldn't have liked that."

"Cursed steps," Takahashi muttered as he climbed the last part of the path, halting beside a colossal grey marble headstone, inlaid with gold. "Here lies Lillian Muromoto, beloved wife and mother," he read aloud.

So informal, he thought. But then, he was never one for showing sentiment through words. If only he'd have told her how he truly felt, that every breath he drew without her by his side was more painful than the one before it. In his heart he knew that she had felt loved, but he had never been one for saying it out loud.

After she had passed, he had tried to change, to be more openly affectionate with his daughter, but she had pushed him aside, not only personally but professionally as well. Over the years she had slowly, secretly gained the trust of the Board of Directors of the Muromoto Group, only to seize power, replacing him as CEO and Chairman of the Board. Strangely, Takahashi felt more proud than disappointed. He knew that she had always blamed him for her mother's death. He only hoped that through her machinations she would find some manner of closure, though he suspected otherwise.

Flakes of snow drifted on the light breeze, starting to melt as they touched the ground. He could feel the tension in his aging muscles. The cold always brought with it such discomfort. As his eyes were drawn to the city's skyline, his thoughts were pulled away from his beloved Lilly. Something was very wrong on Terra. He could feel a change looming in the wind. The war with the Nyari had drawn out far longer than he had anticipated. Though the Terran military had been on Nyramar's doorsteps for almost two decades, and his informants assured him that a relatively small increase in funding and a few strategic assaults could end the war for good, Takahashi knew that the Terran Republic had been withdrawing support from the military, decreasing spending with each passing year, citing much-needed reform and economic aid for the homeworld and the outlying colonies. It wasn't that Takahashi disagreed with the Republic's assessment, but he'd discovered that the funds set aside for such reform were actually being diverted elsewhere. It was difficult to spot, to be sure, but not impossible for a man of his means. But where were they being diverted to? He hadn't yet been able to find out.

Now that his daughter had taken over the Muromoto Group, and his time as director of C-CORE had come to an end, Takahashi was left with far too much free time on his hands. Nothing felt worse than the lack of purpose. He was alone most of the time, despite a constant barrage of servants and unscrupulous callers asking for favors. There was no one he could truly confide in.

The night time was the worst. He never slept. His memories haunted him. With all that he had surrendered for the cause, how could they not? At least he had been successful. By now, Captain Mitchell and the others were probably nearing the end of their journey to some distant world, one so far away that they would never return.

"All things come to an end. What matters is how we use the time we have," he muttered, a phrase his mentor had used frequently. He knew it to be true, though he found little comfort in it now. He had to keep busy. He couldn't let his nightmares get the better of him.

"Sweet Lilly," he sighed. "If only you had known. I would welcome your council now. You always were the wise one."

He fiddled with the strap of his old wristwatch. His limbs had gotten thinner over the years, and it kept sliding either too far up or too far down. He'd meant to remove one of the links, but had kept putting it off. Somehow he felt the act would confirm the true state of his body.

"They're up to something. I can feel it," he murmured. "I'm getting too old for this. Perhaps it's time I stepped aside and told our daughter the truth." He hung his head in regret, a moment of silence as he contemplated his dilemma. "She's strong. Stronger even than I ever was," he admitted. "I know she will not believe me at first, but with time... perhaps..."

He raised his gaze skywards, as if awoken from a dream, breathing in heavily and stuffing his wrinkled hands into the pockets of his coat. A lone tear began to form at the corner of his eye, his lips trembling as his mind was drawn back to the beginning, the very beginning.

"The truth is, I'm afraid," he whispered, his voice cracking and his lips trembling with remorse. "Afraid that I've made a most terrible mistake."

"Sir," his driver interrupted from afar, tapping his wrist to remind his employer of the time. Takahashi shot him an angry glance, forestalling any further attempts at disruption.

Takahashi fiddled with the keepsake in his pocket. He ran his fingers along the smooth curves of the cold metal, hooking his fingers on the delicate chain. He withdrew the circular pendant from his pocket, staring at it briefly as it rested in his palm. He had given it to her during their courtship. He remembered the questioning look she had given him, a brief moment of confusion which she had then tried to hide with excitement.

"Hearts are fickle," he had said, "unimaginative. A circle is eternal, just as my love for you," a momentary stint of sentiment on his behalf, one that would see little repetition in later years. Upon hearing his reasoning, her feigned excitement had become genuine, and magnified tenfold. He remembered her embrace as if it had happened yesterday.

He knelt down at the foot of the grave, laying the pendant to rest on the snow below the headstone, tears swelling in his eyes.

"Our circle is eternal," he whispered. "Forgive me."

Chapter 2

The raging downpour of the previous days had slowed to a half-hearted drizzle.

What the crew of the *Tengri* had found at the end of their journey had been vastly different from what they'd been hoping for, and the weather had done little to brighten their spirits. Marcus had told his fellow clones of his vision: a city among the stars, surrounded by thousands of ships of all shapes and sizes. Given that the coordinates of the star system they'd been travelling to had been gleaned from the navigational crystal of a crashed alien ship, one vastly more advanced than the Terrans' own, Marcus and his squadmates had eagerly awaited contact with advanced civilizations and alien races.

Instead, a planet of primitive humanoids was all that had awaited them. The disappointed Terrans had landed their shuttle a few hundred meters from a haphazard arrangement of huts and tents of wood and hide surrounding a central fire pit. It sat on a broad hilltop amidst soaring trees with leaves so large that the cascading rainwater they collected drizzled down in clear and steady streams, dispersing into the wild weeds below. All around the disembarking crew, the jungle had encroached upon them, so thick and seemingly impassable that they'd wondered if this were the only semblance of civilization to be found on this planet.

The locals had come running upon sighting their shuttle, halting only a half a dozen meters or so from the landing site and immediately falling to their knees, apparently in worship. They were enormous, easily twice as tall as a man. Their stocky frames and limbs, thick as tree trunks, bulged with muscles under taut, pale-greenish hides that looked though enough to stop bullets. A single dark, reflective eye was situated on each side of their bald heads, tucked beneath a protruding ridge. A series of puckered holes along the back of their short, massively-thick necks apparently served as their means of breathing, although their wide, gaping mouths looked large enough to swallow a man whole. One of the support staff – the naturally-born Terrans that ran and maintained the *Tengri*'s systems and sustained her crew – had remarked that they looked like a cross between a man and a frog, though Marcus hadn't been familiar with the animal until he'd looked it up in the ship's database.

Much to their relief, the natives had proved to be gentle beings. 'Golan', they called themselves. It had taken the crew's linguist, Serena Kim, the better part of the two weeks since they'd first landed to get a grip on the basics of their language, although she'd made remarkable progress in the few days since then. Meanwhile, the rest of the crew had spent most of their time aboard the cruiser in high orbit, only a handful choosing to remain planetside, enjoying the hospitality of the Golan tribe.

If it weren't for the near-constant rain and the high gravity, Marcus believed the others would have had an easier time of their brief stay. Still, he was glad of their absence. He found solace in the sound that the raindrops made as they impacted on the canopy of leaves above. This world was magnificent, so lush and green. He'd found the perfect spot to spend his days in silence, enjoying the peaceful nature of this world and its gentle creatures, propping himself up on a set of logs underneath a small tent the Golan used to store firewood.

'Ga'ouna'. What a beautiful name for such a tranquil world. And so far away from home, he pondered. Their ship, the *Tengri*, a Benediction-class exploration cruiser, had brought them thousands of light years from the Terran solar system, further than any Terran had gone since the *Lazarus'* one-way trip more than two centuries before. It had been almost ten years since the survivors of Marcus' squad of clones had said their farewells to Takahashi, the man who had arranged for their voluntary exile and saved them from a fate worse than death at the hands of Division 6, a shadow agency that coveted their unique abilities.

Of course, the squad – and the other crew of the *Tengri* – had spent most of that time in cryo-stasis, so it only felt like a few weeks. Still, Marcus was happy to be free from the constant threat of abduction, or worse. Even if the *Tengri* hadn't found the advanced civilization they'd expected, these gentle creatures offered something Marcus would never have been able to have back on Terra: a life of his own, the freedom to choose for himself.

The only thing he truly missed was Eve, the beautiful clone-woman he'd met in training before his squad had first been deployed, and then again after their near-fatal last stand at the Last Oasis. They'd said their goodbyes there, on New Io, hoping they'd soon meet again. Had he known it was to have been their last encounter, Marcus felt he would have done things differently. The best he could hope for now was that she had forgotten all about him and found someone else, someone better than him. Someone who wouldn't make her a target for Division 6.

The rain kept pouring down from the cloud-cast sky. It felt so refreshing, given the warm atmosphere. Jakunu, the Golan tribal chief, had explained to Serena that the rainy season would soon be at an end, and that his people would have to leave for 'Lo'Mock', a form of tribal gathering.

"Marcus?" He started, only now noticing Serena standing outside his shelter, her long flowing brown hair soaking wet from the rain. "The others are heading back to the ship. Do you want to join them?"

Just then a pair of Golan children ran past them, chasing a plump, purple fly the size of a clenched human fist, giggling hysterically. Marcus smiled, following their playful antics. Even though they were just children, they were almost as tall as he was.

"No, I think I'll stay," he replied.

"Are you sure?" she questioned, her narrow brown eyes crinkling, hinting at her relief. "It will just be me and you then."

She and Marcus were the only ones who seemed more content with the Golan tribe than they did aboard the ship. She was a naturally-born Terran, not a clone, and her delicate features, fair skin and petite frame seemed better suited to a career working in libraries than alien jungles, so Marcus was surprised to see how much she had taken to the Golan people and their primitive way of life. She always wanted to experience all of their customs, taste their food and their wine, take part in their tribal dancing and play with their children. Like him, she seemed more at home in the jungle.

"I'm sure," he assured her, "though I can't seem to get over the rain." he added. "It's amazing."

"The rain?" she asked, confused. "What do you mean?"

As a cloned soldier only a few months old, Marcus had experienced zero gravity, deadly atmospheric conditions on the moon of Triton and assault by alien creatures, but although he had seen rain through the windows of Takahashi's penthouse suite in Sol, this was the first time in his life that he'd been able to experience it firsthand, to feel it on his skin.

"Never mind," he sighed.

Across the central clearing, Jakunu and Jago, one of Marcus' squadmates, appeared from an opening on one of the larger huts, a hexagonal structure whose walls had been painted with symbols of crimson and green, many of which depicted Golan figures dancing around a fire or praying to the sky. Jago was a virtual giant of a man, whose muscular frame was almost too large for his body. He had a broad angular jaw and a monstrous hooked nose, his prominent brow ridge protruding below the dark stubble of close-cropped hair, which was broken by a set of scars.

Despite the clone's towering form, however, he was dwarfed by the enormous chieftain. Jakunu was nothing like what Marcus had expected from a leader. From his experience in the Terran military, Marcus had thought that all leaders were as stern and stubborn as his officers had been. The Golan chieftain was the opposite, a bubbly, cheerful sort who, once Serena had explained to him and his people that the Terrans were not gods but merely travelers from another world, had reveled in the marvels these new friends had to offer. His inquisitive nature was more akin to that of a child. The huge pair circumvented the fire pit, approaching the wood store.

"Marcus, the shuttle is going soon," Jago rumbled. "The boss says we can go back to the ship now."

Jakunu, meanwhile, held one of Jago's cigars in his stubby fingers, rolling it back and forth, trying to devise the nature of the peculiar object.

"I'm staying," Marcus answered. "What's with the cigar?"

"Oh, gift. I think he will like it," Jago explained, obviously enjoying the chieftain's company.

"Hoji hili sahako?" muttered the Chieftain, sticking out his slimy, flesh-colored tongue to lick the base of the cigar.

"No, no," Jago stopped him. "You smoke it. Smoke… it."

Serena shook her head in quiet disbelief.

"He doesn't understand you, Jago. And you shouldn't be giving him that! You have no idea what that thing will do to him. It's not exactly healthy for you either," she scolded.

"Heh, no, no, the Doc gave him one of his cigarettes yesterday. He was fine," Jago retorted, grabbing the chieftain by his massive arm and guiding him back to the tent, leaving Serena standing there with a perplexed look on her face.

"The *Doc* gave him…?" She exclaimed, outraged.

Finally she just shook her head and stormed off towards the shuttle, no doubt to give 'Doc' Taylor – the squad's medic, and the closest thing the *Tengri* had to a medical officer – a stern talking to. Marcus chuckled. If this was to be the extent of their troubles on this new world, then he was all too happy to stay.

A few minutes later, Jago emerged from the now smoke filled tent, stomping off towards the shuttle while the chieftain stood in the doorway waving him off. The bizarre image of the alien chieftain puffing on the cigar, which seemed quite miniscule between his thick lips, brought yet another smile to Marcus' face, a smile that only widened when the smoke wafted from the series of holes on the back of the alien's neck.

Marcus crawled further back underneath the awning sheltering the woodpile. He let his eyelids close softly while breathing in the fresh air. The aroma of wet grass filled his nostrils. The laughter of children in the distance and the soft humming of the tribesfolk preparing the afternoon meal was gentle enough to lull him gradually into a doze. Before drifting off and allowing his drowsiness to get the better of him, Marcus sighed and whispered faintly to himself. "I'm home."

Chapter 3

Taz sat perched on the small metal crate he'd obtained from the ship's stores, hiding behind an open locker door in the far corner of the changing room. He was a shabby dark-skinned man, whose long, narrow face was covered in dark stubble from ear to ear. His close-set brown eyes never strayed far from anyone of the female persuasion, and his plump nose seemed to be permanently stuck in someone else's business. He rubbed his knees with his stubby fingers. His joints ached from having sat there too long. Still, he hadn't chosen the location for its comfort, but rather for the view it would soon offer.

He could hear the water from the shower pouring, splashing against the hard surface of the tiled floor. She must be almost done, he thought as he began unbuttoning his pants, slowly, carefully, without making a sound. Not that she could have heard him anyway, what with the shower running. Still, he'd been bred to be a scout, and was burdened with a high level of innate paranoia. He imagined her standing there, her wet skin glistening as the water streamed down her naked body, washing away the milky white froth that still lingered from the soap.

He froze abruptly, one hand wedged down his trousers, the other firmly holding the locker door in place for cover. Is there someone else here? he thought. He could have sworn he'd heard the hatch to the compartment open. Leaning forward, he tilted his head so he could take in all the sounds with his oversized ears.

Don't even breathe, he reminded himself. If the captain found out what he was up to, he'd be on latrine duty for a month… if he was lucky.

He could hear breathing on the other side of the locker door, rapid and shallow. Was it her? Had she seen him?

Carefully he poked his head around the corner to steal a glance, but couldn't bring himself to open his eyes. His lids clamped firmly down, he waited for the cry of alarm and outrage, but heard only silence… until he felt the warm wet tongue licking his nose.

"Spot!" he gasped, his eyes flying open, seeing the captain's pet, nearly tipping off of his perch on the crate from shock. "Will you get out of here! You're going to get me spaced!"

The little beast looked as if it had just run headfirst into a wall, its comically large eyes set above its squashed snout. The canine tilted its head from side to side, staring vacantly at Taz in bewilderment.

"Shoo!" Taz hissed, letting go of the locker door to wave the little animal away. He knew she was almost done. Any moment now she'd come out of the stalls and into the changing room.

"Get out!" he whispered as loudly as he dared, clambering to his feet with one hand clutching his half-open pants to stop them slipping down, shuffling after the animal which backed away, panting heavily.

At that moment he heard the water being turned off, and immediately sprang forward, rushing for the hatch to the gangway as fast as he could with his pants falling around his ankles, Spot playfully running out ahead of him, tail wagging.

The hatch slammed shut behind him just in time, and Taz found himself leaning with his back against it out in the corridor, staring into the big, blank eyes of the squad's sniper, Reid Albano.

He was a tall man, his muscular frame nearly a foot taller than Taz, his skin an even darker shade than the panicked scout's. Reid stood there, eyebrows raised, arms folded over his chest, a questioning look in his eyes. "Well, I suppose it was only a matter of time," he eventually deadpanned, jerking a thumb to indicated Spot, who was now sniffing at Taz's boots. "You do know it's male, don't you?"

"I wasn't…" Taz began to explain, pulling his pants up.

"I don't know which the captain would find more disturbing, that you were… pleasuring yourself in the women's showers, or that you were doing it while watching his dog."

"Oh fuck off, will you. Kaiden's in there!" Taz hissed, trying to keep his voice down so she wouldn't hear him through the closed door.

"Well, that's a bit less disturbing, but I don't think the captain will like that either. He's got an eye for her himself," Reid chuckled.

"He'll probably space me out of jealousy alone," sighed Taz as he finished buckling his belt. "Not that I'd blame him much! I've never seen anyone like her."

There was truth to his words. Taz had never seen skin so smooth, not that he'd seen that much skin at all, despite his incessant boasting. Aboard the *Tengri*, Kaiden Karell was every man's fantasy. She had lightly tanned skin, long flowing brown locks and an ample bosom. It didn't hurt that her position put her in close physical proximity with the men of the crew on frequent occasion: she filled a variety of roles including the duties of ship's nurse, physical therapist and psychiatrist, her training complimented by her strong and determined character. She was also quite adept at using her good looks to coax those under her care to push themselves to the limit.

"You won't say anything, will you?" Taz begged, grabbing Reid by the shoulder and peering down the gangway to make sure their conversation wasn't being overheard.

Reid stared at him, as if he were measuring him up, tormenting him with silence. Finally he spoke.

"Well… it's not like this is something I really want to remember," he said. "So I guess your secret's safe… at least for now."

* * * * *

"Any more data from the probe?" prompted Captain Mitchell, who'd barely left the bridge in days.

He knew they'd been lucky to have reached upon a world with breathable air, but he'd been expecting more. The lush green world below might offer shelter and sustenance, but with its high gravity it would cause all manner of skeletal deterioration, circulatory problems and other health issues for his crew were they to settle there. It was a shame. Ga'ouna was a tranquil world, with vast clear oceans, teaming with life, though its numerous moons made for some unpredictable weather patterns.

"Nothing new Captain," replied Navigator Wei.

"Hmpfh," Captain Mitchell grunted. His thoughts weighed heavily on his mind. He had hoped that the massive gas giant in the system's farthest orbit might harbor moons more suitable for habitation. He leaned against the railing by the forward viewport, staring at the glimmering ocean on the planet below.

"Serena seems to be enjoying herself," Navigator Wei said, in a vain attempt to appease him. "Her latest reports show that the-"

"I read the reports," the captain retorted, cutting him short. "If it weren't for the gravity, it would be ideal."

"I overheard Dr. Gehringer in the mess this morning. He was mumbling about the possibility of constructing a device that would reduce the-"

"I know. He mentioned it to me," Captain Mitchell snapped, turning his back on the enormous viewport. "It would take years to build, what with our limited resources, and its effectiveness would only be viable over a short distance, assuming he could get it to work in the first place."

Though he appreciated the navigator's attempts to lift his spirits, his own morale wasn't the one that concerned him. Though he had heard no protests or complaints from his crew, it was the silence that disturbed him. Apathy abounded, people's expressions were vacant as they went about their daily routines, routines which held little meaning if this was to be their end. He'd have been happier with another hostile encounter, like the Nyari. At least then they would have gone out fighting, rather than living out the rest of their days in some squalid hut, their bodies slowly crumbling under too-high gravity, of all things. It was not a notion that particularly appealed to him.

When it had been offered, he'd seen the mission as a great honor. Takahashi had made C-CORE hold off on selecting a captain for the ship to make room for his appointment. This could have been his greatest achievement, the farthest that any Terran had ventured since the *Lazarus*. Now it was to be his greatest failure, a footnote in history: Robert Mitchell, Captain of the TES-*Tengri*, embarked on an exploratory mission to Sector 09-09. Status: unknown.

"Unknown," he mumbled. Is there anything more terrifying?

* * * * *

"Is that from a battle?" asked Serena, gesturing to the faded T-shaped scar on Marcus' chest. He had removed his shirt to bask in the

18

afternoon sun on a small hill overlooking the Golan village.

"What?" said Marcus, startled.

"Sorry. People say I can be overly curious," she apologized, standing over him. "I haven't met many soldiers. C-CORE doesn't usually get involved with clones. Not that I have anything against clones. It's just, I…"

"It's ok," Marcus smiled, cutting her short. "Actually this one is from when I was… born."

She looked away, down to the village below, followed by an uncomfortably long silence. Whether it was because of her interest in the Golan tribe, or perhaps because she wasn't a clone, Marcus couldn't tell, but there was something very unique about her, an aura that seemed to follow her wherever she went. She was gentle, but unflinching, like a sapling in a forest glade, fragile yet determined to grow strong and proud.

"This one…" he mumbled awkwardly, feeling compelled to break the silence. "I got this one in battle," he said, pointing to the scar on his cheek, just below his left eye. He regretted it immediately. She would want to hear the details of how he received it. She herself had admitted that she was overly curious.

"It's ok Marcus… It's none of my business," she sighed, a hint of sadness in her voice.

How did she know? Marcus thought. Can she read my mind? The thought had never occurred to him that any of the crew, apart from the captain, might be a telepath. They were supposed to be incredibly rare, but if Division 6 relied heavily on such talents, it wasn't entirely unthinkable that C-CORE might do so as well.

"I can see it upsets you to think about it," she added after a brief pause.

"Oh, I thought…" Marcus began, before stopping himself. "Never mind."

"I'm sorry if I've bothered you. I just thought you might want some company. You're always by yourself," she explained as she turned to leave.

"No, wait!" he called. "You can sit… if you like."

The corners of her mouth curled up into a warm smile.

"Alright then," she replied, taking in a deep breath of the fresh forest air before plopping down beside him.

They gazed over the surrounding landscape. The top of the forest canopy rolled out before them, a blanket of greenish hues which seemed entirely unbroken. Marcus could see mountaintops shrouded by clouds so far away that he imagined it would take weeks to reach them on foot. The laughter of Golan children playing somewhere on the outskirts of the village drew him back from his daydreams.

"He was my friend," he finally sighed.

"Who was?" Serena asked, perplexed.

"The one who gave me this scar," Marcus explained, awkwardly rubbing his left cheek. "He tried to run a knife through my eye… but I… I stopped him." The memories brought with them a rush of emotion. Regret, sadness, anger.

Serena put her delicate hand on his shoulder for comfort.

"It's a strange world we live in, Marcus," she exclaimed, "People will do terrible things, often for the most foolish of reasons."

What could she possibly know of such things? he thought. She wasn't a clone. She knew nothing of war and battle.

"You can't let the mistakes of others dictate how you live your life," she told him. "And you shouldn't blame yourself."

She was right. He knew she was right.

"Is it weird, being a clone?" she asked, unexpectedly.

"I… I don't really have anything to compare it to," Marcus answered, taken aback by her change of subject.

"I suppose it must be nice having so many brothers and sisters, and all of you being born on the same day makes it easy to remember everyone's birthday," she chuckled.

Marcus couldn't help but smile. Her positive attitude was infectious. He'd noticed that Serena smiled a lot. It was as if none of the world's problems affected her in the least.

"Aren't you disappointed at all?" he ventured.

"Disappointed?"

"Well, this, all of this," he explained.

"Marcus, we flew thousands of light years, spent nearly ten years in stasis, all on the remote chance that maybe, just maybe, we might find… something, anything. I don't think the others realize just how lucky we are. We could have wound up on a lifeless ball of dust, or even worse, a system with no planets at all. Even finding microbial life forms would have been a thrill. The Golan are amazing. Did you know the evolution of their society is not unlike our own? Thousands of years ago we weren't that much different from them."

He had to admit, the thought wasn't entirely unappealing to him.

"Although I suppose our history hasn't been quite as peaceful as theirs seems to be," she added. "Even in our infancy, we humans were quite adept at killing each other. The Golan seem to know nothing of war, or hatred, or greed. They live a life of perfect harmony, with nature and each other."

Marcus leaned back on the grass, gazing skyward. Perhaps in time, the others would come to see Ga'ouna as they did, for the paradise it truly was.

21

Chapter 4

By noon the clouds had cleared up, and for the first time in two weeks Marcus could see the bright orange sun lazily soaring across the pristine sky.

Jakunu stood by the fire pit, barking orders at his eldest son, Hanasi, who stood scratching his head as he attempted to get a fire started.

"Huno, huno. Holi livo puto muvuni," shouted Jakunu, kicking a wet piece of wood from the fire pit. Hanasi shook his head in silent protest before scampering off to search for some dry wood.

The shuttle had arrived moments earlier and Marcus was waiting to greet its passengers. Emerging from the bushes, Captain Mitchell and Doc Taylor cleared a path for Dr. Max Gehringer, the lead scientist assigned to their expedition. He was the strangest man Marcus had ever met. Though he looked middle aged, his paper-white skin was delicate and smooth, seeming to almost sizzle in the direct sunlight that washed over him as he stumbled clumsily into the clearing, dropping his datapad. The man had no hair at all, not even eyebrows, and the sheen on his bald head sparkled like moonlight on a still lake. He struggled to extricate his limp little frame from the last of the tangled undergrowth, peering warily in every direction, clearly expecting some savage alien beast to jump him. He cut a ridiculous figure, and Marcus was barely able to contain his laughter when he saw that the scientist was still wearing a stark white lab coat over a plain white shirt and grey dress pants, hardly appropriate gear for the jungle. Even worse, his pale coloring and white clothing made him look ghostlike and utterly out of place.

"Corporal Grey, what… ehm… I mean… these beasts, they are safe, yes?" he stuttered, snatching his datapad from the muddy ground and holding it aloft as if it were some form of shield.

"Yes, it's quite safe," Marcus told him, fighting desperately to keep a straight face. "Come, I'll introduce you to Jakunu."

Marcus could see that the frail man still had his reservations, so he reached out and took him by the arm, leading him towards the chieftain. Serena stood by the hulking giant, her hand covering her mouth to conceal her grin.

"MAX," Marcus pronounced clearly, gesturing to Dr. Gehringer.

The baffled chieftain stared at the cadaverous figure before him. Finally he bent down on one knee, looking the scientist straight in the eye before repeating the name in his thunderous voice.

Dr. Gehringer stumbled backwards in shock upon hearing Jakunu's thundering voice, paling even further.

"It's alright Doctor, I assure you they're quite friendly," Serena proclaimed. "Curious, but friendly."

"Ije livo tompo?" rumbled Jakunu, turning to the others with a questioning gaze.

"No, no. Uhm… Ije livo… nosuli muta. Huno tompo," Serena corrected him.

"He thought that Dr. Gehringer was our leader," she explained to them.

"Remarkable," the scientist gasped. "Do you think it would be possible to borrow one for experimentation?"

This wasn't the first time Marcus had heard the scientist say something so inappropriate. As ridiculous as he was sometimes, Gehringer seemed to suffer a lack of empathy with any living thing

23

that borded on the chilling.

"Most certainly not!" Serena retorted. "These aren't lab animals, they're sentient beings! They are to be treated with respect!" she bellowed, her voice getting louder and louder, clearly infuriated by the thought of what the scientist might have in store. "And just because-"

"I think he gets the point Serena," Marcus interjected, stopping her before things took a violent turn. Given Gehringer's frail physique, Marcus feared a simple slap might leave him bedridden for days.

On the other side of the clearing, Taylor had decided the introductions would hold little interest for him and had wandered off a short distance away from the gathering.

He'd never had much time for military discipline, and his mud-brown hair had grown much longer than the standard crop the other clones still wore. It almost reached the center of his neck, brushed haphazardly behind his ears to reveal his pale blue eyes and freckled cheeks. Despite his tousled hair and three-day stubble, however, he exuded a natural charm and lazy confidence that reassured – or infuriated – those around him.

He'd taken a particular interest in a set of small trees, with peculiar bright green elongated leaves with seven leaflets. Given the intense rain that Ga'ouna had experienced for the past weeks, he'd spent most of his time in orbit aboard the *Tengri*, and had had little opportunity to examine the planet's flora and fauna. Now that he was free to indulge his curiosity, the young medic proceeded to pluck a few of the leaves, feeling their soft texture and sniffing their sharp scent.

"Huno masuko Je'eela, mahando!" bellowed the Golan chieftain, suddenly bursting into action and heading straight for the medic standing across the clearing.

With a startled glance at each other, Marcus and Serena followed

24

him as fast as they could, with Gehringer stumbling along after them at the rear, panting heavily. Captain Mitchell quietly unlocked the safety on the sidearm hanging from his belt, and limped after them in a calm, determined manner.

The chieftain stopped a few meters shy of the startled Taylor, bellowing a series of unintelligible words, which, from the tone, Marcus could only surmise were insults.

"Nivalo livo vanjavi?" Serena pleaded, placing herself between Jakunu and Taylor.

The towering giant flexed his powerful muscles, almost quivering with anger.

"Je'eela livo junuluku! Nutu Golan livo vingani yulluku!" the chieftain proclaimed, thumping his chest with a clenched fist.

"Put the leaves down Taylor," Serena instructed, without turning to look at the astonished clone, both of her arms raised to appease Jakunu.

Jakunu's son Hanasi had come running up behind them and now loomed over Dr. Gehringer, who looked as if he was about to faint, though perhaps no more than usual.

"Friendly?" the gaunt Dr. Gehringer piped, backing away from the grim-faced Golan youth, his legs shaking with fear.

"What's going on?" Taylor asked, slowly bending his knees to gently place the leaves on the ground.

"They're 'Je'eela' leaves, sacred leaves, I think. Only the Golan are allowed to touch them," Serena told him. "Nuvo nutu vave?" she continued, turning back to the chieftain who was now beginning to ease up.

"Ju'ungusi samo nutu Golan janu yulluku Je'eela. Ono vinganu hao vaki ya ju'ungusi. Navo ya ju'ungusi juko umo Ga'ouna, ono guo

25

Je'eela umo ya ju'ungusi," Jakunu explained, waving his hands around him whilst his son stood tensely beside the Terrans.

It took Serena a few moments to decipher the chieftain's meaning, and even then she wasn't sure that she had understood him correctly.

"I think what he's saying is that the gods have declared that only the Golan are allowed to touch the sacred leaves. They collect them for the gods. When the gods come to Ga'ouna, they give the leaves to them… as a form of offering I suppose?"

Captain Mitchell, who had remained silent throughout the scene so far, now felt compelled to speak.

"Gods? They believe that their gods are coming here?"

"I believe so," Serena replied. "And, well… remember how the Golan thought we were gods when we first landed? Could these 'gods' be an alien species of some sort? If they're coming here, they may be able to assist us!"

"When are the gods coming?" Captain Mitchell inquired, genuinely intrigued by the implications of this newfound information.

"Jakunu, navo livo ya ju'ungusi juko?" she asked, her eyes on her datapad making sure that she had chosen her words correctly.

The chieftain's reply was a single word. "Lo'Mock."

"Lo'Mock?" Serena repeated, staring intently at the Golan chieftain, who repeated it yet again in response.

"They're coming to the tribal gathering," Serena informed them.

During the commotion, Doc Taylor had taken the liberty of pocketing one of the sacred leaves while no one was looking. He knew that if any of the Golan people would have seen him, it would have meant serious trouble, but the urge to discover why the 'gods' were so interested in the Je'eela leaves overcame his fear of the consequences. Nothing drove Taylor than being told he couldn't – or shouldn't – do something.

In an attempt to end the debate and draw attention away from his actions, he ostentatiously produced a packet of cigarettes and placed one in his mouth before offering another to the chieftain.

"Then I guess we'll have to wait for Lo'Mock," the captain concluded, releasing his grip on his sidearm. "I just hope it doesn't start raining again. This place is starting to remind me of Nyramar." The captain massaged his knee, the thought of the Nyari homeworld making his old war wound twinge.

"So how long will we have to wait?" Marcus asked, half hoping that the gods would be just that, not aliens at all. He was in no rush to leave Ga'ouna, the world which had brought him such serenity.

"The tribal gathering is supposed to take place at the end of the rainy season," Serena replied, "which could be any day now."

Even though the towering chieftain had knelt down on his knee, Taylor had to stretch up in order to light his cigarette. Jakunu took a couple of long puffs, and wafts of smoke appeared from the holes on the back of his neck. Hanasi looked on in amazement, as if his father were taking part in a magical ritual.

"I'll be in orbit until then," Captain Mitchell proclaimed. "I've had enough jungles to last me two lifetimes." He turned and limped into the trees.

"I think... ehm... maybe it's best if... I join you, eh Captain?" Dr. Gehringer stuttered, his short spindly legs scurrying as he followed the captain much more rapidly than on their arrival.

Chapter 5

The Golan tribe dismantling their huts and packing their tents in preparation for their journey to Lo'Mock made an impressive sight. As the tribe migrated between seasons, they would not be coming back this way after the gathering, but would find a new place to call home. Everything had to be taken with them, and everyone had a task to perform: the children, even the elders, all did their part to ease the passage to Lo'Mock.

Marcus was excited about the journey, although his excitement was mixed with a hint of sadness. If the gods were truly coming to Lo'Mock, perhaps their team might be departing Ga'ouna. He didn't want to leave. He felt so at home here.

The long line of Golan marched through the thick undergrowth of the jungle. It had seemed so still during the excessive downpour, but now the jungle was teaming with life. A choir of squeaks, chirps and wails could be heard from every direction. Reid and Taz had been assigned to take point, walking with the foremost Golan, though their reservation for the task was apparent, as they had little knowledge of which of the jungle's denizens could pose them any harm. Marcus strode along next to Serena just behind the front of the tribe, both of them sharing a moment of silent wonder as they took in all that the jungle had to offer, Taylor stopping periodically to examine particularly weird or interesting examples of local plant or insect life, every so often having to sprint to catch up to them.

Captain Mitchell had ordered the squad – with the exception of

Raven and Jago – to join the march as observers, but of the support staff only Serena had elected to walk with them. The captain himself, between his crippled leg and constant edginess in the jungle, planned instead to return to the ship and follow the migration from orbit.

"I feel sorry for the others," Serena confessed. "They're missing out on all of this."

Marcus didn't reply, he simply smiled, completely at ease.

Taz deftly dodged a long, yellow insect with a segmented torso as it swooped down from the canopy on shimmering wings, narrowly missing the startled scout who gave a shout of alarm and hefted his carbine. Having witnessed the spectacle, Jakunu roared with laughter as the creature performed a sort of rhythmic dance as it hovered around the spooked clone, before skittering further off into the jungle.

"Careful Taz, I think it likes you," Serena joked, shooting Marcus a quick grin and lowering her voice. "None of the creatures we've studied are dangerous to humans," Serena whispered to Marcus. "I would tell him, but that would spoil the fun."

Marcus chuckled. During the course of their stay on Ga'ouna he had come to enjoy Serena's company. They hadn't spoken much, but their mutual respect for the Golan people and their wondrous world meant more to him than he was willing to admit.

*   *   *   *   *

They spent the first night camping in a small clearing. The tents had been arranged in a circle with room in the center for the tribe to gather and eat a meal of an assortment of berries and fruits that had been gathered by the young during their journey. A small campfire provided enough light for them to enjoy the song and dance which

29

quickly followed the evening meal.

A heavy-set Golan female propped herself upon a large rock near the center of the camp, and begun humming in a low droning tone, followed shortly by a chorus of the higher-pitched younglings. The rest of the tribe gathered around them and began a circular dance which lasted well into the late hours of the night. Marcus and the others enjoyed the spectacle for a while, but as the journey through the jungle in Ga'ouna's high gravity had been particularly taxing for them, they quickly succumbed to sleep, not bothering to erect the tents they'd brought in the warmth of the fire.

* * * * *

Perhaps due to the threat of an abrupt departure from Ga'ouna, Marcus slept uneasily that the night. Visions of his oldest and closest friend Steven plagued his dreams.

Marcus had already come to terms with how things had unfolded. There was no other way, nothing he could have done to save him. His friend was already dead before their last encounter. Steven had no longer been the young idealist Marcus had come to know and grown to care for. That thing he had fought at the Strom sensor outpost was something else entirely. There had been so much anger burning inside him, fueling him to do unspeakable things. When they'd first met, Steven had aspired to freedom, not just for himself but for all clones. He'd wanted to offer them a better life, their own choices. How he had ended up on the path he'd eventually chosen was something that Marcus couldn't understand. He probably never would.

A few strands of morning sunlight were already filtering through the canopy overhead when Jakunu nudged Marcus with his stumpy leg, almost sending him flying.

"Kamaso lanji muta," the huge chieftain chuckled.

Marcus followed the Golan's gaze to see Serena lying beside him. Her sleeping bag was only a hair's breadth from his, her normally well-kept long hair now tousled. With a yawn, she sat up.

"Morning, Marcus," she smiled. "Sleep well?"

"...yeah. Not bad," he lied, reluctant to answer the questions he would have to endure if he admitted otherwise.

The tribe had already packed most of their tents and they were getting ready to leave the clearing, so Marcus and the others hastily stuffed their sleeping bags back into their rucksacks and forced their stiff limbs through a quick series of awkward stretches. As they finished, a Golan youngling brought them each a pair of bright orange berries, each the size of a small apple. Their sweet, succulent flesh had a hint of bitterness that Marcus found refreshing. An aroma of honey clung to the air as a misty spray of juices spewed forth with every bite.

"I love these," Serena muttered around a mouthful of the fruit. "We should take some with us when we leave."

Marcus feigned a smile. He didn't want to think about leaving unless it became inevitable. For all they knew the 'gods' might not even exist. Perhaps they were simply some creature native to Ga'ouna, and the Golan had made up all the superstitious rules and laws that governed their religion. As far as he was concerned, there was no need to worry until they knew for sure... or so he tried to convince himself.

*   *   *   *   *

After several days of hiking, the tribe breached the densest part of the jungle and emerged on a small rocky outcropping overlooking the coastline, still half a day's walk away. A short distance to their left, a huge waterfall tumbled from a towering cliff above them, roaring like a savage thunderstorm. Rays of sunlight crested the only cloud visible in the pale blue sky, producing a colorful rainbow, whose bow touched the shoreline of a distant pensinsula.

Marcus was dumbfounded by the breathtaking beauty of the scene that unfolded before him. He stood at the edge of the outcropping, his mouth agape and his eyes wide open, unable to utter a single word. Beside him, Serena started to reach out her hand, wanting to share this moment by connecting with him, but she hesitated, unsure how he'd react.

"Are you guys coming?" Doc Taylor yelled, shattering the peace of the moment, turning to follow the tribe as they made their way down a narrow ledge leading down to the coast.

Shaken from his coma, Marcus reluctantly followed at a slow pace, unwilling to surrender the moment. The procession wound its way onwards along the cliff face for several hours, reaching the sandy shores below around midday, just as the sun was lazily beginning its slow decent.

A stretch of short grass separated the rocky cliffs from the inviting beach before them. Jakunu decided that this would be an ideal spot to take a short break before continuing onwards, and the younglings began distributing fruits and waterskins to the elders who had grown weary from the long travels. Marcus wasn't hungry. He couldn't stop staring at the ocean. The sound of waves beating on the rocks was the most spectacularly soothing sound he had ever heard, and distracted him completely from the shooting pain in his calves. So much water!, he thought. He had never seen so much water before. He felt like running down to the shore, tearing off his clothes and diving into it.

32

Just then, a youngling came rushing by, chasing another one of the plump purple flies. The small Golan leapt comically into the air in bounding strides, reaching out to try to catch the poor creature with its bare hands. Luck struck on the fourth bound as the Golan boy caught hold of one of the insect's wings, tearing the buzzing fly from the sky. The boy marveled at his luck, his wide mouth agape in silent wonder before bouncing off in search of his father. Marcus watched as he proudly presented his catch, and his father patted him on the head in a weirdly human gesture, before fetching a small ceramic jar and squeezing the fly between his stubby fingers until it burst, catching its gooey juices into the jar.

"They use it as an adhesive," Serena told him, following his gaze. "It's remarkably strong. They use it to build their huts."

Marcus smiled at her in reply and focused his attention back on the breaking waves of the magnificent ocean.

After a brief reprieve, the tribe once again continued their steady pace towards Lo'Mock. Before setting foot on the sandy beach, Marcus removed his boots. After tying them together and slinging them over his shoulder, he ran barefooted down the shore. The feeling of the scorching sand giving way to his bare skin was like nothing he'd ever felt, gritty and refreshing, but it was the soothing sea which offered the most surprising sensation. He couldn't believe how good it felt to run along the shore, splashing through the salty waves with each step.

Jakunu roared with laughter from the sidelines, enjoying Marcus' escapades. Watching the paddling clone, the bubbly chieftain noticed an assortment of gigantic clams lying on the beach up ahead and gave a cry of delight, making a beeline for the tasty treats. He ushered the Terrans over as he began prying open a massive shell with his bare

33

hands. It was easily a meter wide, with a pattern of purple veins running along its cream-colored surface and dark spiny ridges bordering the rim of its mouth. As the shell began to give way to Jakunu's tremendous strength, it exuded a loud popping sound before finally snapping in half.

Jakunu proudly offered one half to Marcus and the others while gorging himself on the contents of the other. Marcus grimaced at the thought of eating the raw contents. The others looked at him, waiting for him to try it before working up the nerve to do so themselves. The bluish sludge at the bottom of the shell shimmered in the sunlight, with creamy, membranous globs sporadically covering its surface. Marcus squinted in disgust before finally giving in. He scooped up a portion of the slimy substance with his quivering fingers and put it into his mouth, grimacing with disgust. It tasted awful. It was a briny, viscous substance with a grainy texture and a bitter aftertaste that made him gag as he forced himself to swallow.

"It's not bad," he lied, forcing a smile as he tried to persuade the others to have a go.

"You're so full of shit," Reid chuckled, playfully thumping Marcus on the shoulder.

With the others unwilling to taste of the Golan delicacy, they handed the clam to the nearest Golan who was only too happy to devour its contents, sharing it with his wife and children.

For the next few hours they continued along the coastline, before veering back towards the mainland over a grassy hill just as the horizon took on the first red tinge of dusk. As the hills rolled on before them, weariness set in. The climbing became increasingly more difficult, the heavy gravity weighing them down, and they hoped that they were soon nearing their destination. Finally, as the tribe reached a particularly tall hill, the scene gave way to wide, open plains with a river of clear spring water cutting a clear swath through its center, merging with the breaking waves of the sea a short distance away.

A few tall, solitary trees broke the monotony of the landscape, casting their soft shadows upon the terrain, while on the banks of the river a horde of Golan busied themselves erecting a small city of tents and huts, of all sizes and shapes, a myriad of colors dotting the countryside. From the crest of their hill, the Terrans could hear a chorus of Golan songs being sung. Near the center of the throng, a roaring fire cast bright orange sparks flying into the air where the winds swept them off on an epic journey of their own. They'd finally reached Lo'Mock.

Chapter 6

The diligence of the Golan tribes as they erected their city of tents and huts left quite an impression on the Terrans. In just few short days the primitive natives had managed to organize and construct a vibrant community, complete with temporary homes, tribal councils, eateries, and booths to peddle their wares and entertain patrons. Lo'Mock bustled with commerce, conducted either through barter or by the exchange of colored stones.

Jakunu's tribe had been allocated a stretch of land near the outskirts of Lo'Mock, wedged between a sprawling bazaar and the sparkling ocean, whose waves lit up under the bright reflection of Ga'ouna's many moons. Although the team was weary from their long journey, they were eager to help Jakunu and his tribe set up camp. The sooner they finished, the sooner they could sample the exotic delicacies of the combined tribes, for Captain Mitchell had ordered that they weren't to explore on their own until Jakunu had had the chance to spread the word about them. From the beating of heavy drums in the distance, to the crackling of the massive bonfire and to the myriad of exotic scents filling their senses, Lo'Mock promised to be all they had expected, and more.

Hanasi led the construction efforts, with Jakunu cheerily barking orders to the tribe whilst clutching a large jug full of fermented wine. Marcus was intrigued by the rapid pace at which the Golan worked, and the efficiency with which they reconstructed their collapsible shelters. Large beams of wood were erected and tied together with vines. A layer of gigantic leaves, carried from the jungle in bundles on narrow travois, was then glued onto the beams with the glue extracted from the plump purple flies. Wooden racks for displaying a collection of shells and trinkets were constructed, and a private fire pit was dug in the camp's center.

The tribe worked well into the night, but when they were nearly finished another tribe was spotted on the horizon, heavily loaded with supplies. Jakunu sent his son and a few of the tribe's strongest to aid them on the last stretch of what must have been a long and arduous journey.

Serena and Doc Taylor had already fallen fast asleep, exhausted from the heavy labor. Marcus and Reid sat propped upon a pair of logs near the fire pit, enjoying the stillness of the night as the tribal music died down.

"Do you think these gods are really gonna show up?" Reid asked, staring at a large moon floating low over the horizon, its shape merging with its reflection on the ocean.

"I don't know if I want them to," Marcus confessed. "I'm not sure I want to leave."

Reid smiled, having begun to understand Marcus' fascination with Ga'ouna.

"Marcus," he prompted after a long stint of silence. "Your dream… your vision… it showed a city among the stars, and thousands of ships, right?. Do you really think it's out there somewhere… waiting to be discovered?"

"I don't see why not. We've seen so little of the galaxy, and already we've encountered the Nyari and the Golan. Don't forget the crashed ship on New Io. That's three species we've encountered already," Marcus reminded him. "Who's to say how many more could be out there?"

Reid pondered Marcus' reply and concluded that his friend was most likely correct.

"But then, if there are other races out there waiting to be discovered, do you think they believe in God as we do?" he asked.

"I don't think I'm the right man to answer that, Rev," Marcus joked. "I'm not sure I believe in such things myself."

"But what about our… powers? Those… things… we did on Strom. Don't you think those could have been acts of God?" Reid continued, genuinely puzzled.

"I suppose they could have been… but I think it's far more likely that it's the result of some form of experimentation. Don't forget what Taz heard about Division 6, that they've been trying to breed new types of psionics for decades. Maybe when the W.R.D. made us, they made us different somehow. Division 6 could have tampered with our D.N.A… or maybe the probe we carried to Triton had something to do with it. Or maybe it's all circumstance," Marcus broke off, remembering their painful experiences in the Terran system. "Don't forget why we're out here. Division 6 would be only too happy to get a hold of us. If that happens I really do hope God is real, because he'll be the only one who can save us."

"I suppose you're right," Reid gave in, disappointed, his eyes already half-closed in sleep.

"Get some rest Rev. There'll be plenty of time for religious debate tomorrow," Marcus chuckled, grabbing his pack and heading off towards his tent.

* * * * *

The bustle of Jakunu's tribe preparing the evening meal awoke Marcus from his restful slumber. He'd slept clear through the day, and the shuttle carrying Captain Mitchell and Dr. Gehringer had already arrived, causing quite a stir. Although Jakunu had already explained to the neighboring tribes that these new arrivals were not gods, their camp was filled with new faces, come to catch a glimpse of the sky people.

"Marcus, you're missing all the fun," Taz's voice called. "Muhungu here is just about to bake us up some clams."

A towering female stood by the fire pit, having placed a wooden rack right above the fire, four giant clams hanging from its beams. Despite Marcus' first taste of the delicacy, the smell was quite inviting. Perhaps they'd be better cooked, Marcus thought as he shook off his bedroll and joined the commotion.

The team sat on logs near the fire and enjoyed the evening meal with the tribe. They exchanged cautious looks with their visiting neighbors at first, but soon overcame their shyness. The new children congregated around them, poking and prodding at the most inopportune moments, giggling hysterically as they did so.

With Serena's help, Captain Mitchell was able to gather more information on the coming of the Golans' gods. The tribes had all gathered at Lo'Mock not only to settle disputes and conduct their tribal council, but to make offerings to the gods in the form of the sacred Je'eela leaves. Each tribe had carried with them several sacks stuffed with the coveted plant, and when the gods arrived each tribal chieftain would make his offering and barter passage to the heavens for the tribe's champion. Jakunu had already chosen Hanasi for the great honor of living with the gods, and the youth was only too eager to fulfill his role in Golan history.

"The gods actually take Golan to the stars?" Marcus asked, not really understanding the entire affair.

"It would seem so," Serena confirmed, distressed by the revelation. "They're sounding more and more like a spacefaring species, aren't they?"

"Maybe they'll give us some of those leaves if we take one of them aboard the *Tengri*," Taylor joked, hoping to get his hands on more of the sacred herb.

"Don't even think about it Doc," Serena countered.

Dr. Gehringer began to present his own argument, clearly hoping to be able to examine the Golan in his laboratory, but he was cut short by Serena, who had begun to see herself as something of a self-appointed guardian of the Golan people.

"Do any of the chosen ever return?" Marcus asked, worried about the fate of the Golan champions.

Serena proposed the question to Jakunu, whose reply came simply in the form of him shaking his gargantuan head. Marcus didn't know if that was a gesture the chieftain had acquired from the Terrans or if it was also native to Ga'ouna, but he understood it well enough

"Captain, we have to stop this. These so-called 'gods' are taking advantage of these gentle creatures, and doing... well, God knows what to them!" Serena exclaimed, infuriated.

"Calm down, Kim. We're already here. We'll wait and see what happens. Don't jump to conclusions before we know what we're dealing with," Captain Mitchell replied, trying to reason with her.

"Come on Marcus, let's explore!" chimed Taz, who had grown weary of the conversation and already eaten his full of baked clams.

"I don't think they have any women your size," Reid snorted.

"Very funny Rev," Taz grimaced.

Marcus rose from his log, excited at the thought of wandering through the tribal gathering. Taz led Marcus down a wide thoroughfare, teaming with life. The huge Golan were everywhere, a handful of them, sat on log benches drinking fermented wine from ceramic jugs, shouting cheerful words in their direction as the Terrans passed them by. To one side lay a long fire pit with chunks of meat searing on long stones, while drooling patrons waited hungrily for their portions and the booth's proprietor counted the stones they offered him. A heavy-set Golan female, her bare breasts hanging to her waist, stood in the middle of the path chanting what Marcus could only imagine had to be a form of Golan poetry. A long line of Golan children, their faces painted with streaks of white, yellow and red, ran past them, so excited to be on their way down to the beach to bathe in the warm waters they didn't even notice the two clones.

"Can you ever imagine being so free?" Marcus sighed, admiring the Golan way of life.

"I dunno, it sure looks fun right now, but give it a month and I think I'd be clawing at the walls to get out," Taz objected.

They passed by a few stalls with Golan crafters carving figurines out of sea shells, making pottery from fresh clay and jewelry from colorful stones.

"They don't even have weapons," Marcus noted. "I wonder if they even have a word for war."

"I'm sure they do," Taz protested. "Sooner or later, everybody fights. Maybe their past isn't as peaceful as you think."

Marcus couldn't imagine the Golan tribes at war with one another.

They waded through a maze of intertwining thoroughfares until they came upon a pair of enormous shelters, each easily capable of housing several dozen Golan. The larger of the two was completely

41

enclosed and constructed out of animal skins, painted with ornate symbols in red and white. A pair of muscular Golan stood by the entrance and barred their entry, but the smaller lean-to was open at the front, with a slanting roof made of leaves over wooden rafters. In its center, a lone Golan stood in a deep pit, with a dozen onlookers circling its rim.

Marcus and Taz approached with caution, curious, but unsure of what was about to take place. The spectators wore colored sashes over their shoulders and shouted harshly spoken words in turn, while the pit's occupant looked up at them with pleading eyes, as if waiting to be dealt a horrible fate. The tallest of the spectators suddenly waved his arms and the others fell silent. He slammed his palms together in a thunderous clap, and proceeded to dramatically raise his hands towards the sky. Suddenly, the speaker concluded the affair with a single booming word.

"Vungula!" he shouted, much to the cheering of the others.

Two overly-muscular Golan emerged from the shadowy corners of the shelter and pulled the despondent-looking one out of the pit. Marcus thought he caught a glimpse of a single tear running down his cheek as the guards escorted him out of the tent and down one of the city's busier streets.

"I guess even the peaceful have their black sheep," Marcus admitted as he and Taz moved on, in search of further enlightenment.

Chapter 7

"The field is holding," stated the technician, a blank-faced adolescent whose hands had been entirely replaced with cybernetics. An assortment of wiry tendrils extended from the stubby protrusions where his fingers had once been, dozens of slender mechanized tentacles which tapped away on a console with a vast array of touch-sensitive buttons. His eyes were milky white, as if blinded from birth, but he seemed completely aware of his surroundings.

Behind him, facing the viewport overlooking the Chamber of Seers, stood Captain Virge Intari, whose once-sleek dark hair had now completely surrendered to grey. He had always been lean, and with increasing age his frame was rapidly tending to gauntness. He wore a meticulously-kept dress uniform, dark grey pants and a jacket with an unbroken collar, fastened by a row of silver clasps polished to a high sheen. His square jaw, hooked nose and formidable cheekbones lent him a stern visage, one further amplified by his heavy brow and sunken eyes, which were merciless but full of conviction.

"Increase the output," the captain ordered. "I want the field at maximum capacity."

"Yes Sir," the lab technician confirmed. "The new psi network has already exceeded the results of our initial testing."

The blank-eyed tech engaged a series of sliders on the console just below the viewport, and almost immediately the oval chamber on the other side of the glass was bathed in a dim crimson light emanating from a series of elongated light tubes in the ceiling. They were arranged in a circular fashion around a massive mechanical arm that reached down from the center of the ceiling. A swarm of wiring and tubing jutted out from the numerous sockets on the side of the nightmarish contraption, each one piercing the pale, glistening flesh of one of the seven naked figures lying prone beneath it. The dim glow pulsated softly in succession with the low droning hum coming from the chamber.

Had they been conscious, the figures' expressions would probably have been of sheer terror, but they were all oblivious to their condition. They barely even appeared to be breathing. Three males and four females, some of whom appeared too young to have reached puberty, all of them embedded in man-shaped sockets in the floor, lined with black rubber foam. At some point they had no doubt had hopes and dreams, individual futures, but now they were mere components in one of Division 6's technological marvels, the scrying field.

The Division had used seers before, spying on all aspects of Terran society, but their priority had always been to locate others like themselves for recruitment. Often the seers would lose their sanity from continued exposure. The strongest among them were used to block scrying attempts by other agencies and organizations. After all, the Division's notoriety was dependant on a high level of secrecy, and secrecy demanded countersurveillance. This new device could combine the psi output of several seers – even untrained ones – amplifying their power immensely to form a scrying field, an impenetrable barrier through which not even the greatest of seers could pierce.

Still, even that was just a means to an end. The Division's greatest achievement would have nothing to do with psionics, which were so rare as to be regarded as mere rumor in most of Terran society, yet it would irrevocably change that society forever, bringing with it such wealth and power that it would catapult Division 6 into a seat of true, unrivaled power. No longer would they need to pull strings from behind the scenes to have their way.

"There was an incident with number two this morning," the lab tech mentioned.

"What sort of incident?"

"A breach attempt. The field held, but number two suffered a mild seizure. I've scheduled him for surgery to have his amygdala stripped and a more stable cybernetic component implanted. That should correct the problem," the lab tech explained.

"Won't the field be compromised?"

"Temporarily. Dr. Drechsler has assured me that the procedure shouldn't take more than a few hours. The seer will be re-installed immediately after."

"No," Intari snapped. "The prototype is nearing completion. We must practice utmost caution, or all our work might be in vain. Find a replacement immediately and dispose of the faulty component."

"Yes, Sir."

"And see to it personally this time. Full incineration. Leave no trace."

* * * * *

The interior of the Sol Conservatory had been transformed into a monotonous scene of dull white, everything from tablecloths to long banners hanging from the glass ceiling sporting the faded emblem of the Terran Republic. Long banquet tables lined the hall in front of the central stage, which was adorned with white roses with bleached white stems. The waiters gliding through the crowd, each holding a silver platter piled high with delicate canapés and luscious petit fours, not only wore the same uniform but were identical in every aspect of their appearance. Clones, the lot of them.

The clanking of silverware on crystal was not a sound Leicester Amorosa favored. Usually it meant that his wife was about to give yet another one of her tiresome speeches. He'd heard them all before, and prepared to tune this one out as he always did. His wife was a woman who had taken to every worthwhile cause – as well as some not so worthwhile – just so she could parade around high society functions in the latest fashionable ensembles.

Not that it bothered him much how she spent her time, or his money for that matter. What bothered him was the ritual of having to argue with her before each and every engagement about whether or not he had to make an appearance. He couldn't see how his presence mattered to her at all anyway, as she was always too busy gossiping with her coconspirators or berating the service staff to pay him any heed.

He usually wound up alone in a corner, sucking on his cigar, brooding over his next corporate conquest and pretending to listen to the perverse rants of men whose names he could never remember. Amorosa was a man of great repute, the President of MAier Industries, an enormous conglomerate that held numerous contracts with the Terran military.

"There's no such thing as too young," chortled an elderly man who had the face of an ostrich and the cackling laugh of a chicken. "The madam arranged a twin set for me the other day," he continued. "What a thrill that was. I felt like I was back in my school days."

"I wouldn't think you to have the stamina for such sport," sniggered a wrinkled old man with eyebrows so bushy they nearly covered his eyes.

"That's why they invented Stim-X," scoffed the ostrich. "At our age you might need a blood transfusion afterwards, but it's a price I'm only too happy to pay."

"Leicester," prompted the man with the oversized eyebrows, drawing him out of his daydreaming. "When are you going to introduce yourself to the madam?"

"Oh... I'm not really interested," Leicester sighed. He had heard this diatribe countless times before.

"Don't tell me that wife of yours still gets the old juices flowing," laughed the ostrich. "Mine's as dry as a wheat field on New Io. Not that I'd stick my prick in her if she wasn't, the old cow!"

Leicester was disgusted. He didn't always get along with his wife. Matter of fact, they got on less and less over the years. Still, there had always been at least a modicum of respect between them. He simply lacked the libido of his youth, and even then he'd never been one to chase skirts. He saw it as a weakness, one that made simpering fools out of giants, and he was determined to continue being a giant, at least in the business sense. He feigned a smile as he leaned back, drawing on his cigar.

"It's time," came a voice, one that didn't seem to originate from anywhere in particular.

"Time for what?" he gasped, drawing a startled look from the ostrich and the eyebrows.

"What was that, Leicester?" the ostrich mumbled, somewhat nervously.

"It's time for you to see the fruits of your investment," the voice

47

said, quite calmly, and Leicester realized it was ringing inside his head. A telepathic projection! That could mean only one thing: Division 6.

"Now?" he whispered, unsure whether the unseen speaker could even hear him, wherever or whoever he might be.

The ostrich and the eyebrows scurried off, taken aback by his strange behavior. He scanned the banquet hall hurriedly for any signs that he was being watched.

"Yes. Now." the voice confirmed, and Leicester took note of a well-groomed waiter near the central podium, a blond, gentle looking young man who was staring at him intently while pouring a glass of champagne for Mrs. Orkin, wife of Curtis Orkin, a VP of Aeon Astronautics, his chief competitor.

"What about my wife? She will notice if I'm not..." he began to mutter, only to realize the fallacy of his own words. His wife probably wouldn't notice if he choked on his cigar right then and there. At least not until after the party. And she still hadn't even finished the first half of her torrid speech!

"Your wife will be looked after Mr. Amorosa," the voice assured him. "As far as she'll remember, she had a little too much to drink and you took her home, put her to bed and kissed her good night."

"Don't overdo it," Leicester hissed. "I haven't kissed my wife in years, at least not in private."

"As you wish, Mr. Amorosa. If you would be so kind as to proceed through to the rear third-storey balcony, there will be a hovercraft waiting to take you to a discrete shuttle port."

"Offworld?" Leicester snapped, a bit too loud for comfort. "No one said anything about going offworld."

"Mr. Amorosa," the voice said in a condescending tone. "Matters like these require the utmost discretion. You are about to change the

48

world, after all."

"Of course," Leicester gave in. "My apologies. I'll go at once."

"Wise choice. You won't regret it."

Chapter 8

After four days of constant feasting, Marcus was beginning to hope that Lo'Mock would soon draw to a close. Despite the lighthearted company, exotic cuisine and a never-ending stream of wine and music, Marcus was more accustomed to spending his time in silent thought, and constant bustle was wearing on him. During the last two days, the winds had changed, with a strong wind approaching from the ocean, bringing with it the scent of the fresh sea air and flocks of flying turquoise creatures with orange beaks soaring overhead.

Marcus had enjoyed following a few of the Golan tribesmen as they journeyed out a short distance from the settlement and hunted the birdlike creatures with slings and stones. They were unlike any bird Marcus had ever seen though, more reptilian, with membranous wings stretched between a pair of spindly appendages. They had massive beaks, almost as large as their bulbous bodies.

Although he had initially assumed that, due to their sheer size, the Golan would not be the most dexterous of creatures, he was quickly proven wrong as the first hunter hit his target dead on. As they returned when the day was nearing dusk, carrying over a dozen each of the colorful prey strung together by their spindly appendages, Marcus had to admit that their hunting skills vastly exceeded his own, despite his carbine's superior range.

As the hunting party reached the outlying areas of Lo'Mock they began to see that something was amiss. Everywhere they looked, fires had been left unattended in their hearths, meat still simmering on grills, and there wasn't a single Golan in sight. Nearing the central bonfire, they heard the distant voices of the tribes through the wind, stamping their feet on the ground and chanting what Marcus assumed were prayers. Marcus hurried after the tribesmen as they dropped their prey to the ground and ran hurriedly towards the shore, shouting praise to the darkened skies above.

On a large stretch of grass overlooking the ocean, thousands of Golan had gathered in a wide arch, waving their hands in unison, rising and falling like the waves on the shore. Marcus quickly spotted his squadmates near the edge of the gathering, staring intently at the billowing storm cloud looming eerily overhead. Serena's long, silky smooth dark hair flowed in the wind as she peered worriedly around in anticipation of what was to come.

Marcus quickly joined the others, not far from where Jakunu stood nervously at the forefront of his tribe, his son Hanasi next to him, trying his best to remain calm. As the chanting began to increase in fervor, most of the Golan fell to their knees, all but the Chieftains and their champions.

"Is this it?" Marcus shouted above the chorus of deep droning voices around him.

"It looks that way! The *Tengri*'s scanners picked up a ship entering the system a few minutes ago. The Golan seemed to know before we did, although how is anyone's guess!" Serena shouted, her voice barely breaking through the wall of sound enveloping them.

All around them, Marcus saw the heavily-laden bags of Je'eela leaves, ready to be offered to the approaching gods.

"Marcus, ready your weapon!" Captain Mitchell bellowed. "We have no idea what to expect, so be prepared!"

Marcus sternly nodded his agreement. If these 'gods' were, as it seemed, an alien species with malicious intentions towards the Golan tribesfolk, Marcus wanted to be ready to face them.

The chanting was reaching an almost deafening height. The tribesmen held their arms high in the air, swaying back and forth with the strong wind. Marcus' eyes were drawn to the sky, where the thick, billowing clouds appeared to be merging, forming a deep, dark center right above the beach. They appeared almost magical in the low light, the stark contrast of pitch-black and pure white clouds – as if they were being illuminated from above – simply breathtaking. A roaring thunderclap preceded a bright flash of lightning amidst the densest cloud above, followed shortly by a brilliant bolt striking the sea a short distance from the worshiping tribes.

Marcus couldn't help but feel stunned by the spectacular display. Even though he'd been warned of the ship's approach, he was beginning to doubt that these were in fact aliens. If they were, their level of technology had to be far greater than he could ever imagine. He couldn't fault the Golans' belief that these were in fact the gods coming to visit them. If he'd been born among them, he would have been mesmerized by far less.

The tribes didn't waver, increasing the pitch of their worship to prove to the gods that they were worthy of their presence. Suddenly, the clouds began to part. The outlines of a strange alien craft began to emerge, half shrouded in mist. All the Golan fell silent at the awe inspiring sight, even the Chieftains and their champions collapsing to their knees in silent reverence.

The ship was massive, several times larger than the *Tengri* and easily capable of holding hundreds, perhaps even thousands of passengers. From what Marcus could see of it through the whirling clouds, the ship's shape was utterly unlike anything manufactured by Terrans, or even the Nyari: semi-circular at the stern, its two long flanks merging into a vicious point at the prow, like a dagger cleaving through the clouds as it descended above the throng. Its surface was coated in a shimmering metal that seemed to change hues depending on the angle it was viewed from, first black, then blue, then grey, sleek and hauntingly beautiful to behold, yet lightly tarnished from the rigors of space travel.

The crackling energy he'd taken for lightning was being emitted from the ship's underbelly, and made the hairs on Marcus' neck stand on end and sent shivers down his spine. Bright azure waves caressed the ship's hull, periodically igniting the atmosphere around it, producing popping sounds audible despite the wind of its approach. Slowly the ship began to slow its descent until it hovered in place a mere dozen meters or so above the crowd.

The sound of escaping air could be heard as a portion of the hull began to detach, a blinding white light shining through the cracks. The platform was about the size of the Barracuda, the squad's old dropship, nearly thirty meters in length and ten or so in width, slowly approaching the ground like an elevator, but with no visible mechanics or means of propulsion. Three shadowy figures stood poised in its center, surrounded by halos of light that made it impossible to make out anything but their basic shape. As the lights started to fade, Marcus' eyes began to adjust, until finally he was able to see them clearly.

He had never seen anything so alien. Not the Golan, not the shriekers that had killed most of his squad on New Io, not even the clawed skeletons of the crew of the crashed ship that had brought a menagerie of monsters to the helpless moon. Although upright they were roughly as tall and broad as Terrans, with two arms and a head atop an emaciated humanoid torso, they weren't bipedal at all. The lower part of their body was more akin to that of a snake, a slithering tail flowing from their torso, glistening as if it were covered in a glistening leathery hide. Their orange skin darkened along their tails to a yellowish brown, but on their torsos the skin was stretched so taut over the ridged bone-like protrusions below their chest that Marcus could easily count their ribs, eight in all on each side. Their arms were oddly humanoid, muscular and wiry, ending in three elongated fingers with sharp claws.

Their heads towered over the rest of their bodies, with a forehead that ran up into a majestic flattened crest of curved bone, with jet-black eyes set in deep cavities along the side of their heads. They had no visible mouths, nor ears for that matter. Not even a nose. Instead, a fleshy membrane covered a short triangular snout. Each of the three wore a metallic canister on its back, on which green neon lights blinked on and off in random fashion. Pipes and wires protruded directly from the aliens' flesh, connecting them to the devices.

None of the Terrans knew how to react. The trembling Serena was obviously more unnerved than the others, and she began to back away from the alien gods, her lip quivering as she tried to overcome her fear.

"Nikilosi ja ya ju'ungusi," a thundering, raspy voice boomed from the platform, one of the figures throwing its arms out as if to embrace the kneeling Golan. "Ono vago juko umo natalo vaguna mugijasi."

It wasn't clear to Marcus how they were able to produce the sounds, but the membrane at the front of their snouts seemed to be vibrating back and forth.

"He's welcoming them as his children," Serena interpreted, shouting over the gale winds and the droning sound of the spaceship hovering above, trying in vain to keep her hair from blowing in front of her eyes, but seeming much calmer with something to focus on. "He says they are ready to receive their offerings."

"Screw it," Mitchell bellowed, striding forth defiantly, the motorized brace on his knee whirring with each step.

He pushed and shoved his way through the kneeling tribesmen, resulting in a number of astonished glares.

"Oh almighty alien gods," the captain hollered, not bothering to hide his disbelief, the sarcasm in his tone evident. "Will you hear us?"

Realizing the captain's need for interpretation, Serena reluctantly gathered herself and stepped forward. Marcus accompanied her through the throng of bewildered Golan, who seemed startled that they would be willing to risk speaking to the gods out of turn. Serena came to a halt next to the captain, who was being fixed by what could only be a judgmental glare by the 'gods'. Marcus placed his hand on her shoulder for reassurance as she quailed at the sight of the aliens.

"Ungavi ju'ungusi, ono nidugi ja'ugo vaki ye nujula!" Serena shouted, her feeble voice cracking, barely making its way to the platform.

"Naksi aru tana kaälle kurite Gaian?" The voice boomed again, the god on the left slithering forward towards them.

"I don't understand what he's saying," Serena said, turning a concerned eye towards the captain. "It's not in the Golan language."

"U nayo noku luvanuko vave," she shouted towards the alien gods.

"Vave gashu huno vago juko higo Gaian. Ga'ouna livo ye yanludli lumivuka. Vave latongo nusu!" the alien god replied in a thundering voice.

Serena looked at her datapad, trying to decipher the god's words.

"He says we should not be here. I don't understand it all. Something about it being... protected, I think, and he demands that we leave, immediately."

"Well what the he... tell him we're stuck here. That we'd gladly leave if we could," Captain Mitchell ordered, eyeing each of the aliens in turn suspiciously. Marcus winced.

"Ono livo liagi. Ono doshu huno latongo. Onoguna luhunek doshu huno lunjuko. Doshu vave la'udo?" Serena stuttered, trying to explain with her limited understanding of the Golan language, her task made all the harder by the relentless wind.

The three figures turned to one another for council, seemingly taken aback by Serena's words. After a brief moment of hushed words between them, the aliens turned once more to the Terrans and spoke in eerie unison.

"Nuduko umo vaguna luhunek. Muvile nuduko umo Ga'ouna an ono gashu masuko vave umo Semeh'yone."

"I... I think they want us to return to the *Tengri*. If we promise not to come back, they'll help us. They'll pull us to... I don't understand the last word," Serena told them, skimming through the notes on her datapad.

"I don't think we have much of a choice," the captain muttered. "Tell them we accept."

"Captain," Marcus interjected. "What about the Golan?"

"What about them?" Mitchell barked, shooting Marcus a stern glance.

"These beings are taking advantage of them. We have to stand up for them."

"Can you not see the huge spaceship hovering above you, Grey?" the captain snapped. "They could probably vaporize us in an instant if they wanted to. I say we thank our lucky stars and keep our mouths shut. That means you too."

"But…" Marcus began to argue.

"That's an order Corporal!" Captain Mitchell warned him.

Marcus knew he was right. There was no possible way they could stand up against such awe-inspiring force. Granted there were only three 'gods' and none of them appeared to be armed, but for all the Terrans knew the ship above could be carrying weapons powerful enough to kill them and the Golan kneeling around them in the blink of an eye, and be crewed by a complement of armed soldiers.

Marcus looked at the faces of the Golan nearest to him. They weren't afraid, not of the gods at least. They'd been looking forward to this moment since he'd set foot on this world. Who was he to defy their beliefs? Just because he knew that the gods were in fact aliens, did that give him the right to interfere? Just then he caught sight of Jakunu and Hanasi, and remembered the pride in Jakunu's eyes when he'd told them that his son was to join the gods in the heavens. Could he really shatter his hopes, his dreams for his son? For all Marcus knew, the 'gods' were benevolent beings who meant no harm to the Golan.

No, the captain was right. They didn't have the right to interfere.

As Captain Mitchell began to communicate with the *Tengri*, ordering the shuttle to come and pick up the team on the ground, Marcus and Serena looked to one another for comfort. This world had meant so much to them, with its strange people and customs. It would be a sad farewell.

She took Marcus' hand and led him through the throng towards Jakunu to say their final goodbyes.

Chapter 9

Tears streamed down Serena's soft cheeks as she hugged each member of Jakunu's tribe in turn. Marcus couldn't help but notice the bewildered stares of the surrounding tribes. The entire team had been granted passage with the gods. For them, such a boon was the greatest honor the gods could bestow. Why then, was the Terran female overcome with sadness?

Serena was met only with smiles and warm embraces. The Golan people were obviously not ones for long sad goodbyes, focusing rather on the cheerful moments they had shared with these strange offworlders.

Jakunu himself knelt down and grabbed her lithe frame, rising up to lift her in the air, letting out a roaring chuckle as he gently shook her and pulled her in for a startling bear hug. When he finally lowered her back down, she wiped away her tears and waved them all goodbye.

"Lobaha livo namu vave kodi jia," Jakunu bellowed, clumsily mimicking her wave. "Livo tubuni."

Although both she and Marcus had spent the whole time since the *Tengri's* arrival on the planet, it dawned on Marcus that she had had far more contact with the Golan than he had. He had kept mostly to himself, marveling at the trees, the rain, the animals, content to be alone with his own thoughts. She, on the other hand, had spent the entire time engaged in conversation with the Golan tribe, learning their ways and their customs.

Just then, one of the Golan children ran to her with a small leather pouch full of colored stones. Serena almost couldn't accept the farewell gift. Her lips were quivering, unable to utter a word. The child simply hugged her and ran back to its parents.

Captain Mitchell approached Jakunu, hand outstretched as if about to greet a superior officer. Curiously, the chieftain reached out his own hand, his massive palm upturned. Mitchell grabbed the Chieftain's index finger, which was almost as big as his entire hand.

"Jukuvahi vave Jakunu," he said, mispronouncing the few words he had learned from Serena as he shook Jakunu's finger.

While Taz and Reid stood smiling in the background and waved, happy to be moving on, Marcus felt torn between two worlds. He wanted so much to stay. This world had come to mean so much to him. From its gentle creatures to its raging rainstorms, even its higher than normal gravity, he loved it here. He knew that he couldn't stay. If he would, he knew that not only would he miss his friends, he'd also be letting his squadmates down.

Without knowing quite how to act, Marcus stumbled towards Jakunu, first with his arms outstretched for a hug, then hesitantly lowering one of his arms for a formal handshake. The huge Golan would have none of it, and grabbed Marcus with both arms, giving him the same sendoff as he had Serena.

Marcus warmed at the thought that he'd had such an impact on the proud chieftain. They had not had much contact, but with Marcus' constant presence in their village, he must have touched the Golan in a way he'd not imagined. As Jakunu lowered him back to the ground, Marcus was smiling from ear to ear, not wanting to let go.

The shuttle had landed on the outskirts of Lo'Mock, with Raven eagerly awaiting their arrival. As the team tentatively made the long walk towards the shuttles, Marcus looked back over his shoulder. The chieftains had begun making their offerings. Alongside their champions, they stood by as a pair of females carried the heavily laden sacks of Je'eela leaves to the platform.

What did these 'gods' have in store for the prized herbs?, Marcus pondered. More importantly, given their power and advanced technology, they could easily harvest the entire planet. Why didn't they? Why the ruse? It seemed to Marcus to be an awful lot of effort for maybe a hundred sacks of the stuff. And why did they want to take the tribe's strongest champions? Marcus feared that his questions might never find answers.

He watched from the shuttle's hatch as Jakunu embraced his son and proudly stepped aside to allow him to take his place on the platform of the gods.

"We're leaving Grey. You wanna get left behind?" Raven called from behind him.

"If only you knew," he whispered under his breath before entering the small shuttle craft.

* * * * *

The *Tengri*'s gangways felt cold, and hollow. Polished steel frames lined with deep blue padding were the dominant décor, lit by piercing white lights embedded in the ceiling. Marcus felt strange to be back on the ship. Having spent so much time on Ga'ouna, a warm and welcoming world teaming with life, the *Tengri*'s empty halls were a disheartening sight. Even in his cramped quarters, surrounded by what few personal belongings he had, Marcus felt alone. He emptied the contents of his rucksack onto his bunk and began sifting through the various souvenirs he'd collected on Ga'ouna.

After almost an hour of sulking, staring out into the dead of space through the small square window in his chamber, fiddling aimlessly with a small wooden figurine he'd been given by one of the Golan children, Marcus decided to head to the bridge and see what was happening. Given the presence of the aliens' ship, he had no doubt that most of his squad – if not the whole crew – would be finding reasons to loiter in the *Tengri*'s command centre.

On his way to the bridge he stopped by the galley, whose warmly-lit nooks broke the monotony of the rest of the ship. The galley was cluttered with comfortable chairs, small trees in square black pots, and a range of cupboards and tables. It was situated right below the bridge, at the front of the ship. A wide, arching window opened onto a view of the planet below. It was a sight to behold. Unlike the heavily-exploited planets in the Terran solar system, Ga'ouna's unspoiled forests and pure oceans were truly beautiful.

"You're back," Darryl Knoles, the ship's cook, grunted noncommittally.

Marcus hadn't noticed the surly man as he entered. He slouched by the counter that separated the galley from the kitchen. Marcus had few good things to say about Knoles. The man had a mean blank, unfriendly stare and utterly lacked anything resembling a sense of humor. His sarcastic tone and grim scowl was in stark contrast to the otherwise pleasant room where he served the crew their meals.

"Just what I needed, more work," he moaned, scratching the scraggly mud-colored beard that encircled his thin cracked lips.

"Can I get a quick bite? Preferably something I can take with me to the bridge?" Marcus asked cautiously, unsure of what to expect.

Knoles furrowed his brow, peering at him through his sunken eyes before letting out an exaggerated sigh.

"I think I have a few leftover sandwiches in the fridge," Knoles grunted, dragging his feet as he retreated into the kitchen.

Marcus wondered, not for the first time, how someone with Knoles' sullen disposition had been appointed to a position that required daily human contact. As the cook returned from the darkened corners of the galley, he tossed a pre-packed meal onto the counter.

"Thank you," Marcus sputtered, rushing to leave the cook to brood in private.

Unlike the confined cockpit on their old Barracuda, the *Tengri*'s bridge was spacious, with three main console stations jutting up from the deck and out from the forward bulkhead, which was entirely given over to a deck-to-ceiling viewscreen that doubled as a window and a data display. The three stations took up most of the deckspace, and almost enveloped their operators in their steel frames, upon which controls and displays were mounted.

Copilot Lonnie Gardulo – a bright, eager young pilot whose ebony skin tone, grayish-blue eyes and cheerful disposition set him apart from the rest of the bridge crew – was sat at the copilot's station on the left, while the ship's navigator, Guy Wei a serious man in his mid-thirties with slanting eyes – was at his station on the right when Marcus entered from the main hatch at the back of the room. At the front and centre of the bridge, Zorita 'Raven' Spencer, the pilot from Marcus' old squad, occupied the third station, behind which a central walkway led to a raised platform where Captain Mitchell sat propped on a swiveling chair, an arrangement of buttons and small screens embedded in its armrests. His pudgy, fur-covered pet lazily stretched its paws in the air as it lay on its back on the captain's lap.

The ship's readouts displayed data on Ga'ouna as an assortment of holograms hovering over each station's consoles, with some more technical details glowing on the readout embedded in the forward viewscreen. Judging by the sleek design of the consoles and other electronics, it was clear that the Benediction-class cruiser had been designed much more recently than the basic, functional Barracudas. Marcus had been on the bridge several times before, but he was still no less impressed. It had dawned on him that the soldiers in the Terran military weren't exactly equipped with the best technology that Terran science had to offer. Most of what they had been assigned had been cheap, mass-manufactured gear which would have served its purpose, but it felt odd that non-military personnel such as the *Tengri*'s crew had been equipped with far better equipment.

The barking of the captain's pet alerted the others to his presence. Spot, Marcus mused. What a strange name for a creature with entirely monochromatic brown fur.

"How does it feel being back on the ship there, Grey?" Captain Mitchell inquired, swiveling his chair to face him.

"Its… good," he lied, approaching the center of the bridge. "Any sign of the ship yet?"

"Not yet," Raven replied, pressing a series of buttons on her console. "We're still waiting."

Spot yelped as Marcus came to a stop next to the captain's chair, the little creature panting heavily with its tongue protruding from its squashed snout, its freakishly large eyes staring at him intently. Marcus had found the beast comical from the first moment the captain had introduced it to the team. It had been placed in a cryo-stasis pod prior to their arrival on the *Tengri*, and had proven a welcome addition to the otherwise serious-minded crew. Marcus reached out a hand, holding it a short distance from Spot's nose. Almost immediately the dog caught scent of something new, something it hadn't smelled before, and began to enthusiastically lick his fingers.

"Captain, we've got movement on the scanners," Wei called. "It's the alien vessel."

"Put it onscreen," the captain ordered.

The image of the sleek, shimmering craft appeared suddenly on the forward viewscreen, racing towards them from the planet's upper atmosphere.

"Wei, get as many readings as you can on that ship and send the data to Dr. Gehringer for analysis," Mitchell ordered. "Let's bring the *Tengri* about. They said they'd give us a tow. What that means exactly... well, we're about to find out, but let's be prepared for the worst."

"Yes Sir," the bridge crew acknowledged.

A few moments later Taz and Reid came running through the hatch onto the bridge, having felt the ship's acceleration.

"Is it time?" they blurted in unison, the image on the forward viewscreen already answering their question.

Marcus shot them a wide-eyed smile, pleased to see the pair of them again.

"Damn, she's big," blurted Raven as the alien craft slid closer into view. "She must be at least five times bigger than the *Tengri*."

"Keep your cool Raven," the captain ordered. "Nice and steady."

The alien craft began slowing down as it neared their position, coming to a halt a few hundred meters away.

"We have an incoming transmission Captain," Wei spoke. "Attempting to adjust the frequency."

After a few seconds of fiddling with the controls, Wei was able to play the audio part of the transmission over the bridge's intercom.

"Ono livo ja'aso nusu," came the booming voice of the serpentine aliens.

A sudden jerk shook through the ship as a halo of soft blue light flowed over the forward viewscreen, surrounding the *Tengri*, while the alien vessel began to loom even closer.

"Talk to me! What's happening?" Captain Mitchell prompted anxiously.

"Not sure, Captain," the navigator replied, as the three bridge crew all frantically tapped at their consoles. "It appears to be some sort of gravity generator, a gravitronic beam, although I've got no idea how they're projecting it without interfering with our own artificial gravity."

The captain clutched his armrests with a nervous scowl. Spot seemed to pick up on the sudden tension on the bridge, springing into the air and deftly landing on its tiny feet, scurrying off in search of a safe place to hide.

As the alien craft wheeled across the screen, Marcus felt his stomach lurch as he realized that it was barely moving at all, but was actually pulling the *Tengri* to face it as it pulled away, towing the Terran ship along in its wake.

Without warning, a bright flash of light appeared in the distance, almost blinding everyone on the bridge with its intensity. Tangents of light began to stretch outward from the glaring blaze, enveloping both the *Tengri* and the alien vessel like tentacles pulling prey towards a hungry maw. Suddenly the craft before them seemed to *stretch*, wavering in front of them before shooting forward, pulling the *Tengri* after her at an incredible acceleration. Marcus felt as if his stomach had been pulled out of his body through his back. His lungs refused to breathe, and he gasped for air. His head was swimming and his vision

65

became distorted. It was as if he was suddenly falling at a tremendous velocity, trying to claw his way back into reality.

Slowly the uneasiness began to recede, and Marcus could see that he had not been the only one afflicted. The captain's face was as pale as chalk, and behind him Taz threw up on the deck.

Through the forward viewscreen Marcus could see that they were traveling through what looked like a tunnel made from pulsating waves of energy, the alien ship still visible a short distance in front of them. Grunting at Navigator Wei to send all the logs to Dr. Gehringer for analysis, Mitchell withdrew a small plastic bottle from his pocket. He shook the bottle, rattling its contents before opening it and pouring a handful of pills into his palm, swallowing a few and placing the rest back into the bottle.

"Well… hopefully this journey won't take quite as long as the last one," he proclaimed, visibly concerned. "Though we can use the stasis pods if we have to."

The rest of the crew gathered their composure, and Taz went to clean up the mess he'd made on the floor. Mitchell remained still in his seat, staring intently through the forward viewscreen. He tapped his fingers on the console in his armrest for a while, before finally giving in and leaving the bridge, giving explicit orders that the crew were to remain on high alert and that he was to be made aware of even the slightest development.

Marcus stood stock still, staring in awe of the display in front of him. He had witnessed the incredible speeds Terrans were able to achieve by means of their mass accelerators, cannons large enough to fire entire ships across the deepest regions of space.

This was something else entirely.

Chapter 10

It had been three days since they had departed from Ga'ouna and the alien ship had made no attempts to establish communication. Tension among the crew had magnified with each passing day, and it was starting to show. The bridge crew, under orders from Captain Mitchell, had made several attempts to contact the alien vessel, but to no avail. The captain had also conducted a tactical meeting, preparing the crew for what might await them at the end of their journey, as much as anyone could prepare for such an unforeseeable event. In addition, he had also called a separate briefing for the remainder of Marcus' old squad, one he conducted behind closed doors.

The meeting room was a long chamber on the second deck, next to the captain's office. A narrow table took up most of the deck space, its shiny black surface reflecting the flowing energy waves outside the double-wide window. An enlarged viewscreen took up the whole bulkhead next to the entrance hatch, and was currently displaying a three dimensional rendering of the C-CORE logo that revolved ever so slowly against a golden background. It was the first time they'd all been alone together since leaving Takahashi's corporate suite. It felt good to be there, just the six of them. Technically the captain had only been assigned to their squad after they had lost their former leader, but now, in exile, he was one of them.

"What's wrong boss?" Jago asked, the behemoth of a man, visibly nervous over the secrecy of their meeting.

"Nothing's wrong Ape," the captain replied. "We just have some things that we need to discuss."

"What's so important that you don't want the rest of the crew knowing about it?" inquired Reid, not one for dishonest deeds.

"Your... abilities," the captain answered, silencing the room.

Marcus looked to the others, observing their reactions, looking for some show of emotion. Although he knew that Taz, Jago and Reid had all performed miraculous acts, apart from his brief discussion with Reid on Ga'ouna none of them had really ever sat down to talk about it.

"I don't have any abilities," Raven interjected, a puzzled look on her face.

"Nor do I," said Taylor.

"Not yet, but that doesn't mean that they won't manifest later. All of the other surviving members of your squad have, save for you two, so we'd better work under the assumption that you two will develop them too," the captain warned them. "And when they do manifest, I want you, all of you, to keep them secret."

"Wait, what?" Taz cried. "So I can't flex my awesome muscles to get girls?"

"No!" Mitchell scowled. "Even out here in the middle of nowhere, openly displaying your powers could cause panic. Hand-picked C-CORE personnel or not, the rest of the *Tengri*'s crew are probably still skeptical that humans can develop telepathy, so... whatever it is you all are capable of would almost certainly scare them senseless. Also, we don't know anything about these aliens who so *generously* decided to give us a lift. We don't know where they're taking us or whether they have an ulterior motive for their assistance. Your powers might be the only ace we have up our sleeves if things go sour."

"We haven't really been able to use them since leaving Strom,"

Marcus confessed. "At least I haven't, save for that one dream, and that didn't exactly come true anyway. Not that I've been trying, actually. It scares me just to think about it."

"Just because you aren't able to use them now doesn't mean they're gone," Mitchell consoled him. "When I underwent psi training it took me years to master my ability. In the beginning it came and went. I often thought that I'd lost it completely. Sooner or later, it always came back, until one day, I was able to call it forth at will, harness it, fuel it, make it stronger."

"But, if Division 6 already has people with psionic abilities, then why are they after us?" Taz demanded.

"Because you're different," the captain answered. "Terrans have only ever manifested a handful psionic powers before now. Most of them are like me, capable of reading minds, sensing emotion. A rare few can enhance their senses, see through objects, hear a pin drop from a kilometer away or operate in complete darkness. Only one in ten thousand psi wielders can catch glimpses of the future, and at best what they see is little more than riddles and muddled dreams. Your abilities are unique. No Terran can do what you can do. Division 6 would stop at nothing to get their hands on you."

"But why us?" blurted Taz. "I didn't ask for any of this!"

"I know. None of you did," Mitchell replied. "We may never know who is behind it or even how it was done. Marcus has told me about the probe, the field emitter your squad carried to Triton. That seems a likely opportunity but, it doesn't explain the why or the how. There has to be more to the method than just that exposure. If that were all that was required, whoever did this to you could easily make more clones like you."

"Who's to say that they won't?" Marcus added. "I mean, if these powers are so sought after, and Division 6 knows that the experiment was successful, why don't they just replicate it?"

"Isn't that obvious?" the captain replied, his expression serious. "Division 6 had nothing to do with it. If it had been them, they would never have let you loose out in the world. You would have been caged from the moment you were hatched until the moment they dissected you on an operating table. Someone else is behind this. Division 6 may have found out about the experiment, but they seem to know little more than we do."

"I guess we don't really have to worry about that," Marcus sighed. "We'll never see any of them again anyway."

"Good," Jago muttered, slamming both of his massive fists on the table, which trembled under the weight.

"For now, let's just keep quiet about this," Captain Mitchell concluded. "We can re-address this matter at a later time. But, for now let's keep this between ourselves."

The old squad nodded in unison, acknowledging the captain's order before leaving the meeting room in worried silence. Marcus stood there alone, admiring the repeating pattern of the waves streaming past the window. How far had they traveled? Where were they going?, he wondered. The others were so distressed over the unknown. Himself, he found it rather exhilarating. He just hoped that, wherever they were heading, they'd get there soon.

* * * * *

After a tense few days, boredom had finally set in. Now, seven days after their departure from Ga'ouna, Captain Mitchell sat at his usual table in the galley, in a murky corner near the forward windowpane.

He nursed a stiff drink in a thick square glass, chatting idly with Jago and Reid.

On the far side of the room, Emil Juey, the ship's custodian, leaned against the kitchen counter, listening to yet another of Knoles' tiresome tirades.

"Always together that lot," Knoles ranted. "Don't see them mixing with us support staff."

"So...?" Emil mumbled, his mouth busy wrestling with a half-chewed stick of jerked synthetic proteins, still slightly frozen.

"It's weird!" Knoles insisted.

"Military crew always stick to themselves," Emil countered. "That's just how it is, how it's always been. Even on military ships the combat teams hold back from the support staff."

At that moment, Mitchell's canine pet scuttled into the compartment with a skitter of claws, and started hovering around the captain's chair. He leaned down to pick it up, setting it down on his lap stroking its mottled fur.

"Why did you bring a dog with you?" asked Reid, who found the animal's presence aboard the *Tengri* rather anomalous.

"Can I pet him?" Jago burst out before the older clone could answer, his eyes full of enthusiasm as he eyed the small creature with childlike glee.

"Sure," the captain replied, after a pause while he considered. "Just be careful."

"Why do you even have a dog?" Reid added.

"If you'd have lost as many of your mates in combat as I have, you might want something more stable in your life, waiting for you when you returned from active duty," the captain said, hesitating as he realized that Reid was not unaccustomed to losing people he might

71

have called friends.

To his relief, Reid seemed not to have been offended.

"So why a dog? Why not get married? Have children?" Reid pressed, still trying to understand.

"I don't think any woman would stick around long if she didn't know when, or even if, her husband were coming home. I'm not sure I'd even want to put a woman through an ordeal like that," Mitchell replied solemnly. "So a pet seemed the most logical choice," he concluded, downing his drink.

"Why is a dog that much different? You must spend an awful lot of time away when you're out on tour. Who looks after him while you're away?"

"No one. I keep him in stasis," Mitchell answered casually.

Spot, who had been whining softly, started to growl quietly, drawing the captain's attention to the discomfort he was enduring under Jago's increasingly heavy petting. Each stroke pulled at his fur to such a degree that his eyes seemed ready to pop out of his head at any moment.

"That's enough Ape!" Mitchell warned him, placing Spot back on the ground where he hurtled off at record speed. "Well, I'd better get going. Ms. Karell will give me hell if I'm late for our session," he continued, drawing suggestive glances from Reid and Jago. "Quit it, you two," he rebuked them. "And for God's sake stop wasting time here in the mess. As soon as we drop out of this... whatever the hell you call this-" he gestured to the glow out the window "I want you and the rest of the squad prepped and ready by the forward airlock."

"Yes Sir," Reid deadpanned as Jago smirked.

Chapter 11

"I can't believe I threw my life away for this," Knoles muttered as he rearranged stacks of crated provisions in the cargo hold.

Knoles was not a man who was known for his amicable demeanor. His temper was outright foul on the best of days, and given the course of their mission, his temper of late had been even more appalling. His protruding brow was now permanently locked in a state of resentful worry, pinched together above the ridge of his nose in an ugly scowl. The crew of the *Tengri* had taken to avoiding the galley entirely whenever possible.

"Well aren't you the bright center of the universe," came Raven's voice from the hatchway, startling Knoles, who went stumbling backwards into an unsecured stack of crates, sending them crashing to the deck behind him.

He froze in place, his lips trembling with anger.

"What the hell do you want?" he barked, wiping the grime off of his fingers on his heavily stained apron.

He and Raven had had their share of run-ins since the *Tengri*'s arrival in the Ga'ouna system. Though the clones hadn't had the chance to get to know the rest of the crew before entering stasis, it hadn't taken long for the short-tempered Raven to make a snide remark about Knoles' skills in the galley once they'd awoken. Ever since then, the two had been bickering every few days, each encounter escalating the matter further.

"What are you even doing here?" Raven pressed, eyeing him with suspicion.

"Some of the dry goods were stored in the cargo hold by mistake," Knoles explained. "Not that it's any of your business."

"No, I meant on this ship?" Raven demanded. "You don't seem at all interested in the mission. Or particularly qualified for that matter," she smirked. "I thought you had to be the best of the best to get selected for one of these C-CORE trips."

"Watch it, Zorita," Knoles growled, his nostrils flaring as he instinctively clenched his fists.

"Hmpf," Raven snorted, curling her lip, not backing down.

Knoles knelt down to begin clearing up the mess, but Raven wasn't about to give in so easily. She knew she'd struck a nerve, and after days of being stuck aboard the *Tengri* with nothing to take her mind off of things, this was about as much excitement as she expected to see.

"Why would someone like you sign up for something like this?" Raven pushed. "It's not like you couldn't have stayed on Terra and made crap food for a strangers who despise your cooking just as much as you despise them."

"It wasn't exactly my choice," Knoles muttered, his eyes still fixed on the deck.

"What did you say?" Raven continued, stepping into the hold.

"I said it wasn't my choice!" Knoles shouted at her, springing to his feet and visibly quivering with emotion.

"What do you mean 'not your choice'? *You're* not a clone. Your life is your own," Raven snapped.

"Tell that to my family," Knoles snarled, anger and shame burning in his face.

"Your family?"

"It's none of your damned business!" Knoles fumed, kicking a crate full of canned goods into a nearby bulkhead.

"Oh I see," Raven sneered, "you're here to make daddy proud."

Knoles kept his mouth shut, but Raven thought she could see the hint of a snarl.

"Daddy's little boy gonna be a space man, make the history books. Shame he's too dumb to do anything other than heat a pot full of beans."

"I did it for my sister," Knoles said quietly, not looking at the woman taunting him, "My half sister actually."

"Your sister?" Raven exclaimed, taken aback by the cook's sudden sincerity.

"Father was going to cut her off. It would have ruined her." He still wasn't looking at her, just speaking quietly, as if to the crates on the deck.

"Why?" Raven gasped, confounded. She knew little of family, and she had always thought it to be something desirable, a closeness she could never know.

"I'm my father's bastard son. His weakness made flesh. When my half-sister discovered my existence she demanded he make me a part of the family. He wasn't exactly thrilled at the notion, so he came to me one night. I was working in a diner. I didn't even know who he was. My mother had always told me that he'd died before I was even born," Knoles said. "So when he told me who he was, I was happy. Astonished, but really happy, perhaps for the first time in my life. Then came the threats."

"Threats?" Raven didn't know how to react at all.

This wasn't right. Families were warm, loving things, she was sure of it... just as sure as she'd been that Knoles was a useless, spoilt naturally-born Terran.

"He thought that I'd been in contact with her, that it was my doing that she wanted me as part of the family. I didn't meet her until much later, after a series of threatening calls, harassment by the police everywhere I went. He's not exactly a man without means, you see," Knoles continued. "It wasn't until he threatened her that I started taking him seriously."

"He threatened his own daughter?" Raven gasped, horrified.

"Hard to imagine, right?" said Knoles, finally turning to look at her, raising an eyebrow.

For the first time, Raven saw him as a human being, just as fragile as the rest of them.

"He said either I left, or she'd suffer."

She stared in silence. She didn't know how to respond.

"So I agreed to go on this… journey. It's not as if I was leaving much behind anyway."

"I… I'm sorry," Raven whispered.

Knoles merely grunted in response, kneeling down to begin stacking the crates once more. Raven was about to leave, unsure as to what to make of the measure of guilt she was feeling for her actions.

"I do more than cook, you know," Knoles mumbled.

"What?"

"There's more to it than that, I mean. You might not like the taste, but each meal is prepared according to requests from Ms. Karell. With eighteen crewmembers to care for, each with their own deficiencies and nutritional requirements, it's not as simple as it looks."

The clanking of footsteps approaching interrupted their conversation.

"You two on a break?" came the voice of the *Tengri*'s chief engineer, Nelson Kerr, just before the man himself appeared in the hatchway.

"No Sir," Raven replied, "I was just helping Darryl sort out some supplies." With a cautious nod to the cook, she bent to pick up a crate."

* * * * *

"Bend your knee. That's good. A little further," Kaiden ordered as she pressed the captain's leg all the way to his chest.

"Damnit, Karell, you've got a grip like a seasoned deck hand," Mitchell grumbled, his teeth gritted.

The captain had been showing up at the gym more than was strictly mandatory, though he wasn't the only one. He knew most of the crew thought that the only reason that C-CORE had appointed Karell to her position was her stunning looks, a sure-fire way to motivate the mostly-male crew. Her smooth, silky black hair reached her shoulder blades, framing her hypnotic brown eyes and her delicate, fine-featured face, but her best feature was undoubtedly her lips, voluptuous without being overly pouty. Her slightly upturned upper lip always glistened, subject of many a male crewmember's fantasy.

"You're awfully tense today," she teased, drawing a feigned glare from the captain.

With most of the crew wrapped around her little finger, she could get away with practically anything. Mitchell hid the pain the exercises caused him well, feeling stupid for doing so but not wanting to show any sign of weakness in front of her.

"Captain, you're needed on the bridge," Raven's voice burst over the ship's intercom.

Mitchell sighed, grabbing a firm hold on the rim of the massage table and pushing himself into a seated position.

"Duty calls," he ventured with a grin, relieved at the excuse to get away from the painful calisthenics.

"Of course," Kaiden replied with a seductive wink.

He quickly strapped on his motorized knee brace and threw a towel over his shoulders to keep the sweat at bay as he strode out of the *Tengri*'s small gym. Marcus and the others were already on the bridge when he arrived.

The alien ship had finally transmitted an audio message saying that they would soon be arriving at their destination, but was refusing to answer any further attempts to contact them. As the captain eased himself gently into his chair, the tunnel of energy that had surrounded their ship began to transform, the pulsating waves decreasing in frequency and gaining intensity. The distance between the *Tengri* and the alien craft started to diminish, and the Terran ship's hull began to vibrate ever so slightly, producing a low humming noise.

"What's happening people?" Mitchell demanded.

"We must be coming out of this… slipstream, Captain," Navigator Wei replied. "The power signature from the alien vessel appears to be diminishing."

"Damn. That was fast," the captain acknowledged, rubbing the sweat off of his chin as his mind raced over every conceivable scenario.

"Grey," he decided. "Take the squad down to the armory. I want everyone suited up and ready to go at a moment's notice, just in case. For all we know they could have led us away from Ga'ouna only to tear us apart for scraps."

Reid grabbed Jago by one monstrous arm and pulled him off the bridge, rushing to comply with the captain's orders, but before Marcus and the others could follow them, the tunnel of energy around the *Tengri* collapsed in a blinding flash. The piercing headache and nausea they'd felt when the alien ship had first pulled them into the tunnel of light now returned, although in a milder form. It took only a few seconds for the crew to recover, but once they'd regained their wits the sheer magnitude of the scene that unfolded before them stole their breath away. No-one spoke as, one by one, they stumbled forward, closer towards the viewscreen, some even raising a hand to the glass, as if touching the window made the marvel more real.

Cresting one of two large moons in orbit around a lush green world, whose bountiful landscape was dotted by trailing clouds and sprawling vistas of auburn and golden hues, was the largest space station they could ever have imagined. Even having heard Marcus' description of his vision did little to prepare the clones for the sight before them.

The enormous station dominated the view, tilting generously, as if it had been expecting their arrival and had wanted to provide the most memorable first impression it could. The body of the station itself was made up of three tremendous cylinders, wider than they were tall, stacked end-on-end, each one slightly thicker than the one beneath it, but what drew the eye was what sat atop the broad surface of the uppermost drum: beneath a halo of azure light, a shimmering semispherical force field enclosed an entire metropolis, a city of soaring skyscrapers laid out in grids and circles and districts around a brilliant white central tower that rose from the centre of the city, almost touching the glittering dome of the force field. Even the tallest of the skyscrapers surrounding it was dwarfed by its towering form, a brilliant beacon of light. Beneath the tips of the soaring towers, the depths of the city glowed, uncountable tiny shards of brightness shining in the artificial dusk of the towers' shadows.

As the crew stared, the *Tengri*'s automated systems chimed, throwing estimated measurements across the viewscreen, the digits annotating the view hurtling higher and higher as the ship's computer revised its estimates, finally settling into a readout that said the city was just over 84 kilometers in diameter. Beyond the edge of the glowing dome, a veritable forest of long, spindly joists, arms and girders jutted from the uppermost rim of the station's drum-like body, each long enough to dock a pair of Terran superfreighters. Below them, a cavernous trench circumvented the middle of the station's uppermost drum, with millions of blinking lights piercing through its veil of shadows. Ship after ship came and went, glowing with the flash of engines, swarming to and from the depths of the artificial chasm, flinging themselves along the station's surface and between the spindly docking arms above. Beneath the flashing vessels the station's hull was covered in thick hull plating the size of battle ships, some of which sported veritable forests of small towers jutting from their base at strategic intervals.

Now that the initial shock had passed and he could tear his eyes away from the enormous station, Marcus saw that all around the *Tengri*, thousands of ships of all shapes and sizes streamed in all directions, going about their business in a virtual beehive of commerce and industry. Off their starboard bow, what could only be a grand warship kept a leisurely watch over the busy traffic, its smooth segmented hull gleaming in the light from the system's orange star, broken only by tremendous weapon ports, the enormous cannons half-buried within, each larger than an entire Terran frigate. Near the battleship's aft section, the shimmering hull gave way to dark-grey panels and bulbous protrusions, a bluish glow emanating from the windows, numbering in the hundreds and thousands, lining its surface. She measured over a kilometer and a half in length.

Navigator Wei was so stunned by what he was seeing that it took him nearly a minute to recognize the blinking light on his console, which was displaying an incoming message from the vessel that had brought them there.

"Captain," he finally cried. "The vessel is sending us a signal."

"Uhm... which one?" Mitchell muttered under his breath, gazing out into space. "Ah... put it through."

"Vave livo duey vaguna jia. Nuogi lobaha," the alien voice came over the ship's comms.

"Serena?" the captain prompted, praying that her skills would not fail them on such a momentous occasion.

The faint blue halo of light that had been projected around their ship by the alien vessel finally dissipated, and the *Tengri* began to glide, free from its influence.

"They said we're on our own, and that they wish us luck, Captain," Serena informed him.

The entire crew stared in silent wonder at the spectacle before them. Some had gathered on the bridge, while others had taken up station in the ship's observatory. The moment seemed to last for an eternity, as not a soul aboard the *Tengri* uttered a single word. The ship sailed gently through the sea of traffic in utter silence, a cloud of smaller ships buzzing past them in a hurry to reach their port of call, whilst a hauler the size of a Terran battleship lumbered past them with dozens of gigantic containers in tow.

"Captain, we have another incoming signal," Wei eventually broke the silence.

"Put it through," Mitchell ordered.

After a short moment of static while the Navigator desperately attempted to adjust the frequency and interpret the incoming signal, the noise warbled suddenly before finally clearing up, producing a low-pitched, pleasant voice.

"Kikikun Semeh'yone aukii. Tana no bastakone zijani osuru. Sonodakoy Sarale," the voice droned.

Captain Mitchell looked to Serena for advice on how best to proceed, but the linguist simply shrugged. Having no basis for interpretation, there was very little she could do on such short notice.

"Uhm, this is the TLS-*Tengri*," Captain Mitchell stuttered hesitantly.

There was a pause before the voice responded.

"Welcome TLS-*Tengri*. This is Semeh'yone Traffic Control. You are currently queued for docking at docking bay B-714. Please adjust your course," the voice enunciated carefully in near-perfect Terran.

The crew stared at each other, stunned that the message had been communicated in their own language. Mitchell fumbled with the controls on his armrests, his mind reeling, before finally blurting out."Uhm, Semion traffic control, this is TLS-*Tengri*. Where exactly is docking bay B-714?"

"TLS-*Tengri*, the coordinates for docking bay B-714 have been transmitted to your vessel. Please adjust your course," the alien voice calmly reiterated.

"How are they doing that?" Serena gasped in disbelief. It had taken her two weeks to grasp even the very basics of the Golan's primitive tongue, yet these aliens... whoever they were... seemed to have mastered the Terrans' own language in just a few seconds, without any assistance, or even hard data.

"Captain, they're definitely transmitting some sort of data, but I can't decipher any coordinates," Wei informed him, tapping frantically at his controls.

82

"Semion Traffic Control, we are unable to read the coordinates you transmitted. Please advise," Captain Mitchell replied, an astonished look on his face.

"TLS-*Tengri*, please wait. Deploying docking drones to escort you," the alien voice concluded before audibly shutting off communication.

Less than a minute later a pair of drones the size of small frigates approached their ship. They were little more than metal spheres with thrusters arranged neatly around their aft hemispheres, and what resembled a small cannon mounted at their rounded prows, wedged between a pair of powerful floodlights. They took up position at the front of the ship, one on each side, and, without warning, the same halo of faded-blue light that had brought her from Ga'ouna suddenly enveloped the *Tengri* once again, and the drones began towing them towards the massive equatorial trench on the colossal space station.

As they approached, they began to see openings, hundreds, if not thousands of docking bays, covering the entire inner wall of the trench, some the size of small freighters, others large enough to hold entire battleships. An energy barrier blocked access to each of the docking bays, and as the *Tengri* approached one of the mid-sized openings, the shimmering barrier dissipated and the tow drones began to ease the Terran ship into position for the docking clamps. As a pair of gigantic robotic arms grabbed a hold of the ship's underside, a mechanical docking ramp reached out and aligned itself with their docking hatch, the sound of metal scraping against metal abruptly reverberating throughout the ship, which shuddered to a complete standstill.

Marcus suddenly became very much aware that they had finally reached the destination they'd longed for, the city from his visions.

Chapter 12

The bathroom mirror flickered to life, revealing rows of glowing symbols and a viewing pane depicting a slew of dauntingly invasive and personalized commercials. Takahashi stood by the alabaster ceramic sink, which was as much a sculptured piece of art as it was a fixture. He leaned against the countertop, one hand probing the stubble on his chin as he eyed himself in the mirror, casting wayward glances at the viewing pane. He wore a simple dark-gray cotton bathrobe with a velour weave and a shawl collar, folded back from his neck to reveal his bare skin and graying stubble.

He pulled out a small drawer on the side of the counter, retrieved his shaving utensils and proceeded to eject a stream of foam directly onto his face from the canister, forming a big white smile, above which his eyes betrayed his true demeanor. How pathetic he looked, he thought. If anything, the false smile made his inner sadness even more obvious.

He started to shave, a smooth line of skin down one cheek, tapping the razor on the sink. As he finished his top lip, he caught sight of the end of the commercials, just as the regular program resumed its course. He poked the mute button on the mirror, smudging the glass.

"...over as CEO of the Muromoto Group, Mariko has revolutionized the robotics industry," chirped a female news anchor, whose manner was so cheerful that it could only have been brought about by medication. "Her now-retired father was a visionary designer and engineer in his own time, spurring countless advances in the field of applied robotics: the L4 series labor drone, the Z-16 surgical assistant, even various components of the Golem project were conceived by Takahashi Muromoto."

Takahashi ran the razor under the stream of hot water running from the faucet, doing his best to ignore any coming mention of his departure from his corporation.

"As recent years have shown, however, his daughter Mariko is not without her own vision, transforming how we Terrans view robotics," the news anchor continued, drawing a disappointed sigh from Takahashi, who stared vacantly at the steady stream of hot water.

"There's hardly a Terran household today that doesn't come complete with a set of Muromoto products. With everything from common custodial automatons to robonannies and mechanized guard dogs, household chores are a thing of the past."

Takahashi discontinued the feed and finished shaving in silence.

He'd tried calling her for days, weeks even. She never answered. He could barely remember the last time they'd spoken for more than a minute, and all of their conversations ended with her hanging up on him in anger. She still blamed him, even after all this time. He'd thought that with time the scars would heal, but they'd only festered. If anything, they were more estranged now than ever before.

He dragged his feet as he slouched back through to his lavish bedchamber, pausing momentarily by the raised floor at the foot of the bed, as if climbing the two steps to the mattress were too much of an effort for him to bear. Finally he turned and continued his restless pacing towards the window that made up the entire eastern wall of the room. Lights flickered all over the city throughout the silent night. He felt nothing. He was nothing… no one.

Grudgingly he raised his hand to the small panel attached to one of the window panes, depressing one of button under his fingers. The window in front of him slid to the side, allowing a gust of cold air to fill the chamber, his robe billowing behind him like a cape. Hesitantly, he drew his feet nearer to the edge, inching his way closer. How easy it would be, to end it all. All he had to do was lean forward and let go. He didn't even have to jump.

A man with my means, he thought, letting out a brief, slightly forced chuckle. He should be happy. Everyone always focused on his accomplishments, his wealth. Yet he had failed in so many ways. He'd failed as a husband. He'd failed as a father. And he was about to fail his mentor, the one who had started this all.

"I tried," he whispered, his voice quivering.

Would anyone even care if he died tonight? His wife was gone, his daughter refused to even acknowledge his existence, and he hadn't even heard from any of his old colleagues in months. She would do well, probably even better if she knew he wasn't there anymore to pester her. But… his mentor… would never forgive him. After all, so much was depending on him.

"I can have anything I want," he whispered to himself. "But I cannot afford the luxury of death. There's too much work to be done." He stepped back from the edge.

"Enough," he spat. "This has gone far enough. Stop pitying yourself, you old fool. Remember your purpose. This, everything you see, is just a means to an end."

It had been a tiring time, trying to figure out what Division 6 was up to. Whatever it was, it was something on a massive scale. They had redirected unbelievable amounts of their resources and refocused their blocks, so scrying no longer had any effect. What's more, he suspected they'd been receiving funding from some of his former competitors.

He assumed it had something to do with the wreckage on New Io, all those years ago, but all his attempts to find out what they were planning had been in vain.

He backed away from the window and stormed over towards the bed, grabbing the half-empty bottle of spirits on the bedside table. He stared at it for a brief moment before taking a hefty sip, then smashing the bottle on the floor.

"No more," he said, calm and full of conviction. It was time he reclaimed his legacy.

* * * * *

There was a resounding crash as the tray smashed onto the tiled stone floor, shattering the long-stemmed crystal glasses and half-empty bottles of fine champagne it had held.

"Nyla does it again!" the jovial youth roared. "Careful where you wave that enormous ass," he chuckled, grabbing another bottle from the cooler next to the moonlit pool. He took a huge swallow of the sparkling liquid, then shook the remainder of the bottle's contents all over the face of a naked brown-skinned girl, whose bosom seemed to defy the laws of gravity.

"You jerk," the girl exclaimed gleefully as she helped Nyla, a busty, pale-skinned blonde with a cloud of freckles on her cheeks, back into the pool. "And her ass is not enormous!" she added.

"Thank you, Bianca."

"You would say that," said the boy, grabbing Bianca's exposed bottom firmly. "Sporting a monster of an ass yourself."

"You pig!" Bianca shouted, leaping to the side and smacking him across the cheek.

The young man just laughed, averting his gaze from the two pouting beauties, stretching his arms along the rim of the circular pool, leaning back to arch his head as he gazed at the stars above him in the night sky.

"Ellis…" Bianca said after a long pause, once it became clear he wasn't going to apologize for his boorish behavior.

"Yeah?" he sighed, not taking his eyes off the sky.

"Aren't you even sad that he's gone?" she asked as she propelled herself towards him, wading through the waist-high water.

Ellis raised an eyebrow. What an odd thing to ask, he thought. Weirder still, he didn't know how to answer.

"I know you weren't close, but… he was still your father," she added.

"Good old Mr. Moneybags," he muttered. "The only time my father could tear himself away from his work was when he was fucking his girlfriend, or his mistress, or any of the other… women… he kept around," he finished carefully, not wanting to further offend the girls by sneering at their profession.

His father, Benedikt Bauer, had been the CEO of Garvan Motors, having inherited control of the company when his father, Lukas Bauer, had passed away decades before. The company had fallen on troubled times under Lukas, but thanks to Benedikt's foresight and tireless efforts, Garvan Motors had seen a steady rise in market share and production over the last two decades, so that by the time of his death it was one of Terra's leading manufacturers of ground vehicles and hovercraft. As was common among men of industry, Benedikt's success had come at the expense of his family life.

"The only thing my father was ever good for was buying me things. Now that he's gone, I can do that just as well for myself," Ellis finally retorted with a sneer, attempting to suck more champagne from the empty bottle, shaking it in frustration.

"Laurentz!" he shouted. "We need more wine. And clean up this mess!"

He leaned back, allowing Bianca to sit on his lap. With a sly smile, she started to position herself on top of him, gyrating her hips slowly and biting her lower lip.

"Laurentz," he shouted again, this time loud enough to awaken the entire household.

Finally he heard footsteps approaching the pool, down the path from the estate.

"Senile old fool," he muttered under his breath, closing his eyes as he continued to enjoy Bianca's performance. "Utterly useless."

"What about me?" said Nyla, feigning jealousy. "I want to play t…" her words were cut short by what sounded like soft coughs, followed by a misty spray of liquid across Ellis's face and chest.

Bianca stopped moving, falling limply backwards into the pool.

Ellis opened his eyes in confusion, only to freeze in horrified panic. Bianca's body floated on the water in front of him, blood spiraling lazily into the pool from a hole in her temple. A few meters away on the stone poolside, Nyla lay clutching a gushing wound on the side of her neck, blood gurgling from her open mouth, her teeth stained red and her eyes wide with terror and despair. He couldn't move. Should he run, scream?

Nyla's eyes flickered for a brief moment, finding his, then she slumped head-first into the water, which was now stained with swirls of crimson blood. Finally gathering his thoughts enough to focus his eyes in the direction of the approaching footsteps, Ellis trembled when he saw that it was not his aging manservant that stood at the opposite side of the pool. In his stead stood a young man, tall, yet slender, dressed in simple dark dress pants and a long coat, his sleek blond hair combed back over his head.

"Hello, Ellis."

"Who… who are you? You won't… I have powerful friends!" the youth stuttered, attempting to intimidate the intruder. "If you kill me, they'll find you and boil the flesh from your bones!"

"There's no cause for alarm," this time, when he heard the voice, Ellis realized that the intruder wasn't moving his mouth at all – but Ellis could hear his words perfectly nonetheless. "I'm here to help fulfill your father's legacy."

"What?" was all that Ellis could mutter in terrified astonishment.

"I represent an organization, a very powerful group of individuals, with whom your father invested a substantial portion of his vast fortunes. Now that he is no more – an act which I really must complement you on, by the way," the young man clapped his hands softly and smiled innocently, sending chills running down Ellis' spine, "the return on his investment will be paid to you, his sole heir."

"What… what legacy?" Ellis stuttered, hoping for more information.

"If you want to find out, get dressed and follow me. We have a great deal to discuss. The future of Garvan Motors rests in your hands."

"What about them?" asked Ellis, gesturing towards the dead prostitutes floating in his pool.

"Two whores and a decrepit servant? We'll see to it that they won't be missed. Now come. The shuttle will be leaving soon, and you wouldn't want to miss the show," the voice of the mysterious stranger echoed in his head as he turned to leave.

Chapter 13

As excited as he was anxious about the prospect of making contact with not just one, but a number of advanced alien species, Captain Mitchell paced back and forth on the bridge. The tow drones had already left the docking bay and the force field had been raised, leaving the *Tengri* firmly in the embrace of the docking clamps.

Marcus, still peering through the bridge's forward viewscreen, could see into the adjoining bays through large windows in the bay's walls. The bay to their left was vacant, but a medium-sized cruiser occupied the one on the right. With its hooked nose, tipped, descending wings and multi-barreled cannons, it looked menacing, as well as alien, in its design.

"What do the readings say?" the captain inquired. "Is it safe to breathe out there, or do we need to put on suits?"

"According to the scans I'm reading... 78% nitrogen, 21% oxygen, 0.9% argon and 0.04% carbon dioxide. The outside temperature is eighteen degrees Celsius. It's almost as if it were tailor-made for us, Captain," Wei informed him.

"In that case, I want the contact team in the airlock in five minutes, sidearms only," Mitchell ordered. "Going out there armed to the teeth is bound to send the wrong message. Reid, Jago, you can lose the suits."

"Yes boss," Jago grunted over the intercom.

"Ok, docking hatch in five minutes. Let's move people!" Mitchell concluded, spurring everyone into motion.

The buzzing whir of metal on metal accompanied the movements of the servo arms as they began to open the docking hatch. As the hermetic seal ruptured, a hissing sound cut through the droning as the pressure between the airlock and the docking bay equalized. An open-sided mechanical ramp had already been connected with the ship, allowing easy access to the bay's main platform.

Captain Mitchell ordered Taz to take the lead, urging caution as he followed closely behind, peering through the dim light of the bay. Behind him, Serena seemed overly eager to make first contact, and was pressing up behind him while Marcus, Reid and Jago brought up the rear as the team crossed the wide ramp and started along the wide walkway. Gossamer rays of light pierced the shrouding darkness between the chaotic network of metallic rafters high overhead.

The walkway stretched out for over a hundred meters ahead of them, running the length of the bay, before swerving abruptly to the right to form an L-shaped platform in the corner of the compartment, its long leg running alongside the *Tengri*. A wide metal doorway faced the ship's nose on the short leg of the platform. Marcus leaned over the low metal railing to catch a glimpse of the docking bay's floor, where, almost fifteen meters below, a team of robotic drones scurried about amongst an assortment of hoses, power lines and containers, apparently examining the ship. One of the drones projected an arching beam of emerald light across the ship's flank, as if performing some form of scan.

Marcus followed the beam of light up the *Tengri*'s flank, seeing the ship from the outside for the first time since they'd left Beta Terra.

Unlike most Terran military ships, which were much taller than they were broad, the Benediction-class cruiser lacked the asymmetric over-and-under protrusions and towers that made Marcus think of magazines and pistol grips hanging from a rifle. Instead, the *Tengri* was an eighty-meter long block only four decks tall, slightly wider at her lowest point than her highest, giving her a trapezoidal cross-section that was only broken by two extremely short, stubby wings on each side, the bare minimum required to allow the ship controlled reentry into an atmosphere. Her nose was a blocky, squared-off construction surmounted by huge panels of toughed glass where the bridge sat on the third deck. The ship's hull consisted of a number of segmented plates in a matte, dark-grey color.

The sound of Jago clearing his throat and spitting over the railing went unnoticed before it was too late. Just as Marcus sprang to reprimand the behemoth, a loud hiss rang through the docking bay, preceding the noisy opening of the vast doorway at the end of the walkway. Bathed in light spilling into the dimness of the bay from beyond, three figures emerged from the opening.

"I didn't do it!" Jago muttered automatically, looking both bewildered and guilty.

Shooting him a judgmental look, Marcus turned his attention to the silhouettes. He could see that one of them was clearly humanoid, whereas the other two were different from the first but seemed to be members of the same species as each other. Serpentine, with thick, sluggish bodies, he took them for more of the aliens who had brought the *Tengri* from Ga'ouna.

With Mitchell whispering orders that they stay vigilant, the team advanced slowly. With the exception of Serena, they all kept one hand on their holstered sidearm, prepared to react at the first sign that anything was amiss. The figures ahead of them drew closer, apparently unshaken by their arrival. As the aliens passed beneath one of the strands of light falling from above, Marcus could see them more clearly.

The humanoid one now displayed its alien heritage: well over two meters tall, the alien's frame was bulky with muscles under a thick-looking brownish hide that glistened in the light. Its shape was much closer to a human's body than that of the thick-bodied, short-limbed Golan, but despite the creature's essentially humanoid frame its muscular arrangement was completely foreign, each individual muscle standing out so prominently that it was almost as if each one were covered in its own layer of skin. Its narrow head looked absurdly small atop the huge, muscular body, a curving shield of what looked like smooth bone rising from between its two yellow eyes to cover the top of its head in a protective plate. Its body was entirely devoid of hair, and an almost non-existent chin sat below thick lips that seemed as if they'd never known a smile. As it cleared the corner, Marcus caught a glimpse of a ridge-like protrusion of short bony fins lining its spine, mostly covered beneath a loosely-fitting dark grey bodysuit.

Turning to the other two, Marcus realized that his assumption couldn't have been more wrong. Not only did they lack the distinct heads and humanoid torsos of the Golans' 'gods', these creatures seemed only partly organic. Their bodies were entirely encased in what seemed to be some sort of metallic exoskeleton that left only their heads visible through a glass dome. Beneath the head, which was inhumanly broad and featured a gaping maw lined with rows of small, sharp-looking teeth, set between beady little eyes, these aliens' bodies resembled slugs more than snakes, albeit slugs with faces like something dredged from a primordial ocean.

94

They moved by pushing back against a four-pronged grip that held onto the deck as they shoved their bodies forward, repositioning themselves before pulling the end back in and repeating the process all over again. At the most compact part of their cycle, they were as tall as Taz, the shortest clone in the squad. Most unsettling of all were the aliens' spindly, inorganic arms: a pair of slender robotic limbs tipped with long-fingered hands, large enough to have wrapped entirely around Marcus' head. Set above the shoulder sockets were protruding metal canisters that flashed with tiny blue lights and periodically vented small bursts of some sort of vapor.

From what Marcus could see, none of the three was armed. The humanoid one had a metallic bracer wrapped around its forearm, covered in an assortment of buttons and connectors, but it didn't appear to pose an immediate threat. Still, he knew any of the three might be able to call upon automated defenses, and the slugs' suits looked thick enough to pose a challenge to the stopping power of the Terrans' sidearms.

"I do you welcome to Semeh'yone Station," the humanoid alien spoke as it came to a standstill, its deep voice reverberating throughout the docking bay.

The team came to a full stop a few meters in front of their hosts, and now anxiously awaited the captain's command.

"The... Semion?" Mitchell stumbled.

"It is 'Semeh'yone'," the humanoid corrected. "Heart of Etherium."

"And you are?" the captain prompted, raising an eyebrow.

"I be Ordo'nak. I make customs inspection," the alien replied, pressing a series of buttons on his wristguard.

Suddenly, the metallic bracer produced a holographic interface hovering in midair right before the muscular customs inspector, who proceeded to select a few of the hovering icons with a stubby thumb.

"Excuse me," said Serena, hesitantly, unable to stop herself, "how is it that you know our language?"

"Gaian is not most common language, but is on file," explained Ordo'nak, not taking his eyes off of the holographic interface. "Work customs, must be good with languages."

"Gaian?" Serena blurted. "You mean to tell me that there is someone aboard this station that speaks our language?"

The astonished look on her face was tinged with disappointment, as she realized that she wouldn't be playing as integral a role in their relations with alien species as she'd hoped.

"They is called Gaian," explained Ordo'nak, still peering at his hologram. "They like you, except…"

"Except what?" Captain Mitchell prompted when the humanoid trailed off.

"Except Gaian ambassador say he know nothing of you. Your ship not in databases. I must agree with his assessing," Ordo'nak concluded, pressing another series of glowing icons hovering before him.

A loud thump resounded through the chamber, emanating from the docking clamps.

"I be told I must make lock down on your ship while I make you interrogation. Please to remain here so I be proceeding."

The holographic interface suddenly dissipated, and Ordo'nak stood blocking the walkway before them as the slug-like beings raised their spindly arms and advanced.

* * * * *

The interrogation was conducted in an ante-chamber right outside the docking bay. The whole crew was made to form a line in front of the doorway in the main bay as they were brought in one at a time whilst one of the two cybernetic slugs kept watch on those waiting, a sinister glare dissuading any attempts to get past.

"Is the boss ok?" Jago murmured as he stood anxiously behind Marcus, who was next in line, and was staring, fixated, at the slimy secretion that coated the guard's razor-sharp teeth, dripping slowly into its hideous mouth.

"I'm sure he's fine," Marcus assured him, rather unconvincingly. "They're just asking him some questions."

"What kind of questions?" Jago probed.

"I don't know Ape. They probably just want to know our intentions," Marcus explained.

It had been over an hour and they hadn't heard so much as a sound from the captain the entire time.

"I don't like this," Taz proclaimed. "What if they've taken him somewhere?"

"Taken him where?" Marcus asked half-heartedly, not wanting to give in to Taz's hysterics.

"I don't know. They could be... probing... stuff, even as we speak," he added.

"Shut up Taz!" Marcus cut him off, then hissed at him in a whisper. "There's no reason to think that, and I'd prefer it if you didn't cause a panic. Everyone is nervous enough as it is."

Just then the door to the interrogation room slid open, and a somewhat bewildered Captain Mitchell strode out to greet them.

"Captain, what did they want?" Serena burst out before anyone else had the chance to question him.

Captain Mitchell puffed his cheeks and scratched the graying stubble on his head before answering.

"Well, they just wanted to find out more about us. Although they already knew plenty from examining our ship," he explained.

"What sort of things?" Marcus questioned, somewhat bewildered.

"Well, they know where we stand technologically, which seems to be a big deal. They believe we're somehow related to this Gaian species, although the Gaians apparently are firmly denying any connection," the captain recounted. "They also wanted to know why we're here, and how we mean to support ourselves."

"Support ourselves?" Reid asked.

"Yes. Well, we're stuck here," Captain Mitchell revealed. "They've assigned us a technological rating of zero, which means we're restricted from trading in technology above that level."

"Zero?" bellowed Dr. Gehringer from the rear of the group, suddenly finding the nerve to approach despite the menacing half-mechanical slug looming eerily nearby.

"Apparently their scale starts at a negative. A rating of 'zero' means a civilization can get out of its own solar system, but to get a rating of 'one' we'd need to be capable of full two-way interstellar travel. The 'zero' allows for travel along the lines of our mass accelerators, but given that we can't get home under our own power, I can't exactly fault their logic."

"It's not like we were looking to get back home anyway," Marcus added. "At least, not yet," he added when Serena gave him a curious look.

"True," the captain agreed. "But I would rather have that option available to us in case we need it."

At that point, the cybernetic slug behind them tapped Marcus on the shoulder with its mechanical arm, and gestured to the antechamber. With a deep breath, Marcus hesitantly entered the brightly-lit room, shading his eyes until they adjusted to show him it was little more than an alcove at the opening of a wide, segmented hallway, lined with non-reflective dark metal beams. The atmosphere was close, warm and faintly damp. There, Ordo'nak sat on a portable stool behind a metallic table, across from a small, strangely-proportioned chair, whilst the other cybernetic slug kept watch from the corner. A metal unit, the size of an ammo case, rested upon the table.

"Sit," Ordo'nak commanded as the door slammed shut.

Marcus sat down on the small, uncomfortable chair and squinted to shield his eyes from the piercing light. Ordo'nak's bulbous yellow eyes peered down at him through the holographic interface of his wrist device.

In the corner, the cybernetic slug produced a small, rod-like device and pointed it in Marcus' direction. Marcus threw up his arm in protest, tilting his head to shield himself. For all he knew, he was about to be blasted by a powerful laser, or bombarded with radiation, but before he could react further, device gave off a soft golden glow that produced only a mild tingling sensation as it enveloped him. A few seconds later, the slug deactivated the device and stowed it away.

"Contaminate scan," Ordo'nak explained, without taking his eyes from the hologram.

Marcus eased up.

"Your Captain inform me much what I need. This now just short, you tell some things, I tell some things," the humanoid continued, finally turning his small yellow eyes on Marcus. "You race call itself Terran. Is correct?"

"That's correct," Marcus replied. "What is your race called? Uh, if I might ask?" He hesitated, unsure whether or not he was allowed to ask questions in return.

"I am of the Hrŭll," the muscular alien replied gravely, his expression locked in a permanent frown.

"And the others?" Marcus ventured, gesturing towards the slug in the corner when Ordo'nak didn't immediately continue.

"Dalapian."

"Are they related to the ones that towed us here?" Marcus continued, pressing his luck.

"No," Ordo'nak replied, gruffly. "Eremaran ship bring you, but enough question. You answer, I ask."

"My apologies," Marcus answered, biting his lip.

"Tell me, why you have come here?"

"I… We are a deep space exploration team. We were sent to make contact with other races," Marcus confessed, unsure how much information he should divulge.

"Exploration," Ordo'nak voiced, pressing a sequence of symbols on his holographic interface. "And what weapons you have on ship?"

"Weapons?"

"Yes, weapons. You say exploration, but your ship have cannons, and your people have weapons," Ordo'nak pressed.

"Oh, right. Well we didn't really know what to expect. I… our superiors equipped us with basic weaponry as a precaution," Marcus answered sincerely, deciding it might not be best to admit that the Terran Republic was at war with the only other sentient species it had encountered.

"Small person weapons is allow on Semeh'yone, but only if have proper license. I trust when we make search of ship, we not find explosive or heavy weapons?" Ordo'nak continued.

"No Sir, only personal weaponry. At least, according to our classifications." Marcus confirmed. "Though the, uhm, large individual's weapon packs quite a punch, and there may be some small thrown explosive devices. We call them grenades."

"Make certain they not removed from ship during stay on Semeh'yone station," Ordo'nak sighed before executing another command on his wrist device, which suddenly began to give out a low buzzing sound, then ejected a thin plastic sliver from a slot on its side.

"This is yours," Ordo'nak commented, his voice monotonal, handing the plastic sheet over to Marcus. "Is identification card. You must have with you all times."

"Thank you. I will," Marcus agreed, staring intently at the small piece of plastic which appeared to be entirely transparent, with no markings or imprint visible at all.

Ordo'nak reached over to the metal case on the table, opening its lid and withdrawing a small device, handing it to Marcus. At less than a centimeter in thickness, it was even smaller than one of Taylor's cigarette packets, and light too, but as he grasped its cold metal frame in his palm, it gave off an impression of great durability.

"This is Pamco," the alien said as he handed it over. "Also must keep with you all times."

"Pamco?" Marcus repeated, staring at him inquisitively.

"Put identification card in Pamco at top, and press finger on screen," Ordo'nak instructed him. "Pamco will make sample genetic code and then you access all information to your person: registration, permission, license. It also act as connect to credit accountings and allow pay for goods and service. It also short-range communicate."

"And this is free?" Marcus asked incredulously.

"Yes, basic Pamco is provide free. Is require that all persons who traveling in Etherium space carry Pamco on all time," Ordo'nak added. "You is finished. Please inform Captain that Gaian ambassador have refuse request for audience. You free to go."

Marcus had expected the session to last much longer but was relieved to be let go. As he stood up to leave, Marcus realized just how uncomfortable the bright lights that had been shining directly into his eyes had been, and noticed that he was sweating profusely. The door slid open once more and allowed him passage to the docking bay. As cool as the still air back in the bay was, it made a welcome change to the steamy interrogation chamber.

* * * * *

One by one the crew had each gone through Ordo'nak's questioning, and they'd then been instructed to wait in the docking bay while he reported to the authorities. As there was some confusion as to whether this was in fact a first contact situation or not, the protocols that needed following were apparently in dispute. They had waited for almost four hours, sitting on the deck against the cold steel walls of the docking bay while the Dalapian slugs scoured their ship for any signs of contraband or illegal weaponry. Finally the grim-faced customs official returned.

"I have news," Ordo'nak stated. "Etheran Council will hear you and consider to grant you sanctuary on Semeh'yone. Hearing for you schedule after sixty four cycles."

"Sixty four cycles?" Captain Mitchell asked.

"Sixty four turnings of planet we orbit," Ordo'nak explained. "According to you way of time..." he tapped at his wristguard, "One cycle is twenty seven hour and twelve minute."

"Ah," Captain Mitchell sighed. "And in the meantime, what are we to do?"

"You be give access to New Arrival Zone," Ordo'nak proclaimed. "Please be on best behave, as bad incidents may great affect you plea with Council."

"And the Etheran Council is…?" Serena chimed in.

"Ruling government," Ordo'nak grunted.

"…of your race?" Serena prompted when the Hrūll failed to elaborate.

"No," Ordo'nak corrected. "Etheran Council is combination effort this part of galaxy."

"Well, thank you for your help," Serena smiled. She had been utterly intrigued by the entire encounter, and was bursting to know more, despite her disappointment at the aliens' knowledge of the Terran language.

Ordo'nak simply nodded, his face still locked in a grimace, as if they had somehow wronged him without realizing it. Just then, the Dalapian slugs returned from the *Tengri*, apparently having reported that no contraband had been discovered during their search.

As the crew gathered around, Ordo'nak informed them that they'd now be allowed to leave the docking bay, but reiterated that they would only be allowed access to the New Arrivals' Zone and insisted that they were to leave behind any weapons other than their sidearms, or risk setting off the numerous weapons scanners stationed throughout the spaceport. With a final admonition that they were to keep out of trouble until their hearing with the Etheran Council, the bulky alien strode from the bay, leaving the enormous hatch standing open behind him.

103

"Well, I guess we should go see what this place is all about," the captain suggested, much to the excitement of his crew. "I'm sure you all want to get out and explore as soon as possible, but I'll take the contact team and Dr. Gehringer out for a look around first. The rest of you are to wait on the *Tengri*. It can't hurt to be too careful."

Marcus had almost forgotten all about Ga'ouna and the life he'd imagined for himself on the warm jungle world. His mind was filled with the untold possibilities that Semeh'yone had to offer, and a burning curiosity as to why his visions had guided them here.

Chapter 14

Having been escorted through the maze of windowless back tunnels and passageways that made up the service section of Semeh'yone's spaceport, the team emerged into the New Arrivals' Zone. The sprawling city unfolded before them as they stood on a broad concourse, bustling with returning or would-be travelers. Networks of transparent tubes filled with misty vapors of various colors and opacities intersected one another at intervals, spread out throughout the district and allowing passage to species which didn't share the most common types of atmosphere.

Across from them, a wide chasm was filled to capacity with over a dozen lanes of slow-moving hovercraft that drifted nearly a meter or so from the metallic surface of the road below, lined with rows of blinking lights. A pair of bridges teaming with life spanned the street. Thousands of creatures belonging to dozens of alien species lined the streets, coming and going, greeting expected visitors or peddling their exotic wares. Billowing steam, pouring down from an overhanging vent jutting out from the spaceport's main structure, shrouded a group of peddlers and cutthroats from view. The bittersweet aroma that permeated the area reminded Marcus of a mixture of pungent fish and cinnamon.

Behind them, the facilities of the docking sector bulked large, its upper levels cresting into the city above like rocks poking up through the waves on the beach on Ga'ouna. Ahead, the towering white pillar of the central tower soared high above the rooftops, surrounded by a knot of skyscrapers in the far distance, an imposing monumental landmark that dominated the view. The inside of the domed force field overhead portrayed dark, somber clouds which seemed to shift ever so slightly, stirred by imaginary winds. Marcus couldn't tell whether the light that fell from above was generated by the force field or was the light from the system's star, but it lit the scene well enough for him to see clearly.

Breathing the open air was a tad more strainful than it had been in the docking bay, whose atmosphere Dr. Gehringer suspected had been blended especially for their physiology. This felt heavier, somehow. Still, the city air was apparently within the range of their tolerance.

"Stay close everyone," Captain Mitchell ordered as he surveyed their surroundings.

Marcus was overwhelmed. He'd never felt so small in his life. He was reminded of the time that his old squad had been led on a tour of the promenade, back on Alamo station, when he was only a few weeks old. Fresh from the tanks they'd been grown in, the clones had been overwhelmed by the bright lights of the bars and shops of what was, he now knew, a fairly small centre to keep off-duty troops entertained before they were shipped off to war. How far he and his squadmates had come since then.

"Taz! Get away from there!" Mitchell yelled, noticing their scout had wandered a good twenty yards away and was being beckoned by a pair of... what looked like two human women with slender limbs and curvaceous bodies. Pulling his eyes up from their tight-fitting, low-cut bodysuits, however, he realized with a that their skin was a mottled lavender, and their long, thick hair a purplish colour.

As Taz stood, torn between the captain's orders to return and the voluptuous women who stood by the base of a thick pipe protruding from the platform's floor, Marcus wondered if their skin had merely been painted or tattooed, and if these women weren't the mysterious Gaians. Then the shorter of the two flicked her hair aside in an achingly human gesture, and he saw her face more clearly. Beautiful as she was, there was no way her large amber eyes and broad, nose-less face could be mistaken for a human's, whatever the similarity of their bodies. As if to reinforce the point, her taller companion bent to whisper something to her, and as they turned Marcus saw they had long prehensile tails that writhed in the air behind them.

"What?" Taz shouted back, not noticing the trio of broad, hooded figures looming off to his side in the steam spilling down from overhead.

Mitchell spotted what looked like the glint of metal protruding from the sleeve of one of the looming figures, which was slowly circumventing the scout to come at Taz from behind.

"I said now!" Captain Mitchell roared, and Taz came jogging back with his tail between his legs.

"I could get used to this," Taz proclaimed eagerly to Marcus, not hiding his shame. "At least the girls here seem friendly."

"Yeah, right up until their friends slit your throat," Captain Mitchell countered, pointing out the retreating figures. "We all need to be a lot more careful, especially you two," said the captain, giving Taz and Jago a commanding look.

"Yes boss," chimed the Ape.

The team started nervously across the concourse, Marcus noticing that, as on-edge as the new sights and sounds had made the clones, Dr. Gehringer seemed the most bewildered of them all. The scientist had turned an entirely new shade of pasty white as he peered frantically around him at everything that moved, panting anxiously in barely-suppressed fear.

As they left the concourse fronting the port and made their way across the bridge in front of them, their eyes were drawn to the narrow pedestrian streets that cut through the dense blocks of four- and five-storey structures in straight lines, each building designed to draw as much attention as possible from passers-by on the streets below. With their glowing neon lights, multi-colored streamers and brightly-lit signs written in what could only be a mixture of alien symbols, it was impossible not to feel a strong measure of excitement.

A row of scantily-clad, large-breasted females with purplish skin and devils' tails stood on the nearest street corner, dancing seductively for a small crowd of spectators. Unlike the two Taz had spotted back at the port, some of this group were covered in a variety of body art, inked into their skin or sculpted from their very flesh. Marcus was amazed at just how human they appeared.

The whole team was suddenly startled by a thick, tentacle-like appendage that unfurled down from above them and landed square in the middle of their group. The clones' inborn soldier's reflexes sent them diving for cover, and even Serena and Dr. Gehringer leapt to the nearest wall for safety, unable to utter a single word in shock. Gaping upwards, Marcus saw that the tentacle belonged to a huge cephalopod, drifting a couple of meters overhead as it used its six agile appendages to navigate the busy streets. Its translucent skin revealed veins of greenish blood and purplish muscles, as well as an odd assortment of fluorescent internal organs. Its body was largely enclosed in an artificial transparent shell that contained a sloshing greenish yellow liquid, but its limbs seemed to be covered in a thin, flexible fabric of some sort. Despite the relatively slow movement of the creature's tentacles, its sheer size allowed it to easily surpass the current of passersby, letting out a deep, muffled hum as it loped overhead. When the Terrans realized that none of the alien pedestrians had paid the creature any heed, they regrouped, laughing nervously, and continued to wander the streets, making sure to stick close together.

Wading through the crowded streets, they were completely unaware of the cloaked figure shadowing their every move.

Their path led eventually to a junction, where a street band comprised of all sorts of strange alien musicians were performing a weirdly atonal rhythmic tune, and they hesitated briefly while Mitchell peered down the various streets that spread out, mentally debating which route to take.

Watching the band, Marcus could make out a Hrüll playing some sort of percussion instrument that closely resembled a metal drum with a tuning knob on its side, allowing its user to change the pitch of each blow with one hand while he struck it with the other. A tall, lithe, grey-skinned humanoid with long slender limbs and fingers played a circular instrument lined with dozens of strings, its elongated head bobbing and swaying to the music.

Off to one side, Marcus caught a glimpse of a peculiar creature in a nearby alleyway. It was tall, well over two meters high. Its body was concealed beneath a long, rough brown shell, covered with bulbous protrusions, beneath which three pairs of thick, leathery-looking legs held it upright. A pair of spindly arms with claw-like fingers stuck out from the front of the shell, underneath a head which resembled a large beak with two tiny yellow eyes on each side.

It hunched over a pair of thuggish-looking humanoids with greenish skin and thick features, whose floppy ears listened intently as the six-legged being whispered its ill-gotten secrets for a price. One of the two humanoid thugs was as tall as the Terrans, and more of a mottled brownish green, covered in scars, most of which looked like they'd healed years past. The other was far shorter, and its skin was a more yellowy shade of green. The shorter one stood closer to the street, seemingly keeping watch, with one hand anxiously on the grip of the bulky cannon of a handgun strapped to one side of its belt.

As the team started off into the crowds again, their hooded stalker drew quietly closer, pushing through the throng, closing the distance between them.

They entered a small, round plaza covered in a thin layer of wispy vapors that appeared to be escaping from a monolithic three-storey structure to their left, the walls of which consisted of a combination of tarnished stone and rusted metal. A blubbery, stark-naked humanoid stood defiantly on its front steps, its greenish-brown skin glistening as if it had just emerged from soaking in water. It perked its long, pointy ears to listen to the rustle of foot-traffic. Its bulging stomach and chest were covered in tattooed symbols, and it sported an assortment of jewelry pierced through its pointy ears and nostrils. Its face was not at all unlike that of a human being, though its head was considerably larger, almost comically so. Reflective black eyes were set under a protruding brow ridge on either side of a compact nose, small but broad. Even its mouth looked human, but in lieu of hair, the top of its head was covered in bumps of bone or cartilage atop its skull, and its skin was far from smooth, but rather coarse as uncured leather. Marcus realized that despite the differences between them as individuals, this alien was of the same species as the thuggish two he'd seen in the alley by the band.

Most of the other buildings in the plaza looked shut-up, with closed doors and covered windows, but on the opposite end of the square patrons lined up in front of a building whose front was comprised entirely of dimly-lit, segmented windows, beyond which an assortment of creatures from all manner of species seemed to be offering sexual favors for sale.

Cutting through the dispersing crowd, the cloaked stalker continued its pursuit of the Terrans, inching ever closer to Marcus' back as the traffic thinned out in the plaza, reaching out an arm as it did so.

Suddenly, Marcus felt a tapping on his shoulder and nearly jumped out of his skin.

"You would be wise not to dwell here," the hooded figure addressed them in Terran. "This is not the safest place to be."

The rest of the clones noticed almost immediately, and quickly took up position around Marcus, hands on their weapons as they tried to look as imposing as possible, like a pack of wolves protecting their cub. The spectacle drew the attention of the brutish figure outside the monolithic structure, who watched in seeming fascination.

"You are not safe here," the figure repeated, this time loud enough so all of them could hear.

"Why is that?" Captain Mitchell asked suspiciously.

"That is the leader of one of the Banthalo gangs," the cloaked figure replied, gesturing towards the naked brute on the bath house steps. "If you follow me, I shall take-"

"Who the hell are you?" Mitchell broke in.

"Who *I* am is not important," the figure answered, drawing back his hood to reveal long flowing locks of blond hair and delicate human features. "What I can do for *you*, on the other hand, is very important."

*   *   *   *   *

The cloaked man, who had introduced himself only as Rodan Kesh, had drawn them in off the streets with the promise of a hot meal and helpful advice. The establishment he'd led them to was a rundown formation of tables underneath a canvas awning which hung from crude support beams lashed between the protruding rafters of the building on the opposite side of the pedestrian street and the kitchen itself, which appeared to have been fashioned from an old shipping container. The speckled grey paint on its flat panels was peeling in numerous places, covered in dents and scratches, and the wide window of tinted glass wedged to the side of the main entry was fogged up from the heat.

The clatter of the wait staff scurrying between the tables of the eatery blended with the cacophony of alien voices, deep in conversation about things that Marcus couldn't even begin to comprehend. Their lavender-skinned waiter stood poised at the end of their table, every so often brushing the locks of deep blue hair from his eyes in an unnervingly human manner. His tail held a glass canister containing a bubbly orange liquid which he was pouring into glasses at the table across the gangway, glancing over his shoulder occasionally to know when to stop.

Marcus was having a hard enough time wondering how it was that an alien society would come to adhere to so many of the same practices as Terrans did. Just the fact that they were sitting in a restaurant was cause for consideration, let alone the fact that the restaurant was set in the pedestrian streets of a bustling city.

Rodan ordered for them in one of the alien tongues. The waiter made sure that they all produced their Pamco devices, which he then held up to his datapad, downloading the necessary data to make certain they were only served food and drink safe for their physiology.

At the table next to them, a humanoid with wrinkly gray skin sat poised, its huge milky, lifeless eyes staring into a ceramic bowl, half-filled with what appeared to be some form of grayish meat. The alien's frame was so thin that it looked as if it was ready to collapse from malnutrition. It leaned forward and extruded a short snout, divided in the middle by a groove that ran up the snout and clear across the creature's bald head, and regurgitated a bright yellow gooey substance into the bowl. The resulting chemical reaction produced a thin yellow vapor as the meat slowly began to liquefy, filling the air with the faint smell of sulfur. The emaciated being then quickly ejected a thin straw-like appendage from its snout and began slurping up the concoction. Marcus cringed as he looked away, unable to observe its odd eating habits.

"Never mind him," Rodan explained, noticing the focus of Marcus' attention. "Arangi are harmless."

"Are we not going to discuss the fact that you're human?" Captain Mitchell interrupted him, drawing stares from the entire group.

"I am Gaian," Rodan corrected him carefully. "And you are Terran."

"You'll have to excuse us, but there doesn't seem to be much of a difference," Serena interjected.

"That is not important at this juncture," Rodan insisted.

"Not important?" Taz bellowed. "We've flown halfway across the fucking galaxy only to find humans living with aliens. Not important? I'd say it's the most important topic up for discussion!"

"Pipe down Taz!" Captain Mitchell shouted, drawing glares from a nearby group of Hrūll who were entrenched in a holographic game.

"I have been instructed not to talk about it," Rodan explained.

"Instructed by whom?" Captain Mitchell inquired, starting to get irritated by the mystery.

Rodan's flashing glare spoke more than words. It was obvious that he wasn't about to divulge his secrets to them, no matter how much they persisted.

"First of all, you should know that Gaians are not exactly popular in this part of Semeh'yone. In fact, you are fortunate to have made it this far unmolested," Rodan said, making an effort to change the subject.

"Why is that?" Reid probed, leaning forward in interest.

"Yeah, you seem so open and forthcoming," Taz sneered.

"Because our morals do not mesh well with the criminal element which dominates the New Arrivals' Zone," Rodan explained.

"Point taken," Captain Mitchell said. "I guess that means we won't be popular around here either."

"I fear not. So stick to the more populated areas," Rodan advised. "As long as you remain in a crowd, and you stay together, you should be relatively safe."

"Relatively…" the captain replied, raising his eyebrow.

"I would also advise you to learn Hiodan as quickly as possible. It is the most common language spoken in Etherium space," Rodan added.

"What *exactly* is the Etherium?" asked Serena, who seemed to be the only one among them enjoying the encounter with the self-proclaimed Gaian.

"The Etherium is the name given to an alliance of races which governs this region of the galaxy," he explained.

"This region? So there is more than one alliance out there?" Taz prompted.

"Oh yes," Rodan confirmed. "There are several main powers in this part of the galaxy. You were most fortunate to arrive in Etheran space. Had you ventured into the territories of the Moloukan Empire or the Sereni Sanctum, I am afraid you would not have lived long. At least…

114

not a life worth living."

"What are we supposed to do?" Marcus wondered. "We have no funds, we have no means to support ourselves. Effectively, we're stranded."

"My advice is to tread carefully," Rodan informed them. "You have a meeting with the Etheran Council scheduled, when you will be able to apply for asylum. Until then, I have been instructed to offer some financial assistance. A small sum, but it should suffice to support you until your meeting with the Council. In the meantime, I can guide you to safe and affordable accommodation."

"I think perhaps it's best if we remain aboard the *Tengri*," Captain Mitchell said. "We'll feel a lot safer in familiar surroundings."

"A wise decision," Rodan remarked.

As they took in all the newfound information, Rodan produced his Pamco and proceeded to transfer the credits to Captain Mitchell's account. Almost immediately, the captain's device let out a sharp beeping sound, alerting him that the status of his credit account had been updated.

"The support you are receiving does not come without a price," the blond man warned them. "I must insist that you do your best not to cause trouble. Gaian or Terran, to the other races, we look the same. The Gaian people strive to maintain a certain reputation, and as such I must insist that you help to uphold it."

"You don't have to worry about us," the captain replied. "I'll keep my people in line."

"I hope so. There are many eyes upon you, not the least of which are those of my own people," Rodan cautioned them grimly. "You do not wish to make enemies here, Captain."

As the waiter brought forth an array of exotic dishes, almost all of which were met with high praise, Captain Mitchell stared quietly out at the busy streets. Though he was mesmerized by all that they had experienced, he did not trust the Etherium's agenda. Why make them wait so long for an audience? Who were these Gaians who had sent their emissary to offer their 'support', and why were they so reluctant to reveal their intentions? Perhaps they were the remnants of the first C-CORE colonies, cut off from all communication with Terra once they'd been sent out over a century ago. The possibility was not entirely impossible, though if they'd managed to establish themselves here, surely they could have informed the Republic? Perhaps he was just being an old fool to allow his paranoia to reach to such heights. For now, as far as first contact scenarios went, things could definitely have gone far worse. He only hoped their newfound funds would stretch until their meeting with the Etheran council.

Chapter 15

Ambassador Janosh's audience chamber looked more like a vibrant forest glade than an office. Near a central pool of clear water, occupied by schools of silver and golden fish, the ambassador sat upon a tiled square laid with roughly hewn stone. Trees of all sizes and shapes surrounded the pool, and flowers nearing bloom were allowed to grow freely along the borders of the freshly cut grass. Colorful birds rested on branches, some hidden by the leafy canopy while others, more daring, peered down at the ambassador who appeared deep in meditation. Their song reminded him a gathering of women, recanting gossip and tales of their children's exploits.

The domed roof above the embassy projected an image of a blue sky lit by a bright orange sun cresting the edge of a single formation of clouds. An enormous old tree cast its shadow over the glade, its gnarled branches enveloping the ambassador as if shielding him from the troubles of the outside world. A pair of bright orange butterflies fluttered passed him, as if competing for his attention.

On the surface, he appeared to be a simple man, with simple tastes. One who was in touch with nature, leading a life of perfect balance and harmony. Those who knew him well, however, knew that he also bore a superior intellect, one capable of complex compartmentalization and great strategy. He was respected, even revered, throughout Gaian society, a fact which reinforced his self image and traditional views.

From his stark white and neatly trimmed stubble and receding hairline to his neatly pressed robes of purest white silk, the ambassador was the pinnacle of refinement, taking painstaking care in his appearance and demeanor. His blue eyes exuded a boyish innocence, but hinted at ages of wisdom and experience. His plump nose lent a friendly tone to his otherwise serious façade. Faintly wrinkled skin hinted at the weakness which comes with old age, but he harbored an inner strength few could rival.

A sudden shimmer of light produced a holographic depiction of an androgynous humanoid being of glowing blue light, hairless and dressed in plain robes, standing before the meditating figure.

"Ambassador," the hologram prompted.

"Yes, Thales?" Ambassador Janosh acknowledged, his eyes still closed as he remained unshaken in his lotus position.

"Your disciple has arrived as requested. Shall I send him in?" Thales inquired.

"Please do," the ambassador responded. "Can you have some tea sent in as well?"

"Certainly, Ambassador."

With a flicker, the image of Thales vanished.

After a minute of silence, hurried steps signaled the arrival of Rodan Kesh. As he entered the glade, he bowed down on one knee in reverence.

"I have done as you asked, Master," Rodan informed him.

"Good," the ambassador voiced, without inflection. "What is your impression of the new arrivals?"

"It is still too early to tell, Master. They have yet to prove themselves either way."

Ambassador Janosh suddenly opened his eyes and began to unfold his legs.

"Please, take a seat," he gestured to the tiles before him.

"Yes Master. Thank you," Rodan replied, sitting cross-legged before the older man.

"Tell me Rodan, have you heard of Master Silos?" the ambassador asked him when he'd settled.

"Of course, Master," Rodan acknowledged. "There are few who have not heard of his great deeds."

"During my apprenticeship with Ambassador Silos, I learned some of life's most important lessons. Among them was patience," the ambassador said with a friendly smile. "When we find the strength to wait and watch our opponents, their weakness will ultimately reveal itself."

"Yes Master," Rodan concurred, listening intently to his master's wisdom.

They became aware of the appearance of a young servant girl bearing a silver tray laden with porcelain cups and a decanter of steaming hot water. They waited in silence as she gracefully knelt down beside them and placed the ornate platter on the ground between them. She bowed gently before leaving hurriedly the same way she'd come. Ambassador Janosh leaned forward to pour tea into the pair of ornate cups, the gentle fragrance mixing with the scent of blossoms.

"Of course, patience is not always the best course of action. Sometimes, one must provoke one's opponent into reacting," he explained, and as he spoke, every single flower surrounding the two men bloomed before their very eyes.

The buds of the morning glories spread their brilliant pedals, white lilies swayed under their own weight, their filaments writhing as if they had suddenly gained sentience. A small grouping of butterflies ascended from their hiding places, shaken by the sudden change in scenery. Rodan's attention wandered from his master and with a gaping smile he admired the ambassador's power over the forces of nature.

Janosh passed one of the cups to his aid before taking a modest sip from his own.

"How should we proceed?" Rodan inquired, gently swirling his cup to let the tea blend properly.

The ambassador looked apprehensive, tentatively examining the situation from every aspect in his mind's eye.

"We need to know how many more of them there are, and whether they shall be arriving here," the ambassador decided. "I've been informed that their technology does not allow for two-way travel, which leaves those already here stranded."

"Yes Master," Rodan acknowledged.

"We always knew they would show themselves eventually," the ambassador continued. "But we must know their intentions before it is time to act."

"I shall continue with my observations, Master," Rodan proclaimed proudly.

"We need to make it apparent to the Etherium that there is a clear difference between Terrans and Gaians."

"Yes Master."

With a wave of his hand, Ambassador Janosh dismissed his aid and placed his porcelain teacup back on the tray. He let his eyes fall shut once more and folded his legs back under his body, reaching his hands out with their palms open, facing skywards. His body began to relax, letting go of his conscious mind. He felt his core, his very soul, begin to merge with the surrounding flora and fauna. He envisioned his essence pooling with that of the flowers, the trees, the freshly cut grass, even the fish and the birds.

As his heaving chest took in deep breaths of the freshly scented air, the glade moved with him, writhing back and forth in perfect harmony.

Chapter 16

After four days of sleeping in the ship's quarters and forcing a semblance of routine, the crew was starting to get impatient. It was one thing to travel through space with a purpose, but sitting in dock with nothing to do but wait was another matter entirely. Taz and Jago were taking it the worst. The metropolis lying in wait outside the spaceport was haunting them, and the more the captain denied them access to its opportunities, the more desperate they became to leave the ship.

Tempers flared, and, at the urgings of the others, Captain Mitchell finally gave in and allowed the crew to explore the New Arrivals' Zone, albeit with certain restrictions. They were only to travel in groups, and they had to stay in regular contact with the ship. They were also reminded to be on their best behavior, and to steer clear of even the slightest hint of danger.

Marcus, Taz and Serena were among the second group given shore leave, and they were eager to leave the ship. Also in their group was Dr. Gehringer, who had approached the trip as an opportunity to conduct field research, arriving at the airlock carrying all manner of instruments and scanners, along with his trusted datapad.

"Are you sure you have everything you need?" Serena remarked sarcastically as the scientist stumbled through the hatch to the forward airlock, almost dropping half of his gear.

"I believe so, Ms. Kim," he replied earnestly, apparently unaware of her facetious tone, as he set most of his equipment on the deck and began strapping each piece onto a makeshift shoulder harness. "I've requisitioned some funds from Captain Mitchell in order to conduct my research. If it is at all possible, I would like to find some form of knowledge repository, or a center for learning. A library if you will."

"Figures. We're finally free to have some fun, and the Professor here wants to do some reading," Taz groaned.

"We'll see what we can do," Marcus reassured him, patting the corpse-pale doctor on the shoulder.

* * * * *

It was early evening when they emerged from the docks, and Marcus found himself admiring the mock sky. The sun was setting behind the rim of the docking ring, bathing the cloud-cast sky in brilliant hues of crimson and lavender.

"How do they that?" Taz gasped, following Marcus' gaze.

"My guess would be either a very powerful holographic projector, or some form of plasma being manipulated between twin force fields," Dr. Gehringer proposed.

"Does it really matter how it's done?" Serena intervened. "It's astonishing!"

"I'm a scientist Ms. Kim. It's my job to question everything."

They made their way down one of the busier streets, stopping periodically to allow Dr. Gehringer to record each new species he came across with one of his various instruments.

If it weren't for the language barrier that prevented him asking questions, and Serena's reluctance to work with the doctor, whose insensitivity she was fast developing a distaste for, their journey would have taken hours. Nonetheless, Dr. Gehringer did his best to pose

123

questions to passersby through hand gestures and awkward facial expressions, most shrugging him off as nothing more than a nuisance. Some tried to take advantage, offering up their trinkets as if they were exotic treasures worth their weight in gold. When the clueless scientist eventually wandered too close to a group of Banthalo thugs standing outside what looked like a dive bar, Marcus finally felt compelled to intervene.

"Doctor, are you trying to get yourself killed?" Marcus hissed, running up behind him to grab him by the shoulder.

The entrance to the sleazy establishment was blocked by a two meter tall monstrosity with a large metallic ring through his green nose. As the alien's companions began to take note of the scientist's curiosity, they began to get agitated. One of them, who had been sitting on top of a bike-like contraption hovering a short distance off the ground, furrowed his brow and scowled at them with his large black reflective eyes. Its pointy ears, which had been flapping at the side of his head, were now raised and angled, seemingly to better monitor their conversation.

Marcus pulled Gehringer away, casting an uneasy glance at the massive weapon that rested beside the entrance of the bar, within easy reach of the gang's leader. It resembled a two-handed meat cleaver with a serrated edge and a ball of metal on the end to give it more weight, increasing the force of its impact. Clearly the Banthalo gangs took the station's weapons regulations more as suggestions than laws.

"What are you doing?" Dr. Gehringer demanded, angered by Marcus' interference. "You mustn't interrupt me when I'm performing research."

"Doctor, if your research requires you to have your skull caved in then by all means go and bother the nice doorman," Marcus growled at him.

Dr. Gehringer's expression turned from one flush with anger to one of quiet apprehension. He turned his head cautiously to look over his shoulder to where one of the lower-ranked Banthalo had gone over to the monstrosity by the entrance and was standing on his toes to whisper something in the giant's ear, all the while eying Dr. Gehringer with great interest.

"Oh," the scientist muttered. "I see. Well perhaps I can continue my research elsewhere."

"Very good Doctor," Marcus agreed, hurriedly rushing him off down a nearby side street.

"You know, I find all this isomorphism most intriguing," Dr. Gehringer continued. "There was a sociobiologist back on Earth that hypothesized that most alien life would not only look like humans, but would behave like us as well. His theory was controversial, but here you see it all around you! In the architecture around us – streets, buildings, doors, windows! Even in how they structure their everyday lives: they frequent eateries, bars, seek out entertainment, commerce, all clear indications of extreme convergent evolution."

Taz and Serena had long since started to block out the scientist's ramblings, and were walking a good few meters ahead of them, leaving Marcus to suffer alone.

"I do hope I get a chance to dissect one of them soon," Dr. Gehringer continued. "I'm curious whether their internal anatomy resembles ours as well."

"Let's not go there Doctor," Marcus hushed him. "I don't think they would take too kindly to that, nor would I for that matter."

"Hmm, yes," Gehringer replied absently, his gaze wandering as if he were already making plans for just such an endeavor.

125

"What do you make of these Gaians, Grey?" he asked after a few minutes of contemplation.

"What about them?" Marcus replied, perplexedly.

"Well, they're obviously human. Yet they seem to have been here for some time. Who are they? Where do they come from?" Dr. Gehringer continued as they navigated through a small marketplace, packed with an assortment of exotic wares and street vendors shouting out offers in alien tongues.

"I have absolutely no idea Doctor," Marcus confessed, his concentration fixed on one of the vendors, who was busy trying to clear up a large mess made by a spilled barrel of foul-smelling orange liquid.

"I suppose they could have been sent out here by C-CORE, as one of the earlier missions," Dr. Gehringer hypothesized.

"Hmmm?" Marcus sighed. "Oh, yes. Well, wouldn't they have contacted Beta Terra to let them know what they'd found?"

"Well, obviously they would have tried," Dr. Gehringer agreed. "But sending a communication from here to there could take eons. They're most likely stranded here, just as we are, which is why I find their reluctance to meet with us so disturbing."

"That sounds logical," Marcus proclaimed with renewed interest. "If they've been here for a hundred years or more, they might be afraid that we'll interfere with the life they've built for themselves here."

"Exactly," Dr. Gehringer resounded. "You're not as dim-witted as I'd assumed, Grey. Not that that's a vast improvement."

Marcus simply chuckled awkwardly in response, not sure what to make of the doctor's backhanded insult.

After wandering down a narrow, dingy side street filled with decaying establishments which seemed to have been forgotten by time itself, they emerged onto a massive pedestrian street bordering a busy roadway. At the end of the street, way off in the distance, a wall of shimmering energy blocked passage to lanes upon lanes of hovercraft. Thousands of pedestrians roamed about between spectacular storefronts, most almost a dozen stories tall.

To their immediate left, a jazzy, alien rhythm escaped through the broad entrance of what could only be a popular night club. A queue of several dozen of potential patrons waited in line as a particularly nasty-looking Golan stood imposingly at the front.

Metallic plates had been attached to his head, with tubes and wiring connecting to the base of his skull. He wore a stylish tunic of auburn leather, and a chain-linked belt with a bulky clasp.

"Is that what I think it is?" gasped Serena in surprise, taking a few steps forward to make sure her eyes weren't playing tricks on her.

To Marcus, the Golan bouncer seemed out of place. Not only was he twice as tall as the patrons, the gentle nature of his race seemed ill-suited to such a position. Serena halted briefly, confirming that the hulking figure was in fact a Golan. She tilted her head in disbelief before striding purposefully for the front of the queue. The music grew louder as she neared the entrance to the club, forcing her to shout at the huge alien.

"Nivalo livo vave nayo higo?" she yelled, trying to gain the bouncer's attention.

Without so much as a word, the Golan – who had mistaken her attempt for a ploy to get ahead of the line – shoved her away with the back of his hand, sending her stumbling to the ground.

"Are you ok?" shouted Marcus as he rushed to her aid.

"What's wrong with him?" Serena pleaded, brushing the dirt off her clothes. "He's not like the others."

"I wouldn't do that, if I were you," came a voice from the side lines. "Golansss get very temperamental onccce they've been implanted."

Marcus turned to see a blurry figure approaching them. It was as if his eyes refused to focus, the shadowy being's form shifting and writhing as if made entirely of smoke. As it drew closer, the outlines became more distinct. The haze began to settle, and before them stood a slender humanoid about their own height, clad in the most impressive suit of armor Marcus had ever seen. Unlike the bulky plates worn over a padded undersuit that the Terran Republic issued to its cloned soldiers, this armor was beautifully segmented, each piece sliding smoothly under and over its neighbors, so that no part of the being was left uncovered. Even the three slender fingers on each of its hands wore thick gauntlets, attached to bracers covered with a series of buttons. Boots of fine dark leather lined the figures calves, branching off at the tip of the foot to form two thick toes, but apparently worn over the all-enclosing suit. The shards of the armor itself seemed carved out of a dark, silvery alloy which gleamed with a faintly lavender sheen. Ornate icons of glowing blue – symbols, letters, labels? Marcus wondered – were displayed on each segment. An upright collar formed a neck guard across the being's shoulders, protecting the wearer's slender neck, a halo of cerulean light covering its inner surface. An ornate facemask chiseled from the same dim alloy as the rest of the suit covered the entirety of its visage in a completely smooth, opaque plate.

"Implanted?" Serena blurted.

"Yesss, the Golan are sssuch gentle creaturesss," the shadowy figure continued, its speech smooth, almost hypnotic. "Many of them come here in sssearch of enlightenment, only to wind up working at the docksss. An unfortunate few align themssselvesss with the more

128

disssreputable elementsss of Sssemeh'yone. They implant them with behavioral implantsss. Make them more aggressssive. It isss truly ssshameful."

"That's horrible," Serena exclaimed, horrified at the thought.

"I would go ssso far asss to sssay that it isss an affront to nature," the slender figure continued. "They are enssslaving thessse poor creaturesss to do their dirty deedsss."

"Who are you? What are you?" Marcus interjected, not sure what to make of the stranger.

"I am Rossshana of the Sssheshen," it introduced itself. "You are the Terransss, are you not?"

The group was taken aback by Roshana's awareness of who they were, and looked to Marcus for guidance.

"We are," Marcus answered hesitantly. "How could you tell us apart from the Gaians?"

"It wasss not difficult," Roshana hissed, in a not unfriendly manner. "Biologically the differenccce isss not apparent, but your equipment tellsss a different tale."

"Our equipment?" Marcus replied, looking down to survey his gear.

"Yesss, it isss far beneath that which one might expect of a Gaian," Roshana explained, cackling with a hissing laughter, but not without a modicum of charm.

"But we've only just arrived here. How could you even have heard of us?" Serena pressed, re-joining the conversation.

"My mistresss makesss it her businessss to know what goesss on in the New Arrival Zone," Roshana revealed. "Ssshe would very much like to meet with you."

"Your mistress?" Marcus probed.

"Yesss, mistressss Ssshikari hasss a proposal ssshe wissshes to discusssss with you."

"What kind of proposal?" Taz asked, timidly.

"Not all of my mistresss's dealingsss are for me to know," Roshana confessed. "Ssshe merely exssspresssed an interessst in you and asssked that I procure an audienccce."

Marcus wasn't sure how to react. Roshana had displayed empathy with the poor Golan bouncer, yet there was something in its nature that made the hairs on the back of his neck rise. Despite his reservations, he knew that if they were to be stranded here, they would need allies. He would be foolish to dismiss such an opportunity out of hand. After all, sooner or later, they'd have to trust someone.

"Where can we find this Shikari?" asked Marcus.

"Ssshe awaitsss you inssside Xhalpithia," Roshana proclaimed and ushered them away from the club with the Golan bouncer and into another further down the street.

Chapter 17

The smoky rhythm from the live band reverberated through the shadow-cast foyer, the droning bass so loud it came close to drowning out the clatter from Xhalpithia's enigmatic patrons. A square central stage in the middle of the club's main room housed a peculiar orchestra. A large alien creature with a turtle-like shell and a bird-like head stood at the center, holding a sack-like contraption with dozens of oddly-shaped pipes of varying sizes protruding from it at all angles. The six-legged being held the strange instrument up to its beak-like mouth and blew into a metal straw, using the fingers on its two spindly arms to activate the pipes by means of small levers.

Around the piper, five small furry humanoids with large, bulbous eyes and stumpy limbs jumped up and down and danced around the stage, adding to the intricate jazzy melody by playing bizarre stringed and percussion instruments, their fur painted black with streaks of white, creating a vaguely skeletal pattern. A scantily-clad girl with pale lavender skin and oddly human features – apart from her tail – pranced about, singing and dancing, making sure to show off her slender, curvaceous body at every opportunity.

Surrounding the entire stage was an outward-facing bar with a glass countertop, staffed by a handful of similarly lavender aliens of two genders, apparently male and female, each of them sporting an assortment of tattoos, piercings and odd hair colorings that Marcus had no way of judging were natural or not. The patrons, drawn from many different races, hovered about the dimly-lit club, whose décor was mainly a mixture of pure whites and deep red hues. The walls were clad in a smooth white leathery substance, with three levels of balconies looking down upon the stage, each one lined with booths and tables. Crimson curtains covered arched openings on the far wall beneath the balconies, with some of the more furtive-looking patrons frequenting whatever lay behind them. Disturbing images hung from the walls, most of which depicted nude individuals of various species in what appeared to be horrid scenes of erotic death.

"Up the ssstairsss," Roshana shouted over the booming bass, gesturing them onwards.

Warily, the group made their way through the throng, past the bar, and towards an elaborate staircase, ornately carved from what seemed like a single solid piece of bleached wood. Each step was lined in red velvet, with gold rims running the length of the banister. As they ascended, Marcus paused briefly to take in the spectacle. It was a sight far more debauched than the Zonaka had ever been. Each of the patrons in the secluded booths was carefully cared for by more of the fair-skinned dancing girls, who were enticing their customers to give in to their desires. As he focused on one particularly beautiful dancer gyrating in a booth directly across the stage from him, he felt a firm tug on his shoulder. As he turned, he was greeted by a stern look of disapproval on Serena's face.

They climbed the staircase all the way to the second balcony, where Roshana led them to an area towards the back. Two muscular, reptilian humanoids, armed with sleek yet bulky carbines, halted their procession. The spiny, olive-skinned monstrosities looked weathered, as if they'd seen more than their fair share of war and would be only too happy to find more. Roshana leaned in to whisper into the ear of the closest guard, who stepped aside, signaling for the other to do the same.

"Nerokan bodyguards," the Sheshen explained just as the group passed them. "The very best the galaxy has to offer."

*   *   *   *   *

On a slightly raised platform approachable via three wide steps lay an arrangement of white leather couches surrounding a curving glass table. Seated on the far couch, surrounded by a selection of lavender skinned males with fine, feminine features, lounged Roshana's mistress.

Her segmented suit bore the same lavender sheen. Unlike Roshana, she wore boots and gloves made from the finest white leather, and her mask seemed to have been made from delicate white porcelain, plain and sleek, with no features save for the swirls of black paint surrounding the tinted glass covering the ocular cavities. Long raven-black hair, entwined into thick locks, streamed from the back of her head, spreading out behind her.

"Missstressss Shikari, I have brought the Terransss," Roshana announced, falling down on his knees before her.

Shikari tilted her head to the side, studying her new guests while she nursed a small beaker filled with a translucent red liquid. She crossed her long legs and leaned backwards, gesturing for Marcus and his group to join her. Almost immediately her cohorts rose from their seats and darted past them, obviously not privileged to the conversation that was about to take place. Hesitantly, Marcus took a seat on the couch to her left, with the others cautiously following suit.

"Welcome to Xhalpithia," when she spoke, Shikari's silky smooth voice was every bit as hypnotic as that of her assistant, "the quickessst way to blisss."

Serena and Taz looked at Marcus with questioning gazes, and Dr. Gehringer still stood awkwardly behind a banister at the edge of the raised dais, a safe distance away.

"Pleassse, if there isss anything that you wisssh, you have only to voice it," Shikari proclaimed. "Food, wine, companionsssship?"

"We're fine," Marcus hurriedly refused, and was rewarded with a look of appreciation from Serena, who was obviously feeling very out of place.

"Hold on," Taz stopped him. "I wouldn't mind a…"

"No Taz," Marcus hissed. "That's not what we're here for."

Taz shook his head in disbelief, his face flush with disappointment.

"Temper, temper," Shikari sniggered, clearly enjoying the display.

"Why did you call us here?" Marcus chimed in.

"Hmmm, why indeed?" Shikari mused, pausing briefly to lay her beaker on the table. "I have a proposssal, one that will ssserve usss both greatly."

"What kind of proposal?" Marcus asked, slightly nervous.

"My sssources have informed me that you are stranded here. You have traveled over vassst distancccesss only to find that you have no meansss of returning to your home. Your classssification forbidsss you from purchasssing the drive needed for true interssstellar travel. Like it or not, Sssemeh'yone isss your new home. Without the meansss to earn a living, you will mossst likely end up ssstarving on the streetsss like a common Lenek."

"And I suppose you are going to offer us riches beyond our wildest dreams?" Marcus snapped sarcastically, his hackles raised by the sibilant alien's condescension.

"Not exactly," Shikari giggled. "How would you like to have a sssuperluminal drive of your own?"

"A superluminal drive?" Dr. Gehringer burst out from behind the banister, obviously agog at the implications.

"It isss a drive technology which will allow you to travel between sssolar sssystems in a matter of daysss," Shikari explained. "With it, you will be able to do as you pleassse. You can return to your homeworld as heroesss, or explore the galaxy at your own leisssure."

"Isn't that illegal?" Marcus inquired. "The customs officials warned us we were forbidden to acquire such advanced technologies."

"Legal, illegal, it isss a, how do you sssay, 'grey area'?" Shikari explained. "If we conduct our transaction outssside Etheran ssspace, there isss very little they can do about it."

"And what exactly would we have to do to earn such a prize?" Marcus asked, now fully on his guard.

"I have sssomething of a dilemma," Shikari confessed. "You sssee, our people have been at oddsss with the Hrūll for thousssands of yearsss. They are our closessst neighborsss. They consssstantly raid our bordersss, kidnap our people and sssell them into ssslavery. Recently, a Hrūll raiding party captured an old Sssheshen gasss refinery, a sssmall outpossst orbiting a gasss giant on our bordersss. Membersss of my own family were on board the ssstation when it happened, and they are now being held to ransssom."

"And you want us to go and rescue them?" Marcus asked. "Surely there are other far better candidates."

"Oh, without quessstion," Shikari continued. "The Nerokan, for example, are fiercccce warriorsss. The Zillari are massstermindsss when it comesss to ssstrategy, and the Vreen would rather die than give in to adversssity. Yet they all ssshare a point in common which rendersss them incapable of the job at hand."

135

"And what is that exactly?" asked Serena, still suspicious of Shikari's motives.

"They all have ssstrong tiesss to the Etherium, in one way or another," Shikari explained. "The Sheshen are not membersss of the Etherium, the Hrüll are. This leavesss usss at a disssadvantage. They can call on the aid of the councccil, whereasss our pleasss fall on deaf earsss."

"Why don't you simply rescue them yourselves?" Marcus inquired.

"We fear the retaliation it may bring," Shikari muttered, the sadness in her voice was unmistakable, as was the growing anger with which she spoke. "The Hrüll are a ruthlessss, brutisssh race. In our past, we ssstood up to them, held back their advancesss. The cowardsss called upon the Etherium for aid, and within daysss a mighty armada of shipsss drove us all the way back to our homeworld, where Hrüll dreadnaughtsss bombarded our planet from orbit." She paused briefly to regain her composure. The revelation of her species' history had obviously taken its toll.

"More than three quartersss of our ssspecies was annihilated overnight. Millionsss more died in the following daysss from exposssure to the poisonsss which the Hrüll introduced into our atmosssphere," Shikari continued. "You mussst excuse my show of emotion. It isss difficult for me to have to recount the darkessst daysss of my people."

"There is no need to apologize," Marcus consoled her, as Taz and Serena nodded.

"We know we are not a perfect race. We have our flawsss, asss do the others," Shikari confessed. "We take enjoyment from thingsss such as lavisssh food and intoxxxicants, engaging in bessstial actsss of erotic pleasssure. But are we truly dessserving of sssuch a cruel fate for

136

thisss?"

"Of course not," Serena sighed, beginning to see the problem from Shikari's point of view.

"Pray that you may not find yourssself in our posssition. I would not wisssh it on anyone," Shikari concluded.

"We can't make any decisions without first consulting with our Captain," Marcus explained. "But I will bring this matter to his attention."

"Oh, pleassse do. I wouldn't want to caussse any problemsss," Shikari agreed. "But I beg you to act hassstily. Every day we wait, the chancesss for my family's sssurvival diminisssh."

"I have a question," Taz spoke up. "How can we get to this outpost? Our ship wouldn't get us to even the nearest solar system in our lifetimes. If it could, well, we wouldn't be in the position to need your help."

"That isss no problem at all," Shikari responded, turning her smooth mask to the scout. "I can arrange for a transsssport vesssel which your ssship can dock with. It will take you to the outpossst."

"What about the superluminal drive you promised us?" Dr. Gehringer demanded, still focused on the reward rather than the task at hand.

"Once the facccility hasss been liberated, my freighter will take you to the Sssheshen homeworld, Nos Ssshana, where the drive will be inssstalled. Sssecrecy isss of the utmossst importanccce."

"Don't worry," Serena assured her. "Our lips are sealed."

"We should go and inform our Captain of your offer. Given the need for secrecy, I suppose we'd be better to return our answer in person?" Marcus asked, and when the Sheshen nodded, he added "Then we'll be back shortly."

137

As they stood up from the comfortable, leather-clad couches, Shikari rose as well, embracing them each in turn and thanking them sincerely for listening to her plight, before speeding them on their way back to the *Tengri*.

Chapter 18

Mariko stood poised in the center of the elevator, a statuesque vision in her long, narrow skirt and matching dark jacket. A pristine white blouse pressed to perfection and a tie to match completed her outfit. She always dressed like this. In her mind, her flawless appearance – even down to her sleek black hair, which never had even a lock out of place – reflected the stability of the corporation.

As serene and controlled as she might look on the outside, how she felt on the inside was a different story. Her dulled senses sometimes made it feel as if she were living underwater, although she could still focus quite exceptionally when a pressing need arose, often with the aid of medication. At night she wanted to scream, to lash out with her voice, as if it were the only weapon that could pierce the veil that kept her thoughts and emotions muddled and out of sight. She watched her immaculate reflection in the elevator's glass walls as it rose along the outside of the Muromoto headquarters' inclining walls, and felt... she didn't know what she felt. The elevator's inside wall was made of dark metal, slanting to match the incline of the great ziggurat-shaped structure, its matte finish a far better reflection of her mood.

She had just finished a brief discussion with an investigative journalist and was running late for a meeting with the Board of Directors. What nerve, she thought. The reporter had questioned her motives for moving against her father. He'd even used the term 'insidious' to describe her actions! She found the accusation disturbing. She had always rationalized her decision by convincing herself that it was in best interests of the company, and that it had had nothing to do with her feelings towards her father. She'd never imagined that the outside world would view it any differently.

"Mariko, they're at the meeting. Everyone's ready for you," her assistant, a chiseled young man with auburn hair, impossibly high cheekbones and broad shoulders, informed her. The cheekbones were her idea. She'd had him surgically altered to make him better suited for his role as her assistant. She enjoyed the idea that she could sculpt him to her liking, the perfect vision of devout servitude, an Adonis who followed her every footstep. His only role in life was to see to her needs... her every need.

"Thank you, Adam," she acknowledged in a voice as toneless as the soulless drone of one of the company's androids.

She finally broke eye contact with her own reflection, studying the ever descending cityscape. Outside in the pouring rain, millions of people went about their daily routines. They were the two only constants in the city of Sol, the endless buzzing of traffic, and the rain. It always rained, dark and bleak, just like her mood. Is this really all there is? She pondered.

She was briefly distracted by the beeping noise coming from the assistant's datapad, a device he never let out of his sight, for it contained her schedule, her contacts, her work. That was all she was now, work. In a sense, that datapad was her, her essence.

"A message from your father," the assistant read off the screen. "Do you want me to-"

"Ignore it," she cut him off in the same emotionless tone.

"Yes, ma'am," the assistant replied, lowering his datapad.

The elevator began to slow its ascent, and within seconds it came to a halt on one of the building's uppermost levels. Mariko turned to face the doorway, arching her head to let it be scanned by the internal security sensors before being allowed admission to the structure's inner sanctum. The door drew open with a quiet hissing sound, revealing an elaborate hall that took up the entirety of the level.

The floor was tiled with sheets of black granite. Walkways of roughly-hewn boards of cured elm lifted a few centimeters off the floor reaching across the hall towards its center. Small streams of crystal clear water ran in trenches carved into the stone floor in a seemingly chaotic arrangement, occupied by schools of minute fish which swam freely from one end of the hall to the other, many of them gathering in the shallow moat surrounding the raised island in the chamber's center. The island itself was a platform of the same elm as the walkways, upon which rested a huge round conference table, at which sat the Board of Directors of the Muromoto Group. The lighting around the edges of the chamber was dim, so as to limit the field of view of those inside, but the center of the hall was an oasis of warm yellow light spilling from shimmering globes of various sizes suspended from the ceiling to illuminate the table.

Her father had designed the room. He had wanted it to be something other than the standard dull, cold conference room with its strictly hierarchical long conference table. He'd wanted it to be a source of comfort as well as inspiration, a haven. To Mariko, it was a distraction. Though there were security drones hidden throughout the hall, in various nooks and crannies just out of sight, Mariko felt that the non-invasive nature of the security was a mistake on her father's behalf. It allowed the room's occupants a feeling of comfort which she found disturbing. She preferred her rivals to be on edge when she spoke to them, unnerved and wary. Then she knew how to push them in just the right way to topple them.

"Ms. Muromoto," one of the relics at the table, a decrepit old fool who had been her father's strongest supporter and a staunch advocate that he should have stayed in power, greeted her. "We've been expecting you."

"My apologies, Mr. Barrow," she breathed. "I've been seeing to an important matter relating to Project Isis."

She marched to her seat at the table, taking long strides that even her obedient assistant had trouble keeping up with.

"Gentlemen," she nodded calmly as she took her seat and began preparing herself for the briefing.

"Spare the pleasantries, Mariko," Barrow insisted, defiantly slamming his frail fist on the tabletop. "We demand answers."

"I'm sorry…," she replied in her most patronizing tone. "I wasn't aware that I'd been asked a question."

"Project Isis," Barrow seethed, easing back into his seat, his anger still apparent. "You've kept us in the dark for far too long. You claim this new android will bring this company into the future. No one's doubting your success with the new household lines, but the amount of resources you've diverted to your special project is bordering on lunacy!"

Mariko composed herself, taking a deep breath before trying to deflect Barrow's latest demand for answers.

"As I was about to say, Project Isis is proceeding according to plan. You will have your answers soon enough," she lied.

"That's not good enough," exclaimed Ekker, a prune-faced, middle-aged man whose voice was seldom heard, but always listened to. "Frankly, there are those among us who are beginning to question whether you supplanting your father as Head of the Board was indeed the right decision."

She was in trouble. She had known that she would have to face the consequences sooner or later. But how could she tell them that Project Isis didn't actually exist, at least not in the form she'd lead them to believe. There were no factories, no workers, no research teams devoted to Project Isis, just an account through which she had funneled the resources in order to divert them through to their proper course. If they only knew, they would probably take her more seriously. Still, they weren't ready. If they'd been presented with the same opportunity that she had, they would have discounted it out of hand, as would her father, she knew that much.

"You have a month to produce a viable…" Ekker continued.

"It's time," she heard the voice inside her head, a voice which spoke calmly but with confidence, a voice she had not heard for quite some time. "Head to the roof. A shuttle is waiting for your arrival."

"…or else we will be forced to…" Ekker was still speaking, completely unaware of the voice sounding in Mariko's mind.

"Gentlemen!" Mariko interrupted the elderly man, rising abruptly from her seat and drawing looks of startlement and outrage from Ekker and several others. The members of the Board, particularly Ekker and Barrow, exchanged troubled looks.

"Thirty days," she nodded, pausing dramatically for emphasis. "You will have your answers."

With that, she turned and strode back towards the elevator, leaving the Board to bicker and plot in her absence.

Chapter 19

Rodan Kesh had been slouching on the ornate park bench for a little over an hour, and his nerves were beginning to get the better of him. His contact was late, but given who he was, it was to be expected. Rodan had chosen this particular garden in the leisure district due to its distance from the more popular areas of the sector, and the fact that, following a string of gruesome murders in the last few years, the park was as quiet as the grave after dark.

Shielded from view by a large tree with a thick canopy of branching needles, Rodan stared out at the artificial lake in the centre of the garden, where a fountain emitted an arching cascade of sparkling water, splashing onto a grouping of flat rocks on the far bank. The reflection of artificial moonlight rippled across the water's surface. The lone streetlamp gave the grove where he sat an eerie glow, and Rodan was beginning to wish he'd chosen a spot that wasn't so unnerving for their rendezvous. He kept looking around, frantically aware that the sound of the cascading water could drown out the noise of a stealthy assailant. Where was he?

Rodan hated to have to use his biggest asset for a task like this. If only recent events had unfolded differently. Still, something had to be done. Some things were more important than having an ace up one's sleeve for a future occasion. As he got up from the bench and began pacing about, a stirring in the thick underbrush nearest to him claimed his attention.

"Who's there?" he demanded, his heart suddenly racing with

anticipation.

There was no answer, not a sound save for the splashing of the water. He took a few steps closer to the lamppost, seeking security from the light. He could feel his breathing getting heavier and his mind starting to race. Despite all his rigorous training, he felt completely unprepared.

"Tishun maguri dadukaa, ronohendo. I would not have thought one such as you to have fear for the darkness," came a deep voice resounded from only a few meters away.

Rodan was so startled that he nearly leapt into the air, his lungs frozen and unwilling to take in the cool night air.

"Silence your thoughts, old friend," the voice spoke. "If there were demons lurking in the night waiting to prey on you, rest assured I would have slain them all by now."

With a sudden shimmer of reflected light, the image of a tall, heavily-built humanoid being began to form in the empty air before him. The smooth, silvery suit, lined with panels and devices so numerous that Rodan couldn't even begin to imagine their function, had never ceased to impress him. A visor of opaque darkened glass covered most of its wearer's visage, topped by a metallic skullcap and backed by antennae protruding from the back of its head, towering over his two-meter frame. Although its armor was far heavier and more formidable than that usually worn by its kind, it bore the familiar icon of the Hiodan emblazoned on its chestplate, closely resembling the letter k, duplicated and mirrored, the two halves merging at the base.

"It is good to see you again Hanan Aru," Rodan sighed, relaxing his muscles and breathing a heavy sigh of relief. "Thank you for coming on such short notice."

"The timing was fair," the silvery figure assured him. "I have just returned from my latest assignment."

"That is fortunate," Rodan agreed. "I have a feeling this favor will require some time."

Hanan Aru walked over to the lake and knelt down in front of it, bathing his armored hand in its clear waters.

"Does your kind never tire of wearing those suits?" Rodan inquired.

It was a question that had loomed in his mind for quite some time.

"I have grown accustomed to it," Hanan Aru confessed, "a second skin, you might say."

Rodan knew that in addition to its complement of hidden weaponry and integral equipment, the Hiodan's armor was arrayed with tactile sensors, cybernetically linked to its wearer, so in truth, it really was a second skin.

"You have chosen a good location for our meeting," Hanan Aru praised his friend. "One might think you used to such... shady dealings."

"Thank you Hanan Aru," Rodan muttered, unsure whether he should view the statement as a complement or not.

"So, what is it that you require of me?" Hanan Aru asked, rising up from the banks of the lake to face him.

Rodan couldn't help but pause briefly to admire the Hiodan powered armor. Having seen it on the battlefield up close, he knew full well what it was capable of. Even Ambassador Janosh himself would find Hanan Aru in his suit a worthy opponent.

"Do you remember Cerakan?" Rodan probed, folding his arms in front of him and adjusting his pose.

"I do," Hanan Aru revealed, "although not with fond memories."

"Nor I," Rodan said with a faint smile. "So much pain... and death."

"It was the path we chose."

"True," Rodan paused before continuing. "I fear the consequences of what I am about to ask you. This time you will be on your own. I cannot come with you."

"What is to be my target?" Hanan Aru pressed, without so much as a hint of reserve.

"We have some new arrivals on Semeh'yone-" Rodan started.

"The Terrans," the Hiodan interrupted him, reminding Rodan of his remarkable aptitude for keeping up with current events, despite his long absences from the station.

Rodan nodded in acknowledgement. "We always knew they would show themselves sooner or later."

"It is done," Hanan Aru assured him.

Like an apparition, the silvery figure began to dissipate. If it weren't for the faint impressions the Hiodan left as he strode through the grass, Rodan would never even have noticed him leave. He was perfect for the job. Confident that things were going as planned, Rodan took a moment to gaze up at the moon.

It was a bold move, one that no one would see coming. He would have to take great care to remain discrete. Not only were there eyes and ears in every corner, but he would have to protect his mind from telepathic intrusion as well. Luckily he had always been gifted when it came to keeping people from messing with his head. It was one of the qualities he believed had gotten him this far. His timepiece gave a high-pitched beep, and he glanced down at it.

"Half past two," he read on the chronometer's display. "Time for rain."

He had no sooner processed the thought when the first droplets began falling from the sky. It had always amazed him the great level of detail with which the Hiodan had constructed Semeh'yone. He often forgot he was aboard a space station. He pulled the hood over his head and strolled through the empty gardens, allowing the refreshing rain to soothe the turmoil in his mind.

Chapter 20

Having repeated Shikari's proposal to the captain, Marcus and the others joined the entire crew in the galley for a debate and a vote. Though making decisions in such a democratic method was hardly common practice on C-CORE expeditions, the captain thought it appropriate given the nature of their dilemma. Each crewmember was given the opportunity to weigh in, and, of the objectors, it was the support staff who were the most reluctant to pursue such a drastic course of action.

Having heard each argument in turn, Captain Mitchell was at an impasse. Accepting the offer came with its share of risks. No doubt there was the chance it would anger Rodan Kesh and his people, but seeing as the Gaians had refused even to grant them an official audience, perhaps it was a risk worth taking. After all, the reward for performing Shikari's task could mean everything for them. Not only would it allow the freedom and mobility the advanced drive technology itself would bring, but it would also secure an alliance with someone in a position of influence, at least amongst one of the multitude of races that seemed to inhabit this part of the galaxy. For all they knew, relying on the Council to grant them asylum would come with stipulations and require them to relinquish certain rights. It would probably result in their complete dependency on the Etherium for the foreseeable future, and there was nothing Mitchell hated more than having his fate in someone else's hands.

As far as he could see, Shikari certainly seemed to be the most viable option available to them. At the very least, he decided he ought to arrange a meeting with her, see for himself who he was dealing with. As a highly trained psionic operative he felt confident that he could gauge her true motives. If there were anything amiss he should be able to sense it... or so he hoped. He'd never used his abilities on a non-Terran before.

The crew was given strict orders to remain aboard the ship, while the captain and Serena went to negotiate with Shikari, taking only Jago with them for protection. They waited eagerly. Marcus had wandered up to the observation deck, where he found Dr. Gehringer engaged in a heated debate over the hypothetical origins of the Gaian people with his research assistant, Dr. Linda Haake, outside their workspace.

The first time Marcus had met the woman, he'd found her somewhat cold and distant. Though he could see that, at one point, she'd been a beautiful woman, her looks had faded quite some time ago, and now her once-elegant facial features seemed exaggerated by decades of cosmetic surgery, her skin stretched over her chin and her cheekbones artificially high to hide the decay of age. Her manner was subtly patronizing, as if everyone aboard were beneath her notice. Marcus' position aboard ship had awarded few opportunities for him to interact with the scornful woman, but each time he had had lowered his impression of her.

"They must be among the very first colonists sent out by C-CORE," Dr. Gehringer was saying when Marcus entered.

"I don't see how that could be even remotely possible, Doctor. Those colonists were sent out over a hundred and seventy years ago with only rudimentary equipment. How in the name of the Republic could they have advanced so far?" Dr. Haake countered.

"A lot can happen in nearly two centuries, Linda," the scientist insisted, staring at his own pale reflection in the massive window.

"None of the ships sent out by C-CORE were destined to even leave the Terran sector," his assistant continued. "We're tens of thousands of light years away."

"I suppose they could be an indigenous species, native to the Merillian galaxy," Dr. Gehringer hypothesized, rubbing his smooth, hairless chin. "Who knows? There could be humans all over the universe."

"That's a flawed theory," Dr. Haake argued. "The language similarities are too great. Gaians and Terrans appear to speak nearly exactly the same language. If they were indigenous to this galaxy, their language wouldn't be the same as ours, even if their biology somehow was."

"Hmmm…"

"Could Earth have sent another ship?" Dr. Haake added hesitantly.

"Given the timeframe, I find it highly doubtful," Gehringer responded. "Don't forget that we've only been in the Merillian galaxy for two hundred and eighty four years. And if Earth had sent another ship, they'd have sent it to our coordinates. They would have wanted to know the fate of the *Lazarus*."

The pair of them stood, silently contemplating their hypotheses, but were both eventually forced to the same conclusion: the origins of the Gaians would have to remain a mystery, at least for now.

Having been eavesdropping on their conversation from his position in the hatchway, Marcus turned to leave, feeling somewhat guilty for his furtive behavior, but not wanting to get caught up in a debate where he was sure to be patronized and made to feel a fool.

"Ah, Corporal Grey," Dr. Gehringer cried just as Marcus turned to leave. "Any news from the captain?"

Marcus froze in his tracks, fully aware that he'd been caught red handed.

"Nothing yet," Marcus confessed. "He should be back any moment now."

"Excellent. I do hope he managed to bring back what I requested," the scientist muttered to himself.

"What was it that you wanted?" Marcus asked, stepping in from the gangway now that he couldn't get away.

"Oh, just some data files I was hoping he could procure for me so that I can learn more about these species we have encountered." Gehringer replied dismissively. "Please inform me when he arrives."

"Yes Doctor," Marcus replied, as neutrally as possible.

Though Marcus had his reservations about Dr. Gehringer, the strange-looking little man came highly recommended, despite his obvious shortcomings. He had advanced degrees in several scientific fields, making him an invaluable addition to the *Tengri*'s mission, for all that he seemed oblivious to his own lack of empathy or social skills. If only Marcus didn't find him so very unnerving.

* * * * *

Captain Mitchell and the others returned from their meeting in Xhalpithia shortly after Marcus made his escape from the observation deck. The crew once again gathered in the galley, waiting for news of their negotiations. Jago stood by the kitchen counter, stuffing his mouth with leftovers from their afternoon meal while Knoles stood irately in the corner and watched as the behemoth devoured an entire bowlful of rice and synthesized proteins. Doc Taylor was lounging in one of the comfortable armchairs, a cigarette hanging loosely from the edge of his mouth as he blew wafts of smoke into the air, completely at ease, in marked contrast to Taz, who was leaning up against a bulkhead, tapping his foot with impatience. Marcus had taken up position in the back, near the forward viewscreen, sitting on the wide windowsill just above the primary heating vent. The grim looks on everyone's face revealed that despite their faith in their captain and their acceptance of his decision to agree to Shikari's terms, they weren't ready to depart from Semeh'yone so soon.

"I know it's difficult, people," Mitchell addressed them. "But we can't simply sit idly by and hope that the Etherium will grant us asylum. We don't even know what asylum entitles us."

He paused briefly for dramatic effect, pacing up and down before his assembled crew, his motorized brace whizzing and whirring with each step.

"We have an opportunity to craft our own fate," he continued, "our own destiny. I know this is risky, but some risks are worth taking. You all made the decision to join us on this journey. Look what we've already accomplished!"

Some of the stern looks began to fade, expressions of pride taking their place.

"Since the founding of the Republic, no Terran has ever comes as far as we have. We have seen things none of our people would even have dreamed possible!" Captain Mitchell bellowed. "We cannot simply roll over with our palms outstretched, begging for aid. We are Terrans! We have an opportunity to show this galaxy what we're made of!"

Marcus turned his gaze to the crowd once more. The captain's speech had most of the crew mesmerized. Heads were nodding in unison, lapping up his words, eyes hungry for more. The effect was so noticeable that Marcus couldn't help but wonder whether the captain was using his psionic abilities to influence them in some way. No. Surely he wouldn't do so to his own crew. That would be wrong. Wouldn't it?

"We have the chance to undo a great wrong. One that would call herself our ally, our friend, has suffered a most tragic loss… and she needs our help," Mitchell continued, striking a heroic pose as he hammered in the final blow. "And we're not going to let her down, are we?"

"Sir, no Sir!" the crew shouted in unison, causing Marcus to feel a touch of uneasiness at how easily they were all swayed to the cause.

"I can't hear you," the captain prompted.

"Sir, no Sir!" the entire crew barked in unison, beaming with pride.

The captain scooped up Spot, who had been anxiously hovering around his feet and whispered into the dog's ear. "That's right, Spot. We're going freelance."

* * * * *

The old squad had gathered on the *Tengri*'s bridge to prepare for their departure. Spirits were running high, and Marcus was pleased to see his old teammates so excited. Given all of their experiences in recent months, Marcus realized he'd forgotten one central fact about their existence: they were bred for war. The clones had been designed with a certain mentality, one which might well present difficulties if they were to try to adapt to a life of peace and normality.

Was it so difficult to accept that perhaps their core being would seek out conflict? There was a big difference between being told to

154

fight and being asked to fight. This time, Marcus found himself longing for it, to help free Shikari's people.

Captain Mitchell was seated in the captain's chair on the central dais of the bridge, his pet lounging on his lap with its feet in the air, quivering with each of the captain's not-so-gentle strokes.

"Bridge crew, diagnostics check please," he ordered, spurring Raven and her subordinates into action.

Holographic interfaces appeared over the consoles, and readouts began to materialize on the forward display. Marcus waited impatiently for the diagnostics check to be completed before hearing the familiar sound of the *Tengri*'s engines firing up.

The promise of the coming conflict crept into his mind, waking all too familiar feelings. When he'd left Terra, he had hoped for a simpler life, a life of peace. Initially he had shunned the martial aspect of his old life in the military, dreaming of better days. Now he found himself excited at the thought of standing back to back with his old squad, fighting for a cause they all believed in.

Turning to watch the captain give the final departure order, Marcus was startled to find Mitchell staring at him, smiling. It was as if the captain knew what he'd been thinking. Mitchell gave him an encouraging nod, then returned his focus to the bridge crew.

No... Marcus thought. He wouldn't have...

Chapter 21

The *Tengri* slid silently out of the docking bay into the busy space lanes. Gone was the serenity of empty space. Since their departure from Terra, the crew had grown accustomed to peering out into the darkness with nothing but the stars to light their way. It was only natural that every window was now filled with wide-eyed crewmembers, gaping in wonder at the splendor of Semeh'yone's visitors. Above them, a two kilometer long superfreighter lay docked alongside one of the station's massive docking arms. A horde of worker drones scurried about her like a swarm of bees, detaching the freighter's massive containers, dragging them into an enormous loading dock at the end of the docking arm. Off their starboard bow, a lone frigate so battered it looked more like a piece of scrap than a ship was entangled in a web of energy being projected by a network of drones. A vessel so small it couldn't support more than a crew of two shot passed the *Tengri* on an intercept course, its weapons powering up and trained on the unfortunate rust bucket.

"I guess they're not getting the same royal welcome we did," Taz chuckled.

Captain Mitchell monitored the scene intensely, his keen strategic mind always on the lookout for information that might prove advantageous on a future occasion.

"Wei, set course for the outer rim," Captain Mitchell ordered. "Let's hope our escort won't keep us waiting for too long."

The *Tengri*'s engines flared and sent them racing through the

156

throng of inbound traffic.

*　*　*　*　*

The engineering bay was one of Marcus' favorite places on the *Tengri*, much to the disgruntlement of Chief Engineer Kerr. The man responsible for keeping the cruiser functioning was a robust character, strong and determined. His balding head dripped beads of sweat down his brow to his swollen cheeks, tinted red from exasperation and the heat of the machinery in his domain. His untrimmed beard and grease-stained coveralls were a testament to his lack of hygiene, his suit so filthy Marcus couldn't even begin to guess its original color. He was the sort of man you wouldn't want to get on the wrong side of, foul mouthed and bad-tempered, constantly cursing the apparent ineptitude of his assistant, Ahlain Lyer.

Not that the Junior Engineer didn't deserve it. Marcus had never met a lazier sort in his short life. Ahlain did little more than smoke all day and make up excuses to be sent off on his own, where he would either take long naps where no one could see or engage in flirtatious and often indecent conversation with any of the female crewmembers who would put up with him. Unlike the Chief Engineer's stereotypical appearance for a man of his occupation, Ahlain was always neatly groomed, his black curly hair the only part of him that contained even a drop of grease, and that not the kind that normally belonged in an engineering bay. His coveralls were spotless and pressed even more accurately than the captain's. Even his boots were untarnished. If it weren't for the fact that the man was a virtual library of knowledge on all things related to the inner workings of the *Tengri*, Marcus wouldn't have had much of an opinion of the man.

"Are you stark ravin' mad, boy?" Kerr barked. "You can't replace the primary drive coupling without first disconnectin' the induction field emitter."

Ahlain sat still on the brown cardboard box he'd set on the floor to keep the dirty deck from staining his uniform. He'd removed the metal shielding from one of the bay's many machines, and was about to remove a cylindrical piece of machinery from a wide rubbery tube.

"If I disconnect the induction field emitter while the engine is still active, it'll blow the relays," Ahlain scoffed. "I know what I'm doing, old man!"

"Is that dangerous?" Marcus inquired, sitting on the flimsy metal steps that lead down to the main engine room.

"Remind me what you're doin' here again, Grey?" the Chief Engineer scowled, his cheeks flush with frustration.

"I was looking for Spot," Marcus confessed, leaning forward to prop his elbow on his knee and rest his chin on his clenched fist.

"Spot?" the Chief Engineer asked in confusion, grabbing a large spanner from a drawer full of tools, his eyes fixed on one of the system's primary valves.

"The captain's dog," Marcus revealed, a bit taken aback by Kerr's lack of knowledge. "He likes to wander around the ship, especially into places he shouldn't."

"Huh, is that so?" the Chief Engineer muttered. "Well make sure that mangy mutt don't come into my engine room, or I promise you he won't be comin' out again. You hear me?"

"Yes Sir," Marcus noted.

During their exchange, Ahlain had managed to continue his work uninterrupted, and he now produced a small electronic device, attaching it to the induction field emitter that he and Kerr had been arguing over.

"What are you doin', boy?" the Chief Engineer demanded, puzzled by Ahlain's doings.

"I'm looping the induction field emitter to the power output of the harmonic relays," Ahlain explained, pulling a cable from the small device and attaching it to a jury-rigged plug he'd fashioned out of a broken drill bit.

"And what's that gonna do?" Kerr cried out, getting down on his knees to get a better look.

"It will create a static feedback loop and bypass the power surge when I remove the primary drive coupling," Ahlain said with a self-satisfied grin as he shoved the broken drill bit into the harmonic relay system.

"Is that safe?" Marcus pondered aloud.

"We are about to find out," the Junior Engineer answered as he jerked the primary drive coupling out of its socket.

Kerr panicked, slamming shut his eyes and raising his hands to shield from the blast he expected to tear through the engineering bay. A tense second later, the humiliated Chief Engineer got back on his feet, muttering a stream of obscenities.

"Damned crazy bastard. This is my engine room! You should all know better than to mess with my baby without my say so," he muttered as he wobbled away.

Marcus leaned back against the railing, allowing his mind to wander. Despite the unusual dynamic between the Chief Engineer and his assistant, Marcus found the engine room very relaxing. The sound of the engine, the vibrations, the musky scent, all these things and more gave Marcus a warm feeling which he just couldn't find elsewhere within the *Tengri*'s cold steel hallways.

Marcus felt he was probably the only one mildly concerned about the replacement of their engine. Would it sound the same? Would it still give off the same warm and inviting hum when he visited?

* * * * *

Taylor 'Doc' Vod was enjoying the view from the observation deck. The *Tengri* had long since left the buzzing traffic of Semeh'yone station, and was skirting past the ring system of an orange gas giant. The usual cloud of smoke accompanied the young medic as he slowly paced back and forth in front of the majestic display when the sound of a hatch opening to his right drew his attention.

Turning lazily, Taylor was just in time to see Spot launch himself through the half-open doorway that lead to the laboratory and back down the gangway as fast as his little legs would carry him, the pale visage of Dr. Gehringer peering cautiously through the opening in the hatchway, a guilty look on his face. Upon sighting Taylor, he immediately became skittish and made a poorly-disguised attempt at nonchalance.

"What are you up to, Doctor?" Taylor called, fixing Gehringer with a stare and raising an eyebrow.

"Nothing at all," the scientist gasped. "I was just about to commence a sequence of parallel studies into the magnetic resonance of the gas giant we're passing."

"There must have been some truly remarkable breakthroughs in astrophysics in recent years. I've never heard of any research requiring the use of a dog," Taylor mused.

"Oh... right... well, come in," Gehringer stuttered, waving him hurriedly into the lab.

Taylor crossed over and squeezed himself through the opening, which Dr. Gehringer appeared to be trying to keep as small as possible, as if he were guarding a most terrifying secret. Inside the narrow, white-walled lab, beakers and vials were neatly arranged on the counters running along both bulkheads while a complicated automated scanning device was busy analyzing what appeared to be a blood sample.

"Is that from the dog?" Taylor asked.

"It is, but you must swear you will tell no one," Gehringer urged him.

"Why are you taking blood samples from the captain's pet?" Taylor inquired. "It's not diseased is it?"

"Oh no, perfect health, perfect health," the scientist muttered. "I simply required its genetic code."

Taylor began rubbing his temples, not sure whether he really wanted to know the reasoning behind the scientist's latest bout of madness.

"And why exactly do you need Spot's DNA?" he asked, already regretting his question.

"It's simple really. Studies have shown that females are up to twenty-six percent more likely to copulate with a male who shows a nurturing side, specifically in regards to animals," Dr. Gehringer explained, his eyes shining. "Of course, felines produce higher results, but given the lack of a viable genetic sample, there was really only one option left available to me."

"Wait. Let me get this straight," Taylor gasped. "You want to clone the captain's dog... just so you can get laid?"

"Oh no, not at all. I wouldn't dream of it," Dr. Gehringer stuttered, seemingly appalled at the very thought.

161

"Oh good. I thought maybe-"

"Cloning it would be no good, you see," the scientist continued as if Taylor hadn't spoken. "I'll need to re-sequence the DNA to create a unique specimen. By building on the genetic template procured from the captain's canine, I will be able to create another, different canine. Two identical animals on board the *Tengri* would just be bizarre."

"Yeah. That's what's weird about all this," Taylor sighed, turning to leave.

"You won't tell anyone, will you?" Dr. Gehringer called as he raced after the astonished young medic.

*   *   *   *   *

Almost a week had passed since they had departed Semeh'yone station. The *Tengri* had coasted past the Hiodan planetary system, and now drifted through empty space with nothing around her save for the deep black void. They'd expected Shikari's envoy to rendezvous with them soon, but for almost an entire day they had floated aimlessly, hoping to be contacted at any moment.

Captain Mitchell had taken up position on the bridge, foregoing sleep, fearing that something might have gone wrong. They'd taken a great risk accepting the mission, but, the captain told himself, with great risks came great rewards.

Raven had her legs slung up on the top of her console and had been nodding off for the past hour, Marcus and the rest of the clones clustered at the back of the bridge dozing or murmuring quietly amongst themselves. Mitchell had just swallowed a fist full of painkillers when Navigator Wei noticed the blip on the ship's sensors.

"Captain," Navigator Wei alerted him. "I've got movement off the starboard bow."

"Put it onscreen," the captain ordered, his booming voice startling the others into wakefulness.

The image of a large freighter appeared on the forward viewscreen. It was a dark, sleek vessel, an almost-flat elongated triangle with sharp edges and no discernible bridge – or any other protrusion larger than an antennae – three times larger than the *Tengri*. As it began to adjust its course to intercept, Navigator Wei received an audio communication in sibilant Terran.

"Captain Mitchell, thisss isss Rossshana aboard the *Mitushi Nalphalo*."

"We read you Roshana. This is Captain Mitchell aboard the *Tengri*."

"Excccellent Captain," Roshana proclaimed. "Pleassse ssstand by while we engage the gravitronic beam to pull you into our docking bay."

Without waiting for Mitchell's acknowledgement, Roshana ended the communication.

As the freighter drew closer, her murky hull occluding the stars behind her like a looming shadow, Mitchell ordered the bridge crew to power down the engines. They had barely finished doing so when a vast opening began to appear in the Sheshen ship's mid-section as her docking bay doors started to slide open. The *Tengri* was suddenly enveloped in the familiar energy of what they now knew to call a gravitronic beam. As their course began to shift, aligning them with the freighter's open bay, Captain Mitchell couldn't help but feel an imminent sense of dread.

"Meet a nice alien in a bar. Get eaten by his ship," Taz joked, though no one laughed.

As the freighter began to swallow their ship whole, pulling them

163

inside its dark belly, Mitchell couldn't help but feel that he might have made a terrible mistake.

Chapter 22

Focused streams of emerald light poured from tiny lamps embedded in the dim metal bulkheads overhead, illuminating a tiny part of the docking bay. The old squad, Dr. Gehringer and Serena had assembled on a narrow gangway slung between the *Tengri*'s forward airlock and a wide, circular platform at the end of the gangway. Several intersecting pipes loomed in the shadows beneath them, each one over a meter in diameter. The surrounding darkness obstructed their view.

The sudden release of a jet of vapor announced the sliding open of a tall, narrow door set in the bulkhead on the opposite side of the round platform. The dimly-lit corridor it revealed housed four slender, individual shapes.

"Uriu lo ssshamata osssh," a figure in the middle whispered to its companions, the echo of the docking bay carrying its voice further than it would have liked.

The team was on edge. The three outermost figures were visibly armed with what appeared to be carbine-type weaponry, causing Marcus to grasp his own SGC K-660 more firmly, although he resisted the urge to bring it up to his shoulder.

"Captain Mitccchell," came the voice of Roshana, the central figure. "What a pleasssure it isss to sssee you again."

He stepped forward onto the platform, accompanied closely by a trio of well armed Sheshen bodyguards wearing all-encompassing suits nearly identical to his, save for a lack of the glowing symbols that adorned Roshana's armor. Only one symbol was embedded on their chestplate, no doubt an insignia defining their allegiance.

"Quite a ship you have," Captain Mitchell commented, peering through the darkness at his surroundings, making sure to emphasize his awe.

"Thank you Captain," Roshana hissed. "It isss but one of many in our employ."

"What's with the escort?" the captain asked, eyeing the lean bodyguards.

"Merely a formality," Roshana explained. "It isss more about ssstature than it isss about necccesssity."

"I see. Are you sure you will be able to get us back to the Semayon in time for our Council hearing?"

"Not to worry. We ssshall have you back with ample time to ssspare," Roshana assured him.

Mitchell turned to the team, gauging their reaction, but was met only with blank stares. Sensing the Terrans' uneasiness, Roshana dismissed his bodyguards, sending them back through the door they'd arrived through, before turning to the business at hand.

"Are you clear on the misssion parametersss?"

"Shoot the bad guys, free the captives?" Captain Mitchell replied without missing a beat, fixing Roshana with a dead-eyed stare.

"Your aptitude for sssimplicity isss refressshing," the Sheshen acknowledged. "We will begin by carrying you to the dessstination, a sssystem on the border of the Hrūll and Sssheshen territories. Onccce there, we will part waysss. If the outpost's sssensors pick up readings of a Sssheshen ssship in their vicccinity, the misssion will be over rather quickly."

"Gotcha," Mitchell concurred.

"Gotcha?" Roshana questioned.

"It means 'understood'," the captain explained.

"I underssstand. You will then approach the ssstation on your own," Roshana continued. "When the outpost attemptsss to contact you, you must explain to them that due to mechanical failure, your ssship was dropped out of ssslipstream en route from Natallusss to Voluna. You must persssuade them to let you dock while you attempt to make repairsss."

"What's Natallus?"

"It isss one of the main cultural hubsss of the Etherium," Roshana replied.

"Won't that be suspicious?" Reid called out. "Our ship doesn't have a… slipstream engine or whatever you call it."

"You needn't worry about that," Roshana reassured them. "Given your resssemblance to the Gaiansss, a most trusted ssspecies, they are sssure to allow you to dock without cause for alarm."

"And then what? We just open fire?" Marcus pressed, realizing all was not as it had seemed. Was their resemblance to the Gaians the only reason why Shikari had approached them?

"Where will you be while all this is taking place?" Serena demanded before Roshana had a chance to reply to Marcus' question, seeds of doubt growing in her mind.

"We will hide the freighter behind an iccce planet at the edge of the sssystem," Roshana told her. "When we have confirmation that the misssion has been sssuccesssful, we will return to escort you to Nos Ssshana."

"What if something goes wrong?" Taz muttered from the back of the group.

"It won't," Roshana proclaimed. "I have complete faith in your capabilitiesss."

"Would it be possible to get a copy of your language files?" asked Serena. "I'd be interested in studying your language while we travel."

"Why, of course," Roshana declared. "Although I doubt your sssystemsss will be capable of reading them. If you wisssh, I could lend you one of our datapadsss for the duration of the journey."

"That would be great!" Serena smiled, pleased that she would be able to make good use of her time.

"Of course, the sssilver tongue is a difficult language to massster, essspecially itsss verbal aspectsss. Ssshould you ssso desssire, I could instruct you persssonally."

Serena looked apprehensively at her crewmates for a moment before giving her reply.

"That would be most appreciated," she stated firmly.

"I would also be honored to give you some insightsss into our culture," Roshana added.

"Well, I guess we have a few days to kill, so we might as well make the most of it," Captain Mitchell agreed before concluding the briefing and bidding farewell to Roshana.

* * * * *

"I just don't like the idea of her being alone with him!" Marcus bellowed.

He had stormed into the captain's office to vent his frustration, in the hope that Mitchell would see things his way. Roshana had sent one of his guards to invite Serena to a private audience in his study, and despite her unease around the Sheshen crew, she had been positively giddy at the opportunity.

"Get the stick out of your ass, Grey!" Mitchell yelled right back. "Serena knows how to take care of herself. Besides, I hardly think Roshana would have gone through this much trouble just to fuck with us."

Marcus knew the point to be valid, but something still didn't seem right to him. Perhaps he had just grown attached to the young linguist. After all, of the crew she was the one he'd spent the most time with since they'd left the Terran system. Maybe he was just allowing his feelings to get the best of him.

"At least send someone with her," he begged, leaning against the captain's desk as he tried to convince his superior.

"No Marcus," Captain Mitchell snapped, pausing briefly to swallow a pair of painkillers. "Stop being so damned paranoid!"

*   *   *   *   *

Serena had been pleasantly surprised by Roshana's study. Having been escorted through the dark, foreboding corridors of the freighter, she had been expecting a cold, even sinister, décor, but to her surprise the warmly-lit chamber was extravagantly adorned with crimson rugs and exotic pieces of artwork. Everywhere she looked, paintings depicted alien landscapes and statuettes showed alien figures of various races, some of whom were regal in their pose and demeanor, while others displayed slender figures in erotic poses. A spread of colorful appetizers lay on a gilded platter on top of a small glass table with ornate metallic legs. Roshana himself lounged on a comfortable-looking couch covered in a wine-colored velvety cloth in the centre of the smallish compartment, his arm slung over the edge, fingers swaying in harmony with the sultry music being projected throughout the chamber.

The silent guard who had escorted Serena through the ship's corridors closed the door behind him, leaving her standing awkwardly in anticipation of Roshana's greetings, clutching the datapad he'd sent to her.

"Ah, I sssee you reccceived my gift," Roshana hissed pleasantly, levering himself up to sit on the edge of the couch. "Pleassse take a ssseat. I hope you do not mind, but I took the liberty of having sssome food prepared. It is perfectly sssafe. I had each of the ingredientsss checked againsssst the databasssse to make sssure it would pose you no harm."

Timidly, Serena stepped closer, taking a seat at the other end of the couch.

"Thank you," she said. "You shouldn't have gone to such trouble. We have plenty of food on the *Tengri*."

Although her statement was technically correct, the quality and variety of the *Tengri*'s food in storage left a good deal to be desired. Having survived on the same bland food being prepared by their temperamental cook for several months now, Serena was more than a little excited to have the chance to try some more exotic cuisine.

"Have you been... ssstudying?" Roshana asked, leaning forward to slide the gilded tray closer to her.

"I have," Serena replied. "I think I've been able to grasp the basic grammar and memorize some of the simpler words. You know, it's fascinating, the older a language is, the less complicated the grammar becomes. I suppose it's only natural that things tend to get simpler over time."

She leaned over to take a square of orange, spongy-looking piece of food and pop it into her mouth. To her disgust, it tasted like a mixture of meat and vanilla with a fleshy, grainy texture that seemed to linger on the roof of her mouth.

"Sssuch is true not only with language," Roshana pointed out, inching closer to her.

Instinctively, Serena tried to move to keep the distance between them, but as she was already close to the edge of the couch, she had little room left to maneuver.

"So, shall we begin?" Serena chirped brightly, hoping to steer her host's attention to the matter at hand.

"Of courssse," Roshana agreed. "I sssee you are very determined. I enjoy that in a woman."

Serena was thoroughly unnerved. If he'd been human, she would have been sure that Roshana was making advances to her, but charming as he was, he was an alien. She wasn't one to take romance lightly, so the weird images her mind threw up of engaging in... such acts... with this slender being revolted and horrified her, especially given the depraved acts she'd glimpsed in Xhalpithia.

She decided to ignore the issue, telling herself it was probably just some cultural misunderstanding, instead hefting her datapad and beginning to sift through the Sheshen language files. As she prepared to pronounce one of the phrases she'd been practicing, Roshana startled her by placing his slender hand firmly on her thigh.

His mere touch sent shivers running down her spine, not of excitement, but of repulsion. She began to try removing his hand, but found that her host merely tightened his grasp.

"I... I think you may have gotten the wrong idea!" She stuttered, looking up into the eye holes of his blank mask.

"Not at all," Roshana protested smoothly. "I invited you here to teach you about Sssheshen customsss. What better way than to ssshow you our wayss of intimacy?"

Serena's body quivered with fear and uncertainty, her mind racing. She needed to make it clear to Roshana that what he was suggesting was not only obscene but also highly inappropriate, but she was scared that if she worded it poorly her refusal might come across as an insult.

"Can we perhaps... start with something more... practical?" She finally blabbered, at a complete loss.

"To the Sheshen people, there isss nothing more important than the pursssuit of beauty and pleassssure," Roshana told her. "That isss why we sssurround oursssselvesss with sssuch sssplendor. When I sssaw you, I knew immediately that I had to have you."

Serena's mind roiled with disgust.

"I... I don't think this is really...," she stammered, still attempting to remove Roshana's firm grip from her thigh.

The aggressive Sheshen leaned towards her, placing a finger from his free hand across her lips to shush her. She clamped her eyes shut, leaning back in terror, hoping that this was all just a bad dream. Roshana let go of her leg momentarily to remove his mask, moving in, clearly intending to steal a kiss from his terrified visitor. Serena didn't want to open her eyes. She heard the brief hiss of equalizing pressure as Roshana's armored mask began to open. Finally she couldn't stand it any longer. Reluctantly, she opened her eyes to look upon Roshana's naked visage.

She let loose a horrified scream before pushing the Sheshen aside and fleeing the study as fast as her legs would carry her.

Chapter 23

Having hidden in her quarters for the better part of the day, Serena was finally bracing herself to rejoin the others. Marcus had paced back and forth in front of her door since she'd returned in hysterics, trying to convince her to come out or at least to tell them what had transpired, but to no avail. When she hesitantly emerged, Marcus awkwardly placed his hand on her shoulder in an attempt to console her as she tried to explain what had happened during her 'lesson'.

"What did he do to you?" Marcus demanded, his voice trembling with anger.

"Nothing," Serena tried to convince him. "He... tried to kiss me."

Even now, hours later, she was as pale as a ghost, and for the briefest of moments Marcus thought he caught a glimpse of guilt in her eyes.

"Kiss you?" Captain Mitchell demanded as he came striding down the corridor, Taz bobbing along in his wake. "Is that all?"

"You didn't see him Captain! His face..." she paused, shaking her head in disbelief.

"Couldn't have been much uglier than the Ape," Taz sniggered.

"It was the most revolting thing I've ever seen," she shuddered.

"So he didn't hurt you in any way?" Marcus probed, still not sure whether he was going to let Roshana off the hook.

"No, nothing like that," Serena protested. "He was no worse than any of the men back in Sol. He was just... hideous. I can't even describe it. Just seeing him made my insides feel all wrong, and I felt like I was about to throw up."

"That's probably what that armored suit is for," Captain Mitchell speculated. "They must be very self-aware."

"I guess that's why they surround themselves with such extravagance," Serena added. "But then why remove his mask?"

"I don't know, Serena, but I think it'd be best if you avoid seeing him again," Marcus told her firmly.

"You're right," she agreed. "I don't think I could even stand to look at him, knowing what's underneath that mask."

"You won't have to," the captain assured her.

"If it's alright with you Captain, I'd like to just be left alone for a while," she concluded, already stepping back towards her small room. "I would really just like to spend the rest of the journey studying the Sheshen language, by myself."

"Of course," Mitchell agreed. "Take as much time as you need."

She turned back towards her room, her head hung low. Marcus caught hold of her arm just as she was about to close the door.

"Serena," he pleaded with her quietly. "If there's anything you need, you'll let me know, won't you?"

"Yes," she said, looking up at him with watery eyes, on the verge of tears, but still managing a heartfelt smile. "Thank you Marcus."

"Marcus, have Reid guard her door," the captain ordered, as the hatch swung shut. "Just… in case."

* * * * *

The Sheshen freighter powered down its superluminal engines and the *Tengri* emerged unscathed from its bowels. Roshana had apparently been insulted by Serena's sudden withdrawal from their lesson, and had refused to meet with the captain and his crew, informing them curtly via radio transmission that they'd arrived in the contested system. The Sheshen freighter changed course and pulled away, leaving the *Tengri* on her own, sailing through a nebula of glowing golden wisps, heading towards the coordinates Roshana had provided.

Captain Mitchell gave the order for the old squad to gear up and assemble at the forward airlock. Marcus felt a sudden rush of energy as he ran to the ship's cramped armory and began strapping on his armor, grabbing the familiar K-660 medium carbine. All around him his squadmates were preparing for battle, although Jago was struggling to don his massive armor plating. Reid propped his long sniper rifle up against the bulkhead in order to help the huge man.

This would be their first engagement since leaving the Terran solar system. It had been a long time but Marcus was amazed at how easily they fell into the familiar rhythms.

"Seems our little voyage has made you fat!" Captain Mitchell shouted at the Ape. "I guess I'll have to have a talk with the cook about lowering your rations."

"I'm fine boss," Jago muttered, sucking in his gut so that Reid could fasten the clamps on his chestplate.

The armor provided by C-CORE was nearly identical to the gear they'd used in the Terran military, although it weighed a tad less and was painted a shade of dark grey, with the insignia of the Terran Republic prominently emblazoned in red on the chestplate, rather than the faded yellow of their old gear.

"Move it ladies," the captain bellowed from the hatchway, sending the squad rushing to the airlock.

* * * * *

Raven was now just about able to make out the outlines of the gas refinery, shrouded by the nebular cloud that permeated the entire system. It was difficult to gauge the facility's size from such a distance, but initial indications from the *Tengri*'s sensors estimated that it was over a kilometer in length and almost as tall, but only half as wide. The inhabited part of the station was a long flat roughly-rectangular construction no more than a few levels tall, from the underside of which hung eight massive cylindrical silos in two rows of four which accounted for most of the station's volume. The whole thing was a uniform dark grey in color, although bright yellow stripes ringed the silos, presumably indicating their contents. Plumes of smoke billowed out into space from several exhaust vents.

Along the irregular edges of the station proper, several docking bays, at least two of which were big enough to accommodate cruiser sized vessels, protruded from the kilometer-long edifice that housed the refinery machinery and crew quarters. Raven adjusted her course for one of the larger bays, alerting Captain Mitchell and the assault team that they were minutes away from docking.

"Wei, adjust the scanners," Raven ordered. "I want to know if there are any other ships in those bays. We can't afford to let those bastards get away."

"Scanning now," the Navigator acknowledged, hammering away at his console to configure the scanners for optimum performance.

As the *Tengri* drew closer, a swarm of drones began to appear, each one no bigger than a dot on the horizon.

"How do you suppose they transport all that gas?" Copilot Gardulo wondered aloud, staring intently at the enormous tanks.

"Not now Gardulo," Raven snapped.

"Those things are huge. The docking bays…"

"I said not now!" the pilot barked.

They were drawing nearer to the station, and Raven was beginning to think it was suspicious that they still hadn't been hailed. The swarm of drones she'd seen had gotten larger. They looked like little spiders with eight mechanical legs stretching out in front of them, while behind their bodies dragged bloated containers of gas. The ones heading away from the station were dragging only tiny bundles barely larger than they were, leading Raven to deduce they were some sort of balloon-like contraptions, expanding as they filled up with harvested gas.

"We're receiving a signal," Wei called, turning to look her in the eye. "I hope you lie as well as you fly."

"Put it through," she ordered him with a stern look.

With the flick of a switch, the ship's comms began to warble, producing static, but after Wei made a series of adjustments, the signal became clearer.

"Yalus sakushin, tishun subetsukoy sarale," a thick, brutish voice was saying.

"Ehm, hello. This is the *Tengri*," Raven stuttered. "We require assistance. Please reply."

There was a distinct lack of response from the outpost. As the silence dragged on, the bridge crew stared at one another, unsure how to proceed.

"*Tengri*, what your purpose here?" came the brutish voice once again, this time speaking a distorted but understandable Terran.

"I… eh… our drive system is malfunctioning," Raven attempted to explain. "We were on our way from Natallus to Voluna when our ship experienced engine failure. We need to make repairs and we were hoping you would allow us to dock and make use of your facilities."

"Hold," was the only response.

Raven shrugged her shoulders at the Navigator, who returned a sly grin.

"You may dock Bay 3," came the reluctant reply from the station, drawing sighs of relief from the bridge crew.

"Taking her in," Raven proclaimed. "Wei, what's the status on the scan?"

"Scan completed. All the bays appear to be vacant," he replied.

*　*　*　*　*

As the *Tengri* finished docking, Captain Mitchell prepared the assault team for battle. The atmosphere in the forward airlock was intense. To Marcus, it was an all too familiar feeling. They'd been through numerous engagements together, yet this was the first time they were acting out of choice rather than following orders. He felt his mind begin to wander back to the last time he'd fired his weapon. Their mission on the Strom sensor outpost wasn't so much different than what they were about to do now. The outpost was a remote installation on the edge of the Terran solar system that had been infiltrated by Alpha Terran terrorists, among them the first friend Marcus had ever made, Steven Meer, who had taken the installation's staff hostage, even executing some of them, before rigging the station's reactor to go critical. A lot had happened since then, but thoughts of that day would always weigh heavily on Marcus' mind.

This time will be easier, he told himself. He wasn't facing someone he knew, didn't have to kill his oldest and dearest friend. These were aliens, brutish and inhuman. When it came to it, he assured himself that he would have no qualms about pulling the trigger.

"Ready Captain?" asked Raven over the comm.

"Open the hatch," he ordered.

Armed and ready, the assault team marched out through the airlock. Marcus took the front, he and Taz flanking Captain Mitchell while Jago, Reid and Doc Taylor brought up the rear. Unlike the cold steel plating of the docking bay on Semeh'yone station, what greeted the clones was a harshly-lit compartment with exceedingly rusted and pitted bulkheads covered in pipes and valves, everything stained with oil and grime. They strode down a narrow gangway being held by a pair of robotic arms protruding from a circular protrusion in the floor. As they neared the bottom of the gangway to the rectangular bay's deck, the double-wide door on the opposite side of the bay slid jerkily open.

Four yellow-eyed Hrūll guards, looking eerily like Ordo'nak, the customs official who had interrogated the crew on Semeh'yone station, came out to greet them. If his demeanor was any indicator of his race, the guards they faced would be as unflinching and lacking emotion. These four were wearing black uniforms with faded yellow stripes running down the length of their sleeves and pants legs. Metallic boots with studded toes clanked loudly as they marched towards the *Tengri*, each carrying what appeared to be a cross between a cleaver and a club. Square pouches hung from one side of a metallic belt around their waists, and what looked like a highly-advanced handgun of some sort was strapped to their opposite hips.

The largest of the four halted his advance roughly a dozen meters from the Terrans, the other three spreading out to stand in a line beside him. The harsh looks and intimidating stares they cast at the new arrivals from their blank, expressionless faces would have been enough to break the resolve of most men, and they seemed utterly unimpressed by the assault team's show of force. The clones too had stopped moving forward, and stood staring down at the muscular aliens on the deck ahead of them in uneasy silence.

A staring contest wasn't exactly what Marcus had been expecting. He'd envisioned the team entering the docking bay with guns blazing, tearing through a horde of ferocious adversaries hell-bent on stopping the Terrans from freeing their hostages. He soon became very aware that no one was saying anything.

The clones outnumbered the Hrūll six to four, yet there was no way of knowing how the fight would turn out. Given the larger bulk and hardened appearance of the aliens, he realized they might not be as easy to take down as Marcus had hoped. The silence stretched unbearably as none of the ten figures in the bay moved so much as a muscle. Marcus could feel sweat trickling down his back.

The sound of gunfire blasted through the air as Taz suddenly opened fire. The twitchy scout had lost his composure and squeezed the trigger on his carbine, emptying half a clip into one of the smaller Hrūll. As bullets ripped through its flesh, both sides sprung into action, Jago roaring in defiance, pushing Marcus and Captain Mitchell aside as he charged forward.

As adrenalin surged through his veins and he brought his weapon up to fire, Marcus realized he was grinning like a madman.

Chapter 24

The view from Captain Intari's private suite aboard the orbital space platform was nothing short of breathtaking. A wide window display ranged from wall to wall and floor to ceiling, bathing the chamber in the blue light reflected from Beta Terra.

Captain Intari had been particularly irate of late. Not that he had been particularly calm or even-tempered since he had been betrayed by the man he had considered his closest confidant, Lieutenant Robert Mitchell, almost ten years ago. He stood by the window, admiring the view of world below, surrounded by the chamber's minimal décor. Ten long years. Almost a decade... Intari had never been one to feel comfortable around others. Even when he'd been a child his lecturers – even his own parents – had found him cold and distant. Though they'd never said it, he had seen it in their eyes when they'd looked at him. As if he were somehow broken, different from all the other children. He was different. He didn't view the world as others did, with desire, hated, love, or other strong emotions, but with what could only be described as a morbid curiosity.

They had sent him to Father Maris for tutelage not long after he'd started school, hoping that through religion he might find his place in the universe, and he did for a spell. Or rather, he learned how to pretend he had, to hide his true nature. He quickly learned when and how to fake emotion. He knew to smile whenever Father Maris showed him kindness. He learned to feign reverence during mass. He even learned how to manipulate others into doing his bidding, a skill which he proceeded to use to subvert the authority of those who sought to guide him. When the damage was done, and Father Maris finally saw him for what he truly was, the horrified priest had arranged for him to be shipped directly to the military.

It was not uncommon for Terran families to send their unwanted scions off to the war, but those who did so made sure that their offspring were given rank, or an appointment safely behind the lines. His appointment was not as impressive. He was assigned – quite deliberately, he was sure – to the rank and file as a Private in a squad full of common clones, who had readily mocked his true-born heritage and social ineptitude at every opportunity.

Though his demeanor had done little to help his squadmates warm to him, his superior tactical mind had proved invaluable after the death of their squad leader, Due to the huge attrition rate in the Nyari War, it had not been long after that that he begun a steady climb through the ranks, until Division 6 had approached him with an offer he could not refuse. After all, an organization that relied on secrecy and the subtle exercise of its power was the perfect place for him to hone his own manipulative nature.

When, after decades of service, he was finally awarded his own battleship – one that answered more to the Shadow Council of the Division than to the Admirals of the Fleet – he had named it the TFS-*Genesis*, a reference to the time he'd spent with Father Maris in his youth. When Robert Mitchell had been appointed his second in command, Intari had sensed something amiss. The following months had only helped to further fuel his distrust of the newly-promoted Lieutenant, as he knew full well that Division 6 encouraged rivalries as a means of pushing its agents to excel, often promoting those of lower rank for acts of subterfuge and subversion.

It wasn't long before he felt his paranoia alleviated, as the two had shared a momentary respite on the *Genesis'* observation deck, gazing over the barren landscape of Alpha Terra. Mitchell had spoken first, disrupting the awkward silence, declaring his pure unbridled hatred for the Nyari and the lengths to which he would go to see them all burnt. What had followed had been a philosophical discussion over the future of the Terran race and the measures they were both willing to take to ensure it. Intari had found, to his surprise, that they seemed to share much in common.

What a fool I was, he thought, for all my skill at manipulation, he tricked me so easily. Perhaps it was for that alone he wanted to see Mitchell burnt at the stake.

"Captain Intari," came a call from the chamber's internal comms, interrupting his train of thought. "Dr. Reisner is ready for you."

Intari turned his head, as if to acknowledge the speaker's physical presence, yet he stood alone in the cold steel chamber.

He turned his gaze once more to the world below, a sly grin forming at the corner of his lips.

"Soon," he spoke.

* * * * *

The fluorescent lights illuminating the abandoned platform flickered erratically, casting tinted shadows across the vacant square. Takahashi had never been there before, but he could see it was the sort of place no one would expect him to visit. Hollow ceramic building blocks were lined up against the metal banister, tagged with layer upon layer of illegible graffiti. The pungent aroma of urine hung in the air, momentarily alleviated by gusts of wind.

He leaned against the railing, casting his focus down into the bowels of the train yard. Dozens of maglev tracks were neatly arranged side by side, some of them occupied by the rusting husks of engines and maglev cars. Somewhere deep in the bowels of the yard, in the tunnels beneath the platform, a freight train skidded to an abrupt halt, most likely due to the presence of vagrants or hooligans in the tunnels. He'd read reports of an entire society of degenerates which made the tunnels their home. He had a difficult time imagining how anyone could live under such conditions, shuddering at the thought of a life spent in never-ending darkness.

His contact was late, which wasn't unusual, but given his surroundings it was starting to unsettle him, for all that his driver was less than a couple of hundred meters away, parked just outside the station's southern steps, opposite Harland Park. A sudden rush of air popped somewhere below as an impossibly long passenger train shot out of one of the tunnels. Takahashi started to count the cars but soon realized that the train was traveling much too fast. Given its direction, it was likely passing through on its way to Belforth, a city not too far from the capital.

He nearly leapt over the railing when he felt the tapping on his shoulder.

"Ease up, old fool," came the familiar voice of his contact.

"Harkin! You should know better than to sneak up on an old man like that," Takahashi gasped, clutching his chest as he struggled to catch his breath.

"Hah. You're not the only one the years have treated unkindly," Harkin replied, leaning up against the railing next to Takahashi.

His words rang true, although he hadn't been much to look at in his earlier days either. He was completely bald, with oily skin which

184

glistened under the fickle fluorescent lighting. Deep lines of worry covered his aging visage, and purple veins could be seen prominently on his cheeks, neck and forehead. His oversized ears drooped comically, and his bushy eyebrows had gone completely white.

"So why did you call me this late?" inquired Harkin, stoically.

"I've been out of the loop for a spell," Takahashi ventured. "I need a way back in."

Harkin raised an eyebrow, astonished that his old acquaintance would not only ask such a favor, but to assume that he had the power to grant his request.

"You presume a great deal if you think you can garner enough support to reclaim your old position. Especially having held it twice now," said Mr. Harkin.

"You misunderstand me," Takahashi corrected. "C-CORE holds little interest for me in terms of position or titles. I seek only information."

"Ah," Harkin replied, stuffing his hands in his pockets and fiddling with his coins, something he often did when he felt uncomfortable. "They said you wouldn't leave well enough alone."

"Well, for once they were right," Takahashi replied, smiling faintly. "I thought I could set it all aside, retire with at least a modicum of grace. But there's something amiss."

"Oh?" Harkin probed, stretching his pants pockets outwards in an odd fashion as he continued to play with their contents.

"You can sense it, can't you?" Takahashi urged him. "The war, this... supposed economic reform. Something is stirring... something I fear..." he stammered as he tried to put his thoughts into words.

"You're not entirely incorrect," Harkin confessed, reluctantly.

"You know something?" pressed Takahashi, feeling a rush of relief

185

at the revelation.

"I'm not supposed to. But you know me, I always have my eyes and ears in the wrong places," he smiled.

"Well…?" Takahashi urged him.

"The crystal… the one from the craft on New Io…"

"What of it?" Takahashi demanded, worried about what he was about to hear.

"It's gone missing," Harkin eventually replied, reluctantly.

"Missing?" Takahashi blurted. "How?"

"Misplaced, stolen, I'm not sure. It's all very hush hush. Director Straub has gone to great lengths to make sure no one's aware of the situation. I suspect he's involved somehow… though of course, I can't prove anything," Harkin admitted.

Takahashi felt an uncontrollable urge to lash out. Before he'd left C-CORE a few years before, he'd contemplated disposing of the crystal, thinking it unsafe to leave it in any hands but his own. Yet, in the end, he'd assured himself that if anyone could keep it from falling into the wrong hands, it would be C-CORE. To discover that his judgment had been so deeply flawed was not something he took lightly, and nor were the implications this could have for the future. His mentor's plans depended on it.

Harkin stood there in silence, rolling his feet on the ground, patiently waiting for Takahashi to regain his composure.

"I… I almost can't believe it," Takahashi gasped after a moment. "Division 6?" he ventured a guess.

Harkin nodded in agreement. "I suspect so."

"Then I truly stand alone."

"Don't fret, old man," Harkin said, reassuringly. "I'm still on your side, though I think I should leave you now. There are too many eyes

186

and ears lurking down below, and I believe I see a pair of drones approaching, no doubt to deal with the riffraff in the underpass."

"Thank you, old friend," Takahashi sighed as they parted ways before the hover drones could get within range to record their words.

* * * * *

"The similarities between the propulsion system of the craft and that of the *Lazarus* are astounding," the scientist explained as they passed through the airlock, moving on to traverse the maze of corridors beyond. "As you well know, the original seed ship was outfitted with the alien drive technology scavenged from the craft found in orbit of Mars. Although Earth's scientists did manage to install it on the Lazarus, we never did manage to reverse engineer it once we reached the Merillian galaxy."

Captain Intari was a full head taller than the excitable man, whose nervous facial tics had only intensified the longer he was in his company. The short scientist wore spectacles augmented with sensory devices along the upper rim of the left lens, with which he continuously fidgeted as he attempted to adjust the way they sat on his hooked nose.

"Our scientists were close, very close in fact, to discovering its secrets. But when the Nyari bombarded Alpha Terra, the *Lazarus* was almost completely destroyed, setting us back decades. This new propulsion system is of a similar design, and we believe that true superluminal propulsion is now finally within our grasp, provided-"

"Dr. Reisner," Intari interrupted him, coming to a stop as he did so, forcing the diminutive man to stop with him. "Spare me the historical lecture. Just how fast will this new technology allow us to travel?"

187

"Yes... of course. My apologies," Reisner stammered. "We believe that a vessel equipped with this new propulsion technology will be capable of obtaining speeds several times faster than that of our current mass accelerators. Although just how fast, in practical terms, we haven't yet been able to ascertain."

Intari resumed his stride down the corridor, this time at a speed with which Dr. Reisner had difficulty keeping up, at least not without foregoing grace. A pair of armed guards marched past them, outfitted simply in black uniforms bearing no markings or insignia.

"It is possible that, with continued research, and the appropriate funding of course, we might be seeing a velocity increase of up to twenty times our current maximum," the scientist proclaimed, brimming with pride. "But it will take time."

"Unacceptable," Intari announced, without a hint of emotion or even so much as breaking stride. "I gave you a deadline. I want my prototype."

"That's... not possible!" Reisner gasped, pushing his spectacles further up the bridge of his nose.

In utter silence, Captain Intari came to a stop in the middle of a junction. Corridors stretched out in several directions, some straight and narrow as far the eye could see, others curving slightly, obscuring the view of whatever they led to. A row of heavy metal doors, manned by a team of guards, were laid out evenly along one side of the passage in front of them, and a motorized cart was approaching in the distance.

Dr. Reisner tried to stand perfectly still under Intari's fierce scrutiny, first clutching his arms behind his back, then folding them across his chest, then shoving them deeply into the pockets of his lab coat as he awkwardly tried to remain composed. A young lab technician emerged from a nearby airlock, entranced in the contents of his datapad as he passed them by.

"You," Intari snapped, focusing his gaze on the technician. "Come here."

The technician faltered upon seeing who was addressing him, nearly dropping his datapad in fear.

"Yes... yes Sir," he stuttered, coming to a standstill in front of them.

From his pocket, Captain Intari produced a metal cylinder, no larger than a pen and topped with a focusing lens. He held the device in front of the trembling lab tech, who tried to avert his gaze, but found, to his horror, that he was unable to do so. A flicker of azure light flashed from the device, beamed directly into the man's eyes, which were wide open with terror.

"Interesting piece of technology," Intari murmured, "He's now completely incapable of movement."

After a few seconds, the captain switched off the device and placed it back in his pocket, producing in its stead a small spherical object whose outer shell was lined with a mesh of coppery wires.

"This device, however, serves a more sinister purpose," he explained. "Once activated, it slowly begins to expand, growing up to four times its original diameter."

As much as the technician wanted to scream, to run away as far and as fast as he could, he found his body entirely unresponsive, frozen in place. If he had been paralyzed, he would have slumped to the ground, but instead every muscle in his body was locked, a minute spasm coursing through his frame, keeping him tense and unable to move.

"The Nyari use them on captive soldiers, forcing them to swallow them, causing severe internal bleeding," Captain Intari said, activating the device and watching as it began to slowly expand in the palm of his hand. "I prefer allowing them a moment to grow before inserting them into the oral cavity. That way, they can't be swallowed."

"Captain, I-" Reisner blurted.

"This man," Intari cut him off, grabbing the technician's chin forcefully to pull open his mouth, "Is about to learn what it means to be... expendable."

Reisner watched in terror as the captain inserted the device into the lab tech's mouth.

"It is a lesson I would rather not have to give twice," Intari proclaimed, turning his cold stare on the scientist.

Intari was already well on his way down the corridor when the muffled panting of the technician's spasming lungs was replaced by the popping sound of his head being ripped apart from the inside out.

Chapter 25

The ferocity of the Ape's charge against the Hrūll was unprecedented. Marcus felt as if they'd unleashed a caged beast, starving for blood. Although he'd been carrying his trusted Viking KRS-56, an enormous high-caliber machinegun, Jago used the butt of the weapon to pummel one poor guard into oblivion. With one Hrūll already down from Taz's first frantic shots, the assault team made quick work of the remaining two guards.

Pausing only long enough to tear Jago away from the corpse of the fallen Hrūll, the squad stormed on through the double wide doors leading into the station. The interior was not what the warren of claustrophobic tunnels Marcus had expected. It was one vast container, lined with a row of structures along each side, with a third row along the center dividing the long space into wide streets. The *Tengri* had docked in a bay at the very tip of the installation's long spine, so the clones had emerged into a small area crowded with abandoned barrels and crates, facing the narrow end of these internal buildings, each of which was two or three stories tall, with stairways and walkways connecting them. It somewhat resembled an industrial version of the promenade on Alamo station back on Callisto.

The two streets, which ran the entire length of the station, were populated by hundreds of drones, some the size of trucks, which moved back and forth carrying vats and crates while smaller units busied themselves with custodial duties or maintenance work. Countless overhanging wires and cables spanned the main streets, shoddy maintenance or poor design sending sparks flying through the air at regular intervals. Steam poured out from an array of rusty pipes which jutted out from the walls near the ceiling, pooling on the floor to form a layer of mist. Layers of rust and dirt stained every possible surface, a testament to the poor state of the facilities. The whole scene reeked of sulfur and ammonia, and although the atmosphere was safe enough to breathe, Marcus toyed with the notion of snapping an atmospheric filter into his helmet's chin-slot.

The constant clanging and clamor of metal grinding against metal echoed in his ears, and the dim, yellowy lighting made it difficult to see further than a hundred meters down the path before them, urging Captain Mitchell to signal caution. With a quick brace of orders, the squad split up into two groups of three, with Captain Mitchell, Jago and Doc Taylor taking the left street whilst Marcus, Taz and Reid took the right path.

They'd barely made it more than a few steps into the station when Marcus heard the sound of gunfire from the captain's team. The return fire from the Hrūll did not sound like projectile fire, but rather like bursts of energy, preceded by a soft popping sound, as if the water molecules in the air were instantly becoming superheated. It was difficult to make out, given the loud ambient noise.

Marcus had to make the tough decision of whether to backtrack and assist his squadmates, or continue onwards and try to find a flanking position, and make it quickly. Deciding that the captain had both Jago and Taylor on his side, Marcus chose to move on, even as the gunfire intensified.

The horde of robotic workers streamed back and forth around them, either unaware that the refinery had been infiltrated, or perhaps there was nothing in their programming that suggested any alternative way to react to the situation. Marcus hurriedly led his team through the mist-covered corridor. On each side, structures clearly marked with alien symbols lay vacant. They were crude blocks of metal, stacked side by side or on top of one another. Apart from the steady line of drones, there was no movement in sight. It was as if the station were largely abandoned. If they hadn't run into the Hrūll guards in the docking bay, he would have thought that the entire outpost were completely automated.

The shooting subsided suddenly, ending with a few shots which were clearly projectile in nature, leading Marcus to the conclusion that Captain Mitchell's team had won the engagement.

"Captain, what's your status?" Marcus asked on the comms.

"Two more Hrūll down. The Ape got a little singed, but nothing serious," Mitchell replied, panting heavily.

"Moving on. Out." Marcus acknowledged.

He signaled Taz and Reid to use the slightly uneven walls of the structures as cover, creeping forward up against the walls for a better chance of remaining unseen, and the fireteam began leapfrogging from cover to cover. Some of the structures had wide glass windows with rounded corners, stained with dirt and grime, so Marcus paused briefly every so often to peer through them, making sure that there was no one there to sneak up on them at a later time. They were all empty, but some were obviously meant to house personnel, filled with empty cots and what looked like cabinets, presumably for personal effects. Others were cluttered with all manner of machinery or alchemical equipment.

Suddenly, a door on a structure ahead of them slid open, and out strode a Hrūll less stocky than the ones they had seen before, seemingly unaware of the Terrans' approach. He wore a dark grey bodysuit and held a large datapad in both hands, his concentration fixed on the glowing device as he emerged from the doorway, turning his back on the assault team as if to walk up the street away from the docking bay the *Tengri* had used. Suddenly, the thin Hrūll – who was still significantly more muscular than Marcus – stopped short in his tracks, turning his head slightly to the side, as if suddenly sensing that he was not alone.

Marcus shouldered his carbine with his right hand, giving the others a signal to remain still with his left. The three clones froze. After a tense moment, the Hrūll looked back at his device, poking and prodding at the screen with his plump fingers, as if he'd had a sudden revelation, slowly pacing forwards as he stared at the contents of the screen. Marcus snuck cautiously up behind him. Shooting an unarmed man in the back was not something he was willing to do, even if that man was an alien, regardless of what he may have done to deserve it.

Without warning, the Hrūll began loudly sniffing the air around him, quickly turning in his tracks. Sighting the heavily armed Terrans less than a few meters behind him, the alien instinctively threw his datapad into the air and began sprinting down the corridor as fast as his legs would carry him, shouting unintelligible words at the top of his lungs. Without warning, a well placed shot from Reid's sniper rifle tore through the back of his skull, sending his lifeless body tumbling to the misty floor. Marcus cringed.

He knew that strategically, Reid had done the right thing, but morally he'd have preferred a different outcome. He had hoped that their opponents would all have been armed, capable of defending themselves. Somehow that made pursuing this course that much more just. He hadn't counted on the possibility of unarmed personnel occupying the outpost.

*   *   *   *   *

Having expected more resistance, albeit futile, Captain Mitchell was cautious about proceeding down the street he and his fireteam had taken. Feeling certain that more guards would eventually follow in the wake of those sent to meet the *Tengri*, he gave the order for his team to hustle and make as much ground as possible.

There had to be a security station somewhere, he thought, a central staging area where the Hrūll raiders were keeping their captives and controlling the installation. Given the size of the refinery, there was no telling how large the opposing force could be, so stealth and speed were the keys to success.

Having witnessed Jago's regenerative abilities firsthand on the Strom sensor outpost, Mitchell made the enormous clone take the lead, Doc Taylor and the captain himself leapfrogging behind, taking cover every ten meters or so to scan the surrounding area, clearing the alleyways and quickly peering through windows. Besides, Mitchell told himself, once he started firing it, Jago's weapon was sure to cause enough panic to buy them some time. The firearms the two guards his fireteam had encountered after splitting from the others had used were much quieter, and the roar of the Viking was something even the jaded captain respected.

A few unarmed Hrūll, apparently workers maintaining the station for the raiders, fell prey to the Terran onslaught as Jago and Captain Mitchell made quick work of them, with Doc Taylor trailing behind, trying to keep up, stumbling over the dead Hrūll. The constant stream of robotic workers droning back and forth along the centre of the street was a major distraction, and the clanking and buzzing of machinery made it difficult to hear any approaching guards, keeping everyone on edge.

The central structures gave way to crossing paths every two hundred meters or so, connecting the two primary passages together. With Marcus' team having traveled further up ahead, Mitchell's fireteam had little choice but to keep on moving. Halfway up the station they came upon a junction with a massive crane-like contraption on a sliding base, connected to two sets of rail systems hanging from the ceiling, one set spanning the width of the outpost, the other running the refinery's length, hanging right above the row of structures at the outpost's center.

Stark shadows filled every corner, keeping potential lurkers veiled from view. A series of spiraling staircases led up to the massive crane system every few hundred meters. With so many precarious positions and the possibility of snipers lurking in every corner, Mitchell felt compelled to slow their advance, ordering his team to take cover while he assessed the situation.

* * * * *

Having run into a small ambush a short distance ahead of the looming crane system, Marcus knelt behind a load of abandoned crates. Taz huddled beside him, staying clear of the golden energy bolts zipping dangerously overhead. Reid had managed to sneak away in the initial chaos and had slipped into a narrow side alley, slanting upwards. He crept along a narrow catwalk that protruded from the alley, bolted to the outside of the buildings that ran along the street like an overextended balcony, two stories overhead. The dark-skinned clone maneuvered his way deftly into position, his sniper rifle slung over his back as he crawled out into the open.

A team of four Hrūll had taken cover behind a pair of load-lifters in the middle of an intersection barely fifty meters ahead, disabling the machines' motors to use them as a roadblock. The enemy fire – thin beams of light that flew so quickly that they were barely visible – was so thick that Marcus didn't dare stick his head out, in fear of having it blown clean off. Bolts of energy blasted off the walls of a nearby structure, leaving singed holes in the metal plating.

"What I wouldn't give for a grenade!" Taz cursed, ducking to narrowly escape a bolt which flew into the side of his crate.

"We're inside a space station Taz," Marcus countered. "I don't think using grenades would be the smartest thing to do!"

They watched helplessly as Reid cleared the corner of the catwalk, leaning over the edge and readying his sniper rifle.

"Looks like the Rev's got this one under control," Taz noted.

"Let's make sure it doesn't go to waste," Marcus ordered, inching closer to the corner of the crate, getting ready to provide Reid with covering fire.

The sniper took aim, carefully studying their opponents for signs of a leader. He eventually took aim on a brute who seemed more content barking orders than focusing on his weapon. Reid checked his grip on his weapon, curled his finger around the trigger, and carefully controlled his breathing. At such short range he could barely miss. The shot went off, tearing through the neck of his intended target, whose blood-curdling screams as he fell backwards cut through the clatter of the passing worker drones.

Reid immediately started moving to reposition himself, but it was already too late. The other Hrūll had noticed him, and instantly focused their fire on the narrow catwalk. Sensing the opportunity, Marcus pushed himself to his feet, peering over the edge of his cover, letting loose a hail of rounds in the aliens' direction.

Still, the covering fire did little to dissuade their opponents, who relentlessly fired bolt after bolt of energy in Reid's direction. The sniper roared in agony as one of the bolts nicked his knee, melting straight through most of his metallic armor. He rolled over onto his back, grabbing at his leg, biting down hard on his lip to withstand the pain.

Taz let out a roar of his own at the sight of his wounded comrade, emptying his clip at the three remaining Hrūll, who finally ducked for cover under the scout's accurate barrage. After a second of stillness, during which Taz frantically changed magazines, a bolt of golden energy suddenly blew through one of the supports holding up the catwalk, followed closely by another.

Marcus realized what their change in tactics portended. Firing from the safety of the cover provided by the load-lifters where Marcus and Taz couldn't target them, they intended to bring Reid down to their level.

Marcus frantically scanned his surroundings, hoping to find something he could use to their advantage. It didn't take long for a plan to form.

"Cover me!" he yelled as he ran past Taz, jumping out of cover.

Startled, Taz grabbed at his friend to pull him back into safety, but he was too late. Marcus jumped straight into the steady stream of robotic workers, grabbing hold of one of the larger drones, carrying a large crate filled with canisters, as it rumbled past on large metallic wheels. With one hand he held on tight to the drone's exoskeleton, readying his weapon with the other as the drone raced towards the edge of the Hrūll barricade.

To his astonishment, Taz saw that the Hrūll had missed Marcus' bold move entirely, still focusing on the unfortunate Reid, who was frantically rolling around on the catwalk above, trying to keep from getting hit. Taz fired off a few volleys to try and buy his comrades some time, but their assailants remained unshaken.

As the drone approached the barricade, it veered off to the right, not only shielding Marcus even further from view, but aligning him neatly with the exposed side of the Hrūll roadblock. He only had a few seconds to react before the drone would speed him on his way, so he had to make sure to make them count. He aimed his carbine, training it on where the Hrūll's tight formation would appear when the drone carried him past... then he squeezed the trigger. His weapon roared, firing off round after round in what seemed, to Marcus, to be a never-ending torrent.

Then, all too quickly, he was whisked away by the big robotic worker, and Marcus couldn't even be sure whether he had hit his targets or not. He jumped off the drone, rolling on the floor until he came to a stop at the end of the intersection, drone after drone racing past him.

Marcus scanned the Hrūll barricade and, in between the speeding worker drones, he saw that none of his targets were left standing. As the smoke cleared, he saw Taz running over to help Reid down the closest staircase. He was limping profusely, clutching the short clone's shoulder and weighing him down. He got back on his feet and ran to the others, hoping Reid's injuries wouldn't be too severe.

"Damn it," Reid bellowed as Marcus reached them. "Why am I always the one who gets hurt?"

Chapter 26

Crouching behind a large pipe belching what he desperately hoped was only steam, Captain Mitchell spotted a few more refinery workers dashing into a structure up ahead. Jago leaned up against the wall behind him, brandishing his machinegun and awaiting further orders. Doc Taylor was crouched behind a towering crate at the opposite side of the street.

It felt like the calm before the storm. Their eyes probed frantically, peering into dark corners in the hope of spotting any would-be attacker before they spotted the lurking Terrans. There was nothing. Aside from the swarm of drones whizzing past them at every turn and the periodical release of the steam valve, the area around the crane appeared to be completely vacant.

"Can't be too careful," Mitchell quipped, rising out of cover.

Instantaneously a single focused bolt of searing energy shot through the air, narrowly missing the captain shoulder as it slammed into the wall behind him. The team ducked back into cover as they frantically scanned for the origins of the shot. Judging by the trajectory, Mitchell realized it had to have come from somewhere high up, and saw immediately that strategically their location was less than ideal.

As a team of guards began pouring from one of the structures up ahead and more bolts of energy started flying in their direction, things began to look grim.

* * * * *

"Taz, you have to take him back to the ship," Marcus ordered, eyeing Reid's badly wounded knee.

Fortunately the bolt of energy had singed the flesh, effectively cauterizing the wound, but given the amount of pain Reid was in, and the sniper's inability to walk on his own, Marcus felt it best to get him back safely as soon as possible.

"No way, Corporal!" Reid protested. "You'll need the added firepower more than you need a good pair of legs."

Marcus bit his lip. He knew that Reid's stubbornness would not be easy to overcome, and as he began hearing shots in the distance, that he wouldn't get much time to argue.

"Alright," he conceded. "I'll go ahead. You two follow up behind me as fast as you can. I have a feeling the captain's stirring up trouble."

Without waiting for their reply, Marcus ran off as fast as he could, ducking and weaving between the busy drone traffic. As he cleared the next corner of the intersection, ducking into the other street, he spotted a large crowd of guards, maybe eight or ten strong, rushing to take cover behind one of the massive crane system's vertical support beams. Pausing briefly to gain his bearings, he saw Captain Mitchell and Jago pinned down behind a stand of pipes nearly a hundred meters away in the steam, and unable to react. Moving so much as a few centimeters would put them in harm's way. The bolts of energy sizzling through the damp air from up above alerted him to the presence of the sniper. Fortunately, none of the Hrūll had yet taken notice of his arrival, but he had to act fast.

Marcus darted across the way and jumped on top of a small platform holding a ladder which ran up the side of the crane's support structure. He knew that if he could take out the sniper, they'd have a much better chance of taking out the rest. His heart was pounding, all of his muscles tensed up as he pulled himself higher and higher with a firm grip. As he climbed the rungs, coming up just under the crane unit itself, he looked down to inspect the scene.

Behind the aliens' barricade of metal crates crouched a Hrūll who appeared even more formidable than the others. He wore black metallic plating over his chest and a matching helmet with a yellow visor rather than the thick black cloth of the others' uniforms. Marcus counted eight more Hrūll surrounding him, firing off volleys in Captain Mitchell's direction while their leader shouted orders left and right. One of the guards was finishing assembling what appeared to be a large piece of weaponry from several components he'd pulled from a nearby case. Its body was a bulky piece of hard-edged metal, with a prominent grip protruding from its underside near the front, housing the firing mechanism. Though mostly dark gray in color, a pair of slanting, faded-orange stripes encircled its front end, near where its inverted semi-spherical barrel protruded from the boxy casing of the main body. Once the weapon had been fully assembled, the guard handed it over to his leader, who swung the finished object up onto his shoulder, taking aim at Captain Mitchell's position.

Their cover may have protected them from small arms fire, even the searing laser blasts, but given the sheer bulk of the weapon mounted on the Hrūll leader's shoulder Marcus realized that if he didn't do something quickly this might be the end of Mitchell's fireteam.

"Captain, run!" he shouted into his helmet comms, his voice carrying further than he'd planned, drawing the startled Hrūll's attention to himself.

The astonished Hrūll leader span to face him, and suddenly a continuous beam of energy blasted out of the huge shoulder-mounted cannon, tearing through the platform below Marcus and trailing off to the structures on the opposite side of the street. Captain Mitchell and the others used the opportunity to get to safety, Jago using the butt of his weapon to smash through the large window pane behind them so they could jump into the structure for cover. Seeing them escape, Marcus gave a short cheer. He'd bought them the time they needed to get to safety.

So focused was Marcus on what was happening below him that he didn't notice the fist that came hurtling down towards him. As the Hrüll sniper's blow made contact with Marcus' helmet, the force of the punch threw him off guard, making him lose his grip on the ladder. Completely stunned, Marcus flailed his arms, hoping desperately to grab a hold of anything to stop his fall. His heart stopped momentarily. He felt his stomach pushing up against his chest as he plummeted.

Finally, his fingers connected with the rungs just half a meter below his original position. His, carbine which had been slung over his shoulder, nearly slipped off, and it would have fallen down to the deck some twelve meters below had its sling not tangled on his chestplate.

The alien sniper made out a low grunting sound as he turned to reclaim his rifle from where it had been laid out on the deck of the crane's cab above. As Marcus struggled to gather his composure, the Hrüll turned and stood over the gap in the platform through which the ladder climbed, aiming his rifle straight at the clone below, with barely a meter between the muzzle of the barrel and Marcus' head. The alien tickled the trigger as if toying with him, delaying the kill, still as expressionless as his race ever was.

Marcus was stuck, hanging from the ladder with his carbine still hanging awkwardly off his shoulder and his sidearm safely holstered on his hip. Frantically he searched for a solution, anything he could do to stave off his impending doom. As the alien above him slowly began squeezing the trigger on his weapon, leaning forward to deliver the shot that would no doubt remove Marcus' head from his shoulders, the Hrūll experienced a stroke of truly awful luck.

As he leant forward to ensure his shot was accurate, Marcus' would-be killer snagged his boot on what appeared to be a loose bolt on the crane's deck, causing him to lurch awkwardly forward. Suddenly, the rifle's long barrel was no longer a meter away, but only a hair's breadth from Marcus' fingers, clutching the rung above him. Instinctively, he heaved his body up with his left hand and grabbed at the muzzle of the rifle with his right, pulling on it with all of his might and the weight of his body and gear.

As the astonished Hrūll came crashing down through the open hatch, he barely had time to let out a muddled cry before impacting on the hard surface below. Marcus gasped, clinging to the ladder in shock. He couldn't believe his luck, though the sudden hail of golden bolts fired in his direction from the barricade below sent him rushing up the ladder as fast as he could and into the crane's cab for cover.

Though from his vantage point, Captain Mitchell hadn't been able to see what had transpired, the resounding crash had prompted him to take action. He'd spurred Jago forward, the two of them rushing out the door of the building they'd taken shelter in, guns blazing as they ran clear across the street. His instincts had proven true as the sniper's sudden death had created just the diversion he had been hoping for. As the barrage of bullets raged over the barricade, two of the Hrūll fell limp to the ground, blood gushing from open wounds.

Marcus suddenly noticed a wheeled cart being pushed directly out into the intersection. It was made entirely out of metal plating and looked like it was designed to carry heavy machine parts. Inside it, Reid prepared his rifle for combat while Taz panted as he pushed the cart from behind with all of his strength. Spotting their approach, Jago and the captain immediately ran over to join them, jumping behind the moving cart for cover. Bolts of energy slammed into the cart's flank, showering the entire intersection with sparks.

Marcus let out a sigh of relief. Fortune was finally in their favor. With the focus now shifted back to the others, he began aiming his carbine down at the enemy barricade. Although he understood that the aliens were surprised and surrounded, he still couldn't believe his luck. He had a clear view. He pulled the trigger, emptying his entire clip down upon the crouching Hrüll.

Without even waiting to see how many he'd hit, he immediately dropped to the deck of the cab just as a bolt of energy tore through the window, leaving a gaping hole in the roof of the crane's housing. He knew he wouldn't get another shot off from the same vantage point, so he began to reposition himself. He crawled back to the ladder, slung his carbine over his shoulder and slid down the rails to the ground below, as quickly as he could.

Captain Mitchell and the others laid down covering fire to cover his retreat as he ducked into a nearby alleyway. For once the Hrüll didn't return fire. There was no response. The only sounds they heard were those of the perpetual grinding ambiance of the refinery.

"Captain," Reid muttered from within the body of the cart. "I've got an itch."

"You're not the only one," Mitchell grunted in reply.

Hoping that the alleyway would allow him to double back and flank the Hrüll, Marcus had unfortunately run into a dead end. As he returned, he snuck carefully out of the alleyway in an attempt to catch a glimpse of what their opponents were planning. He could barely see them, but it looked as if their leader were speaking into a small comm device embedded into his wrist guard.

As he peered through the clutter chocking the intersection, Marcus suddenly felt a strange sensation. It was as if he were suddenly getting heavier, barely noticeable at first, but the feeling intensified with each passing moment.

"Zokava rokutti nii-kaäsi totsubunu," a resounding voice boomed from the refinery's intercom.

All the muscles in Marcus' body began to tense. The veins on his neck popped out as he began to buckle under the pressure. He'd experienced high gravity on Ga'ouna, but this went far beyond anything he'd felt there. He could see the others experiencing the same peculiar feeling across the intersection, visibly perplexed.

"Zokava rokutti yne-kaäsi totsubunu," the voice resounded once more.

Marcus felt almost half as heavy as normal, and the effect was still intensifying. What with all the gear he was carrying, including his cumbersome armor, it was beginning to take its toll.

"What the hell's going on?" shouted Taz hysterically.

"Gravity increase," Mitchell bellowed. "They must be messing with the artificial gravity!"

"Zokava rokutti kuro-kaäsi totsubunu," the voice reverberated throughout the outpost.

With his bad leg, Captain Mitchell collapsed, falling to the floor in exhaustion. Seconds later, Taz's knees gave in, sending him crashing to the ground. Beside them, the towering giant Jago still stood, clutching the rim of the wheeled cart for support, his teeth gritted in determination.

206

"Zokava rokutti kachi-kaäsi totsubunu," the voice boomed, sending Marcus to the floor, completely overpowered and writhing on the ground, clutching his knees in pain.

With the entire assault team disabled and on the ground – apart from Jago, who was biting down hard to keep from suffering the same fate – the Hrūll behind the improvised barricade began firing relentlessly. They began leaving cover, circling around for a clearer shot at their prone targets, seemingly less affected by the gravity increase than the Terrans were.

Jago was frothing at the mouth, furious that his own bodyweight would be his downfall. He refused to give in, roaring like a cornered animal, but too proud and defiant to admit it.

With his seemingly unending supply of strength, he slowly managed to heave his machinegun up to the edge of the cart, its barrel just scraping against the rim. His entire body convulsed. His hands were unable to do more than aim the weapon in the general direction of his assailants, who were slowly bearing down upon the cart.

As bolts of energy flew past him, one connecting with his left shoulder pad, Jago unleashed the awesome power of the drum-fed Voss Viking KRS-56 upon them. The machinegun roared as it spewed forth round after round in rapid succession, most of which slammed into a distant wall. The head of the nearest Hrūll exploded into a mist of fleshy goo and fragmented bone as one of the rounds hit home.

A bolt of energy slammed into the inner rim of the wheeled cart as another guard raised his weapon, firing blindly in hopes of shooting over the container. Jago screamed in agony as he turned his weapon, creating an arc of pure death and mayhem. The second Hrūll flew backwards as several rounds blew through his chest, leaving several fist-sized holes.

Before he knew it, the Hrŭll leader in the black helmet was the only one left alive. With a roar, he unclasped an oddly-shaped cleaver from his back, similar to the ones the first guards had carried. He raised it high over his head and sent it sailing through the air towards Jago. It spun twice, full circle, as it arched its way over the wheeled cart before digging itself deep into Jago's left shoulder between his armor and his neck. Jago wailed, but refused to let go of his weapon, despite his crippling injury.

"Zokava rokutti hyusati totsubunu," the intercom boomed again.

Not one to let a blow go unpunished, Jago managed to direct his blazing machinegun to the guard leader before finally giving in to the increasing pressure. The last thing he saw before he hit the floor was his opponent's right arm come clean off his body.

"Turn it off!" Marcus shouted at the top of his lungs from where he lay on the ground, clumsily aiming his carbine at the Hrŭll leader, who was now clutching the stump where his arm used to be.

The wounded alien responded by throwing his helmet to the ground and staring at him with cold lifeless eyes, his face completely devoid of emotion.

"Turn it off now!" Marcus yelled once more, shaking his carbine in his direction.

The Hrŭll slowly raised his good arm and spoke into his wrist device, all the while keeping his eyes locked on Marcus. As the gravity slowly returned to normal, Marcus got back to his feet and began securing their captive while the others saw to the wounded Jago. A moment later Doc Taylor came strolling up from behind them, holding his helmet in one hand and a lit cigarette in the other.

*   *   *   *   *

With the entire base thrown into turmoil, no one noticed the small Sheshen craft approaching the refinery. It had drifted in space for the majority of its journey, its systems powered down to assure it would slip past the station's sensors undetected.

Small maneuvering thrusters on the nose of the dark sleek craft fired off in sequence, flipping the ship over in a matter of seconds. It slowly closed the distance to one of the station's gas silos, and as soon as it made contact, the ship polarized its hull plating, magnetically attaching itself to the surface.

A moment later the ship came loose once more, firing a short controlled burst from its primary engine. As it drifted back into space, it left behind its payload – a tightly packed container of explosives – attached to the enormous gas silo.

Chapter 27

Streaks of light pierced the fragmented glass of the domed roof, its amber and sapphire hues tinting the gossamer rays as they formed a halo of light on the shimmering floor twenty meters below. On many occasions, Rodan had marveled at dome's artistry. He stood opposite Ambassador Janosh, both men dressed in plain black robes, gripping their ceremonial blades.

Rodan had received his only a few years prior, at the culmination of his training. It was a straight blade, as sharp as any he had ever seen, and perfectly balanced. Its hilt was made from the bones of a Nerokan randler, a creature notorious for its ferocity, and highly sought after by poachers, much to the displeasure of the Nerokan noble houses. The bones were engraved with Gaia's blessings and wrapped with crimson ribbons.

"Your sword is an extension of your mind," Ambassador Janosh counseled. "Through its form you can channel your energy, focus it upon your enemy, and release it."

With those words, the ambassador began to channel his essence into his own blade, which began to crackle as waves of energy began to caress its edge, its intensity magnifying with each passing second until finally he released it in a jet of light, cutting through the dimness of the wide circular hall and heading straight for Rodan.

Rodan swiftly swirled his blade in a wide arc, creating a barrier which deflected the beam just as it was about to strike home, hurling it to the edge of the chamber, where it quickly dissipated.

"Well done," the ambassador commended him. "Your skill with the blade has vastly improved since last we sparred."

"Thank you, Master," Rodan said, bowing his head in a sign of respect.

"You have been on several missions for the Triumvirate now," Ambassador Janosh proclaimed. "Your instincts have advanced beyond those of most men of your age, and you have proven your morals to be unquestionable."

"Your words do me great honor, Master," Rodan muttered, blushing at the undeserved praise.

"Tell me, what do you think should be done regarding the Terran threat?"

"I would hardly call them a threat, Master," Rodan countered quickly. "They are only one ship, one crew, and a poor one at that."

"It is not their numbers, or their strength, which concern me," the ambassador confessed. "It is their morality, and how their being here may corrupt the good work we have accomplished."

Rodan pondered the ambassador's words. "What would Gaia do?" he asked rhetorically.

"Our beloved Gaia would indeed know what to do," Ambassador Janosh concurred. "There is not a day that goes by that I do not wonder what happened to her. She was the greatest of us all. I cannot imagine what fate had in store for her. There are many among us who believe that she will one day return to us, though I must admit, I often fear that she is lost to us forever."

Rodan did not answer. The mere thought brought him nothing but sorrow.

"Come now, young one," Janosh smiled encouragingly. "Let us not dwell too much on the past."

He gripped his sword steadily with both hands and took up a defensive stance.

"Your move, Rodan."

Rodan smiled, pleased to have his mind pulled back from the depths of melancholy to more exciting matters. He bent both his knees, lowering his center of gravity, holding his sword off to one side in both hands, twisting his body to hide his intensions. Without warning, he pushed off from the ground, jumping an inhumanly-high five meters into the air, simultaneously whirling his blade into a downward spiral.

Ambassador Janosh grinned, deftly spinning his sword with a quick flick of his wrist so that it was raised parallel with his head. As the two weapons met, a shower of sparks lit up the room. It was as if time had frozen momentarily as Rodan hung in the air, the two blades grinding against one another.

The ambassador let go of his weapon with one hand, clenching each of his free fingers except his index finger. With one swift gesture, Rodan was sent flying backwards through the air, crashing into the shimmering force field that shielded the chamber some twenty meters away.

The old man twirled his blade a full circle before sending it back smoothly into its sheath. Rodan Reluctantly stood up from the floor, sword in one hand and the other rubbing his bruised lower back.

"How did you know?" he demanded.

Ambassador Janosh simply smiled as he paced slowly over to his disciple.

"When you fight, you must guard not only your physical self, but your thoughts as well," he chuckled. "You may think the conflict to be that of the body, yet the mind will always reveal your intentions if you do not keep it guarded."

"You read my thoughts?" Rodan was outraged. "Is that not dishonorable?"

"Honor is a double-edged sword. You must be prepared to fight your opponent on all fronts. Just because you have honor that does not mean that your opponent does as well. A life of honor is one of the highest ideals laid out before us by our beloved Gaia. Honor can prevent battles, but once you are on the field, honor is the rope around your neck by which you can hang."

"Yes Master," Rodan consented reluctantly.

He understood the meaning behind the ambassador's words, but he couldn't help but feel as if the older man had taken certain liberties with his interpretation of Gaia's wisdom. To Rodan, honor was the highest ideal anyone could strive for. Be it in life or on the field of battle, he would rather die pursuing honor than live a life of shame.

"Leave me to my thoughts now," the ambassador ordered. "I must prepare myself for the meeting with the Council."

"May Gaia be with you," Rodan offered, bowing once more in respect before quietly exciting the chamber.

* * * * *

The Council Hall of the Etheran Alliance resembled a gargantuan cathedral spire, its walls tapering steeply upwards in stages until they joined at the top, forming a steeple some eighty meters above its rectangular floor. Its narrow front and back walls consisted of polished black stone blocks, pierced by clear blue crystalline windows. The tapering roof of the chamber above was made of a shimmering white alloy, supported by broad curving metal girders, each of which was emblazoned with a tapestry of ornate runes.

It was built atop a towering square onyx structure, with cylindrical towers perched at every corner. The whole spire was over a kilometer in height, and was the heart of Etheran bureaucracy. Hundreds of drones swarmed its perimeter, monitoring everything that transpired. The top of the tower contained a plethora of landing bays for the hovercraft of visiting diplomats, squares and gardens for leisurely walks ideal for private political discussion, and regiments of statues and fountains in honor of the Etherium's most revered and historic members. The Council Hall was the centre of the tower, and the pinnacle of Semeh'yone's political scene.

Three tall, arching windows towered over the raised platform near the far end of the Hall, the central window slightly taller than the others. Three sets of steps led up to a perfectly plain but flawless throne of solid granite, the back of which rose over a dozen meters into the air. On each side of the throne hung three sets of white banners, which draped all the way from the ceiling to the floor, bearing the emblem of the Etherium alliance: the insignia of the Hiodan formed its base, the mirrored 'k's joined at the bottom and encircled by twin rings and a circle of stars. Hovering over the center of the chamber's polished stone floor was a chaotic grouping of glowing crystals, which bathed the hall in brilliant azure hues.

On each side of the path leading from the chamber's grand entrance, all the way to the steps before the throne, over two hundred broad-chested, long-limbed Etheran Guard stood watch. The elite Hiodan soldiers all stood over two meters tall, as was common for their race, and wore ornate silver armor, segmented to resemble muscle tissue, which seemed to bend and reshape itself as it adjusted with their movements. An arrow shaped from a vibrantly-glowing crystal hung on a silver necklace around each of their necks. The low-slung visor on their gleaming helmets tilted up and around the side to form horns which stood up at the back of their heads. A red cape flowed from one shoulder, connected to the waist on the other side. Each held a ceremonial spear more than twice their own height, which they tilted forward, towards the opposing line of troops.

On the throne itself sat the Shitoru, the highest figure in the Hiodan hierarchy, clad from head to toe in a suit of ceremonial armor that glowed so brightly that a petitioner couldn't help but avert their gaze in his presence. Like most Hiodan headgear, the helmet's faceplate completely obscured the Shitoru's features, but was surrounded by a crescent of metal that swept up from beneath the wearer's chin to tower into delicate points on either side of the helmet's domed crown. A long flowing red cape cascaded down the sides of the throne and rose sharply as if suspended in thin air, forming a pair of enormous draconic wings which writhed faintly without visible cause, the immense power of the Hiodan so supreme that his mere presence distorted the very air surrounding him.

Four tiers of balconies overlooked the central floor of the hall, separated into segregated booths for each of the councilors and their emissaries. There were hundreds of them, completely covering the full height and length of each of the hall's long walls, each one housing the representatives of a race in the Etheran alliance.

His back straight as he stood at the balustrade of the Gaian box, Ambassador Janosh was the picture of defiance as he bore his case before the council.

"We, the Children of Gaia, demand the immediate classification of the Terrans as a separate people, subject to their own hearings, their own pleas," he contested, his holographic representation towering

215

over the central hall and his booming voice echoing throughout the chamber. "The privileges afforded to the Children of Gaia have been earned through years of honourable abidance by the spirit and the letter of the law of the Etherium, as well as outright service in the cause of this alliance. To suggest that these benefits should apply also to the Terrans is ludicrous. They must earn their own place in the Etherium, not inherit ours."

The hologram shifted abruptly to that of Councilor Noga Zhad, the representative of the Eremaran race. His slithering tail section flopped back and forth as he shifted his gaze around the hall.

"The Eremara find it disturbing that you, of all people, would shun those who so obviously belong to you," came the interpretation from the speakers in Ambassador Janosh's booth.

Noga Zhad's visage evaporated in a cloud of smoke as it was replaced with that of councilor Yusol Sulomo, a cephalopod with long flowing tentacles and eyes that took up nearly a fifth of its entire body.

"The Gelvein find this preposterous," its thundering voice shaking the ambassador's stall. "With the Moloukan Empire knocking on our doorsteps, you squabble over internal matters which are of little or no consequence. The Etherium needs to focus on reinforcing the front lines."

The image shifted once more, this time to Councilor Rasha Ke Nahn, a muscular reptilian humanoid with a wide, gaping maw lined with sharp teeth. A nasty scar cut clear through his upper and lower lips on one side of his face, causing his mouth to sag partially open.

"The Nerokan houses agree. We must send more ships to the line. The war with the Moloukan Empire has gone on long enough! It is time we crush our enemies once and for all."

Ambassador Janosh cringed at this turn of events. It was all he could do not to let his rage burst out. After a moment he reined in his anger and rose from his seat, causing the hologram to once more change to his image.

"The war is not the topic of discussion," he snapped. "We may not have been a part of this Council for as long as some of you, but the Children of Gaia have served this alliance with grace, honor and dignity. We deserve to be heard."

His statement resulted in a cacophony of murmurs from all over the chamber, drawing wide-eyed looks from most of the other races. The holographic image faded to that of Councilor Noss Def, a long-faced, slender humanoid with a flat, conical head and large black reflective eyes, cold and inhuman.

"The Zillari agree with the Representative of Gaia. Matters of war are not on the current agenda."

Somewhere in the distance, a fist slammed onto a hard surface, calling forth the holographic image of Councilor Rasha Ke Nahn once more.

"I find it humorous that you, of all of us, would shy away from discussion of the war, what with Zentilla so close to the Moloukan territories! But then, it is well known that your people cater to both the Moloukan Empire and the Mor'row Legion. You cower in fear like herds of Lonwippi, waiting to be culled!"

"That accusation is an outrage!" Noss Def shrieked, throwing up a long-fingered hand to point at the distant Nerokan. "Zentilla merely offers a neutral ground for the Moloukans and the Mor'rowians to settle their disputes without bloodshed. To insinuate that we owe our allegiance to anyone other than the Etherium is a grave insult!"

The hologram phased to the suited image of Kai Käraian, the Hiodan councilor and aid to the Shitoru.

"Calm yourselves. This is not the place for wild accusations. We have come to discuss the status of the Terran newcomers in relation to the Gaian people."

"That is a pitiful diversion," the Nerokan councilor thundered. "The Moloukan threat has gone unchecked for far too long! It is time we commit our full forces to the front."

Kai Käraian appeared once more, shaking his head in disbelief.

"With all our forces on the line, the Rizen Cluster would be vulnerable to attack from the Sereni Sanctum. The Moloukans outnumber our forces ten to one! It is a war that will not be easily won, if at all. To fully commit ourselves to it would be suicide."

Ambassador Janosh was growing weary of all the bickering. He had known beforehand that arguing his cause would be difficult, but he had hoped at least that the Council would evaluate his case with more diligence.

"Councilors, I believe firmly that there is no one amongst us who does not truly see the threat that the Moloukan Empire imposes upon us. Yet, lest I digress, the Terrans are a threat of a different sort. Their corruption, their immorality, will infect the very core of the Etherium. To propose that they share a seat on the council with the Gaian people would open a door which I fear may never be closed again." He raised his voice, allowing his passion to show. "I know, Councilors, that many of you find the Children of Gaia's stance on morals and ethics sermonizing, even pompous, but the Etherium, when all is said and done, runs on our promises, the strength of our word. When we promise to support each other, we keep those promises, promises of military, financial and political aid and support. The Terrans, however, would *not* keep such promises. They would leave us overextended, vulnerable, isolated, if they had the chance to make

218

even minor, short-term gains, even at the expense of their friends. Are these the sort of allies you would bring into the Etherium? Are these the sort of morals you would have us take as the basis of our alliance? Councilors, I sincerely hope not."

Fearfully, he retreated back to his seat, afraid that his plea had fallen on deaf ears.

"This is a sensitive matter, one not to be taken lightly," Councilor Kai Käraian declared. "I do not believe a verdict can be reached on this matter at such short a notice. We require more time to evaluate the Terrans, proof that your words hold weight. I recommend that we reconvene at a later time and revisit the matter."

With that, Ambassador Janosh rose to his feet. With his temper beginning to flare, he chose to leave rather than suffer through the remainder of the session.

Chapter 28

The security station was small and cramped, consisting of a series of rooms, the largest of which was the control center. Rows of computer consoles lined the walls, with lights in every color of the spectrum blinking periodically. Marcus couldn't make heads or tails of all the alien symbols on the ranks of computer interfaces.

The Hrūll operator had surrendered immediately when they'd stormed through the entrance, looking on in expressionless silence as the squad had brought the guard leader in to dress his wounds. Despite his alien anatomy, Doc Taylor had managed stop the flow of blood from his stump.

"Where are the captives?" Captain Mitchell demanded, his sidearm aimed straight at the Hrūll commander's head.

As soon as he had assured himself that the Hrūll wasn't going to bleed to death from the injury Jago had inflicted, Taylor focused his attention on the huge clone's gaping shoulder wound.

"Captive?" the wounded alien moaned with his limited grasp of the Gaian language.

Marcus ran over to help the medic to help remove the behemoth's chest and shoulder plating.

"The prisoners you took when you commandeered this base," Captain Mitchell reiterated. "Where are they?"

Taylor reached for his first aid kit as Marcus tore through Jago's shirt. The towering giant didn't even flinch as the Doc began poking and prodding the wound in order to assess the damage. Blood flowed freely down his shoulder onto his heaving chest at first, but it gradually began to subside.

"I understand not," the Hrŭll sniveled.

"The prisoners!" Mitchell spat out. "Where are they?"

Taylor began pouring a dark, viscous sterilizing agent over Jago's wound.

The Ape bit his lip to stop himself screaming.

"No prisoner," the wounded alien persisted. "We make gas only."

Marcus kept supporting Jago as the medic produced another vial, this one containing a clear liquid to clean the wound with before it could be sewn shut. As Taylor poured the contents over the sterilizing goo and began to wipe away the resulting concoction with a piece of gauze, he was amazed to see the wound beginning to seal itself before his very eyes. Although he'd seen it before, with the Ape's bullet wounds on Strom, it was still a miraculous sight. None of them had been able to use their powers since departing the Terran solar system, and they had all begun to doubt whether they ever would again.

Marcus felt both relieved and concerned at the same time. He had just started to feel normal. Even out here, so far away from home, he had been feeling a semblance of normalcy. However, with the return of Jago's regenerative abilities, he was reminded once more of the terrible ordeals they'd been through. Whatever their origins, their abilities had come at a high price.

"Why the hell can't I do that?" Reid complained, clutching his knee as he stared at the small scar on Jago's shoulder, all that was left from the gaping wound that had bled all over the Doc's hands mere moments before.

"What do you mean, 'no prisoners'?" Mitchell raged, losing his patience. "You took this refinery from the Sheshen and you're holding

221

them captive! We demand that you release them immediately!"

The perplexed tone in the guard leader's voice was unmistakable. "This is Hrūll station. Always Hrūll station," he said. "No Sheshen."

Captain Mitchell wasn't one to give in so easily. If his captive refused to give him the answers he needed, he would have to take them from him by force. He laid his hand upon the alien's forehead, drawing wide-eyed stares from the others as he focused his mind, reaching out to pierce through his opponent's will. To his surprise, the task was far less difficult than he had envisioned, though the thoughts he began to see were much more muddled than those of any human he'd read, and required some degree of interpretation. It was as if he were seeing them through a slick of oil.

"I think we've been had," Taz declared from the sidelines.

"Shhh," Marcus whispered, not wanting to disturb the captain.

Mitchell continued to sift through the Hrūll's memories, but the more he saw, the more he became convinced that the alien was telling the truth, and that this had only ever been a Hrūll-run refinery. After a brief stint, he removed his hand from the alien's forehead, a grave expression on his face.

"Why the hell would anyone send us all the way out here if there's no one to be-" Mitchell began to say, but stopped suddenly, as if struck by a sudden revelation. "We have to get out of here," he cried, visibly distressed by his epiphany.

"What is it, Sir?" Marcus asked.

"It's a trap! Get everyone back to the ship," he ordered, turning quickly to the wounded Hrūll leader.

"Does this base have escape pods?" he demanded. "Escape pods, in case of emergency?"

The Hrūll croaked an affirmative answer, looking at the computer operator for reassurance.

"Get everyone to the pods. Now!" the captain yelled. "Something very bad is about to happen to this base. Get your people away as fast as you can!"

With that, he urged his team out of the security station, rushing them back towards the docking bay where the *Tengri* lay in wait.

* * * * *

The assault team stormed through the forward airlock, Mitchell already shouting over the comms for Raven to fire up the ship's engines and get the ship out of the docking bay as soon as humanly possible.

"I can't believe you took that," Marcus scowled, gesturing to the massive laser cannon that Jago had appropriated on their run back to the docking bay.

Jago shrugged his shoulders in response.

"He won't need it," Jago grunted. "Needs two hands to shoot."

The familiar hum of the *Tengri*'s engines coming online alerted them that the ship was about to depart. They sealed the airlock and dashed straight for the observation deck.

* * * * *

Marcus stared through the window at the Hrūll gas refinery. The atmosphere on the observation deck was tense, loaded with anticipation. The rest of the assault team had gathered to monitor the proceedings, not sure what to expect. Marcus felt wrought with guilt. They had torn through the station, firing upon everything that moved, for no good reason! The image of the unarmed technician stung the most. Although he hadn't personally pulled the trigger, the guilt was still his to bear. It was his fireteam, his command.

Suddenly a blinding flash of light blew through the underbelly of the gas refinery. A massive jet of flaming gas spewed from the ruptured tank, slowly sending the station into a spiral. In a matter of seconds, the fire spread to the remaining tanks, causing a chain reaction of catastrophic explosions which quickly engulfed the entire refinery. Marcus wasn't sure, but he though he saw two small escape pods silhouetted against the fiery inferno. Then again, for all he knew, it could have been nothing more than debris.

What made it worse was that with no other means of returning to Semeh'yone station, they were forced to return to the Sheshen freighter. As they set course for the rendezvous point, Marcus felt so ashamed. They had been used as pawns in a sick game of rivalry between the Sheshen and the Hrüll. Although he was desperate to seek revenge for what they'd been made to do in the name of the Sheshen, he knew that he would have to hold his tongue when he met Roshana, or the whole crew of the *Tengri* could pay for it.

They were at an impasse. Their existence relied on the Sheshen vessel bringing them back to Semeh'yone station. They'd made a deal with the devil and there was no turning back now.

*　*　*　*　*

The dark, foreboding hull of the Sheshen freighter slipped into view. Desperate to call Roshana for his lies and bloody deception, Captain Mitchell ordered Navigator Wei to establish communications.

"Ah, Captain Mitccchell. I am ssso pleasssed that you were able to complete your missssion," the shrill voice of Roshana hissed over the ship's comms.

"Cut the crap," Captain Mitchell snapped. "You used us and you know it!"

"Ssshould I take it that you no longer want your reward?" Roshana snickered softly.

Mitchell glared at the Sheshen freighter, half hoping that his anger would set it aflame.

"If that will be all, then I sssuggest you dock, ssso we can procccceed to Nos Ssshana," Roshana sneered. "I have confirmation that your new engine isss ready to be inssstalled."

"Fine," Mitchell snapped, his brow twitching with rage.

"You did well Captain," Roshana smirked. "Much better than I-"

His message was cut short as the captain cut the communication off.

Having striven against corruption and abuse of power in his work for C-CORE back on Beta Terra, there was nothing that Mitchell liked less than being used.

As the *Tengri* slid back into the gaping black hole of the freighter's docking bay, he palmed a fresh pair of painkillers and threw them down his throat, all the while rubbing his aching knee.

Chapter 29

The journey to Nos Shana was far shorter than the crew had anticipated. After only a few short days of milling around on the *Tengri*, a short burst of disorientation and nausea told them they'd arrived at their destination. Shortly afterwards, one of Roshana's subordinates informed them in broken Terran that the *Mitushi Nalphalo*'s cargo bay doors would soon open, and the Terrans were to bring their ship to a designated shipyard on the surface of the planet below. Captain Mitchell cut of the comms with a snarl as soon as the masked underling had stopped speaking. As they undocked from the Sheshen freighter, still without a word to their host, Navigator Wei input their landing coordinates into the ship's computer.

Marcus was sitting at a table in the *Tengri*'s galley, enjoying a drink with Serena as they observed the scene unfolding before them. A massive dreadnaught kept watch over the busy space lanes above the Sheshen home planet, its sleek, shadowy form easily dwarfing any of the approaching ships. A small dogfight off the *Tengri*'s starboard bow drew their attention. A pair of streamlined fighters had teamed up against a clunky freighter, picking off her primary systems one by one with strategically-placed shots as the agile smaller ships looped around the clumsy cargo hauler. A sudden buildup of energy in one of the dreadnaught's protruding siege cannons hinted at the impending doom awaiting one of the combatants. A few seconds later an intense beam of energy shot from the huge warship's weapon, ripping the helpless freighter apart.

The *Tengri* swung around on a course towards the planet's surface, sliding past countless holographic billboards floating lazily amidst the lanes of traffic, displaying images of exotic drinking containers and scantily clad females of all species. Nos Shana itself drew nearer, its form shrouded in an iridescent green mist, only a few mountain ranges jutting up from the enveloping clouds, specks of black rock on an otherwise engulfed world. The system's orange sun set the planet's horizon ablaze with sickly golden tendrils. As the *Tengri* began her descent, cleaving into the thick layer of clouds, a brilliant network of lights came into view.

"How are your language studies coming along?" Marcus asked Serena, attempting to steer their conversation away from recent events.

"Well," she feigned a smile. "I've hardly left my room these past few days. Not much else to do with my time."

"You should teach the crew," Marcus suggested. "If we are to survive out here, we'd all better learn the language."

"There's more than one," she smiled. "Sheshen's probably not the most useful if we're going back to Semeh'yone."

Marcus smiled shyly back at her. He really had taken to the slender linguist, and not only due to her dark, smooth hair and dark eyes, but also – mostly – due to her compassionate nature. He found her empathy deeply touching, not to the soldier he was bred to be, but to his core being, his very soul.

The network of lights below them transformed into a towering cityscape of decrepit slabs of steel, glass and concrete, most of which loomed over still-thicker banks of swirling green fumes. Shimmering force fields kept the mist at bay, sealing off certain districts of the city from the planet's open atmosphere. A vast network of walkways and platforms dotted the skyline above the mist, teaming with life. It was early evening, yet the splendor of the city's neon lights and holographic projectors filled the city with a permeating glow, tinged a yellowy-green by the ever-present mist.

"They call it Sheijan," she informed him, "the city. It's their capital."

They cruised past an enormous slow-moving cruise liner on a departure course. Through its massive windows, Marcus could see the silhouettes of its occupants as they drank, dined and danced the night away.

The *Tengri* swerved towards a series of open platforms a short distance from the city's center. Marcus felt the familiar rumblings of the docking thrusters firing in rapid succession. As he looked at the decaying structures rising up to engulf the ship, he hoped their stay would not be a long one.

* * * * *

When the *Tengri* landed in one of the narrow, high-walled compounds that comprised the shipyard, Captain Mitchell led the contact team to the airlock, where they were joined seconds later by Raven, who was apparently only willing to leave the ship long enough to ensure that the refit would proceed properly. They were greeted by three dock workers, all of whom, to their surprise, were Banthalo, the same race Rodan had warned them about outside the gang-run bath house on Semeh'yone. A rank odor accompanied the aliens' presence. They were an odd bunch, one was missing a hand, another an ear. Their skin tones were as different as those of humans, ranging from a deep brown to yellow and greenish hues, fitting the ambiance of Nos Shana. Their black reflective eyes, sat beneath a protruding brow, studied them carefully for any signs of malice. Hovering off to the side of the sullen workers was a spherical drone the size of a human head with a range of antennae jutting from its shell, and a focal lens set into its front.

"Sheijan ventosso kar," the Banthalo with the missing ear grunted in its guttural tongue, and the hovering drone immediately began to interpret its words.

"Welcome to Sheijan," it recited in a dreary, monotonous voice.

"Well, that's handy," Doc Taylor noted, eyeing the drone.

"We should get one of those!" Taz blurted without thinking, drawing a concerned glance from Serena, who wasn't too thrilled about the possibility of being replaced by a drone.

"Where's Roshana?" Captain Mitchell demanded, thinking it high time the two of them had a serious discussion.

"Roshana serequie chemo," the drone recited, only to receive puzzled looks from the group of Banthalo.

"Roshana's presence is not required," the drone began to interpret their response. "You are instructed to leave the ship while we tend to the installation process."

"Leave the ship?" Raven flared. "For how long?"

"Seven day cycles," the drone explained.

"Captain, there's no way we're leaving the *Tengri* with these... things for a whole week without supervision!" Raven yelled.

"Agreed," Mitchell said, turning to face the Banthalo once more. "We wish to monitor the installation."

"Nez ceptakisollo," the earless one mumbled.

"Unacceptable," came the reply from the interpreter drone.

"Captain, I don't trust them," Raven grabbed his arm, lowering her voice. "More importantly, I don't trust Roshana. For all we know he could plant a bomb on our ship."

"I'll handle this," Captain Mitchell assured her, and looked the central Banthalo in the eye as he spoke. "We demand to speak with Roshana."

The Banthalo seemed displeased with their response, but the earless one produced a small piece of handheld gadgetry and proceeded to point it at the interpreter drone. The two groups stood in silence for a few moments, before the drone's focusing lens began to glow and then emitted a conical beam of orange light which slowly began to take on shape.

"My dear Captain," came Roshana's shrill voice, as the holographic image began to take on his shape. "To what do I owe the pleasssure?"

"You know damned well I'm not leaving my ship unattended while you gut her and do God knows what to her systems," Captain Mitchell boomed.

"Such distressss," Roshana sneered. "I assssure you, Captain, there isss nothing sssinister here."

"I've heard that before," Mitchell snapped. "I demand that my chief engineer be allowed to supervise the installation."

"I am afraid that isss not posssssible, Captain," Roshana countered. "You will sssimply have to ssshow sssome faith."

"Faith!" Raven burst out. "You piece of sh-"

"Raven!" the captain cut her off, shooting her a commanding stare.

"If our termsss are not to your liking, Captain," Roshana continued, "you are free to sssseek alternative transsssportation off Nos Ssshana. However, you've proved your usefulnesss to usss and whatever you think of the… sssserviccce you performed for usss, we are more than willing to pay the priccce agreed."

With that, the holographic image promptly vanished.

"I curse the day I ever met that infernal cunt," Captain Mitchell moaned.

"As do I," Serena agreed.

Realizing their dilemma, Mitchell was left with no choice but to leave the *Tengri* in the hands of the Banthalo workers.

An hour later, the crew was assembled on the platform, most of them clutching rucksacks and small cases of personal effects and vital equipment. Before they left, the worker with the missing hand gave directions to affordable accommodation before speeding them on their way.

Emerging from the walled-off complex that housed their docking platform, the crew saw the streets of Sheijan with their own eyes for the first time. Unlike the dense, compacted sprawl of Semeh'yone's New Arrivals' Zone, Sheijan was a far more vertical city, and more spacious too. Where the New Arrivals' Zone had clearly tried to make use of every available meter of deckspace, the Sheshen city 'streets' were really concourses, bridges and walkways slung between the upper levels of the towering spires that soared overhead, hanging safely above the greenish mist of the atmosphere below. Between the pitted, crumbling towers, beggars rummaged through the filthy walkways, armed mercenaries bore their weapons openly as loud music spilled out into the streets from a variety of shady establishments, some carved into the ancient buildings, others crouched awkwardly on the concourses themselves, and peddlers sold their ill-gotten wares at every turn. Beggars slept in the streets beneath stained blankets, cowering in fear at each passerby. Alien vermin scrambled for food near the heating vents, competing with the dispossessed for whatever morsels they could find. Marcus even saw a bored-looking, half-naked violet-skinned female fornicating with a male of her race in the middle of a suspended square. Sheijan seemed to be a veritable haven for cutthroats, lowlifes and the destitute.

Fortunately the establishment they had been directed to was not too far from the docking platform, which sat atop a truncated tower, leaving little need to wander through the rancid streets for too long.

As they approached the hotel, Marcus became quite aware that they were drawing a lot of stares from the city's inhabitants. It was the first time since the customs inspection on Semeh'yone that the whole crew had left the *Tengri* together, but their numbers did little to lessen the nervousness that was rapidly building up among them as they traversed the dilapidated city, and peaked when they saw that the hotel sat on a run-down platform, enveloping a small square, its buildings incorporating a massage parlor and a sleazy diner.

"Is this really the best we can afford?" Taz let out, visibly disgusted with the scenery.

"We don't know how far we can stretch the funds we were given on Semion," Captain Mitchell warned them. "We have to use them sparingly."

Marcus peered over the handrail of the walkway, staring into the depths. Dark shadows crept along a series of intersecting catwalks, stairways and scaffolds that disappeared into the abyss below. Screams of agony and despair could be heard faintly in the distance. As grim as things looked to be on the 'surface' of Sheijan, Marcus shuddered at the thought of what lurked beneath.

The captain instructed the crew to await his return while he entered the hotel in hopes of securing accommodation. He brought with him only Serena and Jago, Serena for interpretation and Jago for his intimidating demeanor in case things went sour, or to offer a better position for bargaining. The rest of the crew waited outside under the watchful eyes of Marcus and the other clones, armed and armored against the dangers of the city.

"How about you and me share a room?" Taz whispered to Liana Tinley, the crew's technician.

She was a shy, boyish-looking woman who looked several years older than the clones' apparent age, with short strawberry-blonde hair, a button nose and pale green eyes that seemed to water every time someone met her gaze. Marcus hadn't paid her much attention, most likely owing to her shyness and apparent disinterest in socializing with the cloned soldiers.

Her response to Taz's advance was one of silent retreat as she repositioned herself further away from their womanizing scout.

"Bah, a week in this hell hole?" Taz moaned. "Somebody shoot me now."

"Don't tempt me," Liana muttered under her breath, drawing a light chuckle from Reid, who'd overheard her.

"At least we got to keep our weapons," Taz consoled himself. "I wouldn't want to walk around these streets unarmed."

It wasn't long before Captain Mitchell and the others appeared in the doorway, gesturing for the crew to join them.

* * * * *

To save money, the captain had negotiated shared rooms for most of the crew. Marcus was assigned one with Reid, Taz and Doc Taylor. It was a dingy little chamber, barely large enough to hold a pair of bunk beds. A tiny window on the far wall had been shoddily painted over with a dark, grimy substance, so the only source of light was a thin strip of luminous panels which lined the walls near the ceiling.

"I don't even want to know what that bed's been used for," Taz joked, looking at the none-too-clean blankets.

"At least it's seen more action than your cot on the *Tengri* ever will," Reid teased him, heaving himself onto the lower bunk opposite with a groan.

"We should really find a proper doctor for that leg," Taylor said, kneeling to examine Reid's wound.

The medic had bandaged it as best he could, but the blast had seared all the way through to the bone. Luckily the wound had been cauterized, but there was still the risk of infection and the leg was essentially useless, not to mention the fact that Reid was too reliant on painkillers to be able to function at all.

Dr. Gehringer had offered to attempt to replace the damaged muscles and sinews with cloned tissue, but given the lengthy growth rate and the risk involved with such an operation, perhaps another alternative would prove to be more promising.

"In this place?" the sniper complained. "I don't think they're up to speed on Terran physiology."

"But they might be on *Gaian* physiology," Taylor pointed out. "We still don't know who the Gaians, are or how long they've been a part of… all of this. With luck there might be someone here who can help."

Reid paused to weigh the alternatives. Being left without the use of his leg meant he was forced to steady himself with a crutch or rely on one of the others for support, rendering him pretty much useless.

"It's worth a shot," Marcus agreed.

"Tomorrow," Reid persisted. "Right now I just want to get some rest."

That night they lay on soiled bed sheets, stained with the countless visits of questionable patrons. Taz and Reid were quick to surrender themselves to sleep, leaving Marcus and the Doc alone with their thoughts. Neither of them had much to say to one another as they lay in the half-light of the filthy room. Taylor was too busy inhaling a steady stream of cigarettes and Marcus was still too wrought with the guilt of their last endeavor.

"How many of those did you bring?" Marcus finally asked him, puncturing the awkward silence.

"What, these?" the medic asked, holding his up lit cigarette. "I've got enough."

"Hmmm," Marcus sighed, not particularly pleased to hear that he would continue to be subjected to the medic's unpleasant cloud of smoke.

He stared in silence at the rusted metal ceiling plates. Condensation gathered around the edges, forming small droplets which, every so often, would plummet down to the floor below. He realized that despite all their hopes and dreams, that's all they were. Droplets of water, just waiting for their time to fall.

Chapter 30

Having been ferried offworld from Beta Terra under a veil of secrecy, the assembled dignitaries were led through the station by an envoy of armed guards. The air was dry and stale, but that was to be expected aboard an orbital complex. Somewhere at the edge of the vast network of intertwining corridors, a massive airlock sealed shut with enough force to send a small tremor throughout the corridor.

The guards wore black hard-shell vests, padded arm- and leg-guards and black reflective visors that covered their faces from brow to chin. Though the armed men carried no discernible markings to indicate their origins or rank, each of the new arrivals – except perhaps the youngest – knew who they were, and why they, some of Terran society's most powerful and influential figures, had been brought there.

Pipes and wiring lay exposed along the side walls of the corridors, and the dim lighting did little to lessen their unease at the sudden nature of their summons. Still, it showed that this was a station with a functional purpose that didn't include catering to high-ranking visitors.

They were led down what appeared to be a wide central corridor, their shoes clanking on the rough metal grate underfoot. A stale, warm breeze seemed to permeate the area, randomly changing direction every so often as they passed vents or smaller branching corridors.

"I must admit, I'm surprised to find you here, Ms. Muromoto,"

Leicester Amorosa commented to the small, dark woman as he heaved slightly from the brisk pace, "Especially given the sensitive nature of this... project... and your father's connection to C-CORE."

"I'm afraid I can't say the same for you, Amorosa," Mariko countered with a devilish smile. "I always knew you for the conniving, manipulative bastard you truly are."

Leicester chuckled. It hadn't been often that he'd encountered someone he considered his equal in the corporate arena, and it had been even less often that such figures were women, but he had been monitoring Mariko's recent exploits quite carefully. Her sudden rise within the Muromoto Group, coupled with her appearance aboard this station, meant she was indeed every bit as ruthless as he had suspected.

"What is all this?" bellowed the youngest of the three. Unlike the others, Ellis had inherited his involvement in the project following his father's sudden passing, and it seemed that no one had been willing or able to answer his questions. "I demand you tell me why you've had me brought here!"

The guards didn't so much as hesitate on hearing his outburst, but continued leading them along yet another lengthy corridor, much the same as the ones before.

"You're Benedikt's son, aren't you?" Leicester asked the youth after a moment of awkward silence, slightly puzzled. "I was sorry to hear about your father. He was a great man."

Ellis' reply was a scornful look, one that made it clear he didn't want to hear any further mention of his father, his death, or his accomplishments.

"The Bauer boy?" Mariko chuckled in disbelief. "Here?"

"Can you tell me what this is all about?" Ellis asked. "These morons seem to have lost their tongues."

Their escorts refused to react beyond a stiffening of their shoulders, having been instructed to have no interaction with the new arrivals save to escort them to their destination.

"I think you'll have to wait," Mariko replied. "What little we know won't do you much good. Besides, I think they will want to tell you themselves."

"TELL ME!" the youth raged, losing what little self control he had left.

"Now, now, Mr. Bauer. There's no reason to cause a stir. Besides, knowing would spoil the fun," echoed a crackling voice over the station's intercom.

The dignitaries stopped abruptly, eyeing one another in concern.

"Move along," one of the guards urged, ushering them further into the complex.

A short while later, the corridor widened to reveal a set of double-wide, heavily-fortified doors. A security detail of a dozen men armed with carbines stepped aside to allow them entry. With a series of clanks and whirring sounds, the door ground open, revealing a platform overlooking an enormous cylindrical chamber which ran the entire length of the station. Inside, the TFS-*Genesis*, Captain Intari's battleship, lay berthed beside a lone frigate, dwarfing it several times over in size.

The *Genesis* was shaped much like an elongated locomotive, easily four hundred meters in length and sporting nearly a dozen decks. It towered over them, a dark and twisted block of metal. The sharp outline of its silhouette was broken above and below by the bulges of extra decks and a pair of short, thick towers that clustered towards the rear of its length. The overall shape reminded Mariko of an absurdly large assault rifle, lined with massive segmented hull plating.

Next to the huge warship, the small, twenty-meter frigate was a polished white color and could easily have fit inside the Genesis' cargo bay. Its cylindrical core was only two decks thick for most of its length, bulging above along its rearmost third and at the over-and-under block of its engines at the rear. A veritable swarm of technicians and scientist hovered about on walkways and bridges which spanned the width of the chamber, tending to both ships in a flurry of frantic activity.

On the viewing platform stood their reception party, a small group of Division 6's notables, including the gaunt Captain Intari, the diminutive Dr. Reisner, and the unexpected presence of Senator Yoishi Tomiko. The Senator, a balding middle-aged man with slanting eyes, stood at the forefront of the group, hands held wide to bid them welcome. He wore a grey suit with an almost satin finish and a plain black tie, his disingenuous smile belying his devious nature.

"Almost nine years ago," he began as the three new arrivals came to an uneasy stop just inside the huge hatch, "you were approached with a unique opportunity, a chance to help lead Terra into the future. Although in your case," the senator looked to Ellis, "it is your father's legacy which has brought you here."

The senator cleared his throat as he gestured for Dr. Reisner to prepare for the demonstration.

"I must apologize for having brought you here with such little notice," he continued. "A minor inconvenience, I hope. But it is time that we demonstrate what your considerable investments have helped to create."

In the background, Dr. Reisner had produced his datapad and was entering an activation sequence, turning to inspect the small frigate docked alongside the *Genesis*. A series of tubes and cables began to detach from the frigate's hull, sending billows of steam into the air.

"I should make it clear to all of you that what you are about to witness must kept in the strictest confidence," Senator Yoishi warned, "lest you discover that all of your combined wealth and power is insignificant when compared to the unshakable will of Division 6!"

With that, the Senator turned to face the frigate, whose engines began powering up. At the end of the enormous cylindrical chamber a massive airlock began to open, causing a brief flash of terror across the faces of the new arrivals as they half expected to be sucked into space, along with everyone else present. Instead, they were startled to see a shimmering barrier of pale azure light filling the gap between them and the abyssal void.

The sound from the frigate's engines began gaining in pitch, the sapphire flames spewing from its thrusters flaring intensely. A brief moment later it had vanished, hurled into space at such a speed as to defy all reason, leaving behind only a fading trail of light and the thunderous applause of everyone present.

Chapter 31

On the day following their arrival the crew lay sequestered in their rooms, suffering the tedium of boredom and tormented by the horrid stench that seemed to permeate the entire building. As usual, Taz was the first to begin urging the captain to allow them to go out exploring, despite the apparent dangers, but it didn't take long for the Ape to chime in as well.

"I can keep him safe, boss," he'd muttered, much to the captain's annoyance.

"Did you two not walk through the same city as the rest of us yesterday?" Mitchell snapped at them.

"We're soldiers, Captain," Taz whined. "It's not as if we haven't seen worse, and it's not like we'd be going out unarmed."

Mitchell wasn't about to give in so easily, but over the course of the morning more and more crewmembers joined their incessant whining, and by mid-afternoon he had eventually agreed to grant them permission to go out so long as they stayed within a hundred meters of the hotel unless otherwise instructed, travelling in groups of no less than three, with an armed member of the contact team accompanying them at all times for safety.

After consulting with the surly hotel staff – the afternoon clerk a Sheshen apparently under the influence of powerful narcotics – he doled out a small sum of their funds to each of the crew, enough to buy a drinks and perhaps a warm meal.

*   *   *   *   *

As Darryl Knoles and Emil Juey, the *Tengri*'s custodian, had wanted to venture out for a few rounds of the local brew, Taz had been appointed as their escort. At the last minute, he had managed to persuade Kaiden Karell to join them on their visit to a local watering hole.

It was a single story locale, attached to the outside of one of the city's towering skyscrapers, its walls lined with oval tables of tarnished metal. The place was half-packed with surly patrons, nearly half of whom were Banthalo. The rest were an assortment of freakish beings from all corners of the galaxy. A dimly lit bar near the back wall was being tended to by an elderly lavender-skinned male with a scrawny frame, a tall reddish Mohawk, and a nervous twitch. In the center of the room a shallow pit housed a large holographic projector which displayed a series of action-filled shots of what looked like some sort of brutal athletics competition.

The four Terrans had grabbed an empty table near the bar and Taz immediately went and bought the first round of drinks, returning with stout metallic containers filled to the brim with a fizzy, opaque orange liquid.

"I can't believe I let you talk me into coming here," Kaiden professed.

"Would you rather hang around your sleazy hotel room? Because if you would, I'd be more than willing to keep you company," Taz leered, shooting her a suggestive wink.

A roar of applause erupted, saving Kaiden from replying. The cheerers were a group of Banthalo customers on the opposite side of the bar wearing what looked like grease-stained overalls, their

242

attention fixed on the holographic display, where an intensely muscular member of their race with a missing eye had just pummeled his opponent, an emaciated contestant with four long tentacles protruding from his face, into a bloody pulp. Darryl peered at the image with great interest. It was the first time Taz had seen the gruff cook display even a fraction of interest in anything at all. The one-eyed contestant proceeded to rummage through the possessions of his hapless victim, tearing apart his clothing as if searching for something in particular. He finally stopped short as he produced a shiny medallion on a silver chain, holding it high in the air in defiance before quickly turning to scan his surroundings, apparently making sure he wasn't being watched. The muscular alien pocketed his newfound bauble and reclaimed a savage-looking serrated blade which lay next to the bloody body before scampering off.

"Charming sport," Kaiden remarked sarcastically, burying her face in her drink, which had a sweet aroma, reminding her of spiced mead.

Despite her athletic form and her interest in physical development, the curvaceous brunette was not one for acts of violence.

"I guess you'd rather have your sport with the captain," Taz jeered, catching Emil's eye in the hope of sharing a smirk, but the older man offered only an awkward smile.

"What's that supposed to mean?" Kaiden demanded, her expression fading into one of feigned disgust.

"Nothing," Taz replied sullenly. "But you can't pretend you haven't noticed how he looks at you."

"No differently than the rest of you perverts do!" Kaiden snapped.

"Well if you're not his, then what say you and me-" Taz began, but he was abruptly cut off.

"His?" Kaiden bellowed. "Did your tank on the Alamo have a glitch?

243

Because that might explain your stupidity!"

"Oh come on. You can't dress the way you do and not expect us to look!" Taz chuckled. "Prancing around in your tight little outfits. It's almost as if you want us to-"

He was again cut short, this time by an open-handed slap across the face.

"You know what, I think I'm gonna go someplace where the women are more sociable," Taz snarled. "Maybe find me one of those blue chicks."

"You can't leave," Kaiden snapped. "You're our escort!"

"The hotel is less than a hundred meters away," Taz protested as he pushed his stool back. "If you get scared you can always go crying back to the captain. I'm sure he'd like that."

He looked sternly into Kaiden's eyes for a moment before snatching up his drink, downing the rest of it in one long gulp, slamming the empty tankard on the table and storming out through the door.

"Screw him!" Kaiden burst out, slamming her drink down as well, making a mess as nearly half of it slopped onto the table.

Juey and Knoles exchanged looks in worried silence as Kaiden continued to brood.

"Why are we sitting here by ourselves?" asked Emil.

"What do you mean?" Kaiden growled.

"I mean, we should try to talk to some of these... people," he suggested, gesturing towards the group of Banthalo sports fans.

"Are you insane?" she snapped. "First of all, we don't speak their language. Second, they don't exactly look friendly."

"Oh come on," the custodian argued. "I used to do this all the time back on Sol. The big scary ones usually just want to tell tall tales about all the messed up things they've done. It's good fun."

"You can go hit on the ugly green aliens by yourself," Kaiden spat out, drawing a grin from the otherwise stern-faced cook.

"Fine, sit here by yourself and sulk," Emil conceded. "What about you Darryl? Are you scared too?"

Knoles downed his drink in one go, letting out a long belch as he got up from his chair. The odd pair navigated through the bar, timidly approaching the group of four cheering Banthalo patrons. The smallest of the four was the first to notice them. He threw his drink on the table as they drew near, spilling a fair amount of its contents over the Banthalo next to him.

"Chosey role i, junko?" the short alien growled in his guttural tongue, puffing out his chest in a sign of territorial dominance.

The Banthalo was as ugly as they came, with cracked greenish lips and raggedy ears flopping on the side of his oversized head, his squinting black eyes bearing down upon Emil, causing the Terran to avert his gaze. The thug's breath smelled like it held almost as much alcohol as an entire flask of spirits, and his tight-fitting, grease-stained clothing was covered in spilled drink.

"We Terrans," Emil attempted to explain, using hand gestures to compensate for his lack of language skills. "We… drink with you?"

The aggressive creature thrust his face within a hairsbreadth of the quivering custodian, sniffing his shirt and standing on his toes to look the Terran straight in the eye.

"U sempi gesto labronos repari lon nochi role," he sniggered to his companions as he turned back to the table, drawing a disgruntled chuckle.

The largest of the Banthalo, a hulking giant of a creature nearly the size of Jago, waved the two men over to join them before hailing the barkeep, ordering a round of drinks. Cautiously Emil and Knoles took to a pair of empty seats at the table, their backs towards the door in case they needed to leave in a hurry.

A slightly deformed specimen to their left held a large knife and was busy scraping the dirt from under his short claws. The lavender-skinned barkeep returned momentarily with a tray of shot glasses which he laid to rest at the center of the table, fidgeting as he returned to the bar.

"Repari, Gaian junko. Nochi cirtaki verti chomo i ina sono sivisaney," the large Banthalo declared, grabbing one of the glasses and raising it into the air.

The others quickly followed suit, and waited for their guests to do the same. Apprehensively, Emil and Knoles took a slight whiff before raising their glasses in turn.

"Merito ro huno," the Banthalo all shouted in unison before downing their drinks in one quick swallow, slamming the empty glasses on the table.

The two Terrans, not wanting to upset their new companions, were only slightly behind them. The clear liquid burned the inside of their throats as it slid down, leaving a bitter aftertaste. Emil cringed in disgust, but Darryl only twitched slightly. The little Banthalo cackled like a sniveling hyena at the Terrans' discomfort, looking towards the larger one for recognition.

"Ina juda rigale muardi, mapo gorre massos ile tevere," the malformed individual growled, pointing in the direction where Kaiden sat by herself in silence, eyeing them suspiciously.

"Aloro," the large one retorted, grabbing another glass from the tray.

Emil was less than enthusiastic about sampling the disgusting drink again, but felt uneasy about disappointing their hosts, and so reached out and took another glass from the still well-stocked tray. Darryl snatched a glass and swallowed his drink before everyone else, drawing nods of approval from the others.

Emil hesitantly held the glass up to his lips, closing his eyes in anticipation of the foul taste. Get it over with, he tried to persuade himself. He finally opened his mouth wide and threw back the shot, swallowing it as quickly as possible, hoping that somehow it would taste less foul than before.

Almost at once, he started screaming. His insides were on fire. His digestive tract was in excruciating agony, as if he'd swallowed a bundle of barbed wire. He nearly overturned the table as he jumped back to his feet, knocking over his chair, both hands gripping his throat in a vain attempt to quiet the insurmountable pain, but there was nothing he could do. His insides were already being dissolved by the carefully-disguised, highly-concentrated acid. As blood came rushing into his mouth, he keeled over, his vision fading as he heard the hysterical laughter from his hosts.

As Emil kicked feebly one last time and finally lay still, Knoles instinctively grabbed the knife out of the hands of the malformed Banthalo. As he rose to his feet, he pointed the heavy blade at the group, hoping to deter them as he made his escape. The Banthalos' laughter subsided, replaced by a silence filled with scornful looks and sneers. As Knoles slowly started backing up, making his way towards the exit, the largest one gave a quick flick of his hand, and they all jumped the terrified Terran at once, using their brute strength to overbear him.

The last thing Knoles saw was their leader's fist as it came crashing down on his terrified face.

*   *   *   *   *

"Come with me," whispered a soft voice from behind her while Kaiden watched, horrified, as the Banthalo jumped the retreating Knoles. "Quickly!"

It was another one of the lavender-skins, though this individual's was more of a bluish grey tone, as were his slender, human-like features. He wore an emerald cloak wrapped around his body, with a cowl hiding the top portion of his face. As he stood by Kaiden's side with his hand outstretched, she felt compelled to reach out and grab hold. Before she knew it, the two of them were racing towards the door.

"Wait, what about the others?" she gasped as they escaped to the streets.

"Your friends are already dead," the cloaked figured stated, dragging her into a nearby alley. "You should not have come here," he reprimanded as he drew back his hood, revealing a gentle face, his huge azure eyes gleaming with innocence.

He looked so human, and yet so alien at the same time. His lips were a dark shade of blue with a hint of purple, and the single strip of hair that ran along the centre of his scalp was as black as night, roughly brushed to one side. Instead of a nose, his forehead merged gradually with his lower face forming a smooth nasal ridge running all the way down to his mouth, with three pairs of slitted nostrils running its length.

"What... what happened? Why did they..." she sobbed, suddenly realizing what she'd witnessed.

"It is a game to them," her rescuer revealed. "They call it 'Brut Banthal'. A most distasteful game of chance."

"A… a game?" she stammered.

"I am saddened that luck did not favor your friend on this night," the lavender-skinned man sighed. "As for the other, he threatened them. You must never threaten a Banthalo unless numbers are in your favor. Even then, you would be wise to do so with caution."

"I hate this place! I hate this whole entire planet," she cried, wrapping her arms around her shoulders.

"You are not alone," he assured her. "This is a world where people come to test their luck. They squander away all of their wealth on games of chance, all of which are rigged. Many lose not only their credits, but their fare home as well. Now they're stuck here, indebted to one crime lord or another."

She wiped the tears from her eyes with her sleeves, thankful to have found an honest soul in a sea of villainy.

"Ever since their planet's atmosphere was bombarded with the poison which now covers its surface, the Sheshen have been fighting each other for power, each generation becoming more corrupt than the one before it. It is a sad fate."

"Could… could you escort me back to my… hotel?" Kaiden ventured, looking up nervously at her rescuer. "I don't want to be alone."

He smiled gently, reaching up to gently brush her hair from her eyes.

"How can I deny one in such pain?" he whispered, taking her hand and leading her out of the alleyway.

* * * * *

Knoles awoke to the sound of a roaring motor. His head was

throbbing with pain as he lay on the cold, uneven floor, a feeling that was deeply disconcerting as he realized that he wasn't in his warm bed. How had he ended up lying on a stone floor? As he tried to move, he found that his hands were bound in chains. His momentary confusion was quickly replaced with abject panic.

He tossed and turned, trying to wrest himself free but each tug on the chains only seemed to lessen his resolve. As his vision began to return he saw that he was lying on the floor of what appeared to be some form of large, empty storage space, a hangar or warehouse. On one side, the chain from his left wrist was bound to a thick metal pole set deeply in the floor, and on the other the chain was attached to what appeared to be a large cargo loader on heavy tracks.

He let out a brief whimper as he raised his head to look around at his surroundings. A short distance away from his feet stood the large Banthalo leader, the small cackling hyena at his side, ready to signal the driver of the vehicle that would tear him limb from limb.

"No, please!" he moaned through the pain in his head. "I'll do anything!"

"Anzari romotoros ina!" the small one shouted, giggling with excitement.

As the heavy machine began to move, Darryl let out a horrendous scream as his bones snapped like twigs and his flesh was ripped apart, spraying the ground with blood.

Chapter 32

Hundreds of booths and stalls lined the market plaza, a large circular platform near the heart of Sheijan, selling exotic wares from all corners of the galaxy. Everything from food items and small domesticated creatures to weapons, armor and even illicit drugs could be had for the right price, though most carried trinkets of little or no value.

Doc Taylor had received permission from Captain Mitchell to journey further into the city in the hope of securing a doctor capable of restoring Reid's badly damaged knee to working order. Marcus had been assigned to accompany them, as much to provide protection as to support their limping sniper. Given the importance of their assignment, Serena had been tasked to act as their interpreter.

They'd started out by acquiring the services of a hovercraft driver, who'd informed them in broken Terran that they would likely have trouble finding a healer capable of catering to their race. If they were to have any luck, he'd recommended that they travel to the busy market to seek further guidance.

Marcus had been rather relieved. Although Reid's leg was indeed a priority, he wasn't in mortal danger, and a brief trip to the market could provide them with several of the items that Captain Mitchell had ordered the crew to look out for. The highest on the list was information which could further their life in such an alien environment. Books, tomes, data disks, anything would suffice. Without more knowledge, the crew was simply too vulnerable.

A short hovercraft ride later, the four Terrans were being assaulted by pungent aromas from a variety of sources. Everywhere they looked, merchants shouted at the top of their voices, trying to drown out their competitors as they called out prices and special offers. A particularly aggressive humanoid merchant with small spiny protrusions along the edges of his face and what looked like tentacles of knotted hair jutting out from the back of his bumpy skull waved a small pole with dangling animal carcasses in their direction, shouting at them, presumably encouraging them to come and sample his wares. He wore a tattered skirt held up by leathery straps over his shoulders, while a broad ribbon around his waist supported a series of pouches which bobbed about as he enthusiastically attempted to entice them.

Serena waved her hand to decline his offer, turning her head away in disgust at the smell of the rotting meat. If anything, this only increased the merchant's fervor, the spiny figure dashing after them waving more wares as they tried to advance through the crowd to put more distance between them. Only when Marcus pointedly hefted his carbine did the over-eager merchant finally get the message.

Marcus turned and followed after the others, who had stopped a few meters further on, where Doc Taylor was busy sifting through a crate of used weapons being sold by a heavily-scarred and elderly Banthalo merchant, who was already engaged with another pair of customers. The medic was fascinated with a device that closely resembled a hilt of a sword.

"What does it do?" he asked the preoccupied seller, grasping the cylinder with both hands, shaking and twisting it in hopes of deciphering its use.

Without warning, a shimmering force field shot up from the unit in his hands, forming the shape of a straight blade a meter long. This was followed less than a second later by the sudden ejection of a stream of plasma from within the hilt, rapidly filling the containing force field. Startled, Taylor immediately dropped the glowing blade to the ground in a shower of sparks and hissing of venting plasma.

"Hell, that's way too dangerous," he gasped, turning his back on the stall and stealthily made his way to the others, hoping that no one had noticed his awkward fumble.

Pushing through the throng, Marcus became intrigued by a stall holding a variety of electronics equipment. Small screens, handheld devices, even a pair of wrist devices lined the wall behind a peculiar-looking merchant. The alien was slightly shorter than the Terrans, and had a vaguely humanoid torso that rested above a set of four thick, insectoid legs, each jutting out in a different direction. Its long, slouching arms ended in three very long fingers with the knuckles prominently near the tip. A pale, lime-colored skin covered its naked endoskeleton. The creature's head resembled that of the Nyari, the sworn enemies of the Terran Republic. A profusion of mandibles projected from what Marcus thought was probably the creature's mouth. Sad black eyes were set beneath its low-hanging brow, one of which was obscured by a comically large cybernetic lens, from the side of which wires protruded, angling around to the back of the merchant's small, angular head. A small disk-shaped drone with a series of blinking red lights hovered right next to the alien's head, a small antennae sticking up from its rear.

"What are those?" Marcus asked, pointing at the wrist devices.

Before Serena had a chance to interpret his query into the Sheshen language, the hovering drone beat her to it.

"A wrist computer with a holographic interface and network uplink," the drone announced in a quirky, high-pitched voice.

"Is that an interpretation unit?" Serena inquired, her eyes shining with interest.

"It is an interpreter and messenger drone, cybernetically linked to my neural cortex. It interprets and transmits audio signals directly to and from my brain," the drone informed them.

"That's amazing!" Marcus gasped. "Is it for sale?"

Serena shot him a loaded glare, not bothering to hide her resentment.

"Unfortunately not," the drone proclaimed, drawing the makings of a smirk from Serena. "But everything else you see here is."

"So those wrist devices," Marcus began. "Are they connected to some form of information network?"

"Yes," the drone announced proudly. "They come equipped with access to the Hiodan Interactive Virtual Environment."

"H.I.V.E." Reid remarked, sarcastically. "Seriously?"

"Why yes," the drone proclaimed, clearly not understanding the tall clone's reaction. "Do you wish to make a purchase?"

"Guys, this is exactly what we've been looking for," Marcus said to them. "With this we can hopefully access all the information we could possibly need."

"I agree," Serena concurred. "How much is it?"

"The 4-Matrix on your left comes with a wider holographic field and speedier neural link capabilities. It is produced by Ez'hylar Computer Systems and comes highly recommended. Its price is 6,700 credits," the drone explained, the merchant crouching eerily still behind his counter.

"And the other one?" asked Marcus, slightly taken aback by the heavy price tag.

"The Data Miner 7-Series on your right is produced by Nobus

Electronics and is considered an entry level device. Its price is 2,800 credits."

"That's more in our price range," Serena noted.

Marcus engaged the comms in his helmet and contacted Captain Mitchell, who was pleased to hear of their find. He immediately transferred the sum to Marcus' Pamco device.

After completing the purchase, Marcus was again reminded of their initial objective.

"You wouldn't happen to know of a doctor around these parts who caters to, uh… Gaians?" he questioned.

"I do," the drone voiced. "Not many Gaians make the journey to Nos Shana, but I have heard of a Telorian named Oolan who has, on occasion, treated Gaian visitors."

"Telorian?" Marcus asked, his curiosity getting the better of him.

"Where may we find him?" Serena cut across him, happy to hear that their search would not be a long one.

"I will upload the coordinates to your new wrist computer," the drone sputtered.

Marcus put the device on his wrist and clumsily activated it. To his surprise, the inside lining of the device began to expand, tightening around his armored forearm so as to keep steady. Almost instantly, a glowing orange holographic representation of their surroundings appeared in the air in front of him, projected by a small lens at the base of the device, a blinking red symbol a few blocks away indicating the location of Oolan's practice.

* * * * *

Hanan Aru crept along the edge of a nearby skyscraper. The

chameleon function on his armor rendered him virtually invisible as he shadowed his prey. The target tracker had locked onto their signature as they made their way along a narrow walkway leading from the market plaza to a secluded platform some two hundred meters away.

It was too easy, he thought as he kneeled by the ledge, studying their movements. He was fascinated by Rodan Kesh's interest in the group, and wondered what significance they held. These primitive beings had, he must admit, seemed somewhat capable when he'd shadowed them on the Hrūll refinery, yet they were so obviously out of their element, clueless to all the dangers lurking around them. As one of the best of the Iankari, the Etherium's most capable operatives, he felt that the task he'd been assigned was somewhat beneath him. Nonetheless, he was a man of honor, and his debt needed repayment.

Crouching and holding onto the ledge like a jungle cat, Hanan Aru set his sights on the nearest rooftop, some sixty meters away, across the street below. Without so much as a short run up to gain momentum, he hurled himself into the air, landing on all fours on the other side in absolute silence.

* * * * *

The holographic map had led them down an inclining catwalk that encircled a tall round structure. Its curving wall was covered in rust and layers upon layers of worn paint, streams of greenish sludge trailing down its flanks from overhead. Despite the surroundings, the blinking red dot on the holographic map indicated that they'd come to the right place.

"This is it," Marcus announced as they came to a stop in front of a

256

small alcove at the bottom of the catwalk.

In the recess some unfortunate soul had made its home out of a heap of ragged clothing and scavenged sheet metal. A sliding door of rusted, pitted metal was the only visible mean of ingress. Unable to understand the small keypad on the wall next to the door, Marcus proceeded to bang on the door instead.

After a moment the door slid open to revealing a menacing reptilian creature with coarse greenish-brown skin, clad in dark segmented armor of some thick leather-like material, its bulky frame filling the doorway and barring entry. Its beady eyes were small, and set far apart on the sides of its broad, flattened head, on top of which an array of bristly spikes sprouted from its hairless scalp and curved towards the rear of the creature's head. Rows of small, sharp teeth lined its gaping maw, which spanned the entire width of its head, its intimidating stare glaring down at them. The ominous creature held a short metallic rod in one hand, a glowing blue cylinder protruding from one end.

"Anoshi bansho stugomi?" it snarled, its deep voice reverberating around what looked like a small reception area behind it.

Serena squeezed past the others, clearing her throat as she prepared to answer.

"Shung manshin shio ang kishie cabo Oolan," she said, consulting her datapad for the translation she needed.

The reptilian creature gave her a calculating look, then growled "Bansho shumati so," and stepped aside to let them into the cramped, dimly-lit room.

The huge alien waddled over to the back of the chamber, where a partially transparent curtain seemed to separate the doctor's practice space from the waiting area. Marcus and the others took up position within the dingy antechamber. The only furniture was an uncomfortable-looking couch, standing up against the wall to the right of the entrance, its stained, hard-edged seats doing little to invite them to sit down. To their left, a series of mirrors hung amongst an assortment of strange little trees and flowers growing out of a bed of pebbles, seemingly dug directly out of the floor of the room.

After an awkward pause, the doorman returned, leading a truly bizarre creature into the antechamber.

It bulked even larger than the reptilian alien who'd let them in, its hunching shoulders dragging along massive arms, each easily large enough to overpower Jago, at the end of which huge hands were clenched into fists that the creature planted, knuckles-first, on the floor as it swayed into the room. A series of bony plates ran the length of its thick upper arms and short stubby legs, which resembled small tree trunks propping up its massive bulky frame as it gracefully swung itself forward, almost as if it were walking under water.

A small rounded head protruded directly from its chest, lacking anything that might function as a neck. Bulbous protrusion arose from its shoulders and upper back where the bony plates of its limbs ended, covered in a translucent membrane, but the most peculiar thing was the creature's semi-translucent skin, which seemed to change colors ever so slightly, pink and purple when it first came through the curtain, shifting to yellow and orange upon sighting the waiting Terrans. Four spherical eyes, utterly black from edge to edge, sat in the middle of its small face, giving the creature an air of sadness which, coupled with the way its head hung between its huge shoulders, Marcus would have read as a look shame on a human. Beneath its eyes, a row of membranous tendrils hung from what appeared to be the creature's downward-facing mouth.

"Ehm... I think he must have misunderstood you," Marcus said to Serena, as gently as he could. "There's no way... he... could be a doctor."

Before she could reply, the four-eyed creature stepped forward, the color of its skin shifting yet again to a mix of faded orange and blue.

"I aaam Oooolaaan," it proclaimed, its tendrils writhing as it spoke.

"You're Oolan?" Marcus gasped, not fully ready to accept that such a strange creature could be an expert in Terran – Gaian – physiology.

"What are you?" Reid asked, utterly fascinated.

"I aaam Teeeloooriiian," Oolan replied. "Hooow caaan I fiiix youuu?"

Still astonished that this hulking alien could be the doctor they'd been searching for, Marcus was also taken aback that its fragile, fluting speech was as graceful as its movements.

"What's with the skin?" Reid couldn't help but ask, drawing stern looks from the others.

"Teeelooorian skiiin reeefleeects mooood," Oolan explained, his tendrils forming into what Marcus had the weird intuition was a smile.

The reptilian guardian moved up behind Oolan, holding out its metal rod and prodding him firmly in the back. A brief shock went through the doctor's body, instantly turning its skin to a mixture of green and red tones as its limbs spasmed.

Instinctively, Marcus went for his weapon, training it on the armored guard, but before he could react further Oolan had thrust out a huge arm, pressing the muzzle down to the floor.

"Pleeease, nooo haaarm," he begged. "I aaam ooowned by hiiis maaasteeer," the Telorian explained.

"You're a slave?" Marcus exclaimed in disbelief.

"I aaam," Oolan replied with a hint of sadness in his voice.

"Xio uo wai shito," the reptilian guardian prompted with a sharp-toothed sneer.

"Pleeease, hooow caaan I fiiix youuu?" Oolan pressed.

"Ehm, maybe something for the guy who's missing his knee," Reid gestured as he hung onto Taz's shoulder, gesturing to his wound with his free hand.

Oolan approached, kneeling down slightly to get a better look. He grabbed a hold of Reid's leg with his three gargantuan fingers, probing and prodding with his free hand.

"Thiiis leeeg nooo gooood. Neeeed reeeplaaaceeemeeent," he eventually pronounced.

"Replacement?" Reid asked with a modicum of concern.

"Cloooning wiiill taaake looong," Oolan told him. "Syyyntheeetiiic reeeplaceeement iiis faaaster."

"And you have a compatible cybernetic component?" Marcus inquired.

"Yeees," Oolan replied. "Wiiill neeed neeeuraaal prooocessooor aaalso, tooo iiinteeerpreeet neeeuraaal siiignaaal."

"Fine by me," Reid assured him. "As long as I don't have to be carried around like a sack of potatoes and be jacked up on pain killers all day long then I say we go for it."

"How much will it cost?" asked Marcus, concerned whether or not they could actually afford the operation.

"Eeeiiight thooousaaand creeedits," Oolan announced. "Iiit wiiill taaake sooome hooours aaand heee muuust reeeturn aaa feeew daaays tiiime fooor teeestiiing."

"That should be fine," Marcus conceded. "We don't have much else to do but wait anyway. Let's get it done."

Oolan proceeded to assist Reid into the back room to prepare him for the operation. As the others waited anxiously for his return in the antechamber, the reptilian guardian was never far away, breathing heavily and exchanging intimidating stares with the clones. Marcus knew it was odd that a creature as alien as Oolan had managed to instill them with such feelings of trust – even sympathy – but it felt right somehow. Perhaps, once Reid had recovered, there would be something they could do to help relieve him from his indentured servitude.

Chapter 33

Kaiden's escort had taken her back to the hotel, making sure she arrived safely. The hazy sun had already set behind the towering buildings all around them, and the small square was lit only by flickering fluorescent lights, displaying alien symbols and a series of indecent illustrations. With the vagrants slumbering deep in inebriated sleep, the two were left alone under the makeshift awning outside the hotel's doors.

"You never told me your name," she said to him, somewhat awkwardly.

"Dasaan," he smiled. "Dasaan Ang'wari."

Even though he was slightly shorter than she was, her rescuer had an aura of capability, a quiet confidence that Kaiden found deeply reassuring. He was her white knight. Or, she supposed, her lavender knight.

"What are you?" she ventured.

"I am Ganyatti," he said with a small smile.

"Ganyatti," she smiled, faintly. "We've seen your kind before."

"My people are a common sight in the universe," Dasaan explained, with a hint of sadness in his voice.

"What are you doing on this world? It doesn't seem to suit you."

"Among my people, I am an outcast," he confessed, "forced to wander the galaxy alone. I came here in hopes of finding… something. Now I lack the means by which to leave."

"Why? Did you do something wrong?" she asked, taken aback by his revelation.

"No. I did not do anything at all," he assured her. "I am different from most of my people."

"Different how?" she pressed.

"Just... different," he said, offering no further explanation.

"You might say we have that in common," she admitted after a short pause. "We can never go home again."

"Why not?" he asked, his voiced concerned, his big, innocent eyes sparkling like star fire.

She stared at him for what seemed like an eternity, experiencing an attraction she couldn't comprehend. The draw she felt to him almost compelling in its fierce intensity. She hesitated on the verge of stepping closer to him, but before she had the chance to act further, she felt something brushing up against her leg. Instinctively she looked down, and saw something unexpected.

"You have a tail?" she screamed, jumping away from him.

Thoroughly confused, unable to comprehend her outburst, Dasaan stepped back as well, raising his hands in reassurance.

"Yes. Does that bother you?" he asked, bewildered.

"Of course it does!" Kaiden shuddered. "It's... icky!"

"Icky?" Dasaan frowned, not knowing the word, and unable to see why such a simple appendage would cause such a stir.

"Terrans don't have... tails," she blurted, the look on her face one of embarrassed disgust.

"Well... Ganyatti do have tails," he tried to explain.

"I know. It's just that..." she tried to find the words that would allow her to conclude the conversation without insulting Dasaan even further.

After a long silent pause she finally decided to change the subject.

"Come on. I'd like you to meet someone," she said, taking his hand and pulling him into the hotel.

*　*　*　*　*

Kaiden ventured into Mitchell's small room, having asked Dasaan to remain in the hallway while she explained everything to the captain. As she recounted her harrowing tale, Mitchell began to use his telepathic abilities to gently scan her surface thoughts, taking great care not to reveal his talent. He began to pick up blurred images of events just as she described them.

"Fucking Taz," he stormed. "Always thinking with his cock. I swear, one of these days I'm going to have Taylor cut it off!"

"Yes, Captain," Kaiden murmured, the shock of what had happened hitting her again.

"And Knoles?" Mitchell asked angrily. "Could he still be alive?"

"They took him," she whimpered. "I... I guess... he could still be alive."

Captain Mitchell reached out with his mind, attempting to force a connection with the missing crewmember. Though he had received rigorous psiops training, the distance made his task difficult. Kaiden began to talk, not realizing what the captain was attempting, but he raised his hand to silence her, feigning thought.

Fleeting glimpses began to appear in his mind's eye. He felt a great sense of urgency and despair as he caught a brief glance of the horrific scene as the ship's cook was torn limb from limb, screaming in agony. Just as Mitchell established a firm connection with the dying man's mind, he was interrupted by the door to his room suddenly slamming open.

"Who the hell's the grey guy in the hallway?" Taz demanded out as he sauntered in through the doorway.

"Where the hell have you been?" Captain Mitchell bellowed upon sighting him.

Kaiden stared down at her feet, not wanting to look Taz in the eye.

"I was at the titty bar down the street," Taz confessed, embarrassed at being forced to admit it in front of the beautiful Kaiden. His pronouncement was followed by a long pause. "What?"

"So while you were out burying your ugly mug in some alien's crotch, Juey and Knoles were being brutally murdered," Mitchell declared, his voice flat with rage, fixing the scout with a cold stare.

"I... I... what?" Taz stammered, unwilling or unable to process what he'd just heard.

Mitchell continued to stare at him without so much as a word, deciding that the best – maybe the only – way for Taz to understand the consequences of his actions was to show him. Though all Kaiden saw was the two men staring silently at one another, Taz was being bombarded with telepathic images of Knoles' nightmarish death.

"Give me one reason why I shouldn't leave you on this planet to rot," the captain demanded finally, breaking the silence. "You're lucky Kaiden got out alive, or the death toll on account of your cock would have been even higher."

Taz couldn't speak. He wouldn't have dared to, even if he could.

"Get out of my sight!" the captain commanded, sending the now guilt-ridden Taz ducking out of the room, pulling the door shut behind him.

"Actually Kaiden, how did you get out of there?" Mitchell asked in a more normal voice after Taz had left them.

"That would be the grey guy in the hallway," Kaiden explained, still looking at her feet. "Though he's more of a purple-"

"The what?"

"He pulled me out of there before the Banthalo noticed me," she elaborated. "I don't even want to think what would have happened if he hadn't been there. I brought him back here with me. I was hoping we could return the favor."

"What do you mean?"

"He wants to get off this shithole of a planet," Kaiden explained. "I can't say that I blame him."

The captain gave a deep sigh. "Bring him in," he instructed.

Kaiden went to the door, opening it just enough to invite Dasaan to join them. A moment later he was standing in the middle of the room, looking less dashing in proper light.

"This is Dasaan," Kaiden introduced him after an awkward moment of silence. "He's a Ganyatti."

Captain Mitchell stared at the alien before him, sizing him up and subtly scanning his thoughts to see if he could pick up a hidden agenda, not wanting to risk the level of invasive probing he'd deployed against the Hrüll on the refinery.

"I suppose I owe you my gratitude," he finally grunted.

"That is not necessary. I am simply pleased that your female was not harmed," Dasaan replied smoothly.

"How do you know our language so well?" Mitchell asked.

"I spent time on the beast world of Ferakoon with a Gaian named Tycus Orm. He taught me Gaian, among other things," Dasaan explained.

"Hmpfh. Kaiden tells me you're looking for a way off this world?"

"I am. I would be, as you say, most grateful," Dasaan admitted, looking Mitchell square in the eye.

Captain Mitchell pondered how to proceed for a long time. He didn't much take to the idea of having a passenger aboard his ship, especially an alien one, but nor did he want to leave a debt unpaid. Eventually a solution presented itself.

"Can you cook?"

*　*　*　*　*

Marcus sat on the edge of his bed, so entranced in his new toy that he was unable to even think about falling asleep. Reid was already snoring like a wild boar, having been dosed with enough sedatives to make Doc Taylor green with envy. Marcus only hoped that the accelerated healers would allow his friend to be up and walking within a few days time. His new cybernetic leg was very impressive. It was formed from what looked like a lightweight weave of wiry steel muscles, quite different from the clunky heavy metal pieces he'd seen among the veterans on Alamo station. Taz sat brooding in the corner, wrought with guilt, while Doc Taylor had busied himself with a deck of cards, both of them oblivious to their surroundings.

Marcus fiddled with a series of holographic symbols suspended in midair in front of him. He had already connected with the H.I.V.E., and was browsing through a veritable sea of information.

"This thing is amazingly intuitive," Marcus said to no-one in particular. "It even translates all the information to Terran... Gaian."

He was dumbfounded by the amount of options this little wrist device had made available. He skimmed over a series of topics, finding history, geography, stellar data, linguistics, biology, and hundreds of subsets of each. Where to begin? he wondered.

Following a trail of documents, he finally found something of note, a historical tract relating to a war between the Hrūll and the Sheshen. The document appeared first in strange, alien symbols which sequentially transformed into the Terran alphabet. According to the document, border disputes between the Hrūll and the Sheshen had escalated into a state of war, a war in which the Hrūll had consistently lost ground. After years of combat, when the Sheshen armada was on the doorstep of the Hrūll homeworld, the Etherium had come to the rescue. A joint fleet, twice the size of the Sheshen forces, had engaged them in the upper atmosphere of the Hrūll homeworld, defeating the Sheshen soundly.

The battle had left the Sheshen armada depleted. The last remnants of their forces managed to escape, with the joint Etheran forces snapping at their heels. As the Etheran forces approached Nos Shana, they found the remaining Sheshen forces strategically bombarding their own homeworld with high explosives. After the last remaining ships in the Sheshen fleet had been disabled or destroyed, the Etherium finally discovered the reason for the Sheshens' orbital bombardments.

Hidden on the planet's surface were crumbling detention centers the Sheshen had used to house thousands of Hrūll captives, many of whom had been made to endure horrific experiments at the hands of Sheshen scientists. It became apparent that the Sheshen had long coveted the Hrūll's psionic abilities, and had been willing to stop at nothing to acquire them. Though their experiments had all been in vain, the Sheshen people were condemned to suffer the consequences of their actions.

The Etherium ordered a blockade of the Sheshen homeworld, barring any ship from landing on or departing Nos Shana, enforced by a joint force of Etheran warships. As the years dragged by, the Sheshen people suffered in silence while the Hrūll slowly focused their political efforts on gaining control over the blockade. After nearly two decades of political pressure, the Etherium finally gave in and awarded the Hrūll control over Nos Shana. Since that time, the Hrūll patience for revenge has become legendary.

In one fell swoop, thousands of Hrūll ships blocked out the skies of Nos Shana, disrupting their interstellar communication and blanketing their world with orbital missiles. As the missiles delivered their deadly payload of poisonous gases, siphoned from the Sheshens' own gas giant, more than three-quarters of the planet's population was wiped out in a single night. When the Etherium finally received word of the event, they found that the Hrūll had already gone, leaving what was left of the Sheshen people to their fate.

After the initial chaos, the surviving Sheshen were left without a ruling government. As they struggled to survive, they erected shield walls to stave off the gas in strategic locations throughout their straggling cities, building walkways and platforms high above the toxic mist to allow safe travel between buildings.

The Sheshen adapted quickly. In less than a decade, the survivors had begun vying for power. Mobs rallied behind inspiring leaders, many of whom had been the leaders of powerful Sheshen criminal organizations. The power of these individuals grew exponentially and they seemed content with the status quo. Any attempt to re-establish a form of central government was met with threats, blackmail, or assassination. Eventually the only thing even resembling a form of rulership was the cartels.

Marcus felt so betrayed. Everything Shikari had told them was a lie. Their mission, even the things she had said about the Hrūll. The harrowing details of the Sheshen war crimes reminded him of the fate that awaited him at the hands of Division 6 were he ever to return to Terra. The image of Captain Virge Intari's cold, dead eyes still sent shivers down his spine. Although he could relate to how the Hrūll must have felt, Marcus had a hard time imagining how that justified the fate of the Sheshen people. There must have been millions of innocent lives who had not deserved such a fate.

He turned off his new wrist device and laid down to rest. Though he wondered how reliable the information had been, it certainly explained the state of Sheijan. As he closed his eyes, thoughts of the Sheshen genocide weighed heavily on his mind.

Chapter 34

In the wake of the deaths of Emil Juey and Darryl Knoles, the crew was confined to the hotel. The only ones allowed to venture outside were Jago and Serena, who made twice-daily trips to purchase food from a nearby eatery.

"This shit tastes like cat piss," Jago moaned several days later, stirring a metal container full of orange goop with an eating utensil resembling a cross between a spoon and a knife.

"Been drinking much cat piss lately?" Reid joked, earning a glare from Jago.

Two nights before the *Tengri*'s refit was due to be completed, the old squad had gathered in Captain Mitchell's quarters for the evening meal, all but Taz, who'd chosen to dine alone in his room, unwilling to bear the judgmental looks of his fellow squad members.

"I've had it with this place," Raven spat. "There are things crawling all over me in my sleep, and my room smells like farts."

"You think your room smells bad?" Mitchell protested. "Try sleeping next to the Ape."

"Can't we go out, boss?" Jago pleaded.

"No!" Captain Mitchell put his foot down. "We can't risk losing anyone else."

"What if we all go together, boss?" Jago proposed.

"At least let us get away from Taz," Taylor added.

"I can't believe he just left them there, alone," Reid sighed, shaking his head in disappointment.

"That's not the worst idea," Marcus admitted. "Let him feel what it's like to be left on his own for a change. Besides, I think everyone could use a bit of cheering up."

The captain could see they were all starting to gang up on him, and he was getting just as tired of the hotel as they were. Besides, Taylor was right, they could use a break from Taz. The mere sight of the diminutive scout sickened him.

"Alright, but everyone who wants to go will have to stay together," the captain finally caved in. "That means we go to one place and one place only."

"I know just the place!" Jago howled in excitement.

"Then if it's all the same with you, I think I'll stay in," said Raven. "Someone competent has to keep an eye on the fort and make sure Taz doesn't hang himself," she added with a sneer.

* * * * *

Jago had brought them to a club called Zazunitse. Serena was the only one of the naturally-born Terrans who had wanted to go out with them, but, Dasaan, who had been visiting the hotel once a day to check in with his new crew, had decided to take the opportunity to get to know the team. He'd been fascinated to learn that the crew of the *Tengri* were not actually Gaians at all, and was happy to have the chance to spend time with his new crewmates in more comfortable surroundings than their cheap hotel.

The club was a circular structure rising above a wide platform that stretched up to a tall archway leading inside. An awning above the entrance held several holographic projectors, displaying animated scenes of half-naked Ganyatti females in various striking poses.

Dasaan managed to smooth things over with a pair of mean-looking Banthalo bouncers after Jago's mouth nearly got them into trouble. They didn't bat an eyelid at the armored clones, despite the sidearms strapped to their hips. Inside, a path curved away to the left and right, rising towards the back on both sides, with a wide, cylindrical stage sticking up in the space in its center. The outside wall was lined with stylish booths draped with slick black coverings and glass tables, artfully curved to form various grooves and surfaces. The bar directly in front of the entrance circumvented the entire front portion of the stage, with shelf after shelf filled with exotic bottles of liquor lining the wall behind it.

They quickly made their way to the bar, eyes raised to what looked like a highly inappropriate mating display between a pair of female Ganyatti performers and a young portly Banthalo male with sickly, mud-colored skin.

This early in the evening there were only a handful of shady patrons of various races, all neatly dressed and seemingly unimpressed by the current performance.

Marcus caught himself blushing profusely, having never seen anything quite like it. He realized that he'd seen indications of interspecies relationships all around him ever since Semeh'yone, but ever since Roshana had tried to kiss Serena he'd done his best to ignore the implications. He wasn't at all sure what to make of the idea, but he was frankly shocked at seeing it performed live onstage.

"That's disgusting," mouthed Serena, her mouth agape as she tried to tear her gaze away from the display.

"I don't know," Reid called over the throbbing music. "They seem to be enjoying themselves."

Serena shrugged, feigning a smile.

273

While everyone else was busy ordering drinks, Jago was all but drooling as he stared at the female entertainers. Their bartender was an odd sort, its elongated head topped by a grayish-blue helmet of exposed bone, covered in dark flecks. A pair of expressionless, fish-like eyes were set on the sides of its head, behind a pert little mouth. Its body was distinctively humanoid, though its bizarre head and series of fins running down its naked back suggested that it was most likely amphibious.

"What is he?" Serena whispered in Dasaan's ear, trying not to be too impolite.

"He's a Namidian," Dasaan explained. "They come from an aquatic world called Namala, close to the Axeon Void. I've heard it's quite beautiful."

"I'm still expecting to wake up from a dream at any moment," Serena confessed. "This is all just so overwhelming."

Dasaan smiled sincerely.

"What about your world?" Serena asked. "What's it like?"

Sadness swept across Dasaan's azure eyes as he considered her question.

"I have heard it's one of the most magnificent worlds in the entire galaxy," he eventually proclaimed, a hint of disdain creeping into his voice.

"You've never been there?"

"I am not welcome there," he said, his tone utterly neutral.

Serena decided against pursuing her questioning, as she could clearly see that it was making Dasaan uncomfortable.

"I'm sorry," she concluded. "I'll go get us some drinks."

Reid came over and handed Marcus a clear drink with a light blue tint in a square-shaped transparent container. Marcus was amazed at how quickly the sniper had taken to his new leg, moving without even the slightest limp.

"Come on Marcus, let's go grab some seats," Reid suggested, clapping him on the shoulder.

Marcus hesitated. It wasn't that he didn't want to sit with Reid, but that he'd hoped to find a seat nearer to Serena. He'd finally admitted to himself that he'd grown... fond... of her over the weeks they'd travelled together, and he was beginning to feel the stirring of familiar emotions, emotions he hadn't felt since he'd been with Eve back in the Terra system. Although he missed Eve, he hadn't thought about her for a while. He wondered whether or not he ought to feel guilty for having feelings for another woman. He knew he would never see Eve again, but somehow it felt wrong.

Reid led the way to a booth on the right-hand side of the club with a good view of the stage. As they sat down, Marcus noticed Dasaan making his way along the sloping walkway on the opposite side of the stage, his hand firmly on Serena's shoulder. Only a couple of days with the crew and he was already making his advance, the presumptuous bastard, Marcus thought, giving him the evil eye.

Up until now he'd had no qualms about the captain's decision to take on an alien crewmember, and had even found the idea exciting. Now, however, he was beginning to question it.

At the front of the club where the bar curved back to meld into the front of the stage, Jago was reaching up towards a luscious Ganyatti female who'd just come on stage. She knelt down near the edge, winking suggestively at the huge clone, stroking his chin. Jago was drooling with anticipation, utterly mesmerized.

Marcus' thoughts wandered to the two fallen members of their crew. Having spent so much of his time planetside on Ga'ouna, he'd had far less time to get to know the support staff than his squadmates had. What time he'd spent aboard the *Tengri* following their departure had mostly been spent with his old squad, or wallowing alone in his cabin.

"You know, I'm ashamed to say, I barely even knew them," Marcus admitted, feeling slightly ashamed that Knoles' and Juey's deaths hadn't affected him more.

"That's not what's bothering you," Reid countered.

"What do you mean?"

"What bothers you is that you're beginning to get used to it," Reid added, sipping from his glass.

"Used to what?" asked Marcus, puzzled.

"Death," Reid explained. "I think we all are... a bit."

Marcus didn't answer. He just stared at his friend.

"I think when you've seen as much of it as we have, you're bound to start distancing yourself from it, which is perhaps the saddest part of all," Reid continued. "It's a bit like we're losing the very thing that makes us human."

Though Marcus wanted to deny it, he knew there was truth in what Reid had just proposed. He downed half of his drink in one big gulp, cringing at its sour taste.

Marcus looked back over to Serena and saw that Dasaan was leaning over to whisper in her ear, a sly look on his face. Marcus felt like storming over there, grabbing Serena by the hand and whisking her away from him. What could she possibly see in him? He wasn't even human, and she'd just moments earlier balked at the notion of interspecies... romance. Yet, here she was, leaning towards him, smiling, legs crossed in his direction.

"Marcus!" Reid yelled, right into his face, shaking him out of brooding.

"What?"

"I said," Reid raised his voice, "Do you think the Ape would really get with an alien?"

"I dunno. Probably," Marcus muttered, in no mood for humorous ribbing. "He did get rather friendly with a goat on New Io."

"Are you alright?" Reid pressed. "There was nothing we could have done. Taz is completely at fault."

"I know. It's… nothing," Marcus lied. "What do you think about the new guy?"

"He seems ok, I guess," Reid replied, but before he could elaborate further, the doors to the club burst open. Both clones' heads snapped around at the sudden movement. Quick on the draw, Reid's hand was already on his sidearm.

A pair of thuggish reptilian creatures marched through the wide open door. They bore a striking resemblance to the guards that Shikari had kept in the club on Semeh'yone, as well as the guardian they'd encountered at Oolan's medical practice. What was it Roshana had called them? 'Nerokan'… renowned for their military prowess.

These two were clad in crude heavy armor plating, painted black with an insignia in the shape of a red three-pronged star emblazoned on their chests. Atop their broad, bulging shoulders were pauldrons with what looked like a pair of black talons jutting from each plate. Both humanoids wielded a formidable spear with black, serrated blades, although Marcus noted the handles of what he assumed were some sort of firearms protruding from behind their lower backs, within easy reach. As they each took up position on opposite sides of the entrance, a Sheshen of undoubtable influence strode in behind them. Though he wore a suit of armor that greatly resembled those of his escorts, his was a far lighter, more flexible version, and the insignia

277

embedded in the middle of his chestplate was made from a trio of radiant rubies. His faceguard was a simple black mask with no discernible markings, only a pair of slits allowing him to see.

Almost immediately, one of the lavender-skinned dancing girls jumped from the stage and flung herself into his arms. One of the Nerokan bodyguards proceeded to clear the path to a lavish booth near the rear of the club, one reserved for important guests. As the Sheshen took a seat with his female companion resting firmly on his lap, a male Ganyatti server was already standing by to take his order.

Meanwhile, a wide-eyed Jago was getting pulled up onto the stage by a beautiful, long-legged dancer with small white freckles all over her luscious physique. Once on the stage, she began rubbing herself against him. Another dancing girl joined in and promptly began to undress the huge Terran. Marcus had never seen Jago sport such a devious grin, and was amazed at how unabashed his squadmate was at the thought displaying himself in public. No doubt he was firmly fixated on his prize and not his audience.

As the Sheshen's server walked past Reid and Marcus on his way to the bar to hand in his order, the dark-skinned clone held up a hand and called him over.

"Do you speak Gaian?" he asked hopefully.

"No much," the pale-skinned waiter replied, clearly in a hurry, not wanting to keep the important guest waiting.

"Can you tell me who that is?" Reid inquired, gesturing towards the Sheshen and his Nerokan bodyguards.

"Him be Lishan," the waiter whispered. "Son to Kesha Kun."

"Kesha Kun?"

"Limatoi Rawo... Dark... Sun," the server concluded, hurriedly pulling away so as to not leave his important guest waiting.

"Must be some sort of big shot," Reid shrugged.

The female dancers had removed all of Jago's clothes but his underwear, leaving him grinning from ear to ear in a pair of white shorts, completely oblivious to what was happening behind him as a male Ganyatti started to strip behind him.

Turning back from the departing waiter, Reid noticed the unfolding scene and couldn't contain his laughter as the male dancer came up behind the Ape and began stroking the big man's bare back in a passionate manner, grabbing his hips firmly.

Marcus started laughing as well, and before he knew it he was howling so hard that tears began to swell up from his eyes. He was pleased that the Ape's antics were not only taking their minds off of recent events, but also drawing attention away from Dasaan and Serena, whom he knew he was only torturing himself by watching.

"I think he's in for more than he bargained for!" Reid gasped between gales of laughter.

The female dancers each grabbed hold of one of Jago's arms and raised them up, displaying his athletic physique to a crowd of giggling spectators. The big man's expression slowly faded from one of glee to one of confusion as he realized that the whole club was laughing at him. As the girls began to slowly turn him around to face his would-be partner, he finally saw the reason for all the commotion. He froze in place, his eyes popped open in shock.

Without warning, the huge clone sprang from the stage, landing on his feet and running as fast as he could to claim the empty seat in the darkened booth next to Reid. Neither Marcus or Reid could even managed to sit up straight as they convulsed with laughter.

"Will you please go get my clothes!" Jago finally pleaded.

When the laughter had begun to subside and a new performance

279

had begun on the stage, Marcus spotted Kaiden coming running in through the front entrance of the club, making a bee-line for Captain Mitchell's table. Her serious expression was like a bucket of ice-cold water down his spine, but he couldn't make out what the urgency was all about from so far away.

"Grey!" Mitchell's voice sounded in his earpiece. "Raven's gone missing!"

Chapter 35

In order to safely cover as much ground as possible, Captain Mitchell gathered the old squad and split them up into two search teams. The rest of the crew was confined to the hotel with strict orders not to leave.

Marcus was getting really worried. Although Zorita was known for her independent streak and opinionated attitude, it wasn't like her to pull a stunt like this. She'd left no message or any indication of where she'd gone, slipping out of the hotel when the support staff were all in their rooms, and her comms were turned off. Marcus had a sinking feeling she wouldn't have answered them even if they weren't.

As they scoured the surrounding streets, desperation began to set in, for Taz most of all, who seemed determined to make up for his past failure.

"What about the docks?" Reid suggested as they emerged, empty handed, from yet another sleazy drinking hole.

"She loves that ship more than anything," Taz added, doing his best to contribute.

"She did kick up quite a fuss when we were forced to leave it," Marcus agreed.

"It can't hurt to take a look," Taz concurred.

They ran off as fast as they could in the direction of the shipyard. It was already well into the night, and neither team was having any luck at all.

* * * * *

At such a late hour, the district of the city housing the *Tengri* was largely deserted. Only a handful of dock workers lazily catered to the few ships that still needed servicing, the occasional guard standing sentry outside closed compounds. It was very a different atmosphere to when they had arrived, the bustling shipyard district, now holding only a few aimless souls wandering its streets and concourses.

Marcus and his fireteam hurried along the walkway leading up to the compound where the *Tengri* lay docked. The ship looked strange from this vantage point, her nose peering over a metal fence, windows dark in its lifeless bulk. A pair of Nerokan guards blocked access to the gate, rifles slung carelessly at their sides. One of them was pouring the steaming contents of a thick, polished metal flask into his lizard-like maw as the two bantered to pass the time.

"Shitong ratadishi manshin ono agashiti," the larger of the two announced as the three Terrans approached, its thundering voice stopping them clear in their tracks.

Marcus suddenly realized that they might have come all this way for nothing if they were unable to make themselves understood.

"Do you speak Gaian?" Taz blurted out hurriedly, before Marcus had a chance to react.

The smaller guard pushed the other aside and stomped to within a hair's breadth of Taz, his foul breath overpowering.

"He say, no come here. No allowed," the Nerokan grunted in very poor Gaian.

"We are looking for our friend," Marcus began to explain. "She may have been-"

"No one come here!" the guard interjected, raising his booming

282

voice. "You go!"

The larger guard tossed his metallic flask aside and put one hand on the nasty looking rifle hanging from a sling on his shoulder. Its comically large muzzle looked like something Marcus would have expected to find on vehicle-mounted weaponry.

"We don't mean to cause any problems," Marcus tried to explain. "We just want to find our friend."

"You go!" the guard repeated.

It was obvious that the guards weren't about to listen to their pleas. In the face of such hostility, Marcus led the others away, scanning their surroundings as they left the docking platform, hoping to spot even the slightest sign of Raven's presence.

As they made their way back through the shipyards they noticed an assortment of small bars and saloons catering to dockworkers and the few crew who didn't want to venture too far from their ships. In a city of this nature, there were bound to be all manner of smugglers and lowlifes making short pit stops or simply waiting for cargo or passengers looking for discreet passage off Nos Shana. Marcus directed his team to start combing the sleazy establishments, looking for word of their missing pilot.

After a good hour of information gathering, during which Taz overcompensated for his earlier lapse by trying to rough up anyone who refused to speak to them, they came across a shady looking Sheshen smuggler who claimed to have seen a dark-haired Gaian female sneaking around the dock foreman's office. Excited to finally be on the right track, they called Captain Mitchell to inform him of their progress. The two teams quickly made arrangements to rendezvous at the site.

Marcus and the others waited anxiously outside the foreman's office for the captain and his team to arrive. With no means of determining what they were up against, Mitchell had ordered that they wait until the whole squad was together in case things got rough.

The office itself was a three-storey structure growing out of another truncated tower, connected to the platform adjoining the *Tengri*'s docking bay. Orange light spilled out into the street from the structure's handful of windows, each coated with a special film to prevent anyone on the outside from peering in, and no voices could be heard coming from inside. A tall fence enclosed a large courtyard to one side of the building itself, with stacks of crates and barrels rising up just high enough to be seen.

As soon as they'd regrouped, Captain Mitchell began whispering tactics, ordering Reid and Taz to remain outside to act as lookouts in case anyone tried to flee, whilst the rest of the squad entered the building and began searching for any sign of Raven.

"If there's anyone inside, we're just going to question them," Mitchell insisted, looking pointed at Jago. "Don't make any moves unless they come at you first."

"Yes boss," the huge man agreed, wiping snot from his grotesquely overgrown nose before stuffing his head back into his helmet.

"Good. Reid, you guard the left, Taz, the right. The rest of us will knock on the door and-"

The captain's orders were suddenly cut short as Jago kicked open the door with a roar of rage and charged in.

"Not again!" Mitchell moaned, shaking his head in disbelief. "Ape!" he screamed as they charged in after him.

Inside, a startled pair of Banthalo workers had apparently been engaged in a quiet game of tiles in a large, low-ceilinged room that seemed to take up the whole story of the building. They now stood with their backs against the far wall and their arms raised in terrified surrender. A third had been enjoying a meal of stewed, if questionable, meat, which he'd managed to spill all over himself as he'd fallen off his seat at the sight of the raging behemoth. Jago stormed past the cowering Banthalo on the floor and straight up to the bewildered workers against the back wall, jamming his huge laser right into the nose of the first one he reached.

"Where's Raven?" he bellowed, his lips quivering with anger.

"Chosey cridi i?" the panic-stricken dock worker moaned.

Marcus and Taylor ran to secure the other two, whilst the captain did his best to calm Jago.

"Ape, stand down!" he ordered, putting his hand on the barrel of Jago's massive weapon.

Jago scornfully looked him in the eye and let out an intimidating snarl before finally giving in and backing off.

Although relieved to have been saved from imminent death, the dockworker still trembled in fear as Captain Mitchell started tying his hands behind his back. The squad lined the three Banthalo up on their knees, side by side, as the captain paced back and forth in front of them.

"Do any of you speak Gaian?" he asked, hoping he wouldn't be forced to call on Serena for assistance.

The captives just stared at the ground.

"Grey. Go check their logs. There has to be a terminal or a log book around here somewhere," the captain directed.

"I'm not sure how much help that'll be if I can't read the language," Marcus protested, drawing a grimace from Captain Mitchell. "I'll see what I can do," he conceded.

"Doc, you go rummage around," Mitchell ordered.

The calm-headed medic lit himself a cigarette before slowly starting to search through a collection of crates near the entrance.

"What can I do, Sir?" Taz asked, eager to help.

"You can get out of my way," the captain snapped, pushing the scout aside.

Marcus soon spotted a computer console near a loading door at the far end of the room. He began methodically fiddling with its alien controls, trying to figure out how to operate it.

Captain Mitchell continued pacing back and forth, periodically spurring Jago to hurl a stream of insults and spittle at their captives. After a few moments of this, he knelt by the one whose face and shirt were stained with his evening meal. He looked the foul creature straight in the eye, and even though any mortal man would have trembled at the sight of the hideous alien, the fury burning in the captain's eyes was so intense that even the Banthalo felt forced to avert their gaze.

For a moment, Mitchell attempted to force contact with the Banthalo's mind, but all he could glean was the guttural gibberish of its native tongue and broken, meaningless images. Damn them, he thought. To gain anything useful, Mitchell would have had to lead him along the right path, fool him into recalling what the captain was looking for. To do so would require a dialog, one he couldn't have without knowing the alien's language.

"We know she was here," the captain continued his interrogation. "Tell us where she is and I won't have the Ape here tear off both of your arms."

The frightened captive began sobbing and gestured clumsily towards a metal crate near the loading door, his arms still bound behind his back, spouting unintelligibly slurred words.

A shadow crept over the captain's visage. They wouldn't have...

"Ape, keep them still," he ordered, the hint of fear in his voice was unmistakable.

He went straight for the crate. It looked large enough to hold a human body, especially one the size of Raven's lithe frame. As he laid his hands on the metallic lid, a light tremor coursed through his hands. He closed his eyes, dreading the revelation he feared he was about to endure.

With a quick flick of the wrists, he threw the lid to the side and opened his eyes. The look on his face was one of surprise and relief. He reached into the box and withdrew a handful of small vials no larger than his index finger, each containing a clear yellow liquid.

"What the hell is this?" he demanded, taking determined strides back to his captives, his motorized brace creaking with each step.

"Ti groppis," the captive tried to explain, his oversized face bearing a very human expression of fear.

Captain Mitchell shook his head in quiet resignation.

"What is it boss?" asked a confused Jago.

"Drugs, I'm guessing," Captain Mitchell replied.

"Sir, I've got something," Marcus called, waving him over.

Marcus had managed to bring up the building's live perimeter security feed and then successfully backtracked to show a most revealing piece of footage.

The image was drawn from the security camera in the courtyard beyond the loading door. It showed Raven climbing into the yard from the street and then peering over the three-meter rear wall, clearly trying to get into the secure area where the *Tengri* lay berthed.

The squad stared intently at the screen as a group of Banthalo thugs crawled out of the shadows behind her, moving ever closer, each of them wearing the same type of black armor they'd seen on the Nerokan guards in the Zazunitse club. Raven remained oblivious to their presence as she reached up, seizing the lip of the wall with both hands, then busied herself trying to get her foot over too.

One of the Banthalo took a shiny metallic rod from a holster on its belt and leapt forward, pressing the device against her back, producing a spasm which made her lose her hold on the fence. As she came crashing down, the thugs cheered and squealed with glee, praising each other for their find, their harsh voices recorded by the security equipment and playing back over the consoles tinny speakers.

Raven lay motionless for a short spell. When she regained her senses, she struggled back to her feet, retreating up against the wall to assume the semblance of a fighting stance. The thugs began circling her, back and forth, goading her as if she were nothing more than an animal ready for slaughter.

The squad watched anxiously as one of her assailants withdrew a broad-bladed cleaver from a back holster. Even vastly outnumbered, there was no sign of fear in Raven's eyes. Marcus couldn't help but feel strangely proud. As the sword came crashing down, he feared it would be the end of their brave pilot, but just as the blade was about to make contact with the unarmored woman, a bright flash shot through the air. As if he were no more than a ragged doll, the sword wielder was thrown clear across the yard, landing in a ragged heap with a crash.

In the sudden stillness that followed, Raven stared at her hands. Her fingertips were glowing intensely, as if lit from within. The other Banthalo stared on in astonishment, before starting to shout at her again, clearly attempting to reassure one another. Caught off-guard in her confusion, the remaining assailants were able to fire a net-like contraption in her direction, pinning her to the wall.

As she struggled to get free, she was prodded several more times with the stun rod. Finally, she ceased moving. With wafts of smoke still rising from a searing wound in his shoulder, the wounded Banthalo had managed to recover from the astonishing blow and came to help the others secure their prize, dragging her out of the courtyard.

"Did she just…?" Taz started to ask, his voice trailing off.

"I think so," Marcus replied.

"Did you know she could…?"

"I don't even think she knew," Marcus answered.

"Ape, bring that sorry piece of shit over here," Mitchell ordered, gesturing towards one of their captives.

Jago grabbed the unfortunate Banthalo by the throat and lifted him into the air with one arm. With his hands tied behind his back, there was nothing the prisoner could do except kick his legs and hope that the towering giant would release his grip.

Jago paced slowly over to the console and set the humanoid down next to Captain Mitchell, who grabbed him by the back of the neck and pressed his face into the monitor, pointing at the frozen image of the Banthalo thugs and whispering into his oversized ear.

"Now, you and me are going to have a little chat until you tell me just who these scumbags are, and where we can find them, you understand?"

"That won't be necessary, Captain," Reid proclaimed. "I know who they are."

Chapter 36

"Stock in the Muromoto Group dipped three points today, down for the fourth day in a row," the news anchor reported, the shape of her eyes and her skin tone proclaiming her a woman of mixed Asian and Hispanic descent. "Despite the company's innovative new approach to consumer robotics, the once-booming megacorporation is suffering a serious decline on the stock market due to rumors that their CEO, Ms. Mariko Muromoto, has overextended the company's finances. Furthermore, the-"

Takahashi deactivated the display, with more force than probably necessary. He sighed wearily, peering out through the limousine's window. Outside, the onset of dusk and pouring rain obscured the view.

Could she really go as far as deliberately destroying his legacy, merely out of spite? he wondered. Perhaps he had underestimated her. After all, it was his work which had kept him busy all those years while she was growing up… his work that had caused her mother so much disappointment… his work which had ultimately led to her demise. Could Mariko now mean to destroy it all? Was her hatred for him that great?

The forward windshield wipers were hard at work keeping the torrential rain from obscuring the driver's view. Through the open partition, Takahashi thought he could see the estate in the distance. He'd moved back home, leaving Muromoto Tower entirely. There was nothing left for him there, save for a daughter who went to great lengths to make sure their paths never crossed.

The first night back in the estate had felt odd. So many ghosts of years past had haunted him with each step. It wasn't home to him anymore. Perhaps it didn't help that he kept only a minimal staff. In such a vast house, he could go almost an entire day without running into a single soul. He preferred it that way, but he was even beginning to think that his staff was giving him a wide berth on purpose.

"Beginning our descent, Sir," the driver informed him, altering his course.

A brief moment later, the hovercraft was on the ground and the driver was assisting him to exit the vehicle. How he hated being so frail. He could barely get out on his own, at least not without difficulty.

"Here you go Sir," the driver prompted, producing an umbrella to shield him from the heavy downfall.

"That won't be necessary," Takahashi proclaimed, waving him away and pausing momentarily to allow the rain to caress his cheeks. He had never understood why people felt such a need to keep it at bay. He found every drop a welcome refreshment.

The magnolia trees around the rim of the landing platform were beginning to grow the first leaves of spring, towering giants with gnarled branches which seemed to loom over him, encroaching upon him, their long narrow buds like claws.

"You may retire for the evening," Takahashi declared, dispatching the driver, who hurriedly leapt off towards the service entrance, leaving him standing there alone in the cold.

It was only then that he noticed the second vehicle, parked near the bushes on the other side of the platform. It was a small two-seater, a mediocre model at best. He circled towards it on his way to the entrance, only to find it vacant.

"A visitor?" he lamented, perplexed as to who would have come calling upon him, let alone at such a late hour.

He hurried as he navigated the cobblestone walkway leading up to the entrance, darting between the formidable marble pillars which supported a slanted awning overhead.

"Takahashi," came a voice from behind the nearest pillar, startling him.

"Barrow," Takahashi smiled, recognizing the voice instantly.

The decrepit old man emerged from the shadows with a youthful grin. "Please, after all these years, you still won't call me Julius?"

"Apologies, Julius, old friend," Takahashi responded, "Please, do come in. Let's see if we can't scare up a stiff drink to warm these old bones, shall we?"

Barrow chuckled, baring his prominent gums. They took themselves into the study, a lavishly-furnished hall with a balcony overhanging the right-hand side of the room and a row of framed windows on the other. The décor consisted largely of finely-crafted rosewood, polished to a high sheen.

"The usual?" Takahashi asked, producing a square bottle of emerald-tinted glass, braided with golden thread and a stopper to match, remembering Barrow's preference from the days when they'd worked at the Muromoto Group together.

"Of course," Barrow replied, resting upon an aging armchair by the fireplace opposite the doorway.

Takahashi poured the drinks, then lowered himself into the seat opposite Barrow, pushing one of the glasses across the surface of an ornately carved coffee table, setting the bottle in the middle. He raised his glass in a salute to an old friend. They downed the contents in unison, voicing their appreciation with a pleasing grunt.

"So, old friend," Takahashi finally began. "What brings you here at this late hour?"

Barrow fidgeted in his seat, seemingly reluctant to reveal his purpose.

"Well… speak up old man," Takahashi joked, refilling their drinks.

"It's… uh…" Barrow eventually stammered. "It's about your daughter."

This revelation earned him an inquisitive glance from Takahashi, who paused briefly, then placed the stopper back in the bottle and slid the glass back to Mr. Barrow's side of the table.

"Oh? What has my little angel done this time?" Takahashi remarked, feeling bone tired.

"You know, I've always found it quaint that you don't keep androids as part of your household," Barrow changed the subject.

"I've never had much trust in machinery," Takahashi confessed, perplexed as to what game his old friend was playing.

"Hmpf… you are a contradiction," Barrow feigned a smile as he stared languidly into his glass.

"Am I now?" Takahashi probed. "You didn't come here to discuss my shortcomings, Julius. Get to the point."

Barrow downed his second drink, coughing slightly in the process.

"I trust you've seen the news?" he asked, finally, pushing the glass back across the table.

"I have," Takahashi admitted, refilling the glass.

"This damned Isis business will be the death of us all."

"Isis?" Takahashi asked with great interest. It was the first mention of anything that might prove relevant.

"Project Isis," Barrow sighed, grabbing the glass once more, only to hold it in his hands, nurturing it, rather than drinking. "Your daughter's secret pet project."

Takahashi didn't reply, simply sat staring at him, studying his erstwhile colleague and gauging his expression.

"I suspect I should have turned to you with this matter sooner," Barrow wheezed.

"What matter?" Takahashi pressed.

"She's been funneling resources into a project called Isis, to such an extent that we'll be bankrupt within months if our backers get wind of it. They'll break up the company and peddle the pieces to the highest bidder. There'll be nothing left," Barrow moaned. "Decades of sacrifice, only to have it all ruined by a hot-headed girl with a score to settle."

Despite everything that had happened, Takahashi didn't much like hearing his daughter described with such little regard.

"I hired someone, a few someones actually... very discrete," the old man opposite him confessed, downing his third glass. "They followed the paper trail to a warehouse in East Chesside, near the docks. I was hoping to pierce the aura of secrecy she's kept over the whole thing. But inside... they found nothing! No laborers, no machinery, not even any raw materials, just... nothing."

"She can't be attempting to make away with such an immense-" Takahashi began, but he was quickly interrupted.

"No! I don't believe so. She is financing something. *We* are financing something," he corrected himself. "And whatever it is, it's big."

"I appreciate you coming to me with this. I know it can't have been easy. No doubt my daughter has the Board on a tight leash," Takahashi ventured.

"She does indeed," Barrow admitted, rising to leave. "She has everyone unnerved. Some even claim she's been having them followed. That's why I took the maid's car."

"I still have a few sources I haven't exhausted yet," Takahashi muttered. "I'll give this matter my full attention."

"I knew you would... I knew you would," Barrow repeated as he departed.

Takahashi leaned back in his chair, finishing his drink. Had he been looking in the wrong place all this time? Had he been so arrogant as to assume his daughter was incapable of anything more than petty rivalry? He had an unsettling suspicion, a notion which chilled him to his very core.

He pressed a series of buttons on a hidden panel embedded in the armrest of his chair. A section of the wall slid to the side and a holographic projector emerged, flickering to life and displaying an array of functions hovering in front of the old man. Takahashi engaged the interface. A moment later, the ghostly aura of a man's face and upper torso appeared before him.

Bulging neck veins ran bare underneath his translucent skin and across his bony frame. His muscles were virtually non-existent, a testament to a life spent almost entirely within the grid. A pair of thick cables could be seen hovering behind him, curving upwards to connect with the base of his neck. The few wisps of bleached white hair were almost invisible, giving him the illusion of baldness. He stared vapidly with glazed lifeless eyes.

"It's been a while," said Takahashi with little sign of emotion.

The figure nodded.

"I have a job for you."

Chapter 37

The young servant girl laid the tray, decked with white porcelain cups, a kettle filled with steaming hot water and various other sundries, on the stone floor of the audience chamber. Ambassador Janosh smiled and nodded his appreciation before quietly dismissing her.

"Show me what you have learned Luneia," he ordered as he gazed over the glimmering pond.

Given the ambassador's stature, it was considered a great honor to be taken under his tutelage, and Luneia was a fair bit younger than his previous apprentices. In most cases he mentored those whom others had schooled before him. This was a special case, however, for Luneia was the daughter of Tysob Agashi, a renowned master of the art of energy manipulation, and Janosh's oldest and most trusted friend.

Luneia grasped the handle of the kettle and started to pour its contents into the porcelain cups. She looked no older than fifteen. Her golden hair, lightly freckled cheeks and large, innocent yellow eyes were a welcome sight for the old man's heart, an island of playful naivety in a world full of conflict and distrust.

She laid a pair of napkins at their feet, folding them over twice in a display of finely practiced movements. She then opened a small, ornately-carved box made of cherry wood, varnished to a glossy finish, and poured a small amount of the finely-chopped herbs it contained into a tiny silver tea strainer.

Placing the strainer first inside the ambassador's cup, Luneia allowed the fragrant herbs to soak in the water. The smoky brown and red swirls it produced in the water below began to darken as they both waited in silence. She then tapped the strainer on the edge of the cup three times and poured the spent herbs onto a small plate on the side of the tray before repeating the process with her own cup.

"You forgot to stir," Ambassador Janosh scolded when she finished.

"I was going to stir them both in turn," she argued.

"That is not the correct order," he corrected her. "First we stir for our guest, and then we prepare our own cup."

"Why is that of importance?" she moaned. "I had thought you would teach me the art of the blade."

"Respect, tradition and patience is what I offer you. An undisciplined mind should never wield a blade, for it knows not its own will. You must first learn to wield yourself, and then you will be ready for the blade."

"You make it sound as if the blade has a will of its own," she grinned.

"Some do," he whispered.

"I will start again," she smiled.

They were both wearing the traditional robes required for a Gaian tea ceremony. As the apprentice, hers were plain white with a high collar, while his were crimson, emblazoned with golden symbols along the cuffs, collar and sleeves.

"Is everything well, Master?" she asked, hesitantly.

"Why do you ask, child?"

"You've been very distant of late."

"I have the weight of the world on my shoulders," he explained. "One day you will understand."

"Is it true that you and Father knew Gaia?"

"Why do you not ask him?"

"He refuses to speak of her. I think it saddens him to do so," she admitted.

"Understandably so," the ambassador nodded. "She was the greatest of us, our light in the darkness."

"You knew her closely?"

"Not truly," he confessed.

"Why?"

"I was not worthy of her affection," he confessed.

"Did she not love you?" she gasped.

"Gaia loved all of us without question. It was I who did not feel worthy of her."

"Why?" she asked, her innocent yellow eyes full of wonder.

"She was..." he stumbled over the words, "a goddess. Perfection. Next to her, we are all flawed, but in her name we strive to be better."

"I wish I could have met her," Luneia bemoaned.

"Perhaps you shall," he reassured his apprentice.

"No, she's dead," she stated bluntly.

"There are those who believe she lives still," he told her calmly. "And even if she does not, then surely you will be joined with her in the afterlife. She will welcome you with open arms, forgive all of your transgressions and hold you in her embrace for all of eternity."

Luneia chuckled awkwardly. The thought of an undying entity waiting for her beyond the veil was a difficult concept for her to grasp.

"Father wants me to become... a diplomat, but I find it such tedious work." Janosh caught the very slight catch in Luneia's speech, which, together with the way she looked nervously at him, told Janosh all he needed to know.

He would never hold it against the girl that her father was grooming

298

her as Janosh's replacement. After all, as long-lived as the Gaian people were, no-one lived for ever. Why should she not succeed him when he passed on? At least, as long as she was capable enough.

"Anyway, I would much rather join the Iankari," the girl admitted.

"The Iankari?" the ambassador spluttered, genuinely shocked. "That is no place for someone of your birthright!"

"I thought serving was its own reward. I do not much care for titles or stature. I want to see the galaxy, and fight bravely for those in need."

"But… the Iankari?" he pressed. "Your father will never allow it."

"He would if you were to ask it of him, Master," she allowed herself to propose, forcing a sly smile.

"Focus on your studies, and… well, we shall see," he smiled faintly.

She stirred his freshly-made cup of tea and proceeded to make her own. He waited for her to finish before taking a small sip, reveling in the taste.

"I have heard it said that there are other humans in this galaxy, Master," Luneia proclaimed, revealing her knowledge of current affairs.

"You are well informed. How did you come to know of this?" he asked sternly, with a modicum of surprise.

"The news is all over the station. People are saying they are our long lost brethren. Should we not embrace them as such?"

"I have struggled with that very question," he conceded.

"So that is why you have been so distant."

He smiled.

"What would Gaia do?" she proposed pointedly.

"There is more to this story than you know, child. Things are not always so black and white."

He caught himself envying her simplistic view on life. If only he could let go of his inner turmoil. She was right of course. They were kin. Yet, if she knew Gaia's heart as he did, perhaps she would understand. He only hoped that one day she would be able to forgive him.

"Your tea is getting cold, Master. Should I reheat it for you?"

"Please," he said, as he raised his cup before her.

She laid her hand over the cup, and a flash of energy escaped from her bare palm. As she withdrew her hand, steamy tendrils ascended into the air.

"Luneia, you are indeed the child of Tysob Agashi."

Chapter 38

Once Reid had recounted what he'd heard from the server in Zazunitse, Captain Mitchell had Marcus establish communications with Dasaan, who was waiting with the rest of the crew at the hotel. As their new alien crewmember had been on this world far longer than they had, he no doubt knew a good deal more about the inner workings of its society.

Marcus made use of his newly-acquired wrist computer, transmitting the footage they'd obtained from the docking foreman's console, before establishing a communication link. Within moments a miniature holographic image of Dasaan appeared, hovering in the air before them and looking concerned.

"Dasaan, we need your help, urgently," Captain Mitchell exclaimed. "Reid said that those lizards… things… at that club we were at earlier wore the same type of armor as the Banthalo in the footage. We were hoping they belong to some local faction."

"The 'Dark Sun'," Reid added. "It was something the server in the club said. 'Lishan' and 'Dark Sun'."

With that, Dasaan's expression went from grave to worse.

"Are you certain you heard him correctly?" the Ganyatti asked.

"Positive," said Reid. "Why?"

"If that armor is indeed the same as those of the Nerokan guards in Zazunitse, then Raven's kidnappers belong to the Black Arm, a notorious group. They perform all manner of nefarious deeds for the Dark Sun Empire, Sheijan's ruling cartel. They are essentially a private

301

army." Dasaan explained.

"Why would they want Raven?" Captain Mitchell asked.

"They wouldn't," Dasaan said. "But the Dark Sun Empire certainly would."

"What? Why?" Taz pressed.

"No Sheshen is known to have developed psionic abilities, and most accept this, but the ruler of the Dark Sun Empire is well known to covet them desperately," Dasaan explained. "As such, Nos Shana is not a world where psionics are to be wielded lightly. Those who show such prowess have a tendency to vanish without a trace. Some say he collects them. Most likely, the Black Arm mistook your pilot for a Gaian."

"Why would that matter?" Marcus asked.

"The Gaians are well known for their high psionic aptitude," Dasaan answered.

"That's… just great," Doc Taylor observed from the rear.

The thought of Raven being reduced to a showpiece in some madman's zoo nearly drove Marcus wild with rage. What was worse, he worried that he would also have to overcome her loss, just as he would that of Juey and Knoles. What was it that Reid had said? With each loss, they grow a little more accustomed to death, lost a little more of their humanity.

"What do we do, boss?" Jago muttered, still clutching one of their captives by the neck.

Captain Mitchell perched on the edge of the console, deep in thought.

"Against opposition like that… I really don't know, Ape," the captain muttered under his breath.

"What do you mean you don't know?" Marcus roared. "We go after her!"

"Just like that?" Mitchell chortled.

"Yes. Just like that!" Marcus bellowed.

"It's a suicide mission!" Captain Mitchell snapped. "I'm not going to risk all our lives just to save one, at least not without proper intel."

Marcus felt the rage building up inside him. How could the captain speak that way about Raven? She'd been with them from the very beginning and there wasn't a soul among them she wouldn't risk her life to save. He lowered his head in disbelief. There was no way he would abandon her so easily, no way he would give in to loss and lose another piece of what it was that made him human.

"If you won't save her, I will," he proclaimed defiantly, not raising his head.

"No, Corporal," Captain Mitchell forbade him, using Marcus' rank to hammer home his authority. "You will follow my orders."

Marcus felt his anger beginning to take over, extending outwards, tendrils of pure rage consuming him from the inside out, touching everything in his vicinity. He clenched his fists and tensed his jaw, trying to keep himself under control.

"We're going back to the hotel and that's final!" Captain Mitchell concluded.

With that, the lights in the foreman's office began to flicker. As the others looked up at the luminescent tiles in the ceiling, the windows suddenly exploded outwards, thousands of shards of toughened glass raining down on the streets outside. Marcus barely even noticed, so overcome was he by his emotions.

"Marcus!" Reid shouted, realizing what was causing the bizarre phenomena, his voice barely registering on the raging clone as crates and barrels began to vibrate.

A tremor shot through the floor, shaking the very foundations and breaking cracks in the walls.

"You have to stop, Marcus!" Reid shouted, grabbing him by the shoulders and trying to shake him out of his uncontrollable rage. "We'll find a way! We'll save her!"

Marcus couldn't feel anything. His anger was so all-consuming that it left him numb. It was as if his beaker had been filled with rage, and there was no way to prevent it from overflowing. Reid moved his hands up, grabbing Marcus by the sides of his head, staring intently into his eyes, struggling to maintain his grip.

"Marcus, stop!" he shouted. "We'll get her back!"

Marcus focused his attention on Reid's merciful eyes, drawing strength from his determination.

Slowly, the quakes began to reside, and within seconds, Marcus slumped to the floor, so emotionally and physically drained that he could barely even keep his eyes open. As he slowly began to fall into unconsciousness, he saw Captain Mitchell kneeling over him.

* * * * *

Marcus awoke lying on his bunk back at the hotel. Serena was sitting at his bedside, affectionately wiping his forehead with a damp cloth, her long dark hair gleaming in the dim light of the room.

"Where am I?" he managed to mumble.

"The others brought you back to the hotel," Serena reassured him. "Drink some of this."

She handed him a glass of water, but he could only take a small sip before having to lay it back on his bedside table.

"Where is everyone?"

"They went to that club," she told him.

"The club?" he probed, bewildered. "Why?"

"Reid said something about someone there who might be able to help with finding Raven," she replied.

"Wait, they're not giving up on her?" he mumbled, astonished at the captain's change of heart.

"Give up on her?" she wondered, her eyebrows raised. "Why would you say that? The captain said they'd continue the search until the *Tengri* is ready."

Marcus smiled as he leaned back in his bed. Serena laid her hand on his forehead, running her delicate fingers across his skin.

"What exactly happened to you?" she asked. "The captain said you hit your head, but I can't see any bruises. Even Doc Taylor said you just needed to rest."

It took him a minute to remember that she wasn't privy to their abilities.

"Oh… yeah, I guess I must have," he dissembled awkwardly. "I should get up. I want to go with them."

"No, you should stay in bed!" she told him, pressing her warm hands on his chest. "You're still weak."

"No really. I'm fine," he lied. "I really have to speak with the captain."

As he tried to sit up and reach for his clothes, which lay on a small footstool near the edge of the bed, his muscles ached with every movement. Finally he gave in and leaned back once more.

"I guess you're right," he said. "Perhaps I do need some rest."

She stared at him, clearly wanting to say something, but she held her tongue. As she prepared to stand up and leave, Marcus caught hold of her wrist.

"Don't leave," he said. "I mean… you can if you want to."

"I can stay," she answered with a small smile, sitting down once more, which began another awkward silence.

"Do you… like him?" Marcus asked eventually, immediately regretting it.

"Who?" she asked, tilting her head so that her raven locks swayed away from her kind eyes.

"Dasaan…"

"Of course," she admitted, shooting him a naive smile.

Marcus felt his heart skip a beat. He'd waited too long. He'd had all the opportunities in the world to tell her how he felt, but now she-

"He's a purple alien with a tail," she continued. "He's fascinating! There's so much I can learn from him."

"Oh," Marcus sighed, realizing that her admiration for their new cook might be more academic than anything else.

"I must be starting to get on his nerves, because I honestly can't stop asking him all sorts of questions."

"There is that," Marcus chuckled, suddenly feeling rather relieved, and much better.

* * * * *

The dimly-lit corridor beneath the Zazunitse was lined with arched alcoves along both sides, concealed behind velvety turquoise curtains. A few shady characters occupied the hallway, well-armed and fidgety as they stood guard whilst their employers enjoyed the company of a variety of exotic consorts behind the curtains.

Captain Mitchell spotted the two Nerokan bodyguards near the rear and immediately alerted the others.

"I hope you have a plan Captain," Dasaan urged, "Kesha Kun is the most powerful figure in all of Sheijan, and Lishan is the youngest of his three sons."

"Then we'd best be discreet," Mitchell answered sternly.

As they approached, one of Lishan's bodyguards stepped forth, blocking their passage.

"Kho aygoshi," the reptilian escort grunted, baring its teeth as it hefted its spear.

"We're not allowed to go any further," Dasaan worriedly explained to the others.

"Well, then you'd better explain to him that we're not leaving without first having a word with his boss," the captain instructed him, drawing an even more troubled look from Dasaan.

As soon as he relayed the captain's message, the guard began shoving him aggressively, shouting harsh words in its guttural tongue. Startled by the sudden display of hostility, Taz lowered his hand to the sidearm on his belt.

Almost instantly, the second Nerokan guard twisted the handle of his spear, and in less than a second its metallic shaft had morphed into a nasty-looking sword blade with a keen serrated edge, much better suited to use in the confined quarters of the corridor than his spear had been. He pointed the tip in Taz's direction, gesturing for him to remove his hand from the weapon.

Behind them, Reid saw that other patrons were beginning to take note of the confrontation. "Guys," he said softly. "I don't think this is such a good idea."

Captain Mitchell assessed the situation and saw the futility of their attempt. The bodyguards were clearly no ordinary foot soldiers he could bluster his way past, but highly-skilled mercenaries armed with

307

incredibly advanced weaponry.

"Alright, let's back off," he ordered. "We'll have to find another way."

They raised their hands in the air in a sign of surrender and began to back off slowly, the two Nerokans watching them with cold, reptilian stares.

"No!" Taz blurted out in protest, clenching his eyes shut and tensing his muscles as he tried to shift his focus inward.

The captain grabbed his shoulder, attempting to shake some sense into their upstart scout, but Mitchell's protest only strengthened Taz's conviction. The vein on his neck was throbbing, his whole body begging to tremble as he fought desperately to summon the lethal strength he'd somehow called upon on Strom. He let out a faint groan as he clenched every muscle he could. The closest Nerokan bodyguard tilted his head, staring at him with great interest. Taz focused on his anger, his self-loathing, and felt-

"Are you trying to shit your pants?" Reid asked, his voice disbelieving.

Taz wheezed, inhaling and exhaling rapidly, his muscles relaxing. After a moment he turned to Mitchell.

"Sorry, Sir. I thought maybe if I tried really hard, I could do what I did on Strom," he explained, somewhat embarrassed.

The Nerokan guard let out a deep, gurgling laugh, mocking the scout in his alien tongue.

Taz felt so disappointed. If only he could transform into the same ravaging beast he had become on Strom, he knew he could show these lizards that he was no one to mess with! He glared at the laughing mercenary, who noticed him and stared right back, its mocking laughter ringing in his ears. Without even thinking Taz reached out, seizing to the side of Taylor's belt and grabbing one of the medic's atmos canisters, thrusting the metal cylinder at the Nerokan, his thumb firmly on the protruding valve. Startled, the Nerokan jumped back, as did the rest of the shady patrons close enough to see what was happening.

"Dasaan," Taz said calmly, his eyes locked with those of the bodyguard. "Tell this piece of shit that unless we get to speak to Lishan, I'll blow us all to hell."

It was a tremendous lie. At best, the atmos canister might exude a slight wheezing noise, but certainly nothing that could cause them any harm. However, there was no way his opponent could have known that.

"Isn't that-" Reid began, eyeing the object in Taz's hand.

"Yup," Captain Mitchell cut him off, grinning. "Dasarn, tell them."

After rolling his eyes at the way the Captain mangled his name, Dasaan nervously conveyed Taz's threat in a loud, clear voice. As he did so, there was a rustle of movement behind them as patrons and girls made themselves scarce. Even a wobbling, stark-naked Banthalo tumbled out of from one of the alcoves behind them, hurriedly making his way towards the exit as he tried not to drop his bundled clothing.

"What'll it be?" Taz pressed, wielding the phony grenade in as intimidating a manner as he could muster.

Before the guards could reply, the turquoise curtain at their side slid open just wide enough to reveal the slender hand of the alcove's Sheshen occupant as he calmly handed one of them a piece of bone-white cloth. As the black-armored hand disappeared once more behind the curtain, the disgruntled guard unfolded the fabric and briefly scanned its contents, then tossed it on the floor at Taz's feet.

Dasaan scurried to retrieve it as Taz kept his dead-eyed stare fixed on the Nerokans.

"What does it say?" Mitchell asked as Dasaan returned to his side.

"Guahashou Bath House, tomorrow at eight."

Chapter 39

Marcus awoke to the discomforting feeling of cold steel pressing against his flesh. The chamber was cold and dark. The bitter scent of disinfectant filled his senses. He tried to struggle, but his head, hands and legs were bound tightly by black synthetic straps which disappeared into long narrow slits along the sides of the operating table. He heard a soft thumping as his ankles and elbows slammed into the table as he writhed, furiously trying to break free.

"Tahashiu shalit ish," a voice in the darkness whispered. "Shao stugomi subuchi kho ang mumagi shito sakdoy."

His mind was racing. When he'd fallen asleep he'd been lying in his bed at the hotel, safe in Serena's company. Had he been abducted under the cover of night? Was he alone or had they all been taken? A hundred questions clouded his mind as his heart began pounding harder and faster with each passing moment.

His struggling had slightly loosened the thick strap around his forehead, allowing him to wriggle his head slightly from side to side. Looking around his limited field of vision, he could see all manner of blinking consoles and scientific equipment lining the wall on his right. A tray holding a variety of gruesome surgical tools stood on a stand near the corner of the room, some of them covered in a yellow viscous fluid. The real terror set in when he managed to twist his neck to catch glimpse of what lay on the other side of the darkened chamber.

A lone, slender figure slouched over an identical operating table, its back turned towards him. The sound of metal grinding against flesh and bone sent shivers down his spine. A small puddle of the same yellow liquid he had seen on the surgical tools was pooling at the base of the table, dripping down to the floor.

The shadowy figure turned, revealing its narrow bony head and cold, black eyes as it lurched over to one of the consoles in the far corner of the room, adjusting a series of knobs. Marcus nearly froze when he saw the focus of the figure's work.

A female Hrūll lay strapped to the table, her chest cavity spread wide open and held ajar by a fearsome mechanical arm hanging from the ceiling, her tiny breasts still visible on the slabs of meat that had once formed the front of torso. Rows of spindly manipulators clasped onto flaps of skin and the tips of her ribs, spreading them outwards. A series of transparent tubes extended from the base of the mechanical arm and ran down to her neck and skull, pumping her body full of some God-awful liquid. With a start, Marcus realized he was almost certain that he could hear her heart beating. Whatever was being done to her, she was still alive. He couldn't believe what was happening. It had to be a dream. It just couldn't be real.

The surgeon returned, barely glancing over to where he lay as he resumed his work, cutting through sinewy muscle and bone with no more regard than a mechanic would have exercised when picking apart an engine. Marcus panicked. He screamed at the top of his lungs, crying out hysterically. He had never felt so alone, so helpless, in all his life. He wailed and shouted for what felt like a long time, but inevitably silence finally overcame him.

It wasn't so much death that he feared. He had long since come to terms with the inevitability of his own demise, given the nature of his existence as a cloned soldier in a hostile universe. What he feared was the mask that death had chosen to wear when it came to claim him.

The Hrüll's heartbeat was growing stronger, more frequent. Seemingly alarmed, the surgeon grabbed a new set of tools and began probing and prodding, attempting to prolong the inevitable. Not long afterwards, her heart simply stopped.

The surgeon slumped back, the clanking sound of his tools dropping to the table echoing throughout the chamber. Without so much as a hint of remorse, he turned towards Marcus, pausing momentarily at the sound of what Marcus thought sounded like gunfire from outside the chamber.

The surgeon shook his head, seemingly in resignation, as he pressed a button somewhere on the side of the table's frame. Almost immediately, the horrendous mechanical arm relinquished its hold on the Hrüll's flesh and bones with a sickening series of crunches. Its agile fingers sprung inwards and upwards, like the legs of a nightmarish metallic crab. The entire contraption then slowly began to slide along rails in the ceiling to rest right above Marcus' midsection.

"Shao manshin logasho ang shabinoi," the surgeon whispered, holding up a fresh serrated scalpel, "hut shito manshin banshan adisho yagosh."

The mechanical fingers sprung to life once more, descending slowly upon his chest. Marcus screamed in terror. He tried as hard as he could to muster enough strength to pull his head far enough from the table to get a proper look at what he thought had to be the exit, a featureless metal door somewhere beyond the foot of his operating table, but he couldn't manage it.

Suddenly, he was hit by an unexpected revelation. As he bent his neck to look down along his own trapped body, he saw two fleshy mounds protruding from his chest. It wasn't him after all. It was

313

Raven.

*   *   *   *   *

"Wake up Marcus," came Reid's familiar voice, stirring him from his restless slumber.

The dark-skinned sniper had been standing over him and trying to shake him out of his turbulent dreams. Marcus flailed his arms violently as he awoke, almost knocking Reid to the floor.

"Marcus, Marcus, relax! It was just a dream," Reid shouted.

Marcus breathed a gasp of relief as he recognized his surroundings. Taz and Doc Taylor were both sitting at the foot of their beds rubbing their eyes, having been awoken by Marcus' screams.

"What the hell's going on?" Taylor demanded.

"You were only dreaming. Go back to sleep," Reid told Marcus.

"I was her," Marcus gasped. "I was Raven."

Reid stared at him in bewilderment.

"You're supposed to dream about touching naked girls Marcus. Not about being one yourself," Taz groaned as he crawled back into bed, turning his back on them and pulling his covers over his head.

Taylor lit himself a cigarette, rolling his head as he peered through the darkness.

"I have to tell the captain!" Marcus proclaimed.

"I don't think the captain wants to be woken up just to hear about your wet dreams," the medic objected. "It's the middle of the night, and we've got an important day tomorrow."

"No you don't understand," Marcus insisted. "It was more than just a dream! I could see what they were doing to her."

Shaking his head in disbelief, Reid took a step back.

314

"I know you've had visions before, but are you sure this wasn't just a dream?" Reid asked, half trying to convince him. "We're all under a lot of stress, especially you, after that incident at the foreman's office."

"I'm telling you Rev, this was no dream! They're experimenting on her, cutting into her," Marcus yelled. "I could feel everything! Her fear, her pain! I don't think... she has much time left."

His pronouncement was met with a horrified silence from his squadmates.

"From what I understood of your earlier visions, they're more like premonitions, signs of things to come, right?" Reid said thoughtfully. "So what you saw doesn't have to be happening right now, does it?"

Marcus didn't reply, just stared up at his friend.

"Listen," Reid sighed. "There isn't really much we can do about it now anyway. We have no idea where she's being held, but we have our meeting with what's-his-face tomorrow. Until then we'll just have to wait and pray to God to keep her safe."

Marcus considered Reid's wise words. He knew he was right. So far, his visions had always preceded the events themselves. With luck, and perhaps some help from Reid's God, they might be able to reach her in time.

"Do you think your God would listen to my prayers even if I don't really believe in him?" Marcus asked.

"He's not my God. He's everyone's God," Reid countered kindly, "and of course he'll listen to you. He'll listen to anyone who seeks his guidance."

"Hmpf," Marcus smiled, taken with the idea. "So... how does it work?"

"I'll show you."

They put their hands together, resting their foreheads against one

315

another's. Marcus listened at first as Reid began to recite his prayers, then began repeating them. Even though he found it somewhat strange to be pleading with an imaginary being for the safety of their friend, there was something comforting in the whole experience.

The tension in his body began to dissipate and his mind became clearer, more focused on the task at hand. When he eventually laid his head back onto his pillow for what he hoped would be a more peaceful slumber, he was filled with a renewed confidence. Wherever they were keeping her, her brothers would find her.

Chapter 40

The next morning, Captain Mitchell did not take the news of Marcus' vision lightly. If he'd had any reservations about going after Raven before, they were thrown out the window by what Marcus told him.

"Damn this whole God-forsaken planet!" he had roared, kicking over his bed in a fit of rage.

Waiting for the clock to strike eight proved difficult.

As far as the squad was concerned, they were preparing for war. There was no telling what would be waiting for them at the Guahashou Bath House. For all they knew, it could very well be a trap, but it was a chance they could not afford to dismiss.

When Mitchell had broached the subject with him, Dasaan had elected not to accompany them, fearing the outcome of the engagement. Though he was indeed grateful for being offered a place on the crew, volunteering for a possible suicide mission was not something he believed fell under the duties of the ship's cook. Fortunately, Serena had been more than willing to go with them to act as interpreter, should the need arise.

They spent most of the day cleaning and oiling their weapons, stripping their firearms down to their component pieces on the cleanest of the bed sheets the hotel had to offer, filling every single magazine they'd brought with them from the *Tengri* with rounds from a case Jago had stashed under his bunk. They donned and adjusted their armor, tightening straps and reattaching equipment pouches, jumping up and down to make sure everything fit tightly without restricting their movement. Serena even appropriated the suit belonging to Raven, which had seen little use. Marcus was against the idea of her coming along, but her persistence quickly wore him down, and he eventually helped get her equipped.

Meanwhile Jago was using straps cut from the crews' rucksacks to create a sling for the huge laser cannon he'd acquired on the Hrūll gas refinery, wanting to wield his powerful machinegun for its superior cyclic rate, but still have the heavy alien weapon available to him. Reid had taken apart his sniper rifle and was carefully polish the lenses of its scope, the long barrel of the weapon propped up against the bed beside him glistening with oil. If there were to be any surprises at their meeting that evening, the squad was determined to be ready for them.

* * * * *

From the outside, the Guahashou Bath House was an amazingly conspicuous structure, built on the roof of a small decaying skyscraper. Pillars of stone lined a flagstone path leading to a series of marble steps which climbed up to a tall arched doorway, fill with a pair of heavy metal double doors. The gothic façade resembled an uninviting cathedral more than a place of tranquility and cleansing. The only means of ingress was an extendable mechanical bridge which spanned an urban chasm between two rooftops, soaring above platforms and walkways. Further below, the unforgiving shroud of poisonous gas awaited those who failed to navigate its narrow path.

Outside, an honor guard of eight Nerokan mercenaries stood at attention, wielding serrated spears and dressed in the red and black of the Dark Sun Empire. Two of them barred passage on the public side of the chasm while the other six were stationed between the towering pillars.

When the Terrans approached, the guards crossed their spears in a clear sign that none were allowed to cross the bridge. Captain Mitchell produced the note he had received from Lishan's bodyguard, and, after careful scrutiny, the reptilian aliens stepped aside to allow them passage.

When they reached the pillars, the guards barked at them in Sheshen, which Serena interpreted as meaning that only one of them would be allowed to enter. Without waiting for Mitchell's answer, the beautiful linguist pleaded with the guards to allow her to accompany the captain as his interpreter. She was promptly informed that their master was well versed in the Gaian tongue.

Captain Mitchell weighed his options and finally decided that if the Nerokans insisted he had to go it alone, there really wasn't much they could do about it. Though they were fully armed and armored, there was no telling how many guards could be stationed inside the premises, and if Lishan was in fact willing to render assistance to their cause, going in guns blazing was a sure-fire way of changing his mind.

As he prepared to enter, the Nerokan guards confiscated his weaponry and performed a thorough search of his person for any signs of trickery. The thick reptilian arms were less than gentle, tossing the captain back and forth as they pushed and pulled each piece of his armor to see if anything would pop loose. He felt like a marionette at the mercy of their powerful grip. When they were satisfied, the doors began to part, creaking loudly as they slowly swung open, releasing billows of steam into the dusky evening air.

The captain passed into the veil of mist, each step echoing through

319

the massive chamber beyond. He paused briefly, turning to send his team a reaffirming nod before disappearing from view.

Inside, he was greeted by rows of massive ornate pillars along each side of the huge room, around which lay pools of tranquil waters shrouded in a thin layer of mist. The slanted ceiling above was easily thirty or forty meters tall, rising to a shallow point at the center. Striking statues, hewn from the finest marble, rested in alcoves in the walls, depicting various creatures in erotic poses.

With not a single guard – or any other living creature – in sight, he proceeded hesitantly along a broad path, which lead to a large central pool. Copper pipes poured billows of steamy vapors onto the pool's surface, creating waves of milky clouds which crept along the serene waters. As he ventured farther into the chamber, a lone figure began to take shape in the center of the pool, silhouetted against the stark light source behind it.

The naked figure rose from the gentle waters, exposing its sickly brown skin and weirdly slender limbs. A round, white mask seemingly of fragile porcelain, painted with golden circles around the mouth and eyes, floated about the twisted body. A thick mane of white hair flowed from the very back of the figure's skull, like a writhing nest of serpents poised to strike.

Captain Mitchell paused at the bank of the pool, where a few wide steps descended into the waters.

"Welcome," the creature spoke, its soft, husky voice barely carrying across the water. "I am Lissshan, ssson of Kesssha Kun."

Mitchell looked left and right, peering into each and every dark corner. Surprisingly there were still no guards in sight. Judging by his host's lineage, he would have expected an entire platoon of servants and guardians. As a psiops he'd been well trained not to let down his guard. He reached out with his mind, focusing his will so that he could feel every living being in his surroundings.

"We are alone," Lishan assured him, seeing his hesitation. "You ssseem rather sssurprised."

"I-" Captain Mitchell began, but he was cut off.

"You thought sssomeone of my ssstature would be lessss… vulnerable," Lishan offered. "I am the youngessst of my brethren. I am not afforded the sssame luxuries asss the otherss. That isss not to sssay that I find myself wanting. On the contrary, I rather enjoy the lack of… sssupervision."

"Why did you agree to see me?" Mitchell asked hesitantly.

"Why not?" Lishan countered. "There are few thingsss in thisss world that I find entertaining. Meeting new and interesting people isss one of them."

"Why do you hide your face behind a mask?" the captain blurted out, regretting the question almost immediately as he remembered Serena's experience with Roshana.

"Have you any idea what it isss like having othersss grimace at the very sssight of you? My people are very aware of how the other racesss perceive usss. We go through life terrified of the ridicule we are made to endure if ssseen for what we truly are," Lishan stated, sounding oddly resigned.

"You mean kidnapping scum?" Mitchell snapped, angered by the Sheshen's calm confidence.

"Mossst amusing Captain," Lishan sneered. "I can assssure you, your pilot isss not in my possessssion. It isss my father who hasss that honor."

"I don't give a rat's ass who has her!" Mitchell bellowed. "I want her back, now. I will not allow her to become part of your father's collection!"

"Collection?" Lishan chuckled. "I believe you are misssinformed. My father doesss not collect. He wantsss her powersss."

"Her abilities?" Mitchell asked nervously.

"Precisssely. My father is obsesssed with finding the answer to unlocking the powersss of the mind. He believesss that through... unressstrained exxxperimentation, he will find the way."

"Over my dead body!" Mitchell proclaimed defiantly.

"You care for her?" Lishan probed.

"I care for all of my crew."

"Ssso you are a man of honor?"

"What do you know about honor?" the captain spat. "Your people don't seem to know the meaning of the word!"

"That isss where you are wrong," Lishan announced calmly, wading through the pool to approach him, his long flowing locks writhing in the mist.

Chapter 41

The proprietor of the hotel had his hands full trying to appease the raging squad as they scurried back and forth between rooms, preparing for the assault. Given all they'd already done in preparation for their meeting at the bath house, there was little left for them to do, which only set them even more on edge, and they wanted to get going as soon as possible.

Lishan had proved most forthcoming. In addition to giving them the location of his father's hidden palatial compound, he had promised to provide them with a means of entry to the secure stronghold. Still, the task seemed almost insurmountable. The compound was a veritable fortress several kilometers outside the city, shrouded in the toxic mists of Nos Shana.

"And you really believe we can trust him?" Reid asked, apparently unconvinced.

"If you have a better idea, then let's hear it," Mitchell snapped. "The guy seems to have a real problem with his father. One thing's for sure, we're not going in there without plenty of firepower."

He tore open a case of grenades and proceeded to hand them out to the squad.

"I'm not saying the information he gave you wasn't correct," Reid persisted. "I'm just saying that there has to be a better way to get in. Going down to the ground level and through the... what did you called it?"

"Urdak Nor," Mitchell answered, furrowing his brow.

"What's that?" Jago probed as he clasped his grenades onto his belt harness.

"It's some kind of game. They play it on the lowest level of the city," the captain explained.

"Wait. Do you mean that thing where they beat each other to death over some medallion?" Taz asked, suddenly remembering the holograph of the game he'd seen in the bar on their first trip out in Sheijan, just before his fateful argument with Kaiden.

The captain nodded grimly.

"Captain, that's not so much a game as it is a warzone!" Taz yelled.

"Well, in that case I'd better come with you so you don't get scared," Taylor joked.

"How are we even allowed to go down there?" the scout demanded, clearly desperate to avoid the brutal arena.

Mitchell didn't reply, merely fixing Taz with a cold stare.

"You're not serious?" the short clone whined.

Without taking his eyes off Taz, Mitchell unlocked the safety of his weapon to show that he was indeed dead serious.

* * * * *

Staring down into the abyss, Marcus shuddered at the thought of what awaited them below. The platform the squad was traversing wound its way gently downwards around a cylindrical tower, ending abruptly at an opening in the side wall onto an open platform hanging precariously between two towers, where a pair of other contestants were awaiting their turn to join the game. Descent to the arena below was made possible by three rusting cages, suspended on chains, each of which appeared ready to crumble to dust under even the slightest of pressures.

Of the other two contestants, one was a dwarf-sized Banthalo with a pointy ridged nose and heavily scarred skin. He was holding the end of a chain which was fastened to the collar of a hulking Golan behemoth, larger even than Jakunu had been. The gigantic beast wielded a nasty-looking spiked club the size of a lamppost. Cybernetic implants protruded from his skull, clearly dulling his wits and increasing his aggression. He snarled as they approached, resulting in a quick yank of the chain from his master, who eyed them all suspiciously, sizing them up before the ensuing battle.

"Are you alright Serena?" Marcus whispered, sensing her tension. "It's not too late for you to turn back."

"I'll be ok," she replied, her eyes fixated on the Golan berserker. "I can't believe anyone could do something so hideous to such a gentle creature."

Marcus gripped her firmly by the shoulder in reassurance. Raven's body armor was a bit of a loose fit, but as much as he expected otherwise he hoped there'd be no need to test its durability.

A team of slender, masked Sheshen organizers were there to greet the contestants, making sure that everything was in order for their entry into the arena. Surprisingly, their carbines, sidearms, and grenades passed inspection. Even Jago's massive laser wasn't prohibited in the Urdak Nor.

The midget Banthalo and his hulking slave entered the first poorly-constructed cage, which creaked loudly with each step. The loud clanking noise as the decaying metal frame began to descend was nearly as chilling as the wailing of the Golan inside it as he thrashed about nervously.

"So it's all of us against those two?" Marcus asked, sizing up his team and suddenly not feeling quite so timid.

Taz shook his head apprehensively. "I think the game's already started. We're latecomers."

"What are the rules?" Reid asked, drawing blank stares from a pair of organizers, who apparently understood no Gaian.

"There are none," Taz told him. "Whoever's holding the shiny medallion at the end of the game is the winner."

"We're not here to play," Captain Mitchell whispered, reminding them of their objective. "We're just entering the game so we can reach the R.V. Don't go doing anything stupid. Just stay alive and follow me."

"Tell that to them," Serena muttered, staring at the descending cage.

"You sure you want do this, Serena?" Captain Mitchell voiced. "If you want to go back to the hotel, it's not too late."

"I'm sure. You might need me to interpret," Serena affirmed. "And besides, Taz is more of a girl than I am."

Jago let out a roar of laughter.

"Just make sure to stick to the rear and stay in cover if anything happens," Captain Mitchell commanded.

They entered the second cage just as a pair of Nerokan mercenaries led a small group of malnourished slaves of various humanoid races bound in heavy chains onto the platform, fresh fodder to appease the crowd. Their bleak expressions were a testament to their despair.

The ride down was nerve wracking. Shimmering barriers on each side, erected between the towering skyscrapers, kept the poisonous gases at bay, but they could still see the roiling green-tinted atmosphere only a short distance away. Muffled roars and cries of pain and suffering could be heard over the creaking chains. Somewhere in the distance, a barrage of laser blasts tore through the battlefield below them. The ride seemed to last forever, the level of anxiety rising almost palpably with each crank of the chain. Thunderous explosions rang through the air every so often, throwing up clouds of dark smoke.

Below them, a debris field of cracked cement walls rose out of the night, spreading out between the massive trunks of the skyscrapers, choked with rubble. The ground was littered with all manner of discarded barrels and crates, and even the occasional discarded vehicle or ship's hull. Some areas were lit by powerful floodlights, and there was more than one fire burning. Still, most of the area was in perpetual twilight, the artificial light of the city above filtering down from above, diffused by the thick atmosphere and protective force fields.

Marcus could see shadowy figures dashing back and forth in running battles, some cowering in fear, others snapping of volleys of projectile fire from cover. The most aggressive swung exotic blades, clubs and axes at anything that moved in ferocious charges. As they neared the ground, a walled-off area immediately below them rose into view, enveloping a small oasis of calm before the ensuing madness beyond, its only exit a bottleneck of death and mayhem where a scattering of bodies had already been claimed by the games.

"Ape, you'll have to provide suppressive fire so we can get out of that death trap," Captain Mitchell gestured towards the bottleneck.

A disk-shaped drone a little less than half a meter across came hovering up beside the cage, its absurdly-large central lens recording everything that transpired and broadcasting it out to the masses.

"Yes boss," Jago muttered.

Marcus thought he caught a slight hint of glee in his voice.

The walls rose outside the cage, which clanked to a halt in the midst of a small courtyard floored with mud, enclosed by semi-circular cement walls five meters high, a small sanctuary amidst the carnage.

A pair of armed Nerokan overseers waited anxiously for their arrival. While one opened the cage, the other poked and prodded them with the butt of his spear, cackling maniacally as he ushered them out to join in the games.

Ahead of them, the towering Golan hunched as he strode through the bottleneck, dragging his club behind him as he stumbled towards the thick wall that provided cover for emerging players. His master produced a small laser pistol and fired haphazardly into the air, frothing at the mouth as he tugged on the huge beast's reins.

"Let's give them a moment," Mitchell suggested

The Golan was far removed from the peaceful creatures they'd grown to know and care for on Ga'ouna. Not only had his behavior obviously been significantly altered, but judging by the scars on his back he'd undergone extensive surgery, presumably to make him a more worthy champion for the games.

"Captain," Reid sighed. "I've got an-"

"-an itch," Captain Mitchell interjected. "So have I, Albano. So have I."

After a brief pause, during which the Nerokan overseers grew even more restless and began urging them out onto the field with increased fervor, the squad begrudgingly stalked towards the bottleneck, weapons raised at the ready, prepared for the worst. Marcus felt a surge of adrenalin flow through his body as every muscle tensed up and his focus narrowed, filtering out all other concerns. Serena stayed in the rear, shielded behind Reid and Doc Taylor.

Jago and Taz went on first, with Marcus and Captain Mitchell following quickly behind them. Taz ran up to the head-high barricade in front of the bottleneck, peeking over it to check that the Golan and his master were looking the other way before jumping up and rolling quickly over the barricade's broad top, disappearing into the rubble beyond to scout their route. The rest of the squad moved up behind him, settling in behind the wall and waiting for his signal.

A sudden trail of smoke and fire blew clear through the small clearing beyond the wall, originating from a mound of debris on the opposite side of the cramped space. The rocket-propelled grenade impacted on the other side of the barricade with a bang, blowing up a thick cloud of dust and smoke as shrapnel tore through the area.

Serena gave a short shriek of terror as she huddled between Reid and Taylor, one that was quickly drowned out by a deafening roar as the Golan berserker began smashing through the surrounding debris with his overgrown club, tossing and turning, flailing his chain about with no regard at all for his master's safety.

Crouched safely behind a toppled hovercraft, Taz looked on in horror as the small Banthalo was slammed helplessly into one pile of rubble after another. His cries for help went unheard and soon turned to a wailing sob of pain which quickly died out altogether.

Debris was thrown left and right from the Golan's furious blows as its master was reduced to a bloody pulp. Free from authority, the berserker soon lost interest in the surrounding wreckage. Having either killed or scared off whoever had fired the explosive, and any other opponent in the vicinity, it staggered off in search of more.

In the sudden silence, Marcus noted a swarm of recording drones hovering overhead, monitoring the scene from every angle. After a moment, Taz softly called the all clear.

"Let's move!" the captain bellowed, "Alternating fire teams, left and right."

329

They poured through the opening to the left of the barricade, making sure to navigate the field as far away as possible from the direction the berserk giant had taken. As they moved, Marcus pressed a series of buttons on his new wrist computer, calling up a holographic map of the surrounding area. A glowing dot near the far edge of the field indicated the location of their rendezvous point with Lishan's contact.

* * * * *

Hanan Aru clung to the chains as the throng of wailing slaves below descended through a thin mist of clouds. The chameleon function of his suit made him virtually invisible to onlookers above, and the unfortunate inhabitants of the cage hanging below him had more to worry about than a hidden stowaway.

He adjusted his visor to show the heat signatures of those below, making sure to compensate for the handful of flaming infernos strewn throughout the field. He quickly spotted his targets – the only large group moving with military cohesion – entering the small clearing below, rushing into cover behind one of the mounds of wreckage.

Quickly calculating the trajectory for his jump, aligning himself with the far wall, Hanan Aru eased himself down onto the roof of the cage, crouching still for a moment. Once he was ready, he flung himself into the air, the force of his departure sending the cage swinging back and forth and drawing a chorus of sobs and woeful wails from the wretches inside.

It was an impossible leap, nearly fifty meters in the open air and a drop of almost twice as far. He prepared himself for the impact, adjusting the hydraulics in his suit to receive the blow. The suit's built-in A.I. systems were so remarkably intuitive that he need only think of a command and the suit would carry it out to perfection.

The impact nearly shattered the stone wall, sending cracks rippling out across its surface all the way to the ground, two stories below. Before the Nerokan overseers had a chance to inspect the cause of the crumbling, Hanan Aru was already on his way, dropping to the muddy floor in one smooth motion and lunging through the debris field like a nimble predator catching scent of its prey.

Chapter 42

The squad had trekked through the smoldering ruins and decaying rubble for the better part of an hour, doing their best to steer clear of lurking gladiators in the dim light. There was no telling how many other combatants were still fighting, but judging by the amount of gunfire and screams echoing through the concrete jungle it was safe to say that there were indeed a fair few.

Taz had taken point, scouting ahead to stop them from falling into an ambush, Marcus not far behind him, controlling the squad's route. Reid kept a constant eye on the mounds of debris and lower levels of half-collapsed buildings, watching for hostile marksmen as they slowly made their way to the rendezvous point.

They'd already traversed more than a third of the arena in this formation, with little more than a couple of very brief skirmishes under their belts. Few other players had teamed up as they did, and a force their size did not prove easy for the picking. Most of their assailants had abandoned their assaults, simply running off at the realization they'd bitten off more than they could chew, searching for easier prey. Despite the relative ease of their passage, Marcus had the uncanny feeling that they were being watched at every turn, and had no trouble keeping his guard up.

Taz led them around the remains of a five-meter tall circular cement structure with rusted iron poles sticking out of its walls at odd angles, most of them bent and twisted out of shape. They rounded its bulk in tense silence, emerging in the mouth of yet another small clearing, this one littered with small blocks of rubble. Smoke trailed up into the air at the opposite end of the roughly-rectangular space from the burning husk of a dead body, its race and gender unidentifiable. On the ground, no more than a dozen meters away, a disc-shaped metallic object about twenty centimeters across lay undisturbed in the dirt, a lone green light in its center blinking periodically.

"Trap?" Marcus asked softly, eyeing the device suspiciously.

"Trap," Mitchell agreed. "Reid, how's our flank?"

Reid's long rifle peered over a nearby mound, the sniper stretched out behind it on his stomach, scanning the arena.

"Looks clear, Sir. I've some commotion over to the south-east, and there are a couple of roamers not too far north from here, but nothing we can't handle."

Doc Taylor knelt down to grab a small lump of debris, which he then threw straight at the device. The rock bounced right off its casing, making a loud clanking noise, but having no other visible effect.

"Seems safe to me," he grinned, using the reprieve to jam a cigarette into his mouth between his helmet's chin-plates, lighting it with a flourish.

"We'll go around," Mitchell snapped at the grinning medic, looking back over his shoulder as he pondered possible routes.

Instinctively, Jago made for the device.

"It's no problem, boss," the huge man declared as he strode straight out into the clearing. "It's just a-"

"Ape, no!" Marcus yelled, but it was too late.

Jago turned to see why they were making such a big deal out of such a small object, just as the disc's biosensor triggered the explosives within. With a deafening boom, the explosion tore through the clearing, hitting Jago square in the chest and hurling him through the air and into the mound of tumbled rocks next to the others. Marcus had never seen something so big fly through the air with such ease.

Their ears still ringing from the blow, the squad jumped into action. Reid and Taz flung themselves into cover to protect the rest of the squad, and by the time Marcus reached the huge man Doc Taylor was already at Jago's side, staring at a thick, rusted metal rod that had pierced clean through Jago's hip, pinning him to the rubble. His armor was badly scorched and cracked in several locations, and he was covered in dust, dirt, and blood.

"Idiot!" Captain Mitchell roared, rushing to his aid.

"Is he dead?" Serena cried from the sidelines.

"He's alive!" Taylor pronounced. "Help me get him free."

It took the four of them to pull him lose, and as worried as Taylor was that removing him might cause more damage to his wound, he knew they couldn't simply leave him in the arena. Blood was gushing from the wound, but after careful inspection, the medic was reassured to find that no major organs had been punctured. He had his hands full trying to cauterize the wound, but luckily Jago was unconscious, making it easier for him to work.

"So much blood," Serena gulped, clutching her hands to her chest.

"You ok?" Marcus asked her gently, laying his hand on her shoulder in a comforting manner. "The Ape's tough, he'll pull through."

"Why do you have to call him that?" she snapped angrily, pulling off her helmet to wipe away her tears.

"What, 'Ape'?"

"It's so demeaning!"

Marcus had never really thought about it. It was just a name that had stuck since the very beginning.

334

"I…" he stammered. "It wasn't my idea."

He was prevented from saying more by a sudden flash of light as a pulse of energy burst through their ranks, searing through a fractured piece of hull plating embedded in the mound of rubble.

"Contact!" Reid shouted from on top of the mound, immediately returning fire.

"Take cover!" the captain roared, jumping over a nearby block of cement and crouching behind it.

The team scattered. Marcus grabbed hold of Serena and dragged her to safety just as another bolt of energy slammed into the captain's shelter.

"How many?" Marcus shouted, pinning Serena down behind a slab of cement.

Another shot went overhead, flying wild.

"Two shooters on the north bank, range one hundred and twenty meters, just right of that red drum!" Reid yelled. "A third circling!"

"We've gotta get the Ape into cover!" Taylor shouted, crouching behind a broken steel pillar.

Jago's body lay face down in the dirt next to the spike that had held him impaled. From what Marcus could see from his precarious position, the big clone didn't seem to be breathing.

"Stay down!" Mitchell yelled.

Reid fired a couple of shots, desperately attempting to keep their assailants' heads down.

"Reid, covering fire!" the captain ordered. "Taz, Marcus, back out and see if you can find a way to flank them!"

"Are you crazy?" Taz objected. "There's no time!"

"Do your job!" Captain Mitchell roared at the scout, whose attention was focused on their wounded comrade.

Instead, Taz dropped his weapon, grabbed a pair of fragmentation grenades from his harness and prepared to sprint. Meanwhile, Reid began firing as quickly as he could.

"Taz, no!" Captain Mitchell yelled.

Reid sent a barrage of bullets screaming through the air.

Taz burst from cover, sprinting like he never had before, dodging left and right at random to throw off their opponents' aim. Just as he reached the end of the clearing, he threw the two grenades over the lip of the opposing mound of debris, sliding into the dirt as he flung himself, feet first, into a sliding dive that took him behind a large lump of what had once been a metal bulkhead.

The twin blasts blew up the top of the mound, sending one of their assailants flying through the air. The humanoid figure, its long braided black hair trailing behind it, landed on the jagged rubble of the arena with a sickening crunch. The other, a similar humanoid with a long tail of dark hair, threw itself sideways down the bank of debris just in the nick of time, rolling to the ground and dropping out of sight behind a cracked metal barrel.

Captain Mitchell raised his carbine and sent a steady stream of projectiles after the survivor, most of which bounced harmlessly off the barrel, but at least a few seemed to bore their way through. Marcus and Taylor followed his lead, snapping off shots at the drum as well.

Suddenly the figure behind the barrel threw a small glimmering ball into the air, which hovered momentarily before bursting into a brilliant flash of light, forcing the clones to shield their eyes. When the afterimages faded, they caught glimpse of a shadowy figure disappearing behind the remains of a stone staircase at the far end of the clearing.

"Reid," Mitchell yelled. "Any sign of that third contact?"

The sniper peered every which way, trying to pick up the trail of the missing target.

"Negative," he hollered back.

"Everyone stay down!" the captain ordered.

Taylor had a hard time remaining still. He kept looking at Jago, lying prone out in the open. If there was still time to save him, it was slipping away fast. Finally he couldn't take it any longer and lunged out, diving to his squadmate's aid.

Almost immediately, a stream of silvery needles pierced the air, some of them hitting Jago's broad back, barely missing a startled Taylor, who quickly hurled himself back into cover.

"What the hell was that?" he shouted when he was safe behind the broken pillar.

"Our missing target," Reid whispered, his voice barely audible over the comms, taking aim on a piece of hull plating sticking up from a nearby mound of broken rubble.

Marcus huddled close to Serena, keeping her safe from harm. She trembled as she pressed her body closer to his. He could feel her gentle breath on his neck. He was closer to her now than he'd ever been before. He wanted to say something, anything, but he knew this was neither the time nor the place. Not that he knew what he wanted to say anyway. His heart was racing. He didn't know whether it was on account of the battle or because of her. His right hand gripping his carbine firmly, he wrapped his left around her narrow shoulders, pulling her head into his armored shoulder.

"Everything's going to be ok," he whispered.

Taylor, lying on his back in the shelter of his pillar, picked up one of the needles that had missed its mark, inspecting it. The tip was coated in a clear, viscous liquid.

"Poison," he hissed, shaking his head.

Another stream of needles flew through the air, striking all around the pillar with a patter like rain. Taylor fumbled with the needle, dropping it to the ground as he scrambled to make sure all of his limbs were well covered.

This time, Reid was prepared. As soon as the assailant had popped his head out of cover and began shooting, he squeezed the trigger. The heavy slug sung as it soared a good hundred meters through the air, tearing the target's head clean off its body. The rest of the corpse slumped into the open, spasming violently in its death throes.

"Got him," Reid announced calmly.

"Is it over?" Serena whispered, not wanting to speak to loudly for fear of drawing attention to herself.

"Not yet," Marcus whispered back. "There's one left, but he's injured."

"Watch and shoot, everyone, watch and shoot!" Mitchell ordered, telling the squad to stay in cover and wait for their last assailant to show himself.

Marcus almost didn't want it to end. There was no telling when he'd get another chance to be this close to her.

Taylor reached out of cover, crawling the few meters through the dirt to where Jago lay on his back, perfectly still. Keeping the behemoth's armored bulk between him and the stone steps where their last assailant had disappeared only a moment before. Working as quickly as he could, he loosened the strap that held the huge laser cannon firmly on Jago's back, hoping the weapon hadn't been damaged in the explosion. As soon as it was free, the medic dragged it behind him as he scurried back into cover.

"How the hell does this thing work?" he muttered to himself

breathing rapidly, adrenalin coursing through his body.

He held the bulky piece of hard-edged alien weaponry upright between his legs, his back jammed up against the upright metal beam. A small panel on the protruding shaft near the front housed three distinct buttons which seemed to be the only means of interfacing with the device. His fingers danced back and forth over the buttons as he frantically tried to decide which one to hit.

After a moment's indecision, he decided the one closest to the muzzle was the logical choice, and pressed it firmly. The cannon emitted a faint hum, one Taylor could feel as well as hear as it gained rapidly in pitch. He pressed the second button, only to have a pair of mechanical fins pop out at the front of the weapon's tapering muzzle, surprising him something awful.

Without warning, a burst of shots hit the mound of debris around which the squad was hunkered, fired from different directions as their opponent dashed from position to position, trying to force the Terrans to keep their heads down.

Suddenly, something moved less than a meter from the astonished medic, who was so staggered that he slammed his hand against the last button on the laser without even meaning to, sending a searing hot beam of energy cutting across the clearing, splitting right through rock and metal alike wherever it touched. A loud scream followed by a gurgling sound spelled the doom of their last assailant as he was promptly cut in half by Taylor's lucky shot.

Beside the astonished medic, Jago swayed to his feet, clumsily brushing dirt from his chestplate as he looked around, trying to get his bearings. Finally he caught sight of Taylor holding the laser cannon. The huge man stumbled towards him, knelt down, and with a hand large enough to wrap all the way around Taylor's scrawny neck, grabbed the cannon.

"Mine!"

* * * * *

"How is he still alive?" Serena was astounded. "A moment ago he was lying dead on the ground! Now he doesn't have a scratch on him!"

"The Ape's funny that way," Taz joked. "He's too stubborn to die."

"I'm serious," she insisted. "After what happened, it's not humanly possible!"

"He's not human," Taylor answered her thoughtlessly, helping Jago clean himself up, looking up in time to catch a stern glance from Captain Mitchell. "He's the Ape." He finished blithely.

Once they'd regrouped, the squad made the run across the right side of the clearing, closing in fast on their rendezvous point. Once they were back in the debris field, Mitchell had Taz and Reid leapfrog between mounds, vastly increasing the speed at which they could move. All the while, robotic camera drones hovered in the dimness overhead, monitoring their progress.

The shimmering force field keeping the poisonous atmosphere of Nos Shana at bay was only a couple of hundred meters away now. Just a few more minutes and they would be free from the games, although what lay in store beyond would surely be no easier a task.

The ground dipped slightly before them, revealing an elongated lake of muddy liquid stretching from the barrier walls ahead and to the right back into the arena behind them. Three towering structures rose on its banks, obscuring most of the view, the decaying remnants of what must at some point have been a bridge. As the squad passed between them, they were shrouded in shadow, even the dim, dirty

340

light filtering down from the glow of the city above failing to reach them so far down.

As such, the squad flicked on the infrared filters embedded in their helmets, which immediately proved its usefulness. A lone Banthalo wielding a long, heavy machete crouched near the base of one of the towers, waiting to ambush anyone who ventured to close. Taz made short work of him with a well placed burst of slugs, tearing through his abdomen.

As they emerged from the shadows on the other side of the towering pillars, the spotlights projected by the hovering camera drones blinded them momentarily, just as a club the size of a lamppost came crashing down in their midst.

Chapter 43

Encased in a framework of glass and steel, the chamber that housed the Division 6 Shadow Council hung from the underside of the orbital space platform. Officially, the station was classified as an industrial outpost belonging to one of Terra's numerous mega corps. In reality, it supported a far more sinister purpose.

The room's tall ceiling towered over the raised platform before the primary viewport, an enormous crescent pane of reinforced glass, shielded even further by the energy field that enveloped the entire station. The lighting was kept dim, allowing the natural light reflected from Beta Terra to illuminate the chamber, lending it an even more ominous atmosphere. A row of wide steps lead up to the platform, upon which the Shadow Council would gather to decide the fates of men.

Captain Intari strode defiantly down the narrow anti-chamber that granted access to the council hall, passing a formation of elite guards whose psionic powers were rumored to grant them the ability to see things before they even transpired.

"You summoned me, Senator?" Captain Intari asked as he neared the top of the steps, his throaty voice carried by the chamber's unique acoustics.

Senator Yoishi stood by the crescent viewport, his arms clasped behind his back and his form silhouetted by the dim light source beyond.

"Have they gone?" Yoishi inquired in his callous manner, his arrogance showing as it only did when there was no present whom he needed to flatter.

"They have, Senator," the captain confirmed, moving to stand at the Senator's side.

"Magnificent, isn't it?" the Senator remarked, rhetorically. "I always did want to see the stars, as a child. Now they are within our grasp."

"Yes, Senator," Captain Intari concurred. "But, these-"

"But what, Captain?" the Senator interrupted, shooting him a stern glance.

"These outsiders…" Captain Intari began to speak with a heavy heart, certain the Senator would not understand his concerns. "I understand the necessity for funding, but now that their contribution is complete, why do you intend to allow the corporations to license this technology? Why not dispose of them entirely? Then there would be no risk to the Division."

"Your worries are unnecessary, Intari," Senator Yoishi insisted. "We need corporate backing not only for funding, but also to increase our influence in the civilian sphere. When all of this is complete, Division 6 will be deeply rooted within the megacorps, increasing our capacity to control the populace."

Intari remained silent for a short spell, weighing the Senator's words. This worried him. Throughout his entire career, Division 6 had remained the most closely guarded of all secrets. Only a handful of non-military personnel – all of them key government officials – had ever been inducted into the organization. To bring in actual outsiders, to invite them into the heart of their confederacy, with open arms no less, felt tantamount to betrayal.

"Keeping the technology to ourselves may offer security, that much is certain, but by revealing it, Terrans will take to the stars by the millions. Expansion is inevitable," Senator Yoishi resumed. "There is no greater catalyst for growth than the illusion of free will."

"Then how are we to control it? How do we avoid another invasion?" Intari contested, his visage giving away his doubt. "We are bound to encounter yet more species. We know they exist. Don't forget how we came upon this technology in the first place, Senator."

"Captain Intari, you overestimate our people," Yoishi sighed. "They will always need guidance… leadership. We have seeded our tools into every aspect of Terran politics, and now we will have even greater influence through our corporate allies. Their compliance is as much assured as is their need to draw breath. As for the Nyari invasion, we both know that it was *our* choice which led us down the path to war, a war which will eventually bring us even greater economic prospects on new markets among the stars."

Intari was beginning to understand the Senator's point of view, though he didn't necessarily agree with it. Then again, he was not in a position to countermand the Shadow Council.

"Stay the course, Captain. Have faith in the Division. You have a part to play in securing the future of this organization, and we have complete faith in your ability to see it through. We simply ask that you have the same faith in ours."

"Yes, Senator."

"Go then, Captain," Senator Yoishi urged him, laying a hand on his shoulder. "Your crew awaits you."

* * * * *

In the bowels of the orbital space platform, the TFS-*Genesis* lay berthed alongside the main docking platform. She was a formidable

344

vessel. As intimidating as her enormous bulk was, her true strength lay in the numerous modifications Intari had supervised throughout his many years of command. She was the only ship in the entire Terran fleet equipped with a shield generator, a technology which, for now, was exclusively in the hands of Division 6. Her hidden arsenal of nuclear missiles and siege cannons gave her enough firepower to level entire cities.

Various sections of the ship's hull lay open and exposed as a horde of technicians raced to complete their clearance procedures. Droves of hovering drones buzzed about, ferrying tools and performing routine scans of the ship's various sub-systems. Bundles of wiring and enormous hoses, some the size of freight trucks, venting steam and other vapors into the surrounding chamber, were strung between valves and connectors along the ship's hull and sockets in the platform itself.

Ramps as large as frigates bridged the gap between the platform and the ship's loading bays, where hundreds of support staff ferried provisions to the ship's stores by means of motorized carts. On the platform itself stood a contingent of soldiers, at least a thousand strong, carefully screened and enlisted into the ranks of the Division's private army. They were geared up and standing in formation, awaiting their turn to begin boarding.

The grey-haired Captain Intari arrived standing on the bed of a cargo vehicle with a delegation of his most trusted officers. As they came to a stop near the main entry ramp, he was greeted by his science officer, Dr. Drechsler.

At more than two meters, the doctor was an unusually tall man, towering over the team of technicians who were transporting his specialized equipment; a pair of cold steel operating tables, a tank filled with lime-tinted liquid, and an array of consoles and wiring. Unlike most other scientists, Dr. Drechsler had a naturally stocky build, broad shoulders and a square jaw line. Had he been dressed in anything other than a lab coat, he would have looked more like he belonged at the forefront of a battle than in a lab. The diminutive Dr. Reisner stood at his side, datapad in hand, attempting to familiarize the tall scientist with the new drive technology, though he was having a hard time holding his colleague's attention, which kept drifting to his equipment.

"Dr. Drechsler, I must insist that you take this matter seriously," Reisner was demanding as Intari approached, "The alterations to the auxiliary manifolds and the new reactor calibrations will be crucial to such a long journey."

"14.706 and a correlative increase to the primary plasma injector," Drechsler recited without taking his eye off of a pair of technicians carrying a large glass tank. "Careful with that cloning vat, or I'll see you drowned in it!" He shouted.

"But the injunction field must-"

"-be primed prior to the third cycle," Dr. Drechsler injected, "I read the reports, Doctor."

"Well... I..." Reisner mumbled, both affronted and relieved to hear that his counterpart aboard the Genesis had taken the appropriate measures to ensure that the new drive would run smoothly.

"Don't worry yourself, Dr. Reisner," Captain Intari ordered, his escort forming up behind him. "The Genesis is in capable hands."

At the captain's curt dismissal the short scientist scurried away, leaving the crew to begin boarding. Intari allowed the others to pass on ahead of him, pausing midway up the ramp to peer out towards the end of the docking bay where the enormous docking hatch had slowly begun to open. A shimmering energy field had manifested in its place to keep the enormous chamber from venting into the vacuum beyond. He stared out into the vastness of space. The stars seemed to shine unusually brightly, as if they were calling out to him to come and claim them.

"That ye be not soon shaken in mind, or be troubled, neither by spirit, nor by word," Intari muttered to himself, followed by a heavy sigh, wrought with hesitation.

He let go of the railing and proceeded up the ramp.

Less than an hour later, the *Genesis* was fully loaded and ready to embark on its long voyage. Fuel hoses detached with loud reverberating clanks, docking clamps released their grip, and the *Genesis* began to drift out into the void. As soon as it had cleared minimum safe distance, it adjusted its course, preparing to engage its newly installed superluminal drive.

Captain Intari stood at the helm, gripping the cold metal banister of the balcony overlooking the bridge crew. Drechsler and his team of assistants had just finished going over the calibrations with the engineering crew, and reported the drive ready for operation.

"Lord, grant us your blessing on the journey on which we are about to embark," Captain Intari murmured as he readied himself, preparing to give the command which would catapult them to speeds far greater than any Terran before them.

"Activate the drive!"

Chapter 44

The Golan berserker bellowed in rage. Frothy white bubbles clung to his cracked lips and a long sliver of drool hung from the corner of his mouth. The team had scattered as the blow sent cracks running through the stone underfoot. The long metal club was bent at an odd angle a third of the way from its heavy tip, which was stained red and green from whatever the huge alien had killed on its warpath through the battlefield. On the chain hanging from his neck was an unrecognizable bloody pulp, all that was left of the Golan's former master.

Jumping away from the roaring beast, Marcus had thrown himself out of the blinding spotlights cast by a pair of camera drones. He could see that instinct had kicked in throughout the squad, and most of the clones had run for cover immediately, all except for Jago. The towering clone stood poised in front of Serena, who had frozen in place, her body shaking in fear, clearly too terrified to move. Jago was shielding her with one arm while staring down the snarling beast.

The Golan swung its club back with another mindless roar, reaching forward with its free arm to grab Jago around the midsection. Jago didn't budge, refusing to dodge or dive aside. Instead, he hefted his machine gun and brought the butt end down right onto the beast's knuckles. There was a horrible crack and a sudden wail from the Golan as it reared back, squealing in pain.

"Ape!" Captain Mitchell shouted from the rear, "get her the hell out of there!"

Jago didn't even flinch. Marcus had never seen such an unwavering display of courage. He suddenly became very aware that none of them were reacting to the threat. They were all just staring blindly at Jago, too stunned to move.

Overcoming his initial panic and forcing himself to act, Marcus finally pulled himself to his feet and dived back out into the open space in front of the collapsed bridge, grabbing hold of Serena and pulling her to safety, just as the roaring berserker swept the ground with its club. Jago tried to jump back, but he reacted too late. The tip of the club hit him square in the shoulder, tossing him violently aside, his arms flailing as his machinegun fired an uncontrolled burst, some slugs slamming into the large metal beam Taz was using for cover, hitting a little too close to home.

Marcus snapped off a few rounds as he pushed Serena into cover behind the scorched remains of an abandoned vehicle. His aim was good, but the small-caliber ammunition did little damage as they struck the beast's thick skin. Mitchell and Doc Taylor sprayed the area with enough rounds to take down an entire squad, but the beast merely bellowed in rage, swinging its club wildly as it looked for its next victim.

"Reid, take that monster down, now!" the captain barked, trying to keep it at bay with his carbine.

Reid propped his rifle on a nearby slab of concrete, crouching behind it to steady his aim.

Somewhere amidst the chaos Jago moaned as he attempted to get back on his feet. His body was aching from the tremendous blow. His ribcage felt like it was fractured in several places, and his right arm stuck out at an odd angle, his shoulder dislocated. He slumped back to the ground, fumbling clumsily for his weapon which was nowhere in sight.

*　　*　　*　　*　　*

Hanan Aru reached the top of one of the three towering pillars. He grabbed the edge as he knelt down to survey the scene. His armor shimmered slightly before adjusting to his surroundings.

A lone Vreen tracker was approaching from the west, its thick braids bobbing from the back of its head as it followed a pair of trained Narrkin, picking up the scent of the Golan berserker. Hanan Aru had encountered the creatures before. Although their vicious bite was strong enough to snap the bones of most species clean in half, they were cowardly beasts when confronted alone, foul tempered and twice as smelly.

The Terrans had their hands full, that much was certain. Their tactics were like those of the Yon Ton beetle, backing away from a threat and waiting when they should be pushing. Their sniper fired off a round, piercing the Golan's shoulder. Hanan Aru knew that would only make the huge berserker angry.

There was time still. This fight was nowhere near over, and he was growing tired of sitting on the sidelines. A lone Vreen and a pair of Narrkin were just the diversion he needed to take his mind off the wait.

He grabbed the small pistol-like weapon hanging from the side of his belt and drew it out before him, its outlines barely visible under the camouflage field. With a flick of his wrist, its barrel extended threefold, the body folding outwards to twice its former size. What had looked like a pistol now took on the shape of a formidable carbine.

Under his mirrored helm, an elusive grin made its way across his lips as he took in a deep breath of anticipation. For all its intellectual interests, it had been an uneventful mission so far, and it was high time he got a piece of the action.

Below, the Terrans fought to keep the raging Golan at bay with suppressive fire, while their sniper took aim. Hanan Aru leapt from the pillar, his shadowy form gliding effortlessly through the air towards his unsuspecting prey.

*   *   *   *   *

Jago stumbled to his feet, sweat breaking out on his brow and his right arm still protruding at an awkward angle. Disoriented from the blow, he wobbled over to the base of the closest pillar and bit his lip to keep himself from crying out as he rammed his shoulder into the wall. There was a loud crack as it jammed back into its socket.

Meanwhile, the raging Golan was growing tired of ineffectually smashing its club around and was getting ready to charge in to grab them one at a time.

Ducking down behind the fallen masonry, Captain Mitchell made a desperate attempt to try and connect with the beast's mind telepathically, bombarding him with images from his homeworld in an effort to try and confuse him and buy them some time. Mitchell reached out, and found that its mind was much more alien than anything he'd touched before. Breaking through was not difficult, as was often the case with simpler minds, but he soon found that all of his efforts to try and sway the beast were met with fierce resistance by its cybernetic implant, a device specifically tailored to induce psychotic rage. Mitchell could sense only a faint measure of the gentle being itself. He could feel its suffering.

The fearsome beast labored to regain its senses, shaking off the captain's attempts at telepathic manipulation. It raised its mace high in the air and stormed forward, legs the size of tree trunks thumping at the trembling ground.

Reid fired again, this time piercing the Golan through the hip. The beast buckled as its leg gave way, crashing forward with, its massive club swinging in a wide arc straight for the sniper. Reid just barely ducked away as the mace nearly shattered the cement slab, a hair's breadth away from his head, showering him in fragments of near-pulverized stone.

Marcus jumped up, emptying his clip into the prone beast as it lay writhing on the ground, thrashing its limbs in pain and panic. As he snatched the empty magazine out of weapon and went to swap it out for a fresh one, he was astonished to see Jago come charging in, jumping feet-first right on top of the exhausted Golan.

He thrust the muzzle of his machinegun into the beast's skin, all the while struggling to maintain his balance. He squeezed the trigger forcefully, sending slug after slug directly into the beast's spine, all the while letting out an inhuman roar. Instantly, Jago was showered in a torrent of viscous black blood, pieces of skin and fragmented bone, a fountain of gore spraying from right between his feet. The beast twitched and trembled as the bullets tore through its body, nearly severing it in half.

When the dust had settled and the others began crawling out of their hiding places, Taylor came striding over to Jago, helmet in one hand and a lit cigarette in the other, the latter of which he promptly handed over to the huge man, who stood, dripping in gore, chest heaving. Without so much as a word, Jago accepted the cigarette and took a mighty puff, finishing half of it in one go. Taylor lit himself another and plumped himself down on the dead Golan's shoulder.

"For a second there I thought you were gonna take him hand to hand," he joked as the others approached.

Serena knelt down by the berserker's head, tracing the metal implant protruding from its skull with her fingertips.

"Poor creature," she sighed. "He should never have left Ga'ouna."

"Poor creature?" Taz gasped. "He nearly killed us all!"

"Quiet Taz," Marcus snapped, seeing her distress.

Sometimes he thought they were the only two on the *Tengri*'s crew capable of compassion. He too shared her sympathies. The Golan were being transported off their homeworld with promises of a place among the gods, only to be transformed into these... abominations. He only hoped that not all the Golan offworlders shared his fate.

"We're not done," Captain Mitchell reminded the others.

"I'm pretty sure he's dead," Taylor proclaimed, slapping the dead berserker on the shoulder.

"Not him," the captain scowled. "The camera drones. I don't think Lishan's contact would be pleased to have our R.V. broadcast."

"I'm on it," Reid stated calmly, turning and making quick work of one of the unshielded drones with his rifle.

Captain Mitchell stepped onto the top of a nearby slab of broken concrete. He drew his sidearm, staring defiantly into the lens of the remaining drone as he took aim. He fired, sending the drone crashing into the ground.

"Let's move."

They pulled themselves together and made for the shallow, fetid lake in the dim light of the city above. Serena reluctantly looked over her shoulder at the Golan's remains, saying a silent prayer.

"There was nothing else we could have done," Marcus assured her as he put an arm across her shoulder and pulled her close, comfortingly.

"I know," she admitted, leaning into him. "I just wished... things could have been different."

Taz waded out into the murky waters of the lake. At its deepest, it barely reached his knees. Once he was a dozen meters ahead, the others followed him, approaching the rendezvous point, where something dark lay shrouded on the other side of the shimmering barrier wall.

"This is the place," Marcus confirmed, consulting his holographic map.

"Where's our contact?" Taz probed, attempting to peer through the force field.

"He should be here," Captain Mitchell assured them. "Maybe he ran into trouble, same as us. In the meantime-"

The captain's order was cut off as an intensely bright spot appeared at head height on the force field, gaining in size rapidly. As it expanded, its center became hollow, revealing the sight of a Sheshen wearing a gleaming silver environmental suit.

When the gaping hole in the force field had expanded far enough, he waved them all to hurry on through. They poured through the opening, emerging on the other side inside a large cargo container, apparently the back of a transport vehicle parked right up against the force field. It resembled the inside of the cargo truck they'd travelled in on Beta Terra, a simple sheet-metal box loaded with several large metal crates with a tiny internal hatch presumably leading to some sort of cab at the front.

Marcus was fascinated by the device their contact was holding up to the force field. It was a small, handheld device with four mechanical arms, each one creating a beam of energy focused directly at the force field. Despite this technology, however, it took some time to get Jago through the barrier, as he was worried that he would be too big for the gap. Lishan's contact had to enlarge the hole significantly before the bulky clone accepted that it was indeed large enough for him to fit through.

As soon as they were all aboard, the Sheshen disengaged the device, allowing the force field to spring shut, and reached out to roll the vehicle's door shut. Marcus realized that the cargo container had been backed up right against the barrier so that they could enter without having to risk breathing any of Nos Shana's toxic atmosphere.

"Not that we're not pleased to see you, but couldn't we have met someplace less… inaccessible?" Mitchell asked their contact as he took his seat on one of the crates.

"Princcce Lissshan would know your worth before committing to your aid," the Sheshen hissed, shifting awkwardly as he answered.

"So this was a test?" the captain burst out.

"You mussst undersssstand, the Ssshrouded Kinsssship is a sssmall faction. We cannot afford to take risksss!" the contact explained, clearly terrified that the filthy, blood-stained aliens would punish him for his prince's precautions.

"The what?" Taz demanded.

"The Lessshani resssistanccce," he elaborated. "We ssstrive to rid our world from corruption."

"You're doing a great job," Taz muttered.

"We are few," the contact snapped.

"Why have you risked your lives for us?" Marcus pressed.

"We do not aid you without cause. Kesssha Kun's experimentsss are an abomination, and there isss a priccce for our assssistance."

"A price?" Mitchell pressed. He'd known there had to be a price. He didn't have to be a telepath to see that coming, especially in a society that was as rotten as this one.

"One day, we will call upon you, and you ssshall heed our call," the contact explained, as if that was self-evident. "Now, get in the box."

* * * * *

Having managed to slip through the gap in the force field during the big one's moment of hesitation, Hanan Aru slid past the others and took up position behind the crates. He watched as they opened them one by one and began cramming themselves in as best they could. He took particular enjoyment in seeing Jago trying to squeeze himself into a crate much too small for his size. Once they were all stowed away, the driver climbed to the front of the vehicle and within seconds it was speeding off into the mist.

Chapter 45

As the Council meeting had produced few results, Ambassador Janosh was forced to attempt to sway the Gaian Triumvirate to his cause. His old friend Tysob Agashi, father of his apprentice Luneia, was a triumvir, but that was where Janosh's influence with the Gaian ruling council ended. The others were too driven by decades of suspicion to give his claims the hearing they deserved.

"Thales," he prompted as he marched into the holographic suite, a dimly lit cylindrical chamber with walls of polished chrome.

The virtual servant flickered into view, bowing its head in reverence according to its programming. Ambassador Janosh sat himself on the cold tiled floor, folding his legs together and arching his back.

"How can I serve, Master?" Thales enquired, its glowing image reflected on the walls and smooth floor tiles.

"I must speak with the Triumvirate."

"As you wish, Master," Thales complied, the glowing figure vanishing just as quickly as it had appeared.

Ambassador Janosh closed his eyes. His schedule had been more hectic than usual these last few days. The Etheran Council was in uproar over the bombing of one of Semeh'yone's transport hubs. The Freedom Fighters of Cerakan had already claimed responsibility. Theirs was the world most ravaged by the Moloukan Empire, an independent colony world which had once been home to upwards of four billion people of a range of races.

As the Moloukans had pushed their borders further and further out, they had began raiding the sprawling urban hub of Cerakan in great numbers, claiming hundreds of thousands of colonists as slaves and killing millions with each assault. As Cerakan was a world which had prided itself of its freedom from the strict laws of the Etherium, it was no great surprise to anyone when their calls for help fell on deaf ears.

After centuries of raids, most of the survivors had already relocated to safer parts of the galaxy, leaving only a few thousand die-hard freedom fighters living in squalid conditions amongst the decaying ruins. It had become a popular attraction for the young and foolish, eager to make a name for themselves on the field of battle.

The Moloukans had never bothered to keep a permanent presence on the ruined world. Now it was little more than a staging post for those brave enough to strike back at the Moloukan Empire. These days the Freedom Fighters were little more than terrorists, striking out equally at the Moloukan Empire and the Etherium, in retaliation for their indifference.

Ambassador Janosh rubbed his temples, attempting to keep the ensuing headache at bay.

The entire chamber faded from view, suddenly replaced by the image of the Gaian Triumvirate.

He recognized the interior assembly hall atop Vale's southern tower. There were three towers in all, just as there were three Gaian cities: Vale, the capital; Albion, a magnificent island city and the most popular among visitors to Avalon; and Elysium, shrouded in the deep canyons of Avalon's southern hemisphere.

Seated on three thrones of purest white, before three towering arched windows, sat the Triumvirate, bathed in the earthy, natural glow of Avalon's evening light. They each wore a black half-robe adorned with silver runes along its sleeves and loose white trousers with a wide, shimmering belt made from a series of clasps woven together into a mesh so fine Janosh could barely make out the links. On the left sat Tysob Agashi, Janosh's oldest and dearest friend, whose graying beard had grown since the two had last he seen each other.

In the center sat Jace Rondel, a dark-haired man with a hawk's nose and the vigilant eyes to match. More often than not he disagreed with Janosh on every matter they discussed, though whether this was out of some petty principle or simply because the two men had very different views on almost everything Janosh wasn't yet sure. Last came the ancient Lein Kanter, whose skin reminded him of spotted paper, so thin Janosh could see the web of blue veins on his hands and neck. What little hair remained to Lein was pure white, and he had grown so cautious with age that there was no longer any practical difference between the discretion he always urged and outright cowardice. As far as Janosh was concerned, Lein had long ago proved his ineffectiveness, and the main reason why the Triumvirate said much and did little.

"Ambassador," Tysob greeted him with a respectful nod.

"Triumviri," said Janosh, bowing his head in turn.

"How fares the Council?" Lein inquired, his frail voice trembling.

"As always," Janosh replied, "It squabbles over insignificant matters when more important ones receive as much attention as a beggar on the streets of Rapa Lok Stad."

"With what matter of great urgency do you call upon us?" Jace probed, ever to the point.

Janosh cleared his throat.

"I have confronted the Council on the matter of the Terrans. They were unable to come to a conclusion."

"And this surprises you?" Jace sneered.

"They do not see the threat they impose!"

"Nor do we," Lein stammered. "According to our reports, they are technologically far inferior to the Children of Gaia. Whatever threat you perceive is most likely in your head."

Janosh bit his lip to control his anguish. Could they not see the Terrans for what they were? "Have you forgotten the words of our beloved Gaia?" he demanded, his tone harsh.

"The age of Gaia is past," Jace retorted. "It is high time we decide our own fate."

"I would not speak so lightly of our great leader!" Tysob roared, slamming his fist on his armrest.

"I meant no disrespect," Jace insisted. "But I maintain that if we dwell forever on the past, then the future will escape us."

"Exactly," Janosh seized on the chance to further his argument. "The Terrans may not yet pose a threat, but given time, they will infect everything we hold dear."

"If the Council will not heed your words, why then should we?" Lein scowled.

Janosh looked to Tysob for aid, a gesture of faith – and desperation.

"Perhaps the ambassador's words hold some small merit," the bearded man spoke, placating the other triumviri by belittling Janosh's cause, yet sowing a seed of doubt in their minds by his very reasonableness.

"What do you propose?" Lein probed, raising an eyebrow in suspicion.

"Perhaps a lone scout, cloaked to gauge their strength," Tysob presented. "Surely a mission to gather intelligence poses no harm."

Lein looked towards Jace for guidance, as he often did when he was unsure of himself.

"Do we have the coordinates of their homeworld?" Jace demanded.

"I will acquire them," Ambassador Janosh replied, trying to conceal his triumph. Once they saw the evidence for themselves...

"Then... I consent," Jace confirmed, reluctantly.

"As do I," Lein followed.

"You will not regret this," Janosh smiled, thankful for Tysob's subtle aid.

"For Gaia's grace," the Triumvirate spoke in unison.

"For Gaia's grace," the ambassador replied, bowing his head in veneration.

The image of Vale faded, replaced once more with the cold shimmering walls of the holographic suite aboard Semeh'yone. Janosh stood, stretching limbs he hadn't realized he'd allowed to become so tense. He had work to do.

Chapter 46

Being cramped inside a crate and unable to monitor the driver's heading did not make for a comfortable ride, nor did the anticipation of what awaited them upon their arrival. They knew that Kesha Kun's bunker lay hidden in the mists beyond the city, but how far and what sort of resistance they could expect – remained a mystery.

Marcus pulled his knees as close to his chest as he could, given his restrictive armor. It seemed like they'd been traveling for an awfully long time, and his joints were beginning to ache. He wondered how the others were coping. Surely Jago would be in agony by now, particularly given that the huge man was still covered in the stinking blood and gore of the berserker he'd killed. At least the craft's gravity repulsor offered a smooth voyage, free from contact with the rough terrain.

Fortunately, it wasn't long after that that the squad could feel the hovercraft slowing down. A few seconds later, Marcus heard the hissing voice of Lishan's contact, telling them that they were almost at their destination. The Sheshen warned them that the Dark Sun's electronic defenses would prevent them communicating with anyone on the outside, so they would be completely on their own until he returned after an hour to collect them… if they still drew breath. The truck slowed once again and the muffled sound of a large mechanical door being opened in the near distance alerted them that they'd arrived.

The truck slid into the loading dock and before too long the door was closed behind them. As Marcus lay still in his crate, his heart thumping, adrenaline coursing through his veins, he heard their driver greet someone lazily in the fluid-sounding Sheshen language, and, with a jolt, Marcus realized that the squad was in the perfect position to be betrayed. What if Lishan's goal was simply to deliver the crew of the *Tengri* to his father? The squad was now lying in crates, shipped to Kesha Kun's own compound, and the rest of the crew was defenseless back at their hotel in Sheijan. Just as Marcus was about to jump out of his hiding place, carbine blazing, there was a thump as the contact began unloading his cargo, just as he'd promised he would.

Marcus suffered the heightened discomfort as his crate began to shake in stoic silence, grasping his carbine firmly as the carton rose up and out of the back of the truck, pulled by what he assumed was some sort of load lifter. After a second of lateral movement he was dumped to the ground, and he heard the faint whine of servos as the machine returned to the truck.

As quickly as Lishan's contact must have finished his work, the time stretched unbearably for Marcus, cramped inside his crate. Eventually, however, he heard the sound of the hovercraft's engine starting up and pulling away, followed by the double rattle of the large door opening and closing.

Everything was silent for some time after that. Marcus focused his hearing, straining to hear even the minutest of sounds outside his crate. He wasn't sure, but he thought he could hear soft voices in the distance, speaking the 'silver tongue' of the Sheshen. He was listening so hard that he almost gave a cry of terror when there was a soft crackle in his ear and Captain Mitchell's voice whispered through his earpiece.

"Nobody make a sound," the captain ordered, as softly as he

possibly could.

Cautiously, the grizzled officer raised the lid on his crate a finger's width, peering outside into the space beyond, his sidearm clutched in his free hand. The loading bay the squads' crates were sitting in was much larger than he'd anticipated, easily a hundred meters wide and half that deep, with enough bays to easily accommodate six or seven large cargo vehicles. Theirs were not the only crates resting on the loading platform. Hundreds of crates and barrels were neatly organized into stacks all around them.

A set of steps led up from the vehicle pit, running along the dark stone wall and emerging onto the platform where the crates sat beside a wide doorway. A pair of Sheshen guards in the blackened armor of the Dark Sun Empire stood before it, chatting lazily, compact rifles slung over their shoulders, oblivious to the infiltrators lying in wait. A small group of workers in drab coveralls and the ubiquitous Sheshen masks loitered about, carelessly rooting through crates.

Captain Mitchell lowered the lid once more, considering tactics.

"Right, listen in. Vehicle entrance to our north, two hostiles guarding a door roughly twenty meters to our east, and three or four non-combatants," he whispered softly over the comms. "Lucky for us there's a lot of cover, but we need to take them out quietly. If they manage to sound the alarm, we're screwed, so I wa-"

His orders were cut short by the sound of Jago violently passing wind.

Marcus felt his heart stop momentarily, his eyes wide open in shock as he fought the urge to burst into hysterical laughter.

Mitchell silently cursed the huge clone's lack of restraint before hesitantly raising the lid of his crate once more to see if anyone had noticed. To his horror, a lone dockworker stood with his back no more than a meter from his crate, creeping towards the box containing Jago, his body language radiating puzzlement.

"Ape, stay still and bite your lip!" Mitchell ordered as he slid back down into his crate, hefting his sidearm.

No one dared make a sound. The tense silence seemed to last an eternity.

Jago held his breath, not so much to keep from making a sound as to prevent himself from inhaling his own noxious fumes. Marcus felt his heart pounding in his chest. Two guards and a few unarmed Sheshen weren't much of a threat in themselves, but a compound on full alert was another matter entirely. The best course was undoubtedly one of stealth. If they were discovered, their entire plan would be thrown into chaos.

Just as Marcus thought they'd managed to escape detection after all, the silence was broken by Jago bursting out of his crate, screaming at the top of his lungs and spraying the loading dock with his machinegun.

"Damnit Ape!" Mitchell cursed, throwing the lid of his own crate open and executing the horrified dockworker with a single well-placed shot.

The captain was having trouble understanding how the squad had lasted this long, given the Ape's lack of control. "Go, go!" he yelled.

Marcus sprang free, snapping his head around to get his bearings just in time to see Jago rushing at the astonished guards, still roaring like an enraged beast at the top of his lungs, firing wildly. As he tumbled out of his crate, he realized that the dockworkers weren't as unarmed as the captain had suspected as they each withdrew a small sidearm from their belts and began firing at the squad as they emerged from hiding. Marcus dived behind a low stack of barrels and immediately began firing back at them, the recoil of his carbine reassuring in the rapidly deteriorating chaos of their plan.

"Serena, stay down!" he shouted, not that he had to. The linguist was still crouched in her crate, entirely too terrified to move.

Captain Mitchell had the best angle of attack, and he promptly emptied half a clip at the group of armed workmen, taking down two of them. Two more jumped into cover, laying down suppressive blasts of golden fire that forced Mitchell and Marcus to duck back into shelter themselves.

As he watched Taz and Doc Taylor tumble into cover a few meters away, Marcus thought Reid was still in his crate, until he noticed a shadow disappearing along the back of the service pit. The sniper had gone the other way, and was now circling back around towards them. Taylor sat on the ground, his back against his crate and his legs stretched out in front of him, clutching his carbine to his chest as he looked left and right, unsure how to react. Taz had landed on his feet behind a large stack of barrels and was training his carbine on their assailants.

"Taz!" Marcus shouted to the scout.

Taz heard him and glanced over as Marcus gestured towards Reid. Taz nodded, seeing Marcus' plan of action. The two of them began exchanging single shots with the enemy, firing in turn to keep them pinned down and distracted from their impending deaths.

In the shadows, Reid climbed onto low a platform behind his squadmates, propping his long rifle on the edge of a railing. He held the weapon firmly in both hands, finger on the trigger, lining up his shot.

"Marcus, down!" He called.

Marcus ducked just as a slug tore through the chest cavity of one of the dockworkers. Barely a split second later, the remaining Sheshen slumped to the ground, a spray of blood covering the ground around him.

Once Reid called the all-clear, Captain Mitchell gathered them quickly together and proceeded towards the now-open doorway, where a long, tube-like corridor veered slightly to the right. The only sign of Jago were the corpses of the guards, each with several fist-sized bullet holes.

"Damnit Ape, get back here!" Mitchell shouted into the comms in sheer frustration.

The only reply was the behemoth's barely audible roar, echoing back from further down the corridor.

"I'm gonna kill him," Mitchell snarled, flush with anger.

The squad ran down the corridor as fast as their legs would carry them, Captain Mitchell dragging behind, on account of his motorized leg brace. The bottom of the tube was covered by metal grating, fitting over a series of pipes and wires, whilst the ceiling was made up of dark panels, broken up every so often by a square emitting a dim blue light. On either side of them, the walls of the corridor were clear as glass, opening onto the ruined landscape of Nos Shana. Marcus slowed his pace, coming to a complete stop as he peered out through the darkness.

This far outside Sheijan the lights of the city provided barely any illumination, but he could see that the ground was bleak and barren, shrouded in green mist, eddying gently in the sluggish breeze. A hundred meters or so in the distance, on the very limit of his vision, he could see the silhouette of an enormous towering compound. It was a rough dome in shape, its sides rising steep before tapering quickly towards the top, ridged trenches breaking up its surface. Light spilled from hundreds of elliptical windows, illuminating numerous dark, foreboding structures and installations crouching around the huge building's perimeter. Some were bulky, made from blackened steel, with raised platforms upon which powerful cannons were aimed towards the sky. Others were no more than thin slabs of concrete carrying sophisticated antennae arrays that cleaved through the mist. Pipes and wires ran together in thick bundles, huddling around the rough terrain as they connected each of the structures and installations together.

This wasn't a compound, Marcus realized, his mouth agape. It was a fortress! The others paused beside him, staring out through the window.

"What have we gotten ourselves into?" Taylor said, staring in wonder at Kesha Kun's palace.

Captain Mitchell managed to catch up with them.

"We've no time to waste," he snapped after a quick glimpse out the window. He stomped on down the long corridor that connected the cargo dock with the rest of the compound.

Jago's roars had died down. Either he'd met with a force he couldn't handle, or he'd simply wandered too far for the squad to hear him. As the squad reached the end of the corridor, they found another pair of guards lying dead on the metal grating. Bullet holes covered the doorframe behind them, and the sliding doors stood open, one torn clean out of its tracks.

Mitchell waved the rest of the squad to a halt, and they took cover along the walls of the corridor. Meanwhile, Taz scouted on ahead, deftly ducking under a shower of sparks as he snuck into what appeared to be a security station. Inside, the dim blue lights flickered, wires hanging from the broken doorframe, sparks flying everywhere.

After a few seconds, Taz called back that the room was clear, and the others followed him in, stopping almost immediately, taken aback by the carnage that met them.

The chamber was split in two. The closest section was a circular pit, its outsides walled with a range of consoles, lockers and weapon racks, most of the latter standing empty. In the centre of the shallow basin, the bodies of at least a half a dozen armored guards lay strewn in front of the squad. Some slumped over consoles, others lay on the floor, clutching their weapons. Behind the circular pit, the chamber widened into a wedge, its narrow end falling away from the security station in a long, wide set of steps descending to an underground platform half-cloaked in shadows. A pair of steel pillars split the broad staircase in half, while another tubular corridor led straight to the right from the top of the stairs, no doubt heading off to the main compound. A smaller exit on the left was blocked by a heavy doorway.

Jago seemed not to have been concerned with accuracy during his mad assault. Most of the consoles in the room flickered chaotically, riddled with bullet holes and adding to the steady stream of sparks spilling from damaged cables and lighting panels overhead. He'd clearly strafed the room at large, spraying anything that moved with rounds. The air reeked of gunpowder and the bitter aroma of Sheshen blood. Marcus knelt by one of the bodies, turning it face up to inspect its wounds.

"I can't believe the Ape did all this by himself," he gasped.

"Taz, go check out the platform," Captain Mitchell ordered. "Marcus, see if you can find a working console. Perhaps we can find where they're keeping Raven."

"What about Jago?" Serena pleaded.

"The Ape will have to wait. He's not answering his comms and I'm

369

not running after him blindly. As far as I'm concerned, he just volunteered to play decoy," Mitchell snapped exasperatedly.

Taz crept down the stairs ahead whilst Marcus went to work on the consoles. They were heavily damaged from Jago's slugs, but after a moment of searching, Marcus was able to find one that had escaped his wrath.

"Serena," he prompted. "Can you help me with this?"

She came to his aid, leaning over to read the alien interface.

"What am I looking for?"

"Something medical, or… surgical in nature," Marcus revealed.

Serena's head snapped around as she frowned at the thought. She'd assumed that Raven was being kept in some sort of detention facility.

It was slow work, and the squad was unnerved at having to stay out in the open for so long. There was no telling when a horde of guards could come pouring in from any direction. Mitchell posted the others at the various entrances to the room, but it didn't take long before they were all on edge.

"Make it fast, Grey," the captain urged.

"I'm trying," Marcus answered. "This is a lot harder than it looks."

They were fully immersed in their work when Taz came creeping back up the steps.

"It's a kind of tram," he shouted, a little too loud for comfort. "The tracks seem to go on for quite a bit."

"How fucking big is this place?" Taylor moaned, lighting himself a cigarette and plopping down on a chair in front of one of the broken consoles.

"I think this is it," Serena claimed, pointing at something that had caught her interest on the console.

"What is it?" asked Markus.

"The tram leads to a series of underground research laboratories."

"Laboratories?" Reid repeated.

"Quite large too. There's a whole bunch of them."

"Lab geeks," Taylor grinned. "I like those odds a lot better than storming that fortress."

"Let's hope the Ape thought so as well," Captain Mitchell sighed as he ushered them down the steps to the tram.

* * * * *

Hanan Aru had followed the large one to the security station, witnessing his fury as he single-handedly vanquished any that dared stand in his path. He was magnificent, a worthy opponent.

As soon as he had left, Hanan Aru adjusted his sensors to scan for energy signatures. Glowing blue lines began to appear on his augmented vision, lining the walls, floor and ceiling. A line running through the floor glowed brighter than the others, disappearing all the way out into the corridor behind him.

He smiled under his visor, flicking his wrists and opening his palms, thrusting them out to his sides. Thin strands of energy began to leap out from the broken consoles, dangling cables, wall sockets, and even from under the metal grating on the floor, all of them arching towards him. He raised his face to the ceiling, his whole body trembling as he absorbed the energy, the glowing strands filling the chamber with an eerily blue light.

When he had had his fill, the room fell dark once more, the lights in the ceiling still flickering. Hanan Aru looked again at the surrounding carnage, pondering which course to take. The valor of the big Terran was impressive, even more so than his stupidity. After a moment's

371

consideration, he ran after the berserk soldier, down the tube connecting the security station to Kesha Kun's palace.

Chapter 47

Jago ground his teeth. His path veered to the left, its smooth, curving walls lined with faintly-illuminated panels at regular intervals. An unfortunate group of four guards emerged from one of the many side passageways. A split second later they'd disappeared in a mist of blood and fragments of bone.

The passage came to an abrupt end, and Jago soon found himself in a small, dimly-lit foyer. A pair of staircases soared upwards, continuing up for at least a dozen flights, occasional cross-platforms disappearing into the walls on higher levels. As he craned his neck back to see up, a sudden muddled pain shot through his hip.

He barely glimpsed down at the wound before turning to locate its source, a pair of armed Sheshen kneeling on the far staircase, each of them wielding a carbine-like weapon and firing bolts of golden energy in his direction.

"Hah," he snarled. "Come on, you shit cunts!"

He raised his fearsome machinegun and squeezed the trigger with enough force to break a man's finger.

"Eat this, you shit fuckers!" he roared, swiveling his entire body to shower the staircase with lead.

Aiming was far from his strong suit, but with such a high cyclic rate it hardly mattered. One of the guards was hit square in the chest and flew off the stairs, his mangled body crashing limp to the floor below with a gaping hole in his chest. The other ducked, crawling up to the next floor to avoid Jago's fearsome attack.

The commotion had attracted more Sheshen from neighboring rooms and corridors, and Jago soon found himself outmatched as guard after guard came pouring in. His weapon devoured the ammunition in its huge drum, spitting out round after round, tearing through walls and targets alike. With all the debris, Jago couldn't tell how many he'd hit, not that he particularly cared as long as there were more to fight.

He growled, noticing a sudden movement to his left. He spun to face it, the trigger of his Viking still depressed. The sequential clicking of the hammer alerted him that he was out of ammo just as a bolt of energy singed his shoulder, another slamming into his chestplate a second later. Fortunately his armor took the brunt of the damage.

Jago was undeterred, throwing himself at the nearest foe and ramming the butt of his weapon into his mask. He felt the snap as the Sheshen's neck broke, his head hanging back at an awkward angle as he slumped to the floor.

Almost instantly, Jago took a hit to the lower back, one which sent him crashing to his knees, reeling in pain. With a roar of defiance he staggered back to his feet, turning to face the foyer, where more guards than he could count were closing in on him. With Jago gravely wounded, they were fast gaining confidence and pushing in to surround him.

"Where's the rest of you?" Jago spat, just as his trembling body was blasted again and again by searing bolts of golden energy. "Yeah? Well... I'm prettier!" he mumbled as he collapsed to the floor, twitching briefly before succumbing to his wounds.

* * * * *

The tram was a five-meter long and three-meter wide platform of extruded steel, running on magnetic rails. At each end of the cart stood curved railings, painted a bright yellow and coated with a rubbery substance for grip. A control panel atop a small console protruding from the center of the platform was the only visible means of control.

"Serena?" Marcus prompted, seeking her guidance with the lettering.

Taz was already at the front, peering down the hollow tunnel, carved into the rock beneath the surface of Nos Shana. A chill breeze stirred the black banners hanging eerily over the stairs leading up to the circular security station, each pennant emblazoned with a red three-pronged star, the symbol of the Dark Sun Empire. The only source of light in the tunnel was a handful of illuminated panels set into the ceiling, widely spaced down its length, creating pools of near total darkness along its path.

"I don't like this," Reid murmured. "We're sitting ducks. If there's resistance at the other end, we're as good as dead."

"Then let's hope our aim is better than theirs," Mitchell retorted.

"I have confidence in our aim, it's our numbers I'm worried about," Reid replied, adjusting the heavy scope on his rifle and laying it to rest over the front railing.

He knelt in front of it, touching his forehead, his stomach and each side of his chest in turn as he said a silent prayer.

"Ape," Captain Mitchell called over the comms, hoping for a reply. "Are you there? Ape?"

Taylor lowered his gaze, fearing the worst, when no response came. Mitchell tried as best he could to focus his senses in hopes of making contact with the behemoth's irrational mind, but Jago was nowhere to be found.

"It was only a matter of time before something like this happened," the captain let out. "I suppose he was always destined to meet with a violent end."

Reid lowered his gaze, knowing full well that the captain spoke the truth, no matter how much he wished he could deny it.

"I think I've got it," Serena proclaimed, pressing one of the buttons on the console.

The tram sprang to life with a high-pitched hum, slowly gaining momentum as it accelerated down the tunnel. The rough stone walls whizzed by. The rapid switches between light and darkness were hypnotic to watch, and made it hard to focus.

"Serena, get behind me," Marcus ordered, raising his weapon in anticipation of what lay in wait. "We don't know how long this tunnel is."

"Get ready," Captain Mitchell barked as the tram began slowing down, the tension increasing palpably.

Marcus could feel beads of sweat forming on his brow. A sliver of light appeared on the horizon as the tunnel veered slightly to the left. Without a word of warning, Reid began firing his rifle. Although they were too far out for the others to see what he was shooting at, his sudden actions spelled the certainty of combat up ahead.

"Contact!" he yelled.

He managed another shot before the three remaining guards on the approaching platform came into view of the others. The tram was met with a brilliant display of golden laser fire, most of which impacted on the rocky walls of the tunnel. A few bursts hit closer to home, bouncing off the base of the tram.

"Open fire!" Captain Mitchell bellowed over the fray.

Taz let loose a storm of bullets, with Marcus and Taylor quickly joining in, adding their volleys to his. Two of the guards quickly fell face forward onto the rails, resulting in small explosions of electrical energy as their black armor made contact with the highly charged metal tracks.

The remaining Sheshen suddenly became very aware that he was all alone against a superior force, and jumped behind a nearby pillar for cover. The tram was less than forty meters from the platform, seconds away from docking. Reid didn't dare take his eye off the scope, training his rifle on the pillar, swiveling quickly as they approached the station.

"Fuck this," Captain Mitchell yelled, grabbing a grenade from his belt, pulling the pin and tossing it between the pillars as the tram slid to a halt next to the platform. "Fire in the hole!"

The resulting explosion threw the tattered remains of the remaining guard several meters to the side, slamming him into a nearby wall. The tram ground to a final halt, and immediately Taz jumped from the tram and ran to the unmarked pillar. Reid followed him while the others ducked off the tram, crouching carefully between the electrified rails, waiting for the all clear.

After a moment, Taz waved them forward. Beyond the pillars lay a small antechamber with polished stone walls, a series of slanting metal beams protruding from the walls and digging into the stone floor. To their left, a niche in the room's broad wall harbored the only exit, a wide blast door with no visible means of access. Above the niche, a gleaming lens kept watch like an evil eye, a glowing red light in its center.

Marcus felt a slight vibration, as if they were near an intense source of energy, the deep hum filling him with a sense of looming dread.

"How do we get through?" Serena asked, concerned.

"There has to be a way," Reid insisted.

"I don't think there is. Not from this side at least," Marcus ventured. "I think whoever's on the other side has the only means of controlling the door."

"Then we blow it up," Taz proposed.

"With what? All we have are grenades," Captain Mitchell responded. "Maybe if that obnoxious Ape were here, his explosive flatulence could blow it apart?"

He walked up to the door, staring up at the lens intently. After a short moment, he approached Marcus and pulled him off to the side.

"What do you think, Grey?" he whispered. "I've seen you do some pretty amazing things. Do you think you can do something about that door?"

Marcus didn't know how to react. He'd never intentionally wielded his powers. He didn't even know how.

"I... I don't know," he stuttered. "I'm not really sure how it works."

"If Reid hadn't stopped you at the foreman's office, you'd probably have torn that whole building apart. I know what I saw," the captain urged him, looking him straight in the eye. "I know you have it in you."

"Isn't there another way?"

"Taz's imaginary high-yield explosives? No, Marcus. You're all we have."

"But-" Marcus started to speak.

"Just focus on how you felt then, when you found out they'd taken Raven, that feeling of despair. You were afraid for her. I could see it in your eyes," the captain pressed.

"No. That's not what happened. It wasn't fear," Marcus confessed.

378

"It… it was anger. I… I felt like I was losing control."

"Good," was all that Mitchell said in response.

"Good? What if you hadn't been able to stop me? I could have killed you!" Marcus burst out.

"But you didn't."

"I can't risk that again!" Marcus explained, looking over his shoulder at where Serena stood by one of the slanting beams.

Captain Mitchell followed his gaze, sensing his distress.

"She'll be safe. You have my word. Just focus. Put yourself back in that time and place. Feel the rage burning inside you. Use it, harness it."

Marcus crossed to the huge metal door, and tried as best he could to follow the captain's direction, but to no avail. His nerves got the better of him. He stood in front of the towering portal with one hand laid on its surface, his eyes closed, trying to imagine himself back in that dark place, witnessing Raven's abduction.

"It's not working," he sighed.

"Maybe I can help," Mitchell replied, coming to stand behind him.

"What do you mean? How?"

"Trust me. Focus on the door," the captain instructed him. "It works best if you remove your helmet."

Marcus reluctantly unbuckled his chinstrap and placed his helmet on the ground beside him. He sighed briefly before laying his hand once more on the door, closing his eyes. Behind him, Mitchell stared intently at the back of his neck. As the reached out with his hand and laid it on the back of Marcus' skull, it was as if he were entering into a trance.

By now, the others had taken notice. It was an odd sight, seeing the two men standing there, motionless and so intently focused.

"What are they doing?" Serena asked, turning from where she'd been peering anxiously back up the tunnel.

"You'd best get behind one of those beams," Reid said, suddenly realizing what Marcus and the captain were attempting to do.

"Why? What's-" Serena began.

"Step back," Reid insisted, grabbing her arm and leading her back behind the support beam furthest from the door.

Taz and Taylor mirrored their actions at the far end of the chamber.

Mitchell's eyelids were quivering. The vein on his forehead popped out, pulsating. Probing someone's mind to scan their thoughts was something he was very good at. Having done so often as a mole within the ranks of Division 6, it came naturally to him. Forcing someone to relive their moments of their past was much more arduous and painful, both for himself and the recipient. Even so, he was surprised how difficult he found it to work with Marcus. There were so many instances of pain for such a short life: memories from his training days, moments of love, loss and betrayal. The captain sifted through them all, each one adding its weight to Marcus' suffering.

Marcus was starting to think it wouldn't work, when suddenly the images began flashing in his mind. He saw his old Sergeant shooting Corporal Dimitrov in the head; his fight with Steven in the docking bay of the Strom sensor outpost; the deaths of so many men, women and children in the Last Oasis; the traitor Adam Spielman on the bridge of the alien ship on New Io; and Raven's abduction.

Each display fueled his anger. He felt it building up inside him like a living being, a powerful entity swelling up inside him, taking long empowering breaths as it gained momentum. His hands started trembling with rage. He could feel every muscle in his body tensing. He tried to control it at first, fearful of the consequences if he allowed it to have its way, but as it gained strength he realized that he had to let go. It was the only way.

The door itself started to shake, sending tremors through the walls and cracks through the stone floor. Serena cried out in fear, but Reid held her firmly in place, trying to reassure her that all would be well.

As the last image entered Marcus' mind, he gave in entirely. The furious beast inside him overpowered him, coursing through his body. With a deafening shriek, the blast door ripped apart as if it were nothing more than a sheet of paper.

Before the shards of metal had even had time to hit the floor, Captain Mitchell had grabbed his sidearm and slammed the butt of it down on the back of Marcus' skull.

"You did good soldier. You did real good."

Chapter 48

The Sheshen guards took turn kicking Jago in the gut, making sure that the raging beast was truly dead. Hanging from the underside of the staircase above, Hanan Aru observed. He found their fear amusing, having counted at least half a dozen lethal shots. The large one was dead. Though he should be backtracking to shadow the others, he felt compelled to offer a moment of silence to the brave one who had managed to intrigue him so.

The guards were busy squabbling over who would be tasked with dragging away the body when Jago suddenly gasped for air. Startled, the guards jumped back, quickly turning their weapons back on the wheezing giant, yelling in panic. They were just about to fire off a point-blank volley when their leader suddenly gave the signal to stop.

The wounds on Jago's back, visible through the cracks in what was left of his crude armor, were slowly sealing themselves. Remarkable, Hanan Aru mused. Biogenic regeneration was a rare gift, one usually mastered only by a focused mind after years of meditation. The sluggish oaf did certainly not seem the type.

The senior guard was ecstatic, relaying his findings over his communication link. He ordered the prisoner bound hand and foot with clasps made from the strongest steel. Knowing full well the rumors on the streets of Sheijan, Hanan Aru knew exactly what lay in store for the foolish giant. Kesha Kun would have a new prize to add to his collection.

The secondary security station controlling the blast door had proven to be little more than a lone guard sitting in a cubicle of glass and polished steel, monitoring the feed from the antechamber. No doubt the Sheshen had long ago called for assistance. Captain Mitchell stood over the black-armored body and hoped that wherever the Ape had run off to, he was proving a more immediate threat to the security of the Dark Sun Empire than the rest of them.

Taz and Reid split up as they stalked ahead to the base of a U-shaped intersection, each taking up position at the foot of one of the two parallel corridors stretching out from the tiny security station. Each corridor was lined with over a dozen doors on each side. Mitchell limped along after them as fast as he could, stopping at the intersection, hoping to see some sort of sign as to which way to proceed.

"Reid, this way," he gestured towards the corridor to the left.

"How do you know?" Reid called as he ran to catch up with Taz and the captain.

"The doors on that side have glass windows. When Marcus described his vision, he mentioned a plain steel door."

"Good thinking," said Reid. "You probably shouldn't have hit him though."

"He has the Doc and Serena to take care of him. He'll be fine," Mitchell replied, focusing on the job at hand.

"How do you want to do this?" asked Taz in a low voice, looking at the dozen or so metal doors lining the corridor, which ended in a blank stone wall sixty or so meters away.

The scent of the corridor, bitter and sterile, took him back to his first days on Alamo station, when he'd been a newly-hatched clone. He tried to shrug it off, but it was so disturbing it kept working its way into his mind. Above each door, a lamp cast its stark glow in a semi-circle below. Strange symbols were painted in white on each door, most likely designating what lay behind them.

"Knock them down," Captain Mitchell ordered. "All of them."

Taz and Reid lowered their weapons, switching to their sidearms. They took up position on opposite sides, with the captain slowly marching down the middle, covering the doorways further down the corridor as his troops kicked the doors open and quickly cleared the rooms beyond. The first two chambers were covered in dirt and grime, devoid of furnishings but for a water spout embedded in the rear wall and a circular grating in the floor beneath it, presumably holding cells for Kesha Kun's test subjects. The second two were similar, albeit cleaner.

One of the third pair housed a grotesquely misshapen Telorian, whose once-bright colors had faded to mere muddled hues. The alien squealed loudly as soon as the door flew open, reaching out for the light with disfigured hands. Reid looked at it with pity in his eyes, remembering Oolan, the gentle being who'd operated on his leg. If his tender nature was in any way indicative of his species, then this poor soul had suffered a vile transgression indeed. Reid cringed away as the prisoner stumbled towards him, unsure whether to reach out to help it or take a step back. The malformed Telorian mutely pointed a stubby finger at Reid's rifle, its hand quivering as if that simple action was more than it could bear.

As it came further out into the light, Reid could see that its left arm had been amputated above the elbow, and that three distinct incisions on its chest and abdomen had been crudely stapled closed and left to

384

fester. Another scar circling around the side of its skull was enough to make him gag. Before he had the chance to be sick, a shot rang through the air.

He spun quickly, only to find himself looking down the smoking barrel of Captain Mitchell's sidearm.

"When you see someone in that much pain, you end their suffering," Mitchell told him, his stare cold.

Reid said a silent prayer for the unfortunate soul. It pained him to think of the horrors it had been made to endure at the hands of Kesha Kun's scientists.

When the sniper tried to kick open the door to the next room, his boot skidded awkwardly off its smooth surface as it refused to open. Clearly it was barred from the other side. No doubt its occupant had heard the sound of gunfire and barricaded the door.

"We'll leave that one for last," Mitchell decided, and motioned Taz to position himself outside the next door up.

Having barely recovered from the shock of the Telorian, Reid suddenly heard the sharp cry of a female voice from behind the barricaded door. He shot out the locking mechanism and kicked in the door as quickly as he could.

"Captain!" he shouted.

The dimly-lit lab was cluttered with all manner of consoles and surgical equipment, two operating tables standing in the center. Raven's terrified figure occupied the one closest to the door, a nightmarish mechanical arm hovering above her. The clatter of a metal tray hitting the floor alerted Reid to the presence of the alien surgeon as knives and surgical implements rattled on the hard floor.

The surgeon's large black eyes looked at Reid with terror as the spindly figure tried to get behind the second table, raising his elongated hands in surrender. His fingers were at least three times as long as a man's, and his elongated head swept back from a skeletally flat, nose-less face into a crest of bone.

Reid's eyes were drawn to the eviscerated Hrūll test subject, the sight wreaking havoc on his already upset stomach.

Captain Mitchell pushed past him as he threw up.

"Get me out of this thing!" Raven yelled, pulling at her restraints.

Mitchell went straight for the surgeon, circling the tables with his sidearm aimed right at the frail humanoid's face, his knuckles white on its grip.

"On the floor!" he yelled, hoping the alien would understand him. "Now!"

The surgeon waved his elongated hands in bewilderment, slowly inching its way backwards towards the wall, scanning the room in desperation for a way out.

"Kho hanhomi yama!" it pleaded in a raspy, high-pitched voice.

"On the fucking ground!" Captain Mitchell roared.

"Kho hanhomi yama!" the surgeon shrilled again, throwing its hands up in front of its face, clearly terrified.

Mitchell strode over and grabbed the figure by its spindly neck. It felt so frail, like a twisted doll. He slammed the alien hard into the wall, thrusting the barrel of his gun right into his forehead.

"You sick piece of shit," he shouted right in its face. "I suggest you pray to whatever abomination of a god it is you worship!"

"Kho hanhomi yama," was all it could say, almost sobbing now.

Captain Mitchell couldn't believe that any being, regardless of which hellhole of a planet it originated from, could be as cruel as the inhuman wretch before him. His nostrils flared with rage as he took one last look into its cold reflective eyes. He release his grip on the

386

surgeon's neck, took half a step back, and pulled the trigger.

The feeble body stood, propped up against the wall, for a few seconds, before it finally slid to the floor to sit at an awkward angle, hunched over its gangly legs, which bent out at an awkward angle.

"Get me out of this thing!" Raven screamed frantically.

Taz came to her aid, using his combat knife to sever through the restraints.

"I bet you've never been this happy to see me," he joked with a grin.

"What was it trying to say?" Reid asked, wiping his mouth on the back of his hand.

"Who gives a shit?" Mitchell snapped. "Let's get her the hell out of here."

* * * * *

Marcus started to come to. He could hear muddled voices as he lay on the cold stone. Something was propped under his head, raising it off the floor. Were they talking about him? His eyes slowly started to open, and he was suddenly aware of a throbbing pain at the back of his skull.

"Marcus," Serena shrieked, hovering over him affectionately. "Are you ok?"

"He'll be fine," Taylor said, taking his pulse. "Just a little bump on the head."

"Wha... what happened?" he asked in confusion.

"The captain knocked you out. He thought it best, given the circumstances," the medic revealed laconically.

"How did you do that? I saw it with my own eyes and I still can't believe it!" Serena gasped, kneeling over Marcus, her long dark hair flowing over Raven's ill-fitting pauldrons.

"Do what?"

"You tore apart that huge door as if it were nothing!"

"I did?" said Marcus, attempting to sit up.

"Easy there," Taylor suggested, lighting a cigarette. "You're likely to have one hell of a headache."

Before Serena could press Marcus any further, they heard the sound of hurried footsteps approaching. Instinctively Taylor went for his carbine, and Marcus dropped a hand to his sidearm, but they were relieved to see the captain and the others returned unscathed. Reid supported Raven, who was still too weak to walk on her own.

"You're alive!" Serena proclaimed, jumping to her feet in a rush of enthusiasm and running to embrace Raven in an awkward hug.

Raven frowned. She had never been one for showing affection openly, least of all in front of her old squad.

"Is that my armor?" Raven muttered. "I mean... thanks... I guess I owe you pretty big,"

"Actually, you have Marcus to thank," Captain Mitchell told her. "Without him we wouldn't even have known where to start looking."

She gave him what anyone else would have thought a grimace as she looked over to where he lay and bit her lip, but Marcus knew that showing even that much emotion publically was a huge step for Raven, and he smiled in return, unbelievably relieved to have her back.

"We should hurry," the captain declared. "Doc, help him out. We need to get them onto the tram."

"Maybe if we're lucky Jago will have managed to get back to the loading bay," Serena added, drawing concerned stares from the others, particularly Raven, who looked around, only now realizing that the

388

huge clone wasn't lurking behind one of the pillars.

Taylor grabbed Marcus by the shoulder, steadying him as he rose to his feat, his head throbbing with pain. The squad got to the tram as quickly as they could, and Serena went to work on the console. The second time around it was far easier than before, and within a matter of seconds the tram was already starting to move, rapidly gaining momentum.

"Hey Serena," Reid called from where he'd taken up station at the front of the vehicle. "What does 'Kho hanhomi yama' mean?"

"Kho hanhomi yama?" she repeated. "Why do you ask?"

"Just something I heard."

She withdrew her datapad and began consulting her notes. It didn't take long. "It means 'not my choice'."

"We always have a choice," Captain Mitchell responded curtly, staring into the dark tunnel before them.

Chapter 49

Mariko stood poised, gazing at her own reflection, as she always did when she rode the elevator. Her skin looked paler than usual. Then again, she had been under an enormous amount of stress of late, what with the coming meeting with the Board. A pair of sentry drones buzzed past beyond the glass, performing routine security checks on the perimeter of the Muromoto Tower.

"Are you nervous, Mariko?" her assistant Adam inquired with genuine concern. "I'm sure they'll listen to reason. The deadline they set was way too close, especially given-"

"Strange," Mariko snapped, interrupting him. "I don't recall requesting your opinion."

He bit his lip, taking half a step backwards. She'd been irate of late, more so than usual. She only had twenty four hours left before her meeting with the Board of Directors, and Division 6 had still not given her clearance to reveal the nature of Project Isis.

The elevator stopped on the executive floor, ejecting them into an opulent oval foyer. In the center of the naturally-lit space an enormous sculpture made from ferrofluid, slanted at an awkward angle, loomed over the surrounding seating area. As its animated features twisted and turned ever so slowly, wave after wave, it resembled a nightmarish drill bit, rising and falling. A compliment of elongated, curving ottomans with simple black leather cushions atop glass frameworks were arranged along the outer rim of a lowered depression in the floor around the sculpture. The floor itself was a bleached white wood with a matte finish, though the central seating area sported a dark Saxony carpet of impeccable quality. On their left a reception desk with an illuminated glass counter stood vacant. Its occupant, like the rest of the staff, had gone home for the night.

She preferred this time of day, when the lights had been dimmed and the entire floor was silent. She remembered how she had used to come here as a child when her father had been working late. He had always worked late. Now she did as well.

She strode through the hall, past a pair of diamond-shaped sentry drones hovering in mid-air, her assistant rushing to keep up with her. One of the drones approached them briefly and performed a routine scan as they passed, then floated back to join the other.

"If there's anything I can do to alleviate your concerns-," Adam began to offer, but was choked off by her cold stare.

"I'm getting tired of your voice. You're like a pathetic little mongrel, incapable of independent thought," she belittled him viciously. "In fact, you're more of a drone than they are," she spat, gesturing towards the sentries.

He knew better than to respond. Besides, he was used to hearing her outbursts by now. That's why he cut himself when he was alone, a razor sharp blade drawn across his thigh where no one would see, except for her, during their… sessions.

"Leave me. I'm done with you for the night," she dismissed him as she neared the bend in the corridor which would take her to her office.

He nodded in compliance and returned to the elevator.

Hers was the largest office in the building, taking up a large portion of the eastern side of the storey and a good section of the floor above as well. She entered the darkened room and walked towards her desk, a simple glass countertop sat on an upturned glass frame decorated with intricate golden filigree. The wall behind her desk was entirely made out of a solid sheet of glass, allowing for a spectacular view of the dusky city below.

As she neared the desk, she squinted, peering through the darkness at her chair, a blocky base with a tall back covered in the finest leather. She froze. There was someone there.

For a moment, she imagined the worst. A member of the Board, come to settle a personal score, or an agent of Division 6, there to extinguish her life now that they had gotten what they needed from her.

Without warning, the standing lamps behind the chair on either side of the desk, towering twice as tall as a man, flickered sharply into life, revealing the figure who had invaded her private domain.

"Father?" she blurted out, more surprised at the sight of the old man than she would have been by the presence of a professional assassin.

Takahashi leaned back into the chair, his brow heavy, one hand tense on the armrest, the other clutched in a fist before his mouth as if to stop him speaking his mind.

"Daughter," he mumbled, staring at her with narrowed eyes.

"This isn't the time," she said, forcing her muscles to relax. "I have important work to do."

Takahashi didn't flinch. He simply sat in her chair and kept his eyes trained on hers.

"Did you hear me? I said-"

"Important work," he acknowledged quietly, without moving.

"How did you even get past the sentries?"

He reached into the breast pocket of his shirt, producing a small remote, the size of a large coin, and laid it on the desktop.

"I never thought I would find myself unwelcome in my own house, Daughter," he said, emphasizing the last word.

"I should have suspected you'd have a way past their programming," she smiled slyly, "They are your design after all."

"When were you going to tell me?" he asked, his composure absolute.

"Tell you what?" she groaned.

"Project Isis," he said quietly, his eyes still locked with hers, but his stare suddenly flaring with judgment.

She remained silent, although his words had caused her visible distress.

"Tell me about Project Isis!" he roared, his lips quivering, his placid face distorted with anger.

She had never seen her father so enraged. She'd always thought of him as a weak man. Cunning, but essentially weak. The person who sat before her now was nothing like that man, but was suddenly determined, unwavering.

"I… it's…" she stuttered, retreating before his anger.

He rose defiantly from his seat, circling the desk with a stride that showed nothing of his advancing age, closing the distance between them.

"My own daughter," he practically spat. "How far you have fallen from grace!"

"Me? Grace?" she shrieked. "You're one to talk!"

"Tell me now!" he bellowed, standing before her.

"NO!" she raged, slapping him across the chin in a fit of bitter anger and resentment.

"If you will not tell me, then I will rip it from you!" he howled, reaching out and seizing the top of her skull in one frail hand.

Instantly, she began to spasm, as if waves of invisible energy were coursing through her veins. Her eyes rolled up in their sockets as she screamed in pain, a pain worse than anything she could have imagined. It was as if her brain was aflame, pain spreading like wildfire throughout her nervous system. Her body hung limply from his commanding grip, an impossible feat considering his brittle old frame.

Behind the veil of pain, her thoughts raced back and forth between memories long past. She saw herself as a child, playing with the robotic tortoise he'd made her for her sixth birthday. She saw a vision of her young teenage self sitting alone in the rain on the steps outside their estate, crying after having slipped and scraped her knee.

Her thoughts quickly skipped ahead to the funeral of her mother, where she stood silently by her father's side, refusing to take his comforting hand. Then her mind rushed to the day she'd claimed his position as CEO, and the occasion soon afterwards when she'd stood at the top of Muromoto Tower, greeting a blond youth whose bland smile had masked a compelling purpose. The two of them had stood by the edge of the tower, talking plainly of the future of Terra and the role which the Muromoto Group was to play in its course.

"No…" Takahashi begged, as if he could alter the course of time, "Of all things, how could you have been so stupid?"

Her thoughts wound to the orbital space platform, and the *Genesis* berthed in its docking bay. Takahashi saw Captain Intari and Senator Yoishi standing at the forefront of the assembly. Most importantly, he saw the crowd of scientists swarming around Intari's battleship, and the new drive technology whose installation was nearing completion.

He released his grip. His daughter's unconscious body slumped to the floor with a resounding thud.

He turned to face the view of Sol, walking slowly over to the window, where he raised his hand to rest upon the glass, gazing over the city.

"How could I have been so oblivious?" he sighed. "The worst of our fears, now realized."

He had spent the last few years in apathy, wallowing in quiet surrender, confident in his beliefs that the plans he had set into motion were firmly on course. Now he feared he was too late, that whatever machinations Division 6 had in store for this world would come to pass.

"It's in your hands now, old friend," he whispered to himself. "I pray you are prepared for what's coming."

Chapter 50

"Wahti shong yoni," the gentle voice echoed, the phrase repeated so many times before that Jago was beginning to cringe every time he heard it.

He was strapped upright to a metal rack, his arms and legs spread apart and bound in chains too strong for him to break. His head was arched back, held in place by a thick leather strap. The only thing he was able to see was the ceiling, several stories above him, covered in golden and crimson tiles, arranged in a pattern that reminded him of flames.

He'd been stripped of his armor and most of his clothing. He felt a sharp pain in his chest as the blade sunk in, deeper than before. The first few times he'd bit his lip in defiance, not wanting to give his tormentors the pleasure of hearing him cry out in pain. This time though, he screamed in agony, the sound echoing around the large space.

He heard a gleeful cackle somewhere in the distance, followed by the sound of clapping. Jago returned the gesture, laughing maniacally, a laughter which soon became muddled with fear and faded into a soft whimper. Somewhere off to one side he thought he heard a deep growl, but he was no longer sure what was real and what wasn't. He didn't even know how much time had passed. He'd lost consciousness at least twice, but he firmly believed that his brothers would come for him. After all, they'd come here to rescue Raven. Surely he was no less important to them than she was?

He could feel blood dripping from so many places on his body that he was amazed that he hadn't run out. Perhaps his blood grew back too. Could he even die? As far as he knew, this could go on forever.

"Wahti shong yoni," the gentle voice said again.

* * * * *

The tram sped along its tracks. Despite the successful rescue of Raven, the idea of trading her life for Jago's was not an easy one to accept. Marcus hoped that the big clone's comms had simply malfunctioned and that he would be waiting for them at the loading dock. He pictured him standing there, looking embarrassed and apologetic at his loss of control.

Serena placed her hand on his, reassuringly gazing into his eyes. Marcus smiled.

The tram was about halfway down the track when Captain Mitchell urged them all to put their helmets back on and get ready. There was no knowing what could be waiting for them at the other end.

"What if Jago isn't waiting for us at the loading dock?" Serena asked.

The captain didn't reply. He simply lowered his head, unable to give her the answer she wanted to hear.

"We can't leave him here to die!" Serena pressed. "We have to go after him."

"There isn't time. Lishan's contact will be back in a few minutes. If we want to get out of here, we have to go now," Mitchell told her, his voice soft.

"There has to be a way," Serena insisted, looking to Marcus for confirmation.

Marcus wanted to comfort her. He wanted to storm the palace and bring Jago back safely, but he knew that they'd been extremely lucky up to this point. The Ape should have known better. If he'd only followed the captain's orders, everything would have been ok. Marcus hated him for putting them in this position, for having them make the hard choice.

The truth was, as much as he wanted to rescue Jago, doing so would mean risking all of their lives. Although he was perfectly willing to risk his own, putting Serena in even more danger was not something he would even consider. If only Jago had listened to the captain.

Marcus put his helmet back on and urged Serena to do the same. They were nearing the end of the tunnels. Taylor flicked his cigarette onto the tracks and braced himself against the railing at the back of the tram.

"Captain!" Reid shouted from the front, peering through the scope of his rifle. "We've got trouble."

"What is it?"

Reid gestured for him to take a look through his scope. With a grunt, Mitchell awkwardly knelt down by the front rail and grabbed hold of the weapon. As he did so, Marcus' gaze was drawn to a bright dot on the horizon, where the tunnel gave out.

"Fuck! They've laid out the welcoming committee," the captain barked.

"How many?" Taz asked, checking the magazines in his ammunition pouches.

"Looks like all of them."

The tram started slowing down, signaling their impending arrival at the next platform.

"Everyone get ready," Mitchell ordered. "We're gonna hit them with everything we've got. Marcus, Raven, prep grenades. Taz, suppressive

fire. Reid, pick off any high-threat targets. Serena, stay low. Doc...
look alive."

Marcus could see the platform now. A bright spotlight was being
targeted in their direction. He could see the outlines of around two
dozen men, kneeling at the edge of the platform, weapons at the ready.
The air erupted in a dazzling display of bright blue beams of energy.
These were different from the narrow golden flashes they'd escaped in
the arena, more diffused, looking more like glowing smudges than the
brilliant scratches of light they'd faced before.

The squad returned fire almost immediately. The deafening sound
of every single carbine, rifle, and sidearm being fired in unison was
certainly impressive, lending some hope to their predicament. They
were still too far out for grenades, but Marcus had already got one
clutching in his left hand and was ready to throw it the moment the
opportunity presented itself.

He counted at least three of their opponents keel over as the squad's
barrage hit the tightly-packed Sheshen hard. He ducked just as a
bright blue beam flew across his shoulder – feeling a savage burst of
joy at the realization that the clones might be able to fight their way
free after all – only to feel the flash of energy striking the body behind
him.

"Serena!" he cried out in vain.

The beam had left no mark, but she slumped to the floor as if her
body had simply been turned off. Knowing there was nothing he
could do for her anymore, Marcus focused his fire with savage
intensity and took down two more of their assailants before he
dropped to one knee to exchange clips.

Taz was the next to go down. A well placed shot hit him square in
the chest, sending him to the floor. Mitchell roared, switching out his

magazine quicker than Marcus had thought humanly possible and sending a barrage of rounds at the enemy, killing two and wounding a third. Almost there, thought Marcus, clutching his grenade.

A beam blew clean past Reid, and hit Raven in the head. Taylor grabbed her just as her limp body was about to slip off the side of the tram, the grenade she'd been holding bouncing off down the tracks.

"Marcus, now!" Mitchell yelled.

Marcus pulled the pin and prepared to throw. He arched his back, spinning on his heels to align his body with the path he wanted the grenade to take. Just as he shifted his weight, about to throw, a beam struck him in the shoulder.

He felt no pain. It was simply as if his body had stopped listening to his commands. His arms and legs went limp as he slumped to the floor of the tram, dropping the grenade. He could hear the clanking sound it made as it hit the floor just behind him, bouncing twice before rolling. Even through the gunfire he could hear the gentle rattle as its dimpled surface rolled on the metal deck of the tram. In his mind he screamed as loudly as he could, but his mouth refused to make even so much as a whisper. His eyes were wide open, but he had no control over them. He simply lay there, a prisoner inside his own body.

"Fuck!" Taylor bellowed as he spotted the grenade, his eyes widening in terror.

He jumped over Marcus to grab it, misjudged his leap, knocking the grenade off to one side. Marcus could hear it rolling once more, dropping off the side of the decelerating tram. There was a second's pause, during which Marcus hoped that maybe they'd be far enough away.

The explosion shook through the rails, lifting the rear of the tram almost two meters into the air. Marcus slid along the floor, the ceiling tumbling above him. He could hear Reid and the captain shouting as they desperately tried to hold on to the railings. The tram slammed down hard and out of place. It fell off the rails, and sent an explosion of sparks flying out behind it as it screeched to a halt at the end of the platform, shaking violently and blowing up a thick cloud of dust.

* * * * *

They were dragged back past the circular security station. The dead guards had already been replaced, and a technician was inspecting the damaged consoles, shouting obscenities at an overly-eager assistant. Marcus was being carried by a pair of black-armored Sheshen guards, dragging his feet along the ground. He could see some of the others being borne along in front of him, the procession directed by a fearsome pair of Nerokan honor guards, still wielding their high-tech serrated spears and clad in suits of hard-edged plate armor.

Instead of continuing on through the tube that led to the loading dock, they veered left, taking the passage which connected to Kesha Kun's palace. Marcus gasped as he mentally relived the dream of lying on the operating table, being cut open while the nightmarish mechanical arm loomed menacingly overhead. Unable to see Serena, he worried that she had been injured in the explosion... or worse. No, she had to be alive. He couldn't allow himself to think otherwise.

They were about to be presented to the most powerful and vile figure on Nos Shana, a society renowned for its total lack of compassion. They were soon through the tubular corridor leading to the main compound, and once inside the palace proper, they were dragged through a series of winding corridors past countless guards and servants.

Finally, Marcus heard the sound that sent chills down his spine and shook him to his very core. It was the distant sound of Jago screaming, pleading for death.

Chapter 51

The grand hall of Kesha Kun's palace was every bit as daunting as they could have imagined. Tiles of crimson and golden hues covered the domed ceiling, neatly arranged in patterns of flames dancing around the pitch black orb in its center, a dark sun on a bed of fire. The walls were inlaid with panels of dark grey metal, interspersed with softly-glowing slates of opaque rose-colored glass. Scarlet pennants nearly thirty meters in length hung from shimmering poles in the ceiling, brushing against the black marble floor. Four levels of balconies lined the long side walls, numerous arched doorways opening off the balustraded walkways, all of which were guarded by ceremonial Sheshen guards.

Four wide steps led up to a raised circular dais in the center of the hall, upon which sat a nightmarish black throne of twisted metal. The back of the throne rose maniacally into the air, spreading out at the sides and curving forwards like a canopy. A layer of hellish thorns jutted from around the canopy, spreading outwards like dread, demonic wings. On the throne, slouching backwards over the armrest like a languid tyrant, was Kesha Kun.

Like every Sheshen Marcus had yet seen, the ruler of Sheijan wore a suit that obscured much of his form, but his armor was unlike that of any of the others. His was utterly pitch black and set with intricate filigree of such extravagant detail that it appeared to have been woven rather than forged, pinpricked here and there by tiny dots of red light. Emblazoned on his chest was the emblem of the Dark Sun Empire, a pulsating ruby in the form of a three-pronged scarlet star. From under a pair of dark pauldrons, topped by serrated talons, flowed a wine-colored cape of shimmering silk.

As with the other high-ranking Sheshen the squad had met, Kesha Kun's armor lacked a helmet, but his mask – a white porcelain affair – seemed to cover only the very front of his face. The rest of his head was hidden beneath a cowl that flowed down into the cape that draped the rest of his figure. Apart from its slitted eyes, the mask's only feature was a symmetrical pattern of menacing crimson lines, all the more ominous in their striking simplicity. Perhaps most menacing of all, his hands and neck were exposed, revealing sickly grey flesh and fingernails like sharpened claws, which he tapped on the edge of his armrest.

One each side of the throne stood a fearsome alien beast, vaguely feline in form, the size of a full-grown bear. Around their necks were manes of long thorny spikes, arching towards the middle of their backs. Their powerful front legs bulged with muscles under a thick coat of fur, groomed to a high sheen. Their hind legs were smaller, barely half the size of the forelimbs. Lined with razor-sharp fangs as long as a Terran combat knife, all dripping with saliva, their jaws were large enough to take a man's head clean off his shoulders. A grey membranous tissue connected the upper and lower jaw near the corners of the mouth, with a gaping hole between them. Each of the beasts was as black as the void between the stars, all but for their sunken, milky eyes, the narrow pupils of which seemed to writhe and pulsate with each breath they took, a living nightmare of intelligence and cruelty untempered by the compassion of sentience.

Since the guards had roughly pulled off his helmet and strung him up on a rack, his hands suspended overhead, he'd begun to regain

404

some mobility in his limbs. For a moment, he'd considered struggling, thinking there had to be a way to wrestle free, but his muscles felt weaker than ever.

The terrifying creature on the left side of the throne snarled. The sound echoed throughout the chamber, chilling him to the bone. Marcus didn't dare to look at them for even more than a second, fearing they would tear him limb from limb at even the slightest whim. Marcus used his newly recovered control over his body to gauge his surroundings, seeing all the others, even Serena, lined up beside him, stripped of their helmets, their heads lolling loosely as they began to come round. Though he was momentarily overjoyed to see her still breathing, his relief was soon replaced with the dread at what lay in store for her... for all of them.

He spotted Jago at the end of the line of racks, his huge form covered in blood. They had removed his armor and most of his clothing, binding him firmly to the rack, even his head tied in place. Despite his bulging muscles and massive frame, he looked beaten, a shell of the man he used to be. In front of the huge clone stood a humanoid figure in plain black robes, its head shrouded under an oversized hood. The creature knelt over a small table holding a tray of gruesome instruments, some of which ended in straight blades of varying length and thickness, others, serrated and twisted. The figure placed a blood soaked-knife onto the tray, taking up another, twice as long and half as wide, in its place. It whispered something in a gurgling voice to a nearby guard, who removed the strap which covered Jago's head.

"Wahti shong yoni," Kesha Kun ordered, his voice carrying clearly to the farthest reaches of the hall.

The torturer plunged the knife into Jago's chest, pressing it

405

downwards to cut a full hand's depth into the flesh. The clone let out an inhuman scream as blood poured out of the wound like a fountain. Tears began to form at the corners of Serena's eyes and Marcus could hear Taz muttering hysterically, still not in full control of his mouth. Not that he'd ever been before.

There was a loud whining sound as one of the narrow doors set into the left hand wall, under the lowest balcony, slid open, signaling the approach of a tall Sheshen draped in black robes over a suit of what looked like primitive mail. The new arrival was male, and wore a mask similar to that of Kesha Kun, although his eye slits were lined with blood red streaks, and the lower section had been carved out to make room for a fine metal mesh which bulged obscenely outwards.

He strode across the hall, making his way towards the dais. As soon as he entered, Kesha Kun rose from his throne. As the Sheshen ruler moved, the outlines of his form took on a smoky haze, as if he could only be seen clearly when he was perfectly still. He took a few languid steps down from the raised dais to greet the newcomer, the pair of them stopping within arm's reach of one another.

Kesha Kun raised his hands, gripping the robed Sheshen's shoulders firmly and whispering a few soft words in the silver tongue. The newcomer peered over his shoulder towards the racks, eyeing each of the Terrans in turn. Jago's tormentor withdrew the blade and, within seconds, the wound began to close.

The tall Sheshen strode past Kesha Kun towards Jago, tilting his head as he stared at the disappearing injury. The ruler of the Dark Sun Empire followed the robed figured towards his prisoners and paced back and forth in front of them, reveling in his prize, stopping to peer closely at each of them.

As he came within a few centimeters of Marcus' face, he felt the

Sheshen's bloodshot gaze boring through the slitted mask, piecing his very soul.

* * * * *

Hanan Aru clung to the underside of one of the upper balconies. His suit had kept him well hidden so far, and Kesha Kun's guards had proven easier to avoid than he had anticipated, especially given the Dark Sun Empire's reputation for security.

As far as he knew, Kesha Kun hadn't left his palace for decades, although there were rumors that the leaders of the ruling Sheshen syndicates met every so often on a mothership, dubbed the *Nihilush*, somewhere in the Nos Shana system to conduct their nefarious dealings. Together they formed the 'Iman Sheni', the 'Brotherhood of Shadows', and there were rumors of sightings of the *Nihilush* dating back almost a hundred years, yet none could prove its existence.

Countless agents of the Iankari had perished in the pursuit of bringing the syndicates to their knees, but on the rare occasion they succeeded, a new one simply rose to take its place. Their reach was longer than most could imagine. In truth, the Etheran fleet could easily overpower Nos Shana and declare martial law, rooting out its leaders and establishing a more civilized society, but Hanan Aru knew that not a single councilor would dare call for such a bold move. The retribution for such an act would spell certain death for any who dared propose it, and almost certainly for their families as well. The syndicates were notorious for their ability to strike at anyone, wherever they were. He almost felt honored, perched high above the throne. It was a rare privilege to be standing in the halls of the ruler of the presiding syndicate.

Hanan Aru kept close watch as Shari, Kesha Kun's oldest son and heir to the Dark Sun Empire, stood vigilant before the rack which held the large Terran, mesmerized by his regenerative capabilities. No doubt the others would soon share his fate. Kesha Kun was notorious for his lust for psionic power, whatever the cost. Soon he would want to see if the others possessed similar abilities.

Hanan Aru considered all the possibilities. He faced a choice dilemma. On the one hand, he had given his word to fulfill his mission, yet there, right before his very eyes, stood the most vile and powerful figure on the entire planet. The Etherium would surely benefit from his removal, though such an act would not be without its consequences. Even though Shari would eventually assume the throne, the resulting power vacuum would send the Iman Sheni into turmoil, perhaps even long enough for the Iankari to make their move.

A guard appeared on the balcony above, resting his arms on the railing and peering down at the scene below. Hanan Aru kept perfectly still, not wanting to draw attention to himself. His eyes were drawn to the two magnificent beasts below. They were Eladons, native to the smuggler's haven of Jarrubon. Elusive creatures, but fast and ferocious. Some say they were once a sentient race which devolved into a bestial state, shaking off the shackles of civilization for a life of predation. Despite their shrouded homeworld, their fame was widespread. They could smell the scent of prey several kilometers away. If it weren't for the hermetic seals on his suit, they would surely have sensed him by now. The smugglers of Jarrubon were known to send out hunting parties to capture them, often with disastrous consequences. Any beasts taken would then be shipped offworld and sold to the highest bidder. They were said to be nearly impossible to kill. Many times he had fantasized about testing himself against one, and here there were two.

Chapter 52

Kesha Kun stood arrogantly before them, pondering how best to make use of his captives while his entourage of guards kept silent watch.

"Serena, tell him we want to negotiate," Captain Mitchell slurred. He had regained most of the use of his limbs, and was wrestling with his restraints.

"Negotiate?" Kesha Kun spoke in a clear voice, startling them with his use of their language. "And what you have to give that Kesssha Kun cannot take from you?"

"Let them go," Mitchell commanded. "I'm the one you want," he lied.

"Sssuch arroganccce," Kesha Kun sneered.

Shari grabbed Raven forcefully by the jaw. He tilted his head as he stared into her eyes, then lowered his lascivious gaze to her ample figure. He ran the tip of his gauntleted finger down the seam of her flight suit, between her supple breasts, thrusting it into her abdomen, causing her to gasp. She spat in his face.

Apparently this was not something the young prince had become accustomed to in his sheltered life. He stood stock still for a moment, astounded that someone would dare to defy him so. After his surprise wore off, he thrust out a hand and, without looking, beckoned to a young fair-skinned Ganyatti girl who had been hovering in the background. The girl, who appeared no older than early adolescence, hesitantly approached her master, stretching up when she reached his side and tentatively licking his mask clean. As soon as she finished, backing away with her head bowed and her supple tail writhing around her knees, Shari rammed his fist into Raven's stomach. She reeled in pain, gasping for air.

"You enter my domain, ssslay my guards, sssteal Kesssha Kun's mossst prized possession," Kesha Kun chuckled softly once his son had straightened his robes and regained his composure, "even ssspit in the face of my ssson, and you wisssh to negotiate?"

"We are members of the Terran Republic. If you think you can get away with keeping us prisoner, you are sorely mistaken," Mitchell insisted, his speech clearer as he regained control of his body.

Kesha Kun gasped, letting out a horrendous sound that it took Marcus a moment to realize was malicious laughter.

"Sssourcesss tell Kesssha Kun that your ship isss docked in Sheijan, and isss a most primitive vessssel. Your threatsss carry little weight with me."

"Get me out of here!" Taz moaned as he came round, frantically trying to wriggle free.

Kesha Kun reveled in their misery, turning to Jago's hooded tormentor, "Cut him again," he ordered the crabbed figured, who promptly thrust a blade once more into the huge clone's chest.

Jago screamed, although not as loudly as he had before. Marcus could see that the behemoth was losing strength. He had always thought that the big man would never break.

"I be curioussss to sssee how long he can continue healing. I could ssspend yearsss to listen to his wailsss, but his sssecret shall be mine. All your sssecretsss ssshall be mine. You thought you could stop Kesssha Kun from posssesssing her powersss," he said as he paused in front of Raven. "Inssstead Kesha Kun shall have yoursss asss well!"

In the sudden silence that followed the Sheshen's words, Serena let out an astonished gasp of realization. "Raven, can… you mean… all of you?"

Captain Mitchell silenced her with a glare.

"Let ussss sssee what the girl can do?" Kesha Kun suggested, gesturing towards Serena. "Cut her."

"No!" Marcus shouted. "She isn't one of us!"

Serena was growing hysterical, utterly confused, but aware enough that she knew she was in grave danger.

"She has no powers!" Marcus pleaded with him. "Please, let her go."

"Hmmm," Kesha Kun sneered at him. "No powersss? You must be thinking Kessha Kun be a fool! Yet, if you insssissst, then sssurely I need not be making asss careful with her asss the othersss. If ssshe have no powersss, then Kesha Kun losesss nothing. Cut her!"

Jago's tormentor ceased its probing of the whimpering giant and moved down the line to stand in front of Serena, the serrated scalpel still dripping blood in its gloved hand. The torturer didn't look up at her face at all, the hood of its robes drawn low over its head. Perhaps doing so made the job easier to bear.

"No!" Marcus cried out, "please! Cut me instead!"

Kesha Kun turned his back on them, languidly easing his way back up the steps to rest on his nightmarish throne. The torturer began cutting the straps on Serena's armor, removing the plates one by one. Marcus felt tears swelling up in his eyes at the thought of what was about to happen, but he refused to look away.

Beyond, Marcus could see the robed figure of Shari move over to Reid, leaning in to within a hair's breadth of the sniper's face, staring directly into his eyes. Reid calmly closed his eyes, taking long deep breaths to keep his composure.

"Holy Father, give us the strength to endure our hardships," he began to recite under his breath. "Embrace us with your all-encompassing wisdom and permit us entry into your hallowed realm."

* * * * *

Hanan Aru clutched the edge of the balcony. He knew that if he were to intervene, and fail, it would not only result in his death, but in dire ramifications for the Etherium as well. The rest of the Iman Sheni would find out who was to blame, as they always did. Not only was he Hiodan, his suit, with its distinctive chameleon function, could easily be traced back to the Iankari. A wave of punitive assassinations and retaliatory strikes would wash across the Etherium. As he pondered the best course of action, he realized that there were only two choices available to him: fight or flight.

Flight was the safest option, both for himself and the Etherium, but despite his reservations about the Terrans, he would not wish such a fate on even his worst enemy. The mission, he thought. I still have a mission to fulfill. Among the Iankari, honor was everything. Men in his profession would often give in to honor. It was a double-edged sword, one that could spell the difference between a long and prosperous career and a swift – albeit honorable – death. Though the mission had not been handed down by the Etherium, it was a mission nonetheless. He felt the pangs of guilt stirring as he contemplated retreat. Could he ever face Rodan Kesh again, knowing he had failed him? He had given his word.

His eyes were drawn once more to the Eladons, lounging on the floor next to the throne. Even one would be a formidable opponent, but two? Looking around, he counted over thirty guards in the hall

413

alone. There was no telling how many more would come to their aid. He wanted desperately to fight, yearned to charge in. He even caught himself reaching for the handle of the blade strapped to his back.

I can't, he thought, snatching his hand away. The Etherium comes first. He set his hand firmly back on the stone of the balcony and began eyeing the escape route he would take, a wide passage on the ground floor, currently flanked by a pair of Nerokan honor guards.

* * * * *

Marcus didn't even care what happened to him anymore, as long as Serena got away. They could have him for all he cared. Having been hunted most of his short life, he'd always assumed he would come to one violent end or another.

"If she cannot heal, then she will make a fine meal for my Eladonsss," Kesha Kun sniggered, reaching out to pet the one to his right.

The spined creature let out an almost soothing purr as the last of Serena's armor fell to the floor.

The torturer grabbed hold of Serena's jacket, cutting through the neckline and then ripping it open, tearing away her undershirt in the same swift, efficient movements. Marcus couldn't look. It was a strange feeling. He was both afraid for her life and embarrassed for her at the same time. He turned and looked the other way down the line of racks, seeing that Taz too had averted his gaze, something Marcus would never have expected him to do at the sight of a naked female body.

"No," Serena cried, voice choking on the edge of tears. "Please… stop!"

Steeling himself, Marcus turner back to see what was happening. The torturer was looking over his shoulder, apparently waiting for his master's approval. There had to be something he could do, thought Marcus frantically. He wanted to lash out with his mind, but his thoughts were too clouded by fear. He tried frantically to focus on his anger, his hate, but the more he tried to grasp it, the more easily it slipped through his fingers. Save her, you fool, he thought. You have done it before, why can't you do it now?

"Wahti shyng yoni," Kesha Kun's voice echoed throughout the hall.

"No, please," Serena pleaded in desperation.

The blade pierced her flesh, sinking in deeper with each passing second. The sound she made as she gasped for breath sent Marcus reeling. He thought for sure that it would be her last. Time almost stood still as he hung on the rack, watching the torturer lean forward onto his blade. He squeezed his eyes shut, refusing to look, as he heard the sound of the first few droplets of blood hitting the floor.

How could any living being be so cruel, so utterly devoid of compassion? He hated them, all of them. He wanted to strip the very flesh from their bones. These weren't sentient beings. No sentient creature could do such unspeakable things, let alone actually enjoy them. She was gone. He couldn't look, but he was certain of it. They'd killed her, the shining beacon of light in his otherwise bleak, miserable existence.

Suddenly he felt Mitchell's presence as the captain reached out with his mind, piercing through the roiling mass of emotion clouding his psyche.

"I can't stop you this time, Marcus," Mitchell's voice sounded inside his mind. "But there's no other choice. I've got to pull the pin out of the grenade."

With that, Marcus felt his panic slipping away. There was nothing to fear anymore, no panic, no dismay. It was as if the captain had sealed off that part of his mind entirely. The void in his soul was fast filling up with boundless rage.

Whether he wanted to or not, his feelings for the others were simply gone, nonexistent. He no longer feared the consequences of what his fury might do to them. All he wanted was revenge. His nostrils flared as he drew in deep breaths, his entire body trembling. He couldn't contain it any more.The shackles around his legs and wrists shattered with a series of loud cracks, sending fragments of metal flying in all directions. He lowered his head, dropping his arms to his sides, taking one final deep breath before the chaotic forces brewing inside him seized irrevocable control.

The very air rippled around him as waves of energy coursed through his body. Had they been able to see him, the stars themselves would have trembled in his presence. He was Marcus no more. He was an incarnation of fury and death.

Chapter 53

The Avia were among the finest luxury vehicles in the entire galaxy, and the ambassador's shuttle was one of their most extravagant, built to a sleek and elegant design. Its curved body was a little over a dozen meters in length and a third of that in width, the upper half of which consisted of curved glass, tinted dark for added comfort. Twin thrusters protruded from the rear of the cabin beneath short dual fins that slanted down and outwards in a thin set of wings.

Although the pursuit of wealth for its own sake was a foreign concept to the Gaian people, the acquisition of status was another matter entirely. Ambassador Janosh had always considered his position a means to serve his people to the best of his abilities. For all that, it was an appointment of the highest honor, rivaled only by a seat on the Triumvirate. Selfish gains had always been the farthest from his mind, but he found himself enjoying the little perks that his status afforded him.

"We must hurry. The Council is about to begin," the ambassador urged from his broad seat, leaning forward to retrieve his holopad from the seat across from him.

He'd received the footage while enjoying his afternoon tea, and had known instantly that he finally possessed the leverage he needed to persuade the Etheran Council. The shuttle raced across the cityscape towards the Council Hall. The spire of the Palace of Wisdom towered formidably over the center of the Core district, a glowing beacon of hope for all the races of the Etherium alliance. Though he had wandered its halls on countless occasions, it never ceased to inspire him.

Normally he would arrive early, taking the time to enjoy the majestic rooftop gardens. Strolling leisurely amidst trees native to all the corners of the galaxy, he would enjoy a brief respite from his duties as he marveled at the myriad of exotic aromas and countless statues and fountains, honoring past dignitaries and honoraries of the Etherium. He knew that one day his visage would be memorialized amidst carefully-pruned bushes and towering trees, forever gracing the gardens with his presence.

Today, however, was not the time for such reverie. The Council was about to begin and he loathed late arrivals more than anyone, but the footage he'd been sent had necessitated that he make some arrangements before leaving for the Core. His shuttle banked towards one of the empty landing bays, a circular platform surrounded by pinpricks of azure light that blinked slowly on and off. The ambassador folded a sheath of resistant fabric around the holopad and placed it safely in a compartment within his robes, ready to depart the moment the vessel touched down.

* * * * *

The usual clamor greeted him as he entered the hall. He was met by Rodan and his aide, who had arrived ahead of him to prepare for their latest stratagem.

"They are about to begin, Ambassador," the aide stated, drawing an accusing stare from Ambassador Janosh.

The aide cleared his throat, remembering that the Ambassador was not particularly fond of people who stated the obvious.

"I shall escort you to your seat, Ambassador," he prompted, swiveling on his toes and strutting towards a side passage which led up to the third storey booths.

The opening address was just starting when they took their seats in the Gaian booth. Ambassador Janosh withdrew his holopad, plucking a small data card from one of its sockets and placing it on his armrest.

The assembly began with a heated debate concerning trade legislation, which escalated quickly as reference was made to the recent terrorist attacks. Noga Zhad, the mouthless, serpentine Eremaran councilor, speculated that the attacks were aimed at destabilizing commerce and implied they had actually been perpetrated by corporate competitors on Mott Midahl, the Cerakanese Freedom Fighters simply claiming responsibility to garner publicity for their cause.

It was a ridiculous notion, Janosh knew. While it was true that the corporate interests of Mott Midahl had gained from the inflated prices on trade goods being brought in from outlying worlds, Mott Midahl had more important matters to deal with. Its location so near the border with the Moloukan Empire made the Etherium a valuable ally to them, a relationship their government would never allow rogue elements to jeopardize, no matter the financial gains available. It was clear that Noga Zhad's notion was merely an attempt to divert attention from the fact that it was his predecessors who had been the most outspoken against the issue of rendering aid to Cerakan in their time of need.

"The next speaker is the esteemed Councilor for the Children of Gaia," the Hiodan Councilor and aid to the Shitoru, Kai Käraian, prompted.

"Esteemed colleagues," Ambassador Janosh began, rising and

leaning on the balcony of his booth as he looked around the grand chamber, "I call upon you once more to discuss the matter of the Terran threat."

"This again, Ambassador?" Noga Zhad called. "Is the realm of Gaia so blessed that their only concern is the matter of a few hapless wanderers?"

"The Gelvein agree," came the thundering voice of Councilor Yusol Sulomo, the long flowing tentacles of his hologram writhing in midair above the floor of the assembly hall. "We refuse to dwell on such insignificant matters when war looms over our people."

Janosh was indeed sympathetic to the Gelvein cause, their homeworld having been the target of more Moloukan raids than any other, apart from Cerakan. If it weren't for the harsh nature of their planet, the Moloukan Empire would have made slaves of their entire population eons ago.

"Silence!" Kai Käraian barked.

The clamor dissipated instantly. Though politically he was little more than a mouthpiece for the Shitoru, there were few who would cross the Hiodan councilor, who acted as chair of the assembly, in his presence.

"The Gaian councilor has the floor. Respect the proper course of order," he growled before retaking his seat.

"Thank you, Councilor," Ambassador Janosh bowed in his direction. "In previous sessions, the Gaian people have moved that there be a clear division between the newly-arrived Terrans and the Children of Gaia, citing irreconcilable differences in morals and ideals."

"We have heard this tirade before. Get to the point," the Nerokan councilor interjected, his gaping reptilian maw snarling with impatience.

Ambassador Janosh paused briefly for dramatic effect, ensuring he had the chamber's full attention before finally continuing.

"As you wish," he replied. "The following sequence was intercepted by a remote sensor outpost on the Hrūll-Sheshen border. What you are about to see will prove beyond a shadow of a doubt that the Terrans have evolved along a separate path from the Gaian people. While the Children of Gaia strive for enlightenment and follow strict codes of ethics, the Terrans are no better than the Sheshen or the Banthalo."

He grabbed the data chip from his armrest and inserted it into a socket at the base of a small console by the railing. A second later, the holographic display hovering over the assembly hall faded to a recording from the security feed aboard the Hrūll refinery.

The footage showed the Terran squad emerging from the docked *Tengri*, followed by a series of carefully edited sequences of brutal combat, in all of which the Terrans were the obvious aggressors. The display then showed the image of the refinery breaking up in a series of catastrophic explosions, before ending with a shot of Captain Mitchell standing defiantly on top of a crumbling slab of concrete, his primitive sidearm raised and aimed towards the camera. As soon as he pulled the trigger, the feed was disconnected, leaving only a haze of static hovering over the tiled floor of the chamber.

Ambassador Janosh did not resume his speech once the footage ran to an end, instead allowing whispered debates between the councilors and their aides to grow in intensity for a few moments before shouting out across the Council.

"Councilors!" he called. "What you have just witnessed was an unprovoked attack at the hands of the Terrans. There can be no question that our claims are true. We ask that the Council vote immediately on the matter, and, furthermore, we demand that if and when the Terran race should apply for membership in the Etherium alliance, such application be met with the strictest of reservations and the harshest scrutiny."

The Ambassador's words drew no snide remarks from Councilor Noga Zhad, nor Yusol Sulomo. Even Rasha Ke Nahn remained silent, observing the reactions of his colleagues. The image overhead faded to the broad-shouldered form of Kai Käraian, who rose slowly from his seat.

"This is indeed a grave matter. Despite their small numbers, they are the first representatives of their people. Having requested asylum, the Etherium would have expected them to behave with nothing less than utmost civility. Although I am loath to judge an entire people by the actions of a few of its members, the vast divide between the Children of Gaia and the Terrans cannot be ignored: not only have the Terran emissaries absconded from Semeh'yone having sought asylum with the Etherium, they appear to have assaulted one of our member races as well. Rest assured, Councilors, that this evidence will be presented at their scheduled asylum hearing in a few weeks' time, should they return for it. The Shitoru acknowledges the wise words of the Gaian councilor, and recommends that the notion be passed."

The hall erupted into a heated debate. Ambassador Janosh was certain that he had delivered his argument with perfection. Still, the next few minutes were filled with anxiety as the councilors were allowed to discuss the matter prior to the vote. Finally, Kai Käraian called for the ballot.

A holographic interface embedded at the base of each booth displayed the options available to each councilor. Ambassador Janosh placed his hand over the glowing blue symbol, and waited in nervous silence while the other representatives made their opinions known.

A moment later, the Hiodan councilor rose from his seat once more.

"Esteemed Councilors," he said as the display overhead swirled into a representation of the vote's result. "The motion for classification of the Children of Gaia and the Terrans as separate peoples has been passed."

Ambassador Janosh slumped back into his seat, a sly smile playing across his lips. It had worked. Gaia's legacy would be preserved.

Chapter 54

Hanan Aru kept a watchful eye on the Nerokan guards, biding his time as he waited for an opportunity to make his escape. They stood on either side of the broad passage he wanted to take, painfully close to one another. Though his suit shielded him from sight, such proximity could prove perilous. The camouflage systems were not without fault, causing a rippling effect in the surrounding air which could be detected by a watchful eye when viewed up close.

The sudden sound of tearing metal claimed his attention. He snapped his head up sharply to see that one of the Terrans had torn clean through his shackles. Odd, he thought. Having studied them this long, he would not have guessed that any of them possessed such strength. Still, this was just the diversion he'd been hoping for. This was his chance.

* * * * *

The long flowing banners hanging behind the central dais began to shift, as if shaken by invisible winds. Marcus stumbled down from the metal rack, turning and stretching limbs as the black-armored Sheshen guards rushed to throw themselves at him, clearly planning to bear him down by sheer numbers.

"Ssshao stugomi ssshong haybu!" Kesha Kun screamed from his throne.

Marcus snapped forward, pummeling the nearest guard with his bare hands. He barely felt the impact, but there was a loud crack as his fist smashed through the Sheshen's armor, sending the spindly body hurling a good twenty meters through the air to slam into a wall, where it slid, lifeless, to the stone floor.

The hall erupted as dozens of guards began firing beams of energy in his direction, but Marcus was oblivious to it all. All he saw was his next target. His movements began gaining momentum like nothing he'd ever experienced before. He was a raging whirlwind of death and mayhem as he flung himself between blasts, his fists flying in every direction. Before the others could blink, three guards lay strewn across the floor, limbs broken and chestplates caved in, and Marcus hadn't even slowed down.

"Xio ssshong bansssho changoti!" Kesha Kun shouted.

"Marcus," Captain Mitchell shouted after him. "Cut us loose!"

Dismayed, Kesha Kun's robed son punched the captain square on the jaw and then ran for his life. Captain Mitchell barely flinched.

If he were still Marcus, he would have done anything to free them, but he was Marcus no more. All he could think of was what these animals had done to Serena, and how he would make them all pay with their lives.

The two powerful beasts by the throne paced about anxiously, letting out deep growls as they eyed Marcus. It was as if they were awaiting permission from their master to pounce.

A Sheshen marksman on the top balcony took careful aim, watching as Marcus grabbed another guard by the throat and threw him head on into a third as if he weighed nothing more than an empty suit of armor. The marksman squeezed the trigger, sending a diffused beam of bright blue energy shooting through the air, striking Marcus square in the chest.

425

Marcus didn't even seem to notice, let alone care. He seized another onrushing guard by the head and lifted him off the ground with one hand, squeezing until he heard a distinct popping sound as the Sheshen's skull collapsed. He felt as if he had the strength of a hundred men and the fury of thousands.

Kesha Kun gripped his armrest firmly, pressing the hidden button on its underside. A shimmering semi-spherical force field flickered into life over the central dais, cutting it off from the rest of the throne room, a split second after his son managed to jump onto its steps.

Captain Mitchell was practically snarling in frustration as he watched the hall explode in chaos, leaving the still-bound members of the squad completely ignored, when he heard his restraints snap, as if they'd suddenly been cut in half by an unseen force. He looked down, and gasped in astonishment. He was free.

Not one to question his luck, he immediately tumbled down from the rack and ran to release the others.

Having dispatched all of the guards who'd been foolish to get close to him, Marcus turned suddenly towards the cowering torturer, who was attempting to hide behind the racks, hoping to go unnoticed amidst the firefight, staring at it with eyes burning with hatred. The cloaked figure gave a wordless shriek of fear and ran towards the hall's main entrance.

Marcus reached out with an empty hand and grabbed. Though his hand caught nothing but air, the torturer's hood flew back, as if snagged on an invisible object, and held the writhing creature in place. With a twist of his arm, Marcus pulled the torturer around to face him. Its face looked like it had been made of melted plastic, with cuts and sores all over its mangled flesh, so deformed that its race and gender were unrecognizable. Two huge black reflective eyes stared at

426

him, pleading for its life.

The two Nerokan bodyguards guarding the main passageway to the hall lowered their serrated spears and apprehensively marched towards Marcus, reptilian faces grim. He could feel their fear as if it were a living force, fueling his rage to even greater heights. He yanked on his mental grip on the torturer's hood and the disfigured being shot through the air, landing at his feet.

Marcus bent down over it, completely ignoring the bursts of energy exploding around him, cocking his head as he stared at the hideous thing quivering on the ground before him, its head bowed low and hands outstretched, pleading for its life.

Marcus' indifferent visage turned into a hateful sneer. His lips trembled as he raised his foot and slammed it down hard onto the back of the torturer's head, which exploded into a bloody pulp, sending a shockwave throughout the throne room.

"Helassshi soghoti!" Kesha Kun screamed.

The pair of spined alien predators roared as if suddenly released from an imaginary cage, bowing low as they crawled out into the open. One of them stalked down the side of the hall, angling to approach the escaping Terrans from behind, while the other padded directly towards Marcus.

Marcus turned to face the beast head on as the bright beams of energy continued to pound on and around him. Though they appeared to do him no harm, each burst that struck him caused his skin to glow with a faintly blue sheen.

The Eladon unhinged its jaw, baring enormous razor-sharp fangs, dripping with saliva, producing a sound so deep Marcus felt it as much as he heard it. Marcus let out a roar of his own as he prepared to charge the beast head on, regardless of its size. The nightmarish monster spread its huge front legs and braced itself as Marcus pounded forward, but just as he was about to ram head on into it, the beast let out a peculiar squeal of pain and threw itself away with blinding speed.

Marcus skidded to a stop in confusion, his attention quickly shifted to the gaping wound in the huge creature's side, near its hind legs. The Eladon yelped as it backed away slowly, limping, as it shielded its wound.

* * * * *

Meanwhile, Mitchell had finished releasing Taz and Reid and was starting on Taylor's restraints. As soon as he was free, Taz went for the pile of equipment that had been confiscated from them, dumped carelessly beside the torturer's racks as curios for the Sheshen to examine. He grabbed a carbine and opened fire at the guards. Reid followed his lead, seizing his rifle whilst diving into cover behind the metal racks and starting to take out the guards on the balconies above.

* * * * *

Marcus was suddenly distracted from the injured beast as the two Nerokan guards drew near, holding their spears at arm's length, clearly hoping that the distance would give them an advantage. Marcus sneered, reaching back behind him with both hands, pausing briefly as he eyed each of the fearsome reptilian warriors in turn. Then he thrust his hands forward, gripping the air in his crushing grip.

The Nerokans, some of the most highly trained mercenaries in Etheran space, simply erupted into a mist of blood and torn flesh, what was left of their grotesquely twisted bodies falling to the floor like slabs of meat. Marcus didn't even wait to see them stop twitching. Instead he turned his attention to the throne.

Marcus stepped closer towards the dais, studying the force field.

"Taygionay ssshong!" Kesha Kun screamed.

Shari stood defiantly behind the force field, knowing that there was nothing Marcus could do to breach it.

* * * * *

At the other end of the throne room, Mitchell managed to get Taylor free and immediately ordered him to see to Jago while the officer focused on helping Raven. Behind the racks, the unwounded Eladon had managed to go unnoticed as it crept along the back wall, studying Reid and Taz from behind as they spewed forth a steady stream of rounds at the hapless guards. It crouched low, creeping along the floor in silence, inching its way closer with each step.

A shot hit the rack which Taz was using for cover, making him start back from the gap he'd been firing through. Throwing himself onto his back as he tumbled on the ground, he spotted the stalking beast just as it was about to lunge at the unsuspecting Reid.

"Look out!" he shouted, raising his carbine to spray the monster.

Reid turned to see the horrific creature rearing its head, its maw poised to attack, and froze. Fortunately, Taz's covering fire distracted the huge creature, delaying its attack momentarily. Still, the beast was less than three meters away, and he knew that no matter which way he tried to run, it would get to him first.

Taz snapped off another burst of rounds. Some of them appeared to bounce off harmlessly, but others dug into the creature's thick fur.

Nonetheless, it was not enough to deter it from making Reid its meal.

For a moment, Reid thought he saw a flicker behind the beast. He knew for certain that he had seen... something, but a split second later it was gone. Suddenly, an arc of streaming black blood flew into the air from one of the beast's hind legs. The Eladon wailed, swinging its head sharply around to face the invisible foe, lashing out and slamming its jaw shut as it tried to bite something it couldn't see.

Reid saw the spiny thorns on its back rise as its head moved, revealing the soft skin between them. Instinctively, he jumped forward, ramming his sniper rifle into the creature's side, and pulled the trigger.

The beast yelped in pain just as another flicker on the far side of its body tore through its neck, sending a spray of blood gushing from the mortal wound. The creature reeled, quivering as it slumped to the floor, twitching as it slowly bled to death.

* * * * *

Meanwhile, Marcus was standing in the center of a storm of weapon fire, examining the force field, when he felt his rage beginning to diminish. Not now, he thought. I'm so close! Another flashing bolt slammed into his shoulder, searing his armor. He felt it. It didn't hurt, but the tingling sensation it left behind remained.

"No placcce you can run," Kesha Kun sneered, while his son continued to stare intently at Marcus.

Marcus could feel their mocking gazes, despite their masks.

"You have lossst," Kesha Kun continued, pouring salt in his wounds.

Marcus hated him. He wanted to make him feel his pain, share his loss, deprive him of what he held dearest.

"I have nothing left to lose," Marcus growled, reaching out with his hand.

The sound of tearing metal rung through the air as the massive spiked wings on Kesha Kun's throne began to bend and twist. Marcus focused all of his remaining rage, pushing and pulling with his mind.

"Ssshoot him!" Kesha Kun shouted in a state of panic.

Another blast hit Marcus square in the chest, rupturing his armor and intensifying the tingling sensation that coursed through his veins. Yet another blast barely missed his shoulder. He felt his mental grip on the metal beyond the force field beginning to slip as his body weakened. No, not now!, he shouted in his mind.

A guard on a balcony hit him in the hip, weakening him even further. The faint glowing sheen of blue that had permeated his skin with each blow was fading rapidly. He trembled with rage as he collapsed to one knee, fighting to keep his arm extended as he desperately clung to his mental hold.

He looked over his shoulder at Serena's lifeless body, still strapped to the rack. A puddle of crimson blood had formed beneath her, and the bare skin of her torso was as pale as driven snow. He drew his gaze back to Kesha Kun and made one last effort, pulling with every last fiber of his being.

He had only seconds left. He could see the veins on his quivering arm popping out, his outstretched fingers seeming ready to break. Finally, he heard the snap as the spiked metal wing broke free and flew forward, slamming into Shari's back, impaling him through his stomach, chest and shoulder. The twisted black spikes exploded through his armor as if it wasn't even there.

"Shariii!" Kesha Kun screamed as his son's body remained still standing for a brief second, one last moment of defiance before it slumped to the ground.

Marcus could only imagine the astonished look he must have worn beneath his mask.

Another bolt slammed into Marcus' chest. With nothing left to resist the blow, he slumped to the floor, smoke rising from his smoldering wounds.

* * * * *

Reid stared at the twitching Eladon lying just beyond arm's reach, assuring himself that it was truly dead.

"Run!" a strange voice whispered into his ear, causing him to leap up and swing his rifle to bear on... empty air.

Mitchell had finished releasing Raven from the rack, and the pair of them joined Taylor in helping Jago. The behemoth seemed exhausted and barely conscious, yet vaguely pleased.

At a flash of movement above him, Reid blew the head off another guard on the highest balcony, quickly taking aim at another.

"The passage, run!" he heard the whisper again, and this time caught a flicker of movement off to his side.

Reid grabbed Taz by the shoulder, gesturing towards the wide passageway.

"Let's go!" he yelled.

Taz nodded and ran towards the others, providing covering fire as they grabbed their helmets and weapons. Reid ran out into the open, firing haphazardly towards the balconies as he went, skidding to a stop when he reached Marcus' side and throwing his rifle over one shoulder, bending down to lift Marcus up onto the other.

432

"You will die for thisss!" Kesha Kun screamed at them. "You cannot hide from Kesssha Kun!"

Reid ignored him completely. He saw the others already making their way towards the main passageway leading out of the throne room. Pumping his legs, he powered after them, he somehow managing to jink sideways around an incoming shot as he ran after them, despite the heavy load.

"None can hide from Kesssha Kun!" he heard the shouting once more behind him as he fled.

Chapter 55

They darted down the corridors of the palace as fast as their legs could carry them, taking little heed of the numerous side passages.

Reid held onto Marcus, who lay slung over his shoulder, barely conscious, but completely paralyzed. He couldn't even utter a sound, not that he wanted to. His mind was as exhausted as his body. Serena was gone. The only thought he could muster was a wish that Kesha Kun would share his pain.

Jago stumbled along behind them, aching all over and entirely spent from the torture he'd endured. Taylor tried his best to support him and spur him forwards, fearing that the giant was ready to collapse at any moment, but Jago refused to surrender to exhaustion. Having tasted freedom, his conviction was renewed. Though he was in no condition to fight, he somehow managed to keep with the pace.

As they approached a T-junction, a tall humanoid shape flickered briefly right in front of them. Taz stopped dead in his tracks, raising his weapon.

"What the hell was that?" He shouted, glancing quickly at the others for reassurance.

Captain Mitchell stepped forward and placed his hand on Taz's barrel, forcing his weapon down. "I have no idea, but whoever he is, I think he's with us," he said.

After a brief pause, Taz simply shrugged his shoulders. "Fair enough," he agreed, realizing that this was no time to argue.

"This way," a dry voice called as the figure flickered into view once more, pointing down the left-hand passage.

They ran ahead, encountering the occasional black-armored Sheshen, racing down the passageway to answer Kesha Kun's frantic summons. Taz and Raven made quick work of them. Normally the dark-haired beauty would leave the fireworks to the rest of the squad, but after having been captured not once, but twice, by Kesha Kun's forces, she felt she had a score that needed settling. She gripped her borrowed carbine firmly, screaming as she let loose a hail of projectiles at any hapless guard who was unfortunate enough to cross their path. Every so often they would come across a fallen guard, covered in vicious lacerations inflicted at the hands of their mysterious escort.

It didn't take long before they spotted the opening of the clear-sided tube leading to the first security station up ahead. Realizing that they were about to leave the palace behind, they pushed that much harder.

Racing along the hard metal grating of the cylindrical corridor, they noticed a pair of formidable blast doors blocking their way at the far end. The air in front of the barrier flickered, suggesting a humanoid shape standing in front of the doors with both hands pressing against the metal. The squad came panting to a halt behind it, waiting for whatever it was the barely-visible figure was attempting to do.

As he studied their makeup, Hanan Aru's helmet display began to overlay the doors' mechanical and electrical designs onto its display, revealing its vulnerabilities. He knelt down, reached out with his fingers, touching a small panel at the base of the right hand side of the doorframe. A sudden burst of electricity shot from a device embedded in his fingertip and into the panel. Having disabled its motor, Hanan Aru rose to his feet, gripping the doors with both hands and pulling them open.

As the squad breached the security station the flickering figure accompanying them transformed into a chaotic whirlwind of mayhem and death as it darted about the room, cutting down foe after foe. Taz lent a hand and mowed down a guard who raised a rifle to shoot the ghostly shape in the back.

"Whoever he is, I sure am glad he's on our side!" Taz shouted over the gunfire, staring into the fray.

In a matter of seconds, the security station was still. Four guards lay hacked into pieces on the floor, and two more had fallen to the squad's firearms. The squad watched in wary awe as the tall shape of their benefactor strode to the center of the circular pit. Once there, Hanan Aru turned off his chameleon suite, revealing the hulking form of his silvery Iankari power armor, whose smooth, menacing outlines were far more advanced than anything the Terrans had ever seen.

"Stay back," he warned, reaching out with his hands.

There was a sudden flicker of light as he once more began to absorb energy from the structure's power reserves. Arcs of electricity shot out from the consoles, the torn wiring hanging over the door to the loading dock, and the panels set in the walls, earthing themselves in the silvery suit. Then the room went dark. The only source of light was the dim blue emergency lighting, which exuded a loud buzzing noise. The silvery figure turned to face the squad, its shimmering helmet sporting a visor of opaque, darkened glass, a small antannae rising from behind its head.

Captain Mitchell ventured hesitantly forward.

"What... who are you?" he stuttered, hoping that his assumption that the figure was an ally was in fact correct.

"I am Hanan Aru. Rodan Kesh sent me to watch over you."

Mitchell suddenly remembered the Gaian who'd helped them on

Semeh'yone station. It seemed like such a long time ago.

"I thought he was forbidden to help us?" Taz asked.

"He is," Hanan Aru confirmed. "My presence here needs to remain undisclosed."

"Well if you see him, tell him thanks. I don't know what we would have done without you," Reid said, shifting Marcus' weight on his shoulder.

"We owe you one," Captain Mitchell agreed. "Now... any idea on how we can get out of here? Lishan's contact is surely long gone by now."

"I may know a way, although it will not be pleasant," Hanan Aru revealed. "Follow me."

He led them through the small doorway on the opposite side of the security station. It had been locked when they'd first passed through, but when one of the guards had attempted to flee Hanan Aru's fury he'd opened the door to make his escape, only to be cut down seconds later. They followed their rescuer along a narrow corridor, which soon veered sharply to the left. Mitchell was concerned that the loud clanking sound as Hanan Aru strode down the passage would draw the attention of yet more guards, but none came.

The passage eventually opened into a large, irregularly-shaped chamber with rough cement walls and a high ceiling. A clutter of rusted pipes, some of them were over two meters in diameter, connected various canisters and storage silos before disappearing into the left-hand wall. A plain metal stairway led down two flights to the floor below. The sound of Hanan Aru hastily navigating the stairs echoed through the chamber, sounding as if someone were forcefully banging on the rusted pipes with a metal wrench.

He stopped in front of the first pipe. He reached and laid his hand on top of it, as if trying to sense what lay inside. A few seconds later, he proceeded to the next pipe, which lay level with the raised metal walkway they were standing on, and repeated the gesture.

"This will serve," he announced, grasping the handle of his blade and drawing it from a short sheathe slung over his broad back.

Disappointingly, the blade itself was exceedingly short, no more than a stubby knife embedded in a much more extensive hilt. As the armored figured gripped the handle firmly, the blade sprung forward, increasing in size several times over as segment after segment came rushing out impossibly from the hilt, unfolding smoothly into a sleek length of metal easily a meter long.

Taz gasped, staring hypnotically at the magnificent sword. "Serve as what?" he asked.

"The way out," Hanan Aru proclaimed as he swung his blade a half circle.

It sang as it cleaved through the air, a testament to its keen edge. With his free hand, he pressed down on the pommel and the blade began to glow, faintly at first, then gaining in intensity until it was glowing white with heat. Ripples formed in the air around the sword as Hanan Aru pressed it slowly down into the rusty surface of the large pipe.

To their amazement, the pipe gave way as the blade sank in. He pulled his blade slowly around to produce a hole the size of a clenched fist before finally withdrawing it.

"I don't think I'm gonna fit," Taz quipped.

Hanan Aru's head snapped around, and the armored figured walked up to him, stopping uncomfortably close, sword still in hand.

"I… I…" Taz stammered, hoping he hadn't offended their benefactor.

Before the scout could react, Hanan Aru snatched one of the grenades from Taz's belt, hefted it, and returned to the pipe. He crammed it into the hole he'd made and pulled the pin.

"Move," he announced calmly as he turned and paced away, sending the clones diving for shelter behind protruding pipes and silos.

The ensuing explosion sent a cloud of debris flying into the air, and was followed by the foulest stench they had ever experienced. As he crawled out of cover, Taz gagged, trying to stop himself from vomiting.

"What the hell is that smell?" he gasped.

"Excrement," Hanan Aru replied as he approached the gaping hole in the pipe. "Get in."

* * * * *

They waded through the vilest filth they could ever have imagined. For the most part, it reached all the way up to their hips. Even though they tried to breathe through their mouths, the stench filled their senses. Clumps of feces floated on the surface of the tepid liquid, and small lizard-like creatures swam along the surface. They were at least thankful to have the use of the infrared vision and not have to view the scene in its natural colors.

Reid struggled as he tried to keep Marcus' head above the water, but of all of them, Jago suffered the most. His enormous form had barely fit through the opening, and he was starting to feel anxious and claustrophobic.

"How far is it?" Captain Mitchell called out.

"In your measurements?" Hanan Aru responded from the front,

consulting his suit's built-in A.I., "eight point two kilometers."

Taz vomited, unable to restrain himself at the thought of spending the next few hours in the muck. Although the tunnel seemed to go on forever, the captain urged them to push on. There was no turning back. They were fortunate to be breathing at all.

* * * * *

The suspended streets of Sheijan offered little comfort. Everywhere they went vagrants and vagabonds stepped aside to allow them passage. No doubt the smell was a contributing factor. Fortunately it had started to rain just minutes after they had reached the surface, and the filth was slowly washing off. Marcus had regained control of his limbs and now stumbled along behind his squadmates, a hollow shell of a man, utterly spent.

Hanan Aru had parted ways with them in order to remain hidden, although he swore to keep a watchful eye. He had advised them to retrieve the rest of their crew and find a quiet place to lay low. Luckily, their ship's refit was due to be completed by the following day, and they could finally say farewell to this hellhole for good.

Not that that was soon enough, thought Marcus. He wished they'd taken Serena's body with them. Leaving her in the hands of their twisted captor just seemed wrong. Still, he couldn't fault his companions. There had hardly been enough time for them to make their own escape, and carrying her body would have put them all at greater risk.

"Reid?" he prompted as they made their way along the gloomy streets, rain pouring down their faces.

"Yes Marcus?" Reid asked as he set a hand comfortingly on his shoulder.

"Do you think she's out there... somewhere?"

"I know she is," Reid answered. "And I'm sure she knows how much you cared for her."

"You knew?"

"We all knew," Reid said, giving him an awkward smile.

"Pray for me, Reid," Marcus whispered. "Or at least, for what's left of my humanity."

Chapter 56

They'd barely rushed the rest of the crew out into the pouring rain when Kesha Kun's forces arrived at the hotel. Taz spotted them from an alleyway on the far side of the dismal square, a procession of two dozen of the Sheshen thugs led by a pair of Nerokan enforcers marching straight up to the hotel.

"That you're still alive is a miracle!" Dasaan gasped as they scrambled across a deserted pedestrian way, making sure to stick to the shadows between the feeble pools of light cast by the occasional illuminated sign or window. "How do you plan to get us off this world? Kesha Kun is sure to have his forces waiting at the shipyard."

"We'll cross that bridge when we come to it," Captain Mitchell replied, "Right now I'm more worried about finding a place to stay for the night."

"I know a place," the Ganyatti answered slowly, looking unsure. "It's far from warm, but it will keep us dry and out of sight."

"That'll do," the captain nodded. "Lead the way."

While the armed clones flanked them, the support staff lugged their gear through the torrential downpour, soaked to the bone and exhausted from having been rushed out of the hotel in such a panic. Once the initial shock of their flight had passed, Marcus could see that the crew had not taken Serena's passing well. He could hear soft weeping coming from the throng as they pushed through the darkened streets on their way to Dasaan's refuge. Apart from himself, Linda Haake seemed to have taken it the worst, the older woman's eyes swelling with tears, her chest shaking with gentle sobs. Marcus hadn't realized that the two had been close friends. He remembered seeing them in the galley together on occasion, but hadn't thought it anything more than a working relationship. He reflected on how strange it was that someone he held so dear could have affected so many lives so deeply without him even realizing it.

Dasaan led them down a series of spiraling walkways, diving underneath the main streets above, eventually stopping before an underpass beneath a less conspicuous part of the city. The outlines of a pair of humanoid derelicts, their races and genders invisible, lay sleeping inside a small crumbling cargo crate just inside the underpass, sheltering from the rain. Inside the underpass, the rough ground was strewn with rubbish and small creatures crept along the walls, searching for morsels of food to drag back to their lairs.

"We should be safe here for now," Dasaan told them.

Marcus was sure that the loudmouthed Taz would be the first to complain, but to his amazement there were no objections. Taz even took the initiative and made himself useful, organizing the support staff to create a makeshift shelter out of pieces of metal sheeting they found further inside the underpass.

One of the derelicts woke from his stupor and started making noise, crying out in a language Marcus didn't recognize. Dasaan knelt by the leathery flap which served as the doorway to the decrepit cargo crate, slipping the poor creature a bit of currency, laying the matter to rest.

Marcus found himself standing in front of Jago, who was sitting quietly on an overturned pillar of cement. He stared at the huge man. He was the reason. If he hadn't...

"She's dead because of you," Marcus blurted out, his voice low and bitter. "The next time you charge off without thinking, I'll shove a grenade so far up your ass that no amount of regeneration will save you!"

Jago didn't reply. He merely lowered his head in shame as Marcus walked away.

"Fourteen hours," Captain Mitchell announced. "Then we're out of here."

"What about the Rev?" Taylor asked, sitting on a small crate and enjoying a cigarette, his back turned to the torrential rain.

"What about him?"

"His leg… He's supposed to see Oolan, the doctor, before we leave."

"Even I'd forgotten about that," Reid confessed. "It's not worth the risk, Captain. It can wait until we get back to Semeh'yone station."

"A checkup after invasive surgery performed by an alien doctor, using alien meds and cybernetics, not to mention having trudged through eight clicks of sewage, thereby exposing your wound to God knows what? Nah… you're right, it's not important. It can wait," Taylor sneered, taking a big puff and attempting to blow a smoke ring.

"Point taken Doc," Mitchell said. "But I'm not sending you alone Rev."

"I'll go with him," Marcus mumbled from where he was leaning up against the wall, his chest still heaving with anger.

"No Grey, you need to rest," the captain ordered, worried about his mental and physical condition.

"I'm fine, Sir. I'd rather do something than sit here and wait."

"I'll go as well," Taylor added, rising from his crate. "But we'd best wait until the crack of dawn."

Falling asleep proved almost impossible, and they ended up huddling together for warmth. The rain didn't let up the entire night, and Marcus found himself replaying past events in his mind. The

444

more he dwelled on it, the more he became convinced that Serena's death was his fault. Had he just convinced her to stay behind, she'd still be alive.

Dawn brought little comfort, as their departure was still more than seven hours away and the uncertainty kept them all anxious. For all they knew, Kesha Kun could be waiting for them at the *Tengri* with a whole regiment of his best soldiers.

Marcus and Reid had found a pair of stained sheets amongst the heaps of rubbish, and using their combat knifes, had fashioned them into makeshifts cloaks to disguise their appearance. Dasaan instead had lent Taylor the use of his own emerald garment As they pulled their disguises on over their armor, Captain Mitchell had wished them luck, and ordered that they keep radio silence as there was no telling who might be monitoring their communications.

As the new day dawned, they set out under the cover of the downpour and made their way to the market plaza. It was a lot less crowded than it had been on their previous trip, only a handful of merchants braving the weather, too foolish or desperate for business to take the day off. Marcus could count the number of customers on the fingers of one hand.

It wasn't long before they stood in front of the heavy door to Oolan's practice. The same foul-tempered Nerokan ushered them in from the rain and pointed them towards the seats in the waiting room while Oolan finished with another patient.

A short while later, a brutish Banthalo with an oversized cybernetic arm emerged from the operating room, clenching and admiring his new fist of chromed steel. The Nerokan escorted him out, and the two exchanged whispered words in the doorway.

Oolan came out into the waiting room and seemed pleased to see the Terrans, the colors of his skin shifting from a light pink to a deep orange with splotches of bright yellow.

"Weeelcooome baaack," he said lengthily, sitting back on his haunches to open his huge arms.

Reid rose from his chair and was just about to greet him when the Nerokan doorman returned from the entrance to the clinic, shoving him aside and slapping Oolan hard across the face with his open palm. The alien doctor's color shifted to a deep green as he stumbled backwards, rubbing his chin with a hand the size of Marcus' torso.

"Shya manshin kho hansayo wai banshan babavashi! Kumchi qusy mahieu shoro," the reptilian guard growled as he turned away from the Telorian.

"That's enough!" shouted Marcus, jumping up from his seat, Taylor standing to back him.

"Pleeease, dooon't," said Oolan. "Iiit waaas myyy faaault."

"Your fault? How was it your fault?" Reid demanded, flustered.

"Paaatieeent nooot saaatiiisfiiied."

Marcus eyed the guard with a glare, angered at his lack of empathy and casual violence. The Nerokan's only response was an intimidating snarl, baring a mouthful of pointed teeth.

"Pleeease, cooome," Oolan gestured towards the operating room, breaking the tension.

Reid and the Telorian disappeared into the other room, and Marcus slowly lowered himself back onto his seat and resumed waiting, shooting the hulking reptilian guardian a wayward glance every once in a while. After a quarter of an hour or so the bestial creature closed his eyes and started giving off a deep rumbling as he drifted off to sleep.

It was little over half an hour before Reid and the doctor returned from the operating room, waking the guard from his nap.

"Everything alright?" Taylor asked.

"Everything's fine. He gave me a cream to rub around the edges. Should help with the inflammation," Reid explained.

Oolan escorted them to the doorway leading out into the rain, feigning a smile as he waved them off, his color slowly shifting to a pale pink. The Nerokan gave the doctor a savage push, sending him crashing aside, as the lizard-like alien prepared to usher them out into the rain, his maw contorted in what could only be a sneer.

Without even thinking, Marcus drew his sidearm and shot the hulking guard through the head. The expression of shock on the enforcer's face was almost comic as he slumped heavily to the floor, collapsing in a pool of blood. Marcus felt nothing. No remorse. He wasn't the same Marcus anymore.

Before his astonished companions had a chance to react, he fired again, then again, emptying his clip into the Nerokan's skull. Reid and Taylor just stood there, unable to utter a single word.

Oolan's color shifted to a bright yellow as he too refused to move, lying crumpled awkwardly next to his former jailor, shifting his gaze between the corpse on the floor and Marcus' face, waiting in resignation.

Marcus finally broke the silence.

"You wanna get out of here?" he asked the astonished doctor, his voice completely neutral, devoid of empathy.

Oolan didn't seem to know how to reply, but his color shifted to a mix of orange and brownish hues.

"Off this shithole of a planet?" Marcus reiterated.

"Marcus-" Reid began, but Marcus raised a hand to silence him.

"We're leaving in a few hours and there's room for one more," he explained to the prone doctor.

"Iii aaam hooonoooored," Oolan finally said. "Buuut myyy thiiings?"

"Guys, give him a hand," Marcus ordered.

"What are you doing, Marcus?" Taylor hissed.

"Too many good people have died. I'm saving one. If anyone has a problem with it, they can kiss my ass!" Marcus snarled. "Now grab as much stuff as you can carry."

With Oolan telling them what might be of most use, they raided the operating room for whatever they could carry. They emptied the medicine cabinets, grabbed surgical tools and the medical scanner. Marcus even managed to fill a crate with all manner of cybernetic gear.

"We have to go," Taylor prompted after a few minutes. "The ship will be ready soon and who knows what sort of attention this little... scene might have drawn."

Marcus nodded his approval, and together they escorted Oolan out into the rain, free from his indentured servitude.

Chapter 57

"We're not exactly running a charity here," Captain Mitchell sighed upon their return, "but then again, a proper surgeon on our crew, particularly an alien one, could come in handy, no offense Doc. Do you trust him?"

Marcus looked over to where the Telorian doctor stood uneasily in the rain, too shy to venture closer.

"I do," Marcus answered.

"Fine. He's in," Mitchell proclaimed, waving the awkward doctor in from the rain. "Besides, it's a kick in the teeth for whomever he belonged too, and something tells me they had it coming."

Marcus forced a smile.

"I only hope you got away clean," Captain Mitchell added. "We've got enough heat on us as it is."

Oolan was drawing curious stares from the rest of the exhausted crew, particularly from the pale-skinned Dr. Gehringer, who was ecstatic to have such a marvelous and exotic creature in their midst. Seizing his handheld scanner and datapad, he seemed to completely forget the cold, wet, sleepless night he'd endured, examining their new crewmember with as much tact as they'd come to expect. Oolan's hide changed to a shade of pale blue as he followed the crazed antics of the socially-inept scientist.

"Where's Dasaan?" Taylor asked, noticing that the dark-skinned Ganyatti was nowhere in sight.

"He's gone off to meet Lishan. Hopefully he can help us escape."

Mitchell muttered. "He should be back any time now, as long as-"

The sudden appearance of a sleek, silvery vehicle hovering over the entrance to the underpass cut him off, its engines exuding a steady high-pitched whine as it began to descend.

"Take cover!" Captain Mitchell yelled, sending the crew diving for their weapons.

The clones waved the support staff into the scanty cover available and assumed kneeling stances as they prepared for the worst.

For all they knew, Dass'an could have been compromised, or worse... he could have betrayed their location to Kesha Kun for promise of a hefty reward.

The two derelicts – a shabby discolored Nerokan drunk and a decrepit Banthalo crone – kicked up quite a fuss as they fell out of their cargo container, snatching at their few possessions before scuttling hurriedly away from the underpass.

Captain Mitchell was relieved when the vehicle touched down and a smiling Dasaan emerged from a gull-wing door, followed closely by Lishan, who was without his usual entourage of Nerokan bodyguards.

"Stand down!" the captain yelled as he hurried out to greet them. "Lishan! I didn't expect you to show up in person."

"I will not ssstop long. I have businessss to attend to. I came only to warn you," Lishan replied.

"Warn us?"

"Father has had the docking clampsss on your vessel locked, and isss currently gathering hisss forcesss. Your asssault on his compound last night decccimated hisss personal guard, and bringing the Black Arm to heel alwaysss takesss time, but you must make haste."

"How can we get out if the ship is locked down?" asked Mitchell.

"With the accessss code to the docking clampsss I have brought you," Lishan revealed, his voice unmistakably mischievous.

"Why are you doing all this?" Marcus demanded, unable to understand why Lishan would betray his own father for a handful of strangers.

"Long ago, our people were not asss they are now. We were a proud and compassssionate race, free from the corruption which now dominatesss every facccet of our exxxissstenccce. The Ssshrouded Kinssship would sssee that time returned. For thisss reason, I have pledged myself to their cause," Lishan explained. "It is sssomething my father will never comprehend, and would probably have me exxxecuted for if he were to dissscover it."

"Looks like you have your work cut out for you," Taz scoffed.

"You are correct. The challenge we faccce is not a sssmall one, though that doesss not mean it lacksss merit. Now go, you mussst hurry."

"You heard the man," prompted Captain Mitchell. "Gather your gear. We're moving out in five!"

Lishan prepared to leave, returning to his hovercraft.

"Lishan," the captain stopped him. "Thank you… for everything."

Lishan looked back over his shoulder and gave him a brief nod before remounting his vehicle and speeding on his way.

* * * * *

Kesha Kun's surviving troops had formed up in the throne room. Over a hundred men, dressed in blackened battle gear and wielding laser rifles, stood ready for inspection while their lord paced back and forth in front of them, awaiting the arrival of his second born.

An escort of four heavily-armed Nerokan bodyguards preceded the arrival of Osha Kun, who came bursting into the hall in a sweep of robes.

"Where isss hisss body?" the new heir to the Dark Sun Empire shouted. "Where isss my brother?"

Osha Kun's appearance was much the same as his older brother's had been, save for his mask, and a stocky build which was uncommon among his race. His was a plain porcelain mask, painted black and embedded with ocular enhancements that glowed a bright red.

"Removed. There will be time to tend to it later," Kesha Kun told him. "Have you done as I asssked?"

"I have, Father. They are awaiting our arrival."

"And the tracking device?"

"Already inssstalled. If they do manage to get past my guardsss and break the lock, we ssshall be able to follow their every move."

Kesha Kun paused in his pacing and turned to admire his new heir.

"Well done, my ssson. Essscort the men to the ssshipyard and recapture the prisonersss."

"Yesss, Father. I will do asss you command," Osha Kun proclaimed, falling to his knees in a sign of fealty.

"I will hear their ssscreams before thiss day isss at an end," Kesha Kun decreed before storming out of the hall.

A few moments later, the large docking hatch on the roof of the domed palace slid open and four heavily armed transport vehicles emerged, climbing into the misty sky and racing towards Sheijan.

* * * * *

"Hurry!" Mitchell urged as they neared the shipyards.

The crew had been trotting through the rainy streets for the better part of an hour now, and many among them were getting fatigued, although, to Marcus' surprise, Oolan was able to move not only with great endurance, but also great speed when he had to.

The fenced-off compound where the *Tengri* lay berthed came into view, the ramp leading up to its open gates empty in the drizzle.

"Where are the guards?" Marcus asked as they slowed down to catch their breath.

"Lishan said his father was still assembling his men," Mitchell panted.

"Yes, but there were two of those Nerokans stationed out front when last time we came. Now they're gone."

"I've got an itch," Reid added. "This doesn't smell right."

"I agree," the captain concurred. "Everyone else waits here. Marcus, take Reid, Taz and Jago, go secure the yard."

"Yes, Sir," they bellowed in unison.

Jago ran on in ahead of the others, but slightly slower than usual, apparently practicing what he thought was a fair degree of caution after Marcus' reprimand. Marcus lead Taz and Reid down the short concourse that lead between the walled-off yards and compounds to the bay where the *Tengri* stood, while the captain and Taylor shepherded the support staff back around the nearest corner. The three clones stalked quickly and quietly up the gently-sloping ramp, which ended in a wide gateway where the Nerokan guards had stood only two days prior.

Reid stopped just short of the tall fence, kneeling down behind an empty barrel, prepping his rifle for combat. Taz and Marcus each stopped on opposite sides of the opening, their backs flat against the metal paneling of the wall, checking to see if the path ahead was clear, ready to provide covering fire if the need arose.

Inside, the *Tengri*'s bulky form lay in a spidery scaffold of extruded metal beams, dwarfing the handful of small storage shacks and workshops that huddled around the external wall of the yard, an ordered detritus of cabling, sheet metal, tools and containers strewn against their inner walls. Marcus couldn't see the ship's aft or engines from where he stood, but the general impression of the yard was that of a job completed.

For a long moment, the only movement was Jago's hesitant charge, which, in the absence of foes, had deteriorated into a stubborn trot. Just as the huge clone reached the center of the yard and started to slow down, a sudden burst of blue energy blew clear across the platform, hitting Jago square in the chest, but doing little to slow his momentum.

The behemoth howled as he changed course, diving to the left to charge towards the source of the blast. Taz lent him covering fire, aiming towards a small grouping of crates, from behind which a pair of Nerokan guards targeted Jago with their laser rifles. Jago roared, gaining speed. It was a good two seconds before his assailants realized the need to fire their stun rays again.

"Reid, move up!" Marcus shouted, waving him forward.

Jago was hit once more. He stumbled momentarily as his legs stiffened but was able to regain his pace, throwing himself into the air over the crates and came crashing down on his attackers.

One of them managed to escape by diving out into the open, giving Taz and Marcus the opportunity to send a hail of projectiles in his direction. The sound of bullets ricocheting off metal rang through the air as the desperate Nerokan ran for cover.

Meanwhile, Jago rose from up behind the crates, holding his assailant by the neck, squeezing and forcing the reptilian humanoid's scaled head to one side. Jago growled like an animal, applying as much pressure as his bulking muscles allowed until he finally heard the distinct crack as his attacker's neck snapped in half.

Reid came running up to the entrance, switching places with Taz, who ducked into the yard to assist Jago.

"How many?" Reid asked, shouldering his long rifle and peering through the gateway.

"I counted two," replied Marcus. "The Ape got one, but the other's still on the loose."

It wasn't long before Taz was dodging laser blasts coming from the other side of the *Tengri*. The missing Nerokan had taken cover behind the docking clamps – a heavy-looking block of machinery somehow tangled up in the network of struts that made up the ship's cradle – and was making use of the open ground to keep the scout pinned down.

It didn't take Reid long to spot him, and within seconds the sniper had him in his crosshairs, but the heavy rifle was a difficult weapon to fire while standing and his aim kept wavering. Meanwhile, the Nerokan's shots were coming in awfully close and Taz, crouched behind a roll of cabling much smaller than he was, was hard pressed to keep out of harm's way.

Marcus saw what was happening, and knew that the only way to give Taz a chance was to provide a distraction. He took a deep breath, hefted his carbine, and ran straight into the yard, yelling and firing as he went.

The remaining Nerokan spotted him immediately and popped up out of cover, getting ready to send a searing bolt of energy into the running clone, when Reid's high-caliber round pierced his skull.

"Clear!" Reid called on the comms as Marcus skidded to a halt beside a grinning Taz.

Without wasting a second, Captain Mitchell began barking orders for everyone to get aboard the ship as fast as possible.

Taz helped Jago up the *Tengri*'s docking ramp while Marcus and Reid ran to the shipyard's gate to cover the rest of the crew as they hurried on board.

"Straaange deeesiiign," Oolan proclaimed as he halted in the gateway, taking in the ship's angular, blocky shape.

"You have to hurry, please!" Marcus rushed him, urging him up the ramp.

As soon as they were all aboard, Mitchell closed the docking ramp and made straight for the bridge, where Raven and the rest of the bridge crew were busy trying to figure out how to disengage the docking clamps.

"Captain, the sequence!" she demanded as soon as he arrived, gesturing to her console.

Marcus burst onto the bridge right behind Mitchell and ran to the front of the chamber, staring out of the forward viewscreen to make sure that Kesha Kun's forces were nowhere in sight.

"I don't know what the fuck it says!" Raven shouted, trying to figure out the interface for the clamps. "I can't read Sheshen!"

Mitchell got on the ship's internal comms. "Dasaan, report to the bridge, immediately!" he shouted.

Marcus suddenly spotted four distinct dark spots on the horizon, only just visible through the low clouds, but getting larger by the second. Though he hoped desperately they had nothing to do with the crew of the *Tengri*, something told him otherwise.

A moment later, Taz came rushing onto the bridge, a worried-looking Dasaan in tow.

"How can I assist?"

"The docking clamps! It's all in Sheshen," the captain gestured towards Raven and handed him the scribbled note he'd received from Lishan.

Dasaan went to work immediately, leaning forward to tap away at the console's controls. The four dots on the horizon were getting bigger, taking on distinct shapes that something buried in Marcus' resonant memories told him could only belong to attack vehicles.

"Captain!" Marcus bellowed. "We've got incoming. They're coming... fast!"

Captain Mitchell rose from his seat, approaching the window.

"Any moment now would be fine Dasaan!" he shouted, spotting the inbound craft.

"Working as fast as I can!" the Ganyatti barked.

Two of the Sheshen vehicles began descending, while the other two retained their altitude. They were close now, very close.

"Almost there," Dasaan cried.

Two of the craft made abrupt landings on the concourse outside the shipyard, and dozens of Kesha Kun's men began pouring out, racing towards the *Tengri*.

"No, not almost, Dasaan, they're already here!" the captain shouted. "We need to go, now!"

The other two ships whizzed by overhead, no doubt turning around in case they managed to get airborne.

"Got it!" the Ganyatti yelled.

"And here I was almost getting worried," Taz whimpered as he slouched against the bulkhead while Captain Mitchell practically threw himself back across the bridge to his seat, calling up screens of data.

There was a distinct clanking sound as the docking clamps began to release their hold on the ship. Kesha Kun's forces burst through the gate to the yard below, showering the ship's hull with laser fire as it began to lift off the ground. Twice the circling craft strafed the *Tengri* with their underslung weapons, shaking her to her core and sending tremors through the hull as she inched slowly out of the docking cradle.

Raven was sweating profusely as she grabbed hold of the controls and began pushing the ship into a steep climb.

"All our money's on you, Raven!" Mitchell bellowed encouragingly.

Another blast shook the ship as they pierced through the veil of clouds. The ship's sensors were beeping steadily to indicate that they were being pursued, but the *Tengri* had no aft-facing weaponry.

"I hope those bastards can't do vacuum!" Raven roared as she pushed the engines to their limit.

Marcus peered through the viewscreen as they raced through the clouds. The atmosphere began to darken and another pair of energy blasts shot passed them. As the stars began to dominate their view, their pursuers began to lose distance, and a brief moment of weightlessness as the ship's artificial gravity kicked in, signaled their escape from the planet's atmosphere.

"They're turning away," Copilot Gardulo informed them. "We're in the clear!"

"Make the calculations for Semion Station," Captain Mitchell ordered. "Kesha Kun might have ships lying in wait further out in the system, and I want us out of here before they get a chance to spot us... and Raven, excellent flying."

Chapter 58

"Iiit iiis doone," Oolan proclaimed as he ran his stubby fingers over the outline of the implant.

Marcus sat up from the surgical table in the *Tengri*'s medical bay, rubbing the back of his neck.

"How does it feel?" Mitchell inquired, sounding concerned.

At first, he'd been hesitant to allow the operation, but, owing to their need for a new interpreter, he'd agreed in the end. There was no knowing how long Dasaan would remain in their service, and Marcus himself had jumped at the opportunity, seeing it as his way of honoring Serena's memory.

"It feels strange. Cold," Marcus replied as he looked out through the window.

Never before had a Terran vessel traveled at such tremendous speed under its own power. The tunnel of flowing energy surrounding the *Tengri* was an inspiring sight. Its hypnotic patterns evoked a soothing sensation, particularly knowing that each passing second put them farther and farther away from Nos Shana.

"Thaaat wiiill paaass," Oolan told them.

"But is it working?" prompted Captain Mitchell.

"Tsuuudähmeee taaana jiiiteraaa sakiiilo?" Oolan voiced in a strange alien language.

"I... I do understand," Marcus replied in astonishment. "Will I be able to speak also?"

"Yeees. Iiin tiiime," Oolan professed.

"How many languages does it store?" Mitchell asked .

"Iii haaave iiinpuuut ooonlyyy ooone," Oolan explained. "Thiiis mooodeeel caaan taaake seeeveeen laaanguaaage fiiiilesss. Buuut Iii haaave ooonlyyy Hiiiooodaaan."

"Well I guess we can always buy more," the captain shrugged.

"We should all have these," said Marcus. "If we're going to live out here, we have to be able to speak the language."

"All in good time Marcus. All in good time."

They had gotten to know a great deal more about their new shipmate since leaving Nos Shana. Dr. Gehringer had discovered, as much by asking Oolan as by physical examination, that the Telorian species were more plant than animal, shooting down roots into soil and basking in ultraviolet light for nourishment, a process that they need only partake in once a week under optimal conditions. The crew had arranged for a two by two meter square crate to be built in one of the cargo holds and filled with the soil from the few potted plants that had occupied the *Tengri*'s hallways, an ultraviolet lamp strung high above so that Oolan could sustain himself on the long voyage ahead. They'd even learned that although the bizarre doctor usually spoke and moved at the speed of a garden snail, this was more to preserve energy than a limitation. In fact, he could move and speak just as quickly as they could, but chose not to, as doing so would necessitate more frequent nourishment.

Marcus had taken to the gentle surgeon, having spent some time with him in preparation for the delicate surgery in the weeks since the *Tengri*'s hasty departure from Nos Shana. He mused glumly that he ought now to spend some time with Dasaan, practicing the use of his new implant, but he knew that would be hard. He'd been avoiding their new cook since Serena's death.

460

With a sigh, he laid himself back on the operating table and allowed Oolan to run the diagnostic routines the Telorian had prepared.

* * * * *

The whole crew had crowded onto the bridge, dressed in their finest clothing for the ceremony that was about to take place. Though the suggestion had been Reid's, Marcus knew that it was as much for his benefit as for anyone else's.

Captain Mitchell had found the idea appropriate at the time, but the arrangements had proven more troubling than he'd anticipated. Dr. Gehringer had been reluctant to leave his research, and Dasaan had been slaving away in the galley, trying to understand Terran culinary traditions in preparation for the meal they'd be having.

Still, they'd managed to organize it eventually, and now the support staff were lined up on one side of the bridge, while the military personnel lined up on the other. Navigator Wei sat firmly in his seat, as he had his own role to play in the ceremony. By the forward viewscreen, Reid stood with his back turned towards the tunnel of light, dressed in his most formal grey uniform, as he prepared to recite his speech.

"Today we gather to commemorate the fallen, Emil Juey, Darryl Knoles and Serena Kim," he addressed the gathered crew, pausing briefly after each name. "They will be sorely missed, both as colleagues, and as friends."

Marcus could see Dr. Haake tearing up.

"Though they are no longer with us in person, their eternal spirits will always be with us, in our hearts."

Though Marcus could feel the truth of Reid's words, it was small

461

consolation. He was overcome with sadness as he tried to picture Serena's presence aboard the ship, her unwavering smile, her effortless grace.

"It is with the greatest honor that I commit our fallen to the void," Reid concluded.

Navigator Wei activated the forward cannons, sending brief tremors through the ship as he fired into the abyss, once for each of their fallen comrades.

Once the ceremony was complete, the crew retired below to the mess hall, where Dasaan's feast awaited them, a buffet of meat, freshly baked breads, and frozen vegetables cooked into a variety of fine pastes.

What had once been a clear divide between the support staff and the military personnel was now fading fast. Jago sat next to Captain Mitchell and Kaiden Karell, deep in conversation, attempting to overcome the sadness they were feeling with cheerful banter. Taz and Ahlain Lyer, the *Tengri*'s assistant engineer, were both busy trying to flirt with the ship's technician Liana Tinley, despite the inappropriateness of the timing, and she was playing the two off against each other with great enjoyment. The bridge crew had formed a group near the forward window, where Raven was doing her best to prove her superiority to the two men by recounting tales of her former exploits, much to their delight and disbelief.

Oolan sat quietly in the center of the Galley, engaged in a lengthy conversation with Dr. Gehringer, who was taking advantage of the socially-sanctioned discussion to interrogate the alien surgeon about every imaginable aspect of Telorian physiology and sociology.

Marcus had hesitantly approached Linda Haake as she sat quietly in the far corner, wanting to offer his sincere condolences. She started tearing up all over again and Marcus soon found the situation too uncomfortable to stay. In the end he wound up claiming the empty seat between Jago and the captain.

"This is good meat," bellowed Jago, tearing through a strip of succulent flesh from what looked like a small thighbone.

"I didn't know we had any meat in the freezer," Mitchell professed. "Knoles must have been holding out on us."

Marcus feigned a smile. He didn't really feel like eating. He found himself gazing out through the window, listening half-heartedly to their conversation as he reminisced about his time on Ga'ouna with Serena. How he wished they'd stayed behind when the *Tengri* had left. He began fantasizing about what their lives would have been like, but it only made him sadder.

Dasaan entered the galley with a bowl full of fried rice mixed with green beans, chopped onions and small chunks of meat.

"Would you like to try some?" he asked as he approached the captain's table. "I don't yet know the names of all of the ingredients, but I find that cooking is the same in all corners of the galaxy. All that's required is a good palate, and a healthy dose of patience."

"I want," Jago mumbled with his mouth still full, lifting his plate.

"I was under the assumption that we didn't have any meat on board," Mitchell said as the Ganyatti spooned out a serving onto Jago's outstretched plate. "Knoles used to say that it spoils too quickly for long voyages."

"That is *most* strange. I found meat rather quickly," Dasaan replied with a puzzled look.

"Really?" Kaiden said, surprised that their old cook could have lied to them about their supplies.

"Do you know what kind of meat it is?" the captain asked.

463

"I think it's called 'spot'," Dasaan answered proudly as Jago made appreciative noises around a big mouthful of his latest dish. "Is it to your liking?"

"Spot?" Mitchell gulped, dropping his fork and suddenly gagging as he rose from his chair.

"Is he alright?" Dasaan pressed, looking over the galley in search of Taylor or Oolan.

"Can I have some more?" Jago mumbled, without realizing.

"You cooked Spot?" the captain yelled, still struggling to breathe.

"I do not understand. Have I prepared it incorrectly?" Dasaan asked perplexedly.

Marcus caught sight of Reid, who'd apparently overheard them and was now rushing off to the bathroom.

"You cooked the captain's dog," Marcus replied, astounded at Dasaan's incomprehension.

"Yes, the spot," Dasaan replied. "I do not understand why you would keep only one of such a skinny animal. There was not a lot of meat on it."

"That was the captain's pet," Marcus explained, just as Mitchell stormed out of the galley, on his way to join Reid in the bathroom.

Suddenly Kaiden could control herself no more and burst into laughter.

"It's not funny Kaiden!" Marcus insisted, but her infectious laughter soon began to spread.

Without warning, Jago let out a chuckle which soon erupted involuntarily into roaring laughter. Soon, Marcus found himself laughing along as well.

"I hated that mangy mutt," Kaiden professed, still giggling. "It was always peeing on the exercise equipment."

Jago laughed even harder.

Even as he laughed, Marcus gave a sigh of relief, knowing that despite their great loss, they could still find cause for hilarity.

Chapter 59

Ambassador Janosh sat in the lotus position on the cold stone floor underneath a canopy of multicolored glass. A metal cylinder stood on end beside him, shimmering under the starlight. The hour was late, and he'd made certain that his staff was long gone. Even Thales had been shut down for the night, in contravention of usual practice. The downstairs lobby had been cleared, the only remaining protection a pair of drones whose memory core could be erased after the meeting he was about to conduct.

"She has arrived," the ambassador proclaimed, his voice carrying to the far reaches of the vast chamber. "I can sense her presence."

Rodan placed his hand on the handle of his blade in preparation. Although the ambassador was a powerful figure, both politically and in terms of psionic and martial prowess, Rodan did not like the idea of him conducting a meeting in so vulnerable a state. It had taken some convincing, but the ambassador had finally consented to have Rodan act as his sentinel, on the condition that he stay hidden for the duration of the meeting.

"It is time," Janosh said softly, and Rodan stepped into the shadows.

A moment later they heard the sound of approaching footsteps, echoing gradually louder and louder throughout the chamber. It didn't take long after that for the alluring female form to appear, silhouetted by the intense light source out in the corridor.

"You men and your ssshadow play," she remarked snidely. "Your influenccce isss outweighed only by your paranoia."

"It is good to see you again, Shikari," Janosh lied. "Please take a seat."

She had arrived unescorted, as he had requested, a state that obviously unnerved her, for all that she was doing her best to appear otherwise.

She lowered herself to the floor, resting on her knees in front of him, tilting her head ever so slightly as she studied him, attempting to appear amiable.

"I would offer you refreshments, but…"

"But your ssstaff ssseemsss to have gone home for the night," she finished his sentence.

"Indeed."

"I heard the Councccil voted in your favor," she prompted after an awkward silence. "I trussst that meansss the recordingsss played their part?"

"They did," he replied. "You performed admirably."

"And isss that my payment?" she gestured towards the metal cylinder.

"As requested," he acknowledged, handing it to her.

She reached out to take it from him, but he held on tight, refusing to release the metal object.

"I trust you have not forgotten the second part of our arrangement?" he reminded her.

"My dear Ambassssador," she teased. "Shikari doesssn't mate and tell."

"Hmpf," he snorted, the imagery enough to make him retch.

He released his grip and immediately she snapped the cylinder from his grasp, rising promptly to her feet. She strode towards the exit, pausing briefly to blow him a kiss before she disappeared into the

467

night.

"Master, why must you resort to dealing with the likes of her?" Rodan said as he stepped out of the shadows.

"A necessary evil," the ambassador assured him.

"But what does it serve to discredit the Terrans?"

"To allow the Terrans a position in the Etherium would be a travesty. It could spell disaster for the Gaian people, and the Merillian galaxy as a whole. Now at least the Council will think twice."

"There has to be another way, Master. I cannot feel comfortable with this," Rodan professed.

"Had the Council but heeded my words in the first place, none of this would have been necessary."

"But-" Rodan began to argue.

"But nothing," the ambassador cut him off, his expression suddenly turning grave. "I have gone through proper channels, pleaded with them to hear my words... Gaia's words.... but they would have none of it. An example had to be made. They need to know the true nature of the Terrans."

Rodan lowered his gaze. Although he did not agree with his master's methods, the ambassador was following Gaia's will. Rodan only hoped that he would not surrender his humanity in the pursuit of his goals.

"As you wish, Master."

"When the Terran vessel returns, I need you to infiltrate their ship and hack into their navigational computer. As soon as you have the coordinates of their home system, you are to relay the coordinates to the Triumvirate. I want that scout vessel on route as quickly as possible."

"Yes Master," Rodan agreed, bowing his head in reverence.

* * * * *

Taylor walked into the *Tengri*'s laboratory just in time to hear Dr. Gehringer ask Dr. Haake if she would be interested in participating in a mating ritual with him, to be followed by copulation. The medic had never seen anyone turn that particular shade of red. She slapped the pale little scientist clear across the cheek before storming out of the lab.

"Practicing your seduction techniques, Doctor?" Taylor joked from the doorway.

"I think I'm getting the hang of it. I believe I've discovered a direct correlation between the female's reaction and the strength of the graviton field!" Dr. Gehringer revealed, buzzing with excitement and completely oblivious to the clone's sarcasm.

"The what?" Taylor asked, completely confused.

"I've recalibrated the ship's artificial gravity, reducing it by a factor of 0.2 percent. Don't tell me you hadn't noticed!"

"I... uh... yes, of course I noticed," Taylor lied.

"This time, she only slapped me once," Dr. Gehringer proclaimed, bursting with pride.

"I see," Taylor said, shaking his head in disbelief. "Anyway, now that you're... between repetitions, Doctor, I was wondering how the cloning process is coming along?"

"The cloning pr... oh, the canine!" Dr. Gehringer cried, running over to one of the small cloning vats standing in a corner of the laboratory, which he'd covered with a black tarp.

He removed the shroud, peering into the tank.

"He's coming along nicely," the scientist said. "Shouldn't be more than a few days now."

469

"Good. Don't you think you should give it to the captain?" Taylor suggested, appealing to what little empathy the scientist might possess. "After all, it was his dog whose genetic sample you took. Without his permission, I might add."

"But I had planned to test my theory of-"

"It's not going to work Doctor," Taylor warned him. "If you want a girl to like you, you should just be yourself…" he began, immediately regretting his words.

What little he knew of the cadaverous scientist's character didn't seem at all suited to appeal to the opposite gender… or any gender, come to that.

"How?"

"Let the captain have the dog and perhaps I can teach you a thing or two."

Dr. Gehringer grinned from ear to ear as and stretched out a limp-wristed hand.

"I accept!"

*   *   *   *   *

As the *Tengri* slid into the busy space lanes surrounding Semeh'yone station, Hanan Aru disabled his magnetic hold on the ship's outer hull. His suit not only offered protection from the harsh elements of space, but was also capable of acting as a stasis pod, and he had programmed it to awaken him the moment the ship disengaged its superluminal drive. He waited until he had drifted far enough away that no-one would notice before he engaged the suit's small built-in thrusters, making his way towards the lower docking ring, a section of the station restricted to the Etheran military.

Fortunately, his position within the Iankari afforded him unrestricted access.

*　*　*　*　*

Their journey back to Semeh'yone station was at an end. After almost a month at superluminal velocity, Captain Mitchell sat quietly in his office, finishing Engineer Kerr's report on the new drive and getting ready to head up to the bridge for the *Tengri*'s final approach. He'd been pondering the possible ramifications of his decision to leave Semeh'yone rather than waiting patiently for their asylum hearing with the Etheran Council, particularly now that they were returning having acquired a superluminal drive of their own, albeit semi-legally. Well, he thought, I suppose we'll find out in a few days, won't we?

He grabbed the half-full bottle of pills from his desk and swallowed a small handful, rubbing his aching joints.

"Captain," the voice of Navigator Wei came from outside in the hallway.

"Come in," Mitchell called.

The navigator had a worried air about him as he hurriedly closed the hatch behind him.

"I was about to head up to the bridge, so whatever this is, it had better be important," Captain Mitchell muttered, trying to see how many painkillers he had left in the bottle.

Wei stepped forward in silence and placed a small data disk on the captain's desk before coming to attention.

"At ease," Mitchell told him. "What's this?"

"Captain, I was reconfiguring the nav computer. Not really a necessity, but if we were ever to return to any of the locations we've visited since leaving Terra then I thought it might save us some time on astrogation."

"Hardly a pressing matter," the captain said, picking up the disk. "These are the new parameters?"

"No, Captain," Navigator Wei replied. "While I was rummaging through the computer's subroutines, I came across something... a glitch... perhaps, though I'm not certain. It has all the indications of having been inserted there deliberately."

"Explain," Mitchell demanded, his patience wearing thin.

"It appears that there was a hidden subroutine in the nav computer. Had we entered stasis for our journey back to Semeh'yone station – or any subsequent journey, from what I can tell – the ship's nav computer would have automatically redirected the ship's course."

"To where?"

"Back home, Captain. To Beta Terra."

"What?" Captain Mitchell yelled, slamming his fist onto the desk and startling the navigator.

"If we'd entered stasis, we would've been completely unaware of it Captain. Most likely, we'd have woken up in orbit above Beta Terra without even realizing it."

"I thought a trip like that would take hundreds of years, if not thousands? What would be the point?"

"In the past, Captain, yes, it would have. There would presumably have been very little point," the Navigator agreed. "But with our new drive technology, the trip from Nos Shana to Terra would only take several months, perhaps a year. This, uh..." Wei cleared his throat awkwardly. "...leads me to believe that whoever reprogrammed the nav computer knows about our new drive, and is therefore aboard the ship."

"A mole... on my crew?" Mitchell sighed.

"It would appear so, Captain," Navigator Wei confirmed.

"Tell no one of this," the captain ordered. "Until we're in a position to root out this... traitor, we will keep this information contained."

"As you wish, Captain."

Wei turned to leave while Captain Mitchell stared blankly at the bulkhead. He couldn't believe that even this far away from home, Division 6 remained a very real threat. There was a traitor amongst them... but who? Though he'd done his best to hide it, he'd scanned the mind of each and every one of the crew. A sleeper agent perhaps? One who didn't even know that they were working for the Division? Such practices weren't unheard of in the Terran intelligence community. I should never have underestimated Captain Intari, Mitchell thought. The man is as vile as he is cunning, and his wrath knows no bounds.

*   *   *   *   *

Everyone apart from the captain and the bridge crew had gathered in the galley to enjoy the view as the *Tengri* approached Semeh'yone's docking ring. From its gigantic docking arms to the white tower in is center, the massive hub was a beacon of light at the end of a perilous journey, and the mood was festive. Taz even raised a sardonic toast to a job well done, which some found inappropriate, given the high price they'd paid.

Marcus stood in a shadowy corner, looking at the exuberant faces of his colleagues. He wondered who would be the next to go. Perhaps it would be him.

Despite this small but costly victory, there was still a huge range of challenges that they would have to face. They were a long way from home, and Semeh'yone, though unarguably more pleasant than Nos Shana, still felt like nothing more than a way station. Perhaps in time they would come to call it home, but something inside him suggested otherwise.

As he *Tengri* approached the docking bay they'd been assigned, the shimmering force field disengaged to allow them passage, the now-familiar tow drones pulling the ship into position. As the sound of the docking arm grabbing hold of the ship's underbelly reverberated through the hull, the crew cheered.

Marcus suddenly felt his eyes drawn to something outside the window, something entirely unexpected. He walked clear across the galley, pushing people aside as he strode forward, spilling Dr. Gehringer's drink down his lab coat as he pushed through a small knot of his crewmates. In the adjoining bay, through one of the massive windows that divided the docking ring into its numerous berths, Marcus saw the last thing he had ever expected to see at Semeh'yone. The TFS-*Genesis*.